Love is Alluring

By

Dr. Jessica Jude Ziegler, Ph.D.

&

Jackie Farrugia Masotto, M.A.

Dedication

For the love of my life, Dennis James Ziegler

"The Real Cowboy"

Love you

J Bear

Acknowledgments

I have no words to thank my dear friend Kristen Jackson, who has not walked this journey with me. Her passion and fire of the characters was really unstoppable. I would not be here if not for all the inspiration and creativity of my dear friend Jackie Masotto. It goes without saying I would not be where I am with you, my dear husband, Denny, who has to endure me in my craziest moments. I also need to thank all of you, my friends, for supporting me, keeping me grounded, and spreading the word about the work. I am so very grateful to everyone. I love to hear from all my readers and hope you continue to enjoy the work.

"The thing that matters is others way beyond yourself. Realize they're a lot of great people to be grateful for and a loving God," –Robin Williams

Keep reading and stay kind,

Jess

About the Author

Dr. Jessica Jude Ziegler PhD

Dr. Jessica Jude Ziegler was born in the heartland of St. Louis and raised landscape of Costa Rica, Dr. Ziegler's passion for storytelling emanates from her unique perspective forded during her 24 years as a cop. Balancing her full-time career while earning a PhD from Walden University was just one of many challenges to reach her goal as an author. Jessica lives a peaceful and happy ranch life along her wonderful husband Dennis, and loving pets, Copper, Loretta, and Chuggy. Prepare to be enthralled by Dr. Ziegler's tales woven where adrenaline meets love, and the pulse of each heartbeat yearns with raw authenticity and a sprinkle of spice.

Jacqueline Farrugia Masotto M.A.

Farrugia Masotto has been a School Counselor for over 20 years. Originally from NYC, she attained her undergraduate and graduate degrees from New York University. She lives in the Tampa Bay area with her ever-loving husband, two wonderful daughters, as a good boy named Beau. She enjoys traveling, 80's music, and long naps.

Contents

Chapter 1

Introduction

The night evening had come upon Kyle, who was returning to Rob's and Ellis' ranch. His mind was recalling basic training along with Rob so many years ago. Kyle started laughing to himself, thinking of the time when the Drill Sergeant kept dinging them because instead of saying, "Noyes," Kyle would respond, "Maybe." Suddenly, he noticed, just a few miles outside of town, a broken-down car with the hood up. Kyle could tell it was a young woman who was kicking the side of her car. He decided to pull over and offer assistance, but something in his gut told him she was trouble. He parked several yards in front of her, and he walked towards the female. As he approached, she raised a tire iron.

"Whoa, I come in peace. I was just wondering if you needed help. I really don't need my head smashed in," Kyle said, raising his hands.

"Sorry, I am a nervous wreck. This piece of shit car just decided to quit on me. I tried everything to get it going, but no dice, "she responded as she kicked the car once more.

"Well, I can take a look at it if you like. Or I can call AAA for you," Kyle said, slowly getting closer to the vehicle, "I am going to be sticking my head underneath the hood. Do you mind putting the weapon down?" he said.

"Oh, sorry, I wasn't thinking. Thank you so much for stopping. A trucker pulled over earlier, but he looked sketchy, so I waved him off," she responded as she placed the tool on the ground.

"No worries, I see what the problem is with your water pump. You have no fluid. It is an easy fix, just a quick replacement. You just need a new pump and more fluid," he said.

"Great, an easy fix is just another thing to deal with. I think this trip was just a huge mistake," she said while pacing up and down," I have no idea what you are talking about. I guess I'd better call my Dad for help," she said with tears of frustration rolling down her face.

"Hey, it's okay. We all have bad days. I am Kyle Noyes, by the way, and you are?" he asked, reaching his hand out to shake hers, "Oh, sorry, I guess we can't shake. My hands are covered in oil."

She reached out and took his hand, handing him a rag. "I am Atlas Martin. It's nice to meet you."

"Well, Atlas, do you want to call a tow truck?" he asked as he walked around to the back of the car.

"Nope, I don't have the money for either one. I used my last bit of cash to fill my gas tank, and now this Crap. I think God hates me. Do you have a cell phone I can borrow? I dropped mine somewhere, so there is that one as well. I did not plan for any of this. Holy shit, my father is going to kill me," she said as Kyle handed her his cellphone.

"You got Missouri plates. What are you doing so far from home?" Kyle asked as he closed the hood.

Atlas grabbed the phone and began dialing. She said, "Can you believe I packed everything I owned to go to the police academy here? I saw they advertised a $5,000.00 sign-in bonus. I didn't even tell my parents I had just quit my job, drained my savings, gassed up my car, and drove. Impulsive, right?"

"Put the phone down, Atlas. I don't mind helping you, and if it doesn't work, then we will call your Dad," Kyle said, reaching for his cell phone.

"Why would you help me? You don't even know me," she responded as she wiped a tear rolling down her face.

"Mainly because I am a nice guy, but we are going to be classmates. I also saw the same billboard. You start next Monday, right?" he said, taking her keys and locking the doors.

"Come with me to my friend's ranch just a few miles up the road. We can get help there for your car and calmly figure things out. What do you say?" Kyle said as he opened his car door for her.

"Are you sure your friends won't mind?" Atlas said as she sat inside of the car.

"You're good," Kyle said with a smile as they started driving to the ranch. Kyle pulled up to the house and parked. He immediately jumped out and opened the door for Atlas.

"Hey, thought you were grabbing your gear, not your girl, Maybe," Rob said, walking towards them.

"Oh, I am not his girl. We just met. I am Atlas Martin," she said.

"Rob, I hope you don't mind. Atlas is one of my classmates. I found her. She was stranded on the side of the road. I needed some parts from town to repair her car, but it was getting late. I think they might be close," Kyle said.

"A relaxing room is something we have plenty of." Ellie said, "Come on, what did you say? Your name is Atlas. That is a very unusual name. I am Ellie, and I believe we will be classmates as well at the academy," Ellie said with a big smile.

"Really? You guys are very nice. I was going to see if I could find a place to rent while I go to the academy and a part-time job near town. Well, if my car holds up. I kinda leaped before I thought things through," Atlas said with some embarrassment.

"Well, let's see if the boys can go and tow your car here tonight. I will set you up in one of the cabins. We can ride together to the academy, and I will speak to Ben to take you on as a hired hand. Can you ride? Rob is training the horses. We could use all hands on deck," Ellie said, signaling to Rob to help with the car.

"She is the boss. Come on, Kyle, let's earn our keep. We can take the truck and pull the car," Rob said, kissing Ellie goodbye. Rob made sure to give her a passionate, lasting kiss and hug.

"Wow, Ellie, that is some kiss. You guys are very lucky to be together," Atlas commented.

"It was hard work to get us together, but he is worth it," she said.

"I hope one day I can find someone who will love and miss me every second we are apart. You know that someone who thinks about me more than himself. You get me, right?" Atlas said.

"Oh, I get it. You will the moment you stop looking. There they are, "Ellie said with a warm smile.

"You know, Ellie, this journey seems almost impossible. I am not sure if I am doing the right thing. Maybe I should just call my father and go home," Atlas complained.

Ellie took her hand, leading her into the house. She turned and said, "You know we always look at the mountains ahead of us and forget the mountains behind us were just as difficult to climb. Why don't you rest a bit, get something to eat, and then decide what is best for you?"

By the time the guys had returned with Atlas' car, the two girls had fallen asleep on the couch. Rob and Kyle decided it was best not to wake them. They quietly walked outside and headed to the stable. "I guess you are sleeping in my cabin tonight, Kyle. The cabin is on the other side of the ridge. You can unpack in the morning once we are done with the ceremony. Yep, Ellie and I are getting married." Kyle nodded in agreement, and the two men made their way to get a few hours of sleep.

DAYS LATER: Rob and Ellie emerged from the honeymoon suit to get their lives started. They walked hand in hand towards the house, enjoying the cool evening air. When they got closer to the house, Ellie could see the group had started the traditional bonfire. She looked at Rob with a scared look. "God, no, you are not deploying, are you?"

"No, my love, I am not. In fact, I already submitted my paperwork requesting early retirement. I am staying on to work with Ben while you go off and protect our community," he responded.

"Do you think it's Kyle? Ava can't because she was medically discharged, and I put my papers in. Maybe Levi? Lord, I hope it is not Levi. He and Ava are just getting to know one another. I am not sure what she would do if it was Levi," Ellie responded, almost in a panic.

"Ellie, my love, I love you, but you need to slow yourself down. Put your fears away until we know something. Let's just walk up there and hear them out," he said, holding her hand tightly as they approached the group.

"Well, it's about time you two came out for fresh air," Barb said as she wrapped herself in a blanket.

"Now, Barb, let the young couple be. You just have never experienced that type of love. It is all-consuming, all-knowing, all..." Ben responded and stopped catching himself, "you know what I mean."

"Oh, I know what you mean, all animalistic. I have, but to be honest, it's been a while. I don't mind being reminded," Barb said with a smile.

"Are you two a couple?" Atlas asked, but neither Ben nor Barb would give up any information.

"What gives? Why the bonfire? Ellie is worried someone got called up for duty," Rob said as Ellie shot him with a dirty look.

"No, no one got called to serve abroad. I thought it was time for new traditions. Since you three are going to the academy, I thought service is service. So here we are, ready to laugh, sing, and tell tall tales," Ben said as he handed Rob his guitar.

"Man, I forgot you could sing. I remember you dragging us to a gig or two during basic," Kyle said.

"Don't be shy, Kyle. I remember you could hit a note or two as well. Country, wasn't that your thing?" Rob asked.

Kyle did not respond. He just simply watched the fire as Rob began to play. When he looked at Kyle and said, "Remember this one?" as he started playing a few notes," You always killed it. Come on."

Kyle looked at him and started to sing: *"I believe in ghosts. Most people don't. I swear it on my grandpa's grave. I've seen them in the trees, I've seen them in my dreams, and I still can't stay away. My heart wants to wander here, and yonder, I let you come along and take it. Baby, you're the right one, the right one by my side. Maybe you're the one that is going to break it."*

"That was amazing. Whose song is that?" Atlas asked

"Jackson Dean Fearless, right?" Rob interjected as Kyle seemed to shake himself off from a trance.

"Let's not waste this beautiful fire. Come, let's go grab us some food and drinks," Barb said, pulling Ben up and walking to the house.

"Hey, what is their deal? Are they together or not? I cannot figure it out," Atlas asked the group.

"Barb is like the wind, and Ben is like the mountains. They just simply work well together. Come on, Rob, let's go help them before she starts bossing him around. You know how he starts twisting his face when she does that," Ellie suggested. Ava pulled Levi to go in as well.

"So you think they did that intentionally?" Atlas remarked, looking around.

"Did what?" Kyle said, staring at the fire, almost hypnotized.

"Leaving us together. Like we are here all alone," she said.

"You know Atlas, you are very young. Things aren't always the way that you think," he said without looking at her.

"I guess. I do hope one day I find the kind of love they have here," she said.

"I hope you do as well. Life is fun and easy when you are young. You are careless with your heart. Never knowing if you are truly in love or not, you just give it away," Kyle explained.

"What do you mean?" she asked.

"One day, you will get it, but for now, if I am honest, you are simply too impulsive. Impulsive makes you dangerous," Kyle responded.

"Well, that's it for me. I don't want to make you feel uncomfortable. I will simply excuse myself and walk to my cabin," she said in a furious tone, standing and walking away.

"Like I said, impulsive and dangerous," Kyle said, walking behind her.

"Stop following me!" she yelled at him.

"What is all that commotion?" Ava asked from inside the house.

"Love," Barb replied.

"No way Kyle is way too old for Atlas," Ava said.

"You were too young for me, and here we are," Levi said, reaching for her hand and giving it a kiss.

"What are your plans, Ava? Are you next to jump the broom?" Barb asked.

"Well, it's a bit complicated. I need to convert from Christianity to Judaism, and it is going to take time," Ava said, "for Levi, I would walk to the moon," as she looked tenderly at Levi.

Ellie tried to look out the window to see what was going on outside, but Rob pulled her away, "Now, Darling, let them figure it out."

"Did I not tell you to stop following me? I know the way. I don't need an escort," Atlas shouted as Kyle continued to follow her away from the house and towards the trail that led to her cabin.

"You know Atlas, I hate repeating myself, but you are careless," Kyle said and stopped.

Atlas turned and yelled, "What? How?"

"Do you know anything about this state? Did you forget you are in Wyoming? Well, young lady, for your information, Wyoming is filled with bears. You are currently residing next to a national forest with bears. Bears, who might not know they are trespassing into Ben's ranch," Kyle said calmly. "Now let me walk you to your cabin before you get mauled to death." He then abruptly grabbed her arm and pulled her closer toward him.

"I don't hear them anymore. Do you?" Ellie asked.

"The coast is clear. We can go back outside if you all want?" Rob said with a huge smile.

"Why don't you gentlemen go ahead and carry the cooler? We will be out shortly with the food," Barb suggested.

Once the men stepped outside, Barb gathered the two women and said, "You mark my words, that is a lot of man for such a young girl. I am so glad her name is Atlas, and she can carry the weight of the world on her shoulders. I hope she quickly realizes that man has it all: looks, manners, and a kind heart."

"Barb, don't start with your predictions. She is a wild mustang, and it takes strength and determination to tame one. Even then, a Mustang is a Mustang, no matter if they are saddled. In their heart, they are free," Ben said, sticking his head through the doorway.

"Well, you just wait and see you, Old Devil. Barb here knows what she is talking about. You just wait and see what happens next," Barb said, walking out to the porch. "Just wait and see. Their story will be a wild one. Can't wait for it to be told you know love is alluring."

Chapter 2

Love is Alluring

Atlas walked quickly, trying her best to stay ahead of Kyle, who was holding the flashlight. She was furious at him for making her feel like a child. She could see the cabin just ahead. Atlas turned around and said, "Happy I made it to the cabin. See no bears. You are free to leave." Atlas looked at Kyle, wondering why he had stopped dead in his tracks. She turned to see several pieces of her clothing all over the ground.

"Wow, I am not sure what happened here?" Kyle said.

Atlas turned to see most of her clothes scattered throughout the yard. Stepping forward, she could tell a critter had eaten through her boxes and bags.

"What the heck, Atlas? What were you thinking? Why didn't you take your stuff inside? Why did you leave your things out here?" Kyle illuminates the yard with the light.

"Crap! Crap! Crap! I just dropped everything on the front porch and went to get the keys from Ellie. She did not tell me anything about animals in the area. I don't know anything about bears. You think it was a bear? What the hell was the bear looking for in my stuff?"

"Food?" Kyle said with some astonishment.

"What? Are you kidding me?" Atlas said as she started picking up her items.

"Where are the keys to the cabin? I will get the door open and then help you gather your stuff," Kyle stated as he opened the door, which was not locked. "Hey, the door was open. Why didn't you check it before you went to get the keys?"

"I just assumed it was locked. So I dropped my stuff and went to look for Ellie or Ben to get the keys," Atlas said as she bent over to pick up items.

Kyle turned on the lights, and one could see her garments scattered throughout the field, "as I said, you are careless. Because you are careless, things like this happen to you. You are too impulsive. You need to stop and think before you do." Kyle walked over and began helping her grab her stuff.

"How was I supposed to know that this was going to happen? I am not from here. I don't live in the woods. I am from St. Louis City, for God's sake. I didn't join the Girl Scouts. I have never been camping. I didn't even sleep in the backyard. So, I simply did not know. Okay!" she yelled out of frustration.

"If you don't know, you need to ask. I can help you if you let me, but I am telling you you are going to get yourself or someone else hurt if you don't grow up, son. Being a cop is not just looking good in a car. It is not like in the movies. You could get into a fight, stabbed, shot," Kyle said, handing her some clothing, "people are going to look at you for answers. You get it?"

"Stop scolding me. I get it. I was willing to learn it was just a stupid mistake," Atlas said, pulling clothes from Kyle's arms.

"Well, it looks like I am going to have to wait until you get it through your thick head," Kyle said as he walked to another pile of clothes.

"Don't bother, I can get this stuff myself. I don't need your help. I thought we were going to be friends, but I guess I am simply too dumb to hang out with you," she said, walking into the cabin.

"Look, Atlas, you are not dumb, and I never called you dumb. You are just naive, and I don't want you to get hurt. You are out here all alone, and I worry about you, that is all," Kyle said, following her into the one-bedroom cabin.

"Really, I can gather my clothes. I will figure it out, "she said in a furious tone.

"Do you even have a flashlight?" Kyle asked.

"No, but I guess because I am young, I have my cell phone. All cell phones have a flashlight feature. So you can go. I got it," Atlas said while frantically looking for her cell phone.

"I thought you said you had misplaced it. Do you want help looking for it? Or do you want help getting your clothes inside before a raccoon gets your Victoria Secret's undergarments?" Kyle said with a half-laugh.

"Don't bother! Just don't bother! I don't care! Whatever!" Atlas yelled as she pushed Kyle out. "Seriously!! This trip sucks!"

"Oh," Kyle said. "I think the raccoon found your cell phone," he said, illuminating the grass a few feet away from the cabin.

"Great," she said, running to get it, "Crap, it's dead. Do you see the charger?"

"Well, I think it might be this," holding up a well-chewed-up wire.

Atlas dropped her head back and felt tears rolling down her face. Kyle did not want to be pushed again, so he did not even try to comfort her. Instead, he picked up a box and walked inside. He returned outside, pointed at the entrance, and said, "Why don't you go on in and relax? I will pick up the rest of your stuff and throw it inside for you."

Reluctantly, she went inside and dropped into the bed, crying uncontrollably. Kyle cleaned up the yard and brought the items inside. He could hear Atlas sobbing in the dark room. "Are you alright? Do you need anything?" Kyle asked almost in a whisper.

"No, just go away," she yelled back between tears.

He walked into the bedroom and sat next to her, gently stroking her hair, "Don't stress so much. You are not alone here. I mean, we got you. You are with good people. Just calm down."

"Calm down. Are you patronizing me? Don't tell me what to feel. How do you feel? I don't want to calm down. Whoever told you to talk to a woman that way? Calm down!" Atlas said, raising up from the bed, causing Kyle to stand at attention.

"Woman? You? Who are you kidding? I have scars older than you. Woman, she says," Kyle responded without missing a beat.

"Get out! Get out! I don't want to talk to you anymore. I thank you for your assistance, Sir, but now I am asking you to please exit my room," she said, pointing to the door. Kyle walked out without saying a word, taking his flashlight. He stood on the porch for a second, contemplating leaving the flashlight, when he heard a loud "tonk."

"Crap!" he heard Atlas shouting.

"Are you alright, Attie?" he said, wondering if she had broken something like her toe.

"No, I am not alright, but I will figure it out. Didn't I tell you to leave? And I am Atlas, not Attie," she shouted.

"Wow, alright, Attie, I mean Atlas, the woman. I am leaving the flashlight here so you don't stumble and kill yourself in the dark," Kyle shouted back as he placed the flashlight on the window frame of the small cabin and began walking away.

Atlas was furious as she heard his words. She ran outside, grabbed the flashlight, and chuckled it at him, but she was missing. "I guess we will need to work on your aim and temper. This is going to be a long academy, Attie," he said, walking away.

"Oh, shut up! Just shut up," Atlas said, walking to the flashlight, grabbing it, and going back inside.

Kyle made his way over the ridge as the group was having a great time at the bonfire. Ava looked up and said, "Hey, Kyle is walking back alone. You think he is coming back?"

"Na, not after that lover's quarrel," Barb responded with a huge grin.

"Maybe I should see if he is alright and if he wants to rejoin us?" Rob asked the group.

"No, I would not. If you look closely, that man is walking in the shadows. I can see the spirits of his past are chasing him. Why don't you let him be? You too, Barb, I am asking you not to start giving him any ideas," Ben warned.

"Ideas," Barb said, rolling her eyes, "You see spirits. I see sparks. I just call it like I see it."

"Well, don't be calling it something it is not. Kyle is haunted, and I am not sure Atlas is strong enough to handle it," Ben said, reaching his arm around Barb and pulling her close to him.

"Let us not forget Atlas is the god of strength and endurance," Barb said.

"Strength and endurance. Atlas? She is impulsive and immature. Don't get me wrong. I like her and all, but all she got from Atlas is the name," Ellie interjected.

"We'll just have to wait and see, Doll. I tell you, that man is smitten," Barb said, cuddling to Ben.

"Great Spirit helps us all if that is the case. Atlas is wild, and Kyle is haunted. Untangling them just might be a group effort," Ben said, letting out a contagious laugh.

The next morning, Kyle found himself walking in the direction of Atlas' cabin. He could still see clothing scattered all around. He decided to pick it all up and simply place it on her front porch. Kyle looked at his watch and noticed it was 3:45 A.M. He tapped, pushing it open. He walked into the cabin, shaking his head while making his way to the bedroom. There, Atlas was sleeping peacefully, tucked into the covers, snuggling her pillow as if it were a person. Kyle looked around and noticed she had only unpacked a few things, such as pictures, a few books, and stuffed animals, making him smile and almost chuckle.

Kyle took a deep breath and sat on the edge of the bed. He tenderly stroked her long brown hair, whispering her name, "Attie, Attie, come on, you need to get up." But Atlas did not budge. He tried it again, but nothing. Atlas kept sleeping as if nothing was happening. Kyle looked at his watch again and then started shaking Atlas by pushing her shoulder. He thought of pulling her covers off but rethought it since he could not tell if she was dressed. He hoped she was, but he did not want Atlas to think he was a "creep."

Atlas finally started to open her eyes, saying, "Come on, Dad, five more minutes."

"Attie, get up! Come on!" Kyle said in a strong tone, standing up from the bed.

Atlas opened her eyes, looked around, and noticed the time, "You have got to be kidding me. It's like 3 A.M. What the hell, Kyle? Why are you getting me up at this hour?"

"Attie, wake up! There is lots to do before daybreak. Come on, you are late getting dressed," he instructed.

"No way, it's too early," she said, rolling over and pulling the covers over her head.

"Good Lord, I hope you are dressed because I am pulling the covers off you," Kyle said, reaching for a handful of blankets.

"You would not dare. I could be naked. I am too tired! Kyle, so go away!" she responded.

"As you wish. I don't care if you are naked. I have seen my share of naked women. I mean girls," he said, pulling off the covers with such force that Atlas fell to the floor. She was wearing a white silk sheer tank and matching boxers.

Atlas was furious. She looked at Kyle from the floor and yelled, "What the hell are you doing, Kyle? Why can't you let me sleep?"

"Look, Attie, you are now employed at this ranch. You need to be grateful for the food and shelter these people are giving you. I got you this job, and you will not make me look like a jerk," he said.

"Alright, but do you know what time is? Why do I have to wake up so early?" Atlas said, trying to stand.

Kyle reached out his hand and pulled her up on her feet. He noticed the sweet, flowery scent, which was soft but alluring. He immediately pushed her away, saying, "Great, we are late. Come on, you need to put on some proper clothes. I will wait for you outside for 90 seconds."

Atlas ran to the bathroom, brushed her teeth, and threw on some jeans, a sports bra, a white shirt, and a pair of tennis shoes. She ran out, and the cool air cut through her body like a knife, making her shiver. Atlas started rubbing her hands over her bare arms when a coat was thrown at her.

"I knew you didn't even bother to bring proper clothing to this adventure, did you? Don't bother answering me. I know the answer. Careless, Attie simply careless. You need to get more appropriate clothes and proper pyjamas. You will catch a cold. Now come on, we are late," Kyle barked at her as she struggled to keep up.

"Where are we going? Can you at least tell me that? And is there coffee there? I am dying for a cup," Atlas said.

"Attie, you are at a working ranch. You need to be at the barn at least by 3:45 each morning. If I was a betting man. You should really plan to be here by 3:30. Ben needs to know you are serious and grateful to be here. Come on, step it up," he said.

"I don't mind working, but why so early?" she complained.

"Amazing! I got you a place to stay and a job, and you are throwing a tantrum," Kyle said.

Atlas took a deep breath, acknowledging her behavior. She waited a second or two and then said, "I am sorry if I came across as ungrateful. I am not; I have never worked at a ranch. Can you please explain the time thing? Why so early?"

"Horses are not tied to a clock like you and I are. They have an internal schedule. So, if Rob and Ben are breaking them in, you will need to train them to have a timeline. A routine, do you understand? The mustangs need to get used to people, and you will be the first person they see every morning," he replied.

"I kind of get it, but, "she said.

"But nothing, Attie. This is your part, and that is it. I will show you what to do, but it is up to you to do it, period," Kyle said in a strong tone.

"I guess I should say thank you," she said smugly.

"Yes, you should," he responded without missing a beat

They walked into the barn, and Atlas smelled a mixture of hay, stale water, and manure. She could not help but say loudly, "Gross."

"Yep, this is a ranch. Get used to the smell. You might as well see if you can slip into those boots, as there are coveralls over there. Just put those over your clothes. Tie your hair up or something so it's not in the way. And for God's sake, hurry up. I want Ben to see us working when he gets here," he said.

"Us? You're working here too? Are you staying here? I didn't think you were going to move in?" she said while trying to pull the oversized coverall over her clothes as her hair cascaded over her shoulder. Kyle watched as Atlas flung her hair back, and with little effort, she pulled her hair back into a ponytail. She smiled when she noticed Kyle watching her. "I am ready to learn."

"Okay, put these gloves on. Wait! You need to push your pants legs inside of the rubber boots," he growled at her.

"Why?" she asked as she bent over, almost falling into Kyle.

"Lord, you are a mess," he said as he pushed her into a bench and did it for her, "you need to stop asking so many questions. Keep them in your head, do the task, and then you will have your answer. Do you understand?"

"Kind of," she said almost under her breath.

"Look Attie, law enforcement is paramilitary. You need to get it, or you will have a hard time at the academy," he said as he helped her up, "Now, put those gloves on and grab that rake. We will start by cleaning the empty stall. Then, we will focus on the horses. Each horse needs to be brushed. Do you know how to do it? Never mind, I better show you how to do it right," Kyle said.

Atlas rolled the wheel barrel near the first stall, took the rake, and started clearing the piles of dung. She spent about five minutes completing this task. She tossed the clean shavings aside. Atlas had a little experience dealing with horses, but she knew that the wet spots needed to be mopped up or dried. She found cat litter in the corner near the front door and poured it over the spots. Finally, she raked hay shavings and then moved the horse into the clean stall. Atlas continued in this matter until every stall was clean and ready. She placed her hands on her hips with pride as she noticed Ben walking towards her with a cup of coffee.

"Good Morning, Sir. Kyle and I got an early start," she said with a huge smile.

"You were late, but no matter what, you will do better tomorrow," Ben said, handing her the cup. Ben then walked back towards the main house.

Atlas took a sip of coffee, "what the hell? I was late. He never told me what time to be here."

Kyle walked next to her, grabbed the cup out of her hand, drank the coffee, and handed her back the cup.

Atlas was shocked at this behavior, "You drank it all?"

Kyle smiled at her, saying, "Come on, we will move the horses down, clean up, and have breakfast."

Atlas smiled and followed him. Kyle grabbed the cup out of Atlas' hand and replaced it with a brush. He led Atlas to the left side of the horse, stood behind her, and placed his hand over hers, saying, "Always start on the left. Everything with horses always starts on the left. Got it? Alright, use long, sweeping strokes in the direction of the hair growth to whisk away any particles left by the dandy brush and smooth down the hair." Kyle placed his left arm around Atlas's waist, reaching her side as she leaned on him. He used his tactic to maneuver her easily as they continued to brush until they were done. "For the lower legs, use shorter sweeping strokes, but always make sure the horse is nice and comfortable. Remember, whatever you are feeling, the horse will feel."

"Huh?" she said without thinking. Atlas felt as if she was just in a trance, bracing herself against Kyle's body.

"Horses are very spiritual animals, and they perceive changes in feelings. If you are nervous, it will be transferred to the horse. If you are happy, the horse is happy, and so on," Kyle said as he moved Atlas to the other side, and together they brushed the horse with large strokes.

"You really believe that?" she asked.

"Yes, so if you are nervous, anxious, or scared, don't brush them. Horses are great animals. They are very grateful for your tender care. They are great listeners and are always happy to see you when you are lonely," Kyle said.

"So what you are saying is if you are feeling like a jackass, then the horse will feel like one too?" Atlas responded, then chuckled, "Get it? Turning a horse into a mule or an ass."

Kyle stopped guiding and released her hand, stepping back, "Attie, you need to take this job seriously. It will help you get through the academy and life. This is important."

"Do you ever let up? I mean, you got me up in the middle of the night. For heaven's sake, you drank all my coffee. You could at least have a bit of a sense of humor," she responded, turning towards him. Then, walking back towards the wall with supplies.

"Well, that is not the point. This is not the time for games or jokes," he said.

"Wow, what a crab ass," she said, grabbing a bucket of water and tossing it at him.

"What the hell, Attie?" Kyle yelled, and the commotion caused the horse to kick and try to pull away. Making all the other horses nervous, so they started kicking their stalls. Kyle pulled the horse back, attempting to calm it down. After several minutes, he finally was able to make the horse comfortable again. He then proceeded to scold Atlas, "You are so silly. This is no place to play. Don't you know horses are unpredictable and dangerous? Get your act together, Attie!"

"I am sorry I forgot. I was trying to loosen you up. Stop treating me like a child!" she yelled back.

"I will when you stop acting like one, Attie," Kyle said, walking away and heading to his cabin.

Atlas could not let him have the last word, so she ran out and yelled as loudly as she could, "Stop calling me, Attie. My name is Atlas!"

Chapter 3

Heartbreak

The shouting from the stables carried over to the main house, where Rob and Ellie sat on the porch enjoying their morning coffee with Ben. Ben stood and walked to the railing, saying, "Those two are going to be the death of me. Their childish fights are going to spook the mustangs, and we will get nothing accomplished today."

"Give them a minute, and I am sure they will settle down. Besides Ben, the mustangs need to get used to the noise if they are going to the rodeo," Rob said, trying desperately to ease Ben's fury.

Ben stood stoic, just waiting to step into the barn and raise hell.

"Why don't you go and take Barb her breakfast in bed? I know how much you enjoy that?" Ellie said with a huge grin.

"You know, Ellie you talk too much," Ben said, walking inside of the house.

"Don't forget her flower," Ellie yelled in, laughing and turning to Rob," what you know, he loves it."

"Ellie, you are bad. I guess I should go and check on Kyle and Atlas," Rob responded with some hesitation.

"What is his deal anyway? I heard Ben talking about how Kyle walks in the shadows," Ellie asked, placing her hand on Rob as if telling him to stay with her.

"You get everything wrong, girl. I said he was haunted. I came to cut a flower for Barb, as you suggested, while the coffee is brewing," Ben said, walking outside one more time.

"Well, I don't know the whole story. I recall that, during basic training, Kyle was one of the youngest recruits. I want to say he was maybe 16, and his parents had to sign for him to join. I remember that well because he was the youngest to join. Our Drill Sgt. made it a point to tell us to watch out for him. As a tradition, on the first night of basic training, we sat around and got to know one another. The drill sergeant said it was good for us to have the chance to join. Most of the recruits said they joined because they loved the county or because they wanted money for school. That was the reason I needed the money for college.

It was not Kyle Noyes; he was quiet and did not volunteer his story at first. The Sergeant said Noyes was an exceptional student who graduated from High School at the top of his class. He was an All-American, given both football and baseball scholarships all over the country. Noyes was one of the most sought-after players. Academically, he was given a Rhodes scholarship, which would pay for any University in the United States the full ride. One of the recruits asked why he had joined.

Kyle was mesmerized by the fire, staring at it, and without missing a beat, he said, "I need to pay back a debt. I made a promise to Isa, and I will keep my promises." We were all curious to hear the rest, but we waited, and a few minutes later, Kyle explained that he was dating a girl who had recently moved to Tennessee with her family. They had gone on two, maybe three dates, nothing serious. Kyle invited her to Homecoming, which was a big deal for the school because of his status. Isa had agreed, but she did not tell him her father did not approve. They met at the party and had a good time until her family came and dragged her away.

A few days later, at school, he noticed she had bruises on her arms. She explained her father was furious because of the dance. In her culture, women are more sheltered, and it appeared that Isa had been promised to an older man in marriage. Her father did not want her to embarrass the family name by dating, least of all an American. Kyle said he did not understand what the big deal was, but he respected her wishes. For the next few months, he would see her at school and sometimes at her job.

One evening before graduation, he asked her to go to prom, which was another tradition Isa had not experienced. She was very excited about attending. Kyle even paid for her dress so she could go. They were going to meet at Prom, but Isa never showed up. Kyle went to her job and was told her father made her quit. He did not understand what had happened and why she was not there. Days later, he was told that Isa had returned to his country of origin to get married. Kyle was sad but understood there was nothing to be done; however, one of Isa's friends later told him Isa had been killed.

Kyle stopped speaking for a bit. All the recruits were shocked at the news. The silence was broken by the Drill Sergeant, who told him to get it off his chest and burn it in the fire.

"Tell us the rest, son, how was Isa killed? What happened to her?" Sergeant asked.

"When Isa got back home, her father had discovered that we were dating. Dating is not even true. I had not even kissed her. We were just friends. They are good friends, but just friends. Her Dad did not believe her. He put her on a plane and sent her back so she would be murdered. According to their beliefs, if a female brings shame to the family, the only way to cleanse their name is with blood, her blood. I can't understand those traditions and how people can be so cruel to one another. When I heard the news, I promised Isa I would defend girls like her from such savage practices. I could not do that through academics or sports. So here I am. That is my mission."

Needless to say, we were all stunned by his testimony, but we understood what was driving him. Kyle's commitment to the military was impeccable. He was selected right after basic to join the Special Forces, but I lost track of him. Every once in a while, I would hear about a mission or two where girls had been rescued, and I wondered if it was his unit. In my heart, I knew he was charging in to get them out. Now, I am surprised to see him here."

"Why do you say that?" Ellie asked.

"Well, to be honest, I am not sure if he has acclimated himself back to society. Military life, especially an elite unit like his, requires a lot of discipline. Civilian life is not rigid," Rob said, standing up.

"So you think that is what is haunting him?" Ellie asked.

"Probably not," Ben interjected, "But he sure is going to have his hands full with that girl," as he walked inside the house carrying a beautiful rose.

"Roses are my favorite," Ellie said, chuckling.

"Shut up before I send you to referee the fireworks at the barn," Ben responded.

"You think he will be alright at the academy? Are you worried about him?" Ellie asked Rob, who was looking at the barn.

"Not sure if Kyle got Isa out of his system. I hope he found peace with that," Rob said as he watched Kyle walking out of the barn and heading towards his cabin.

"Looks like he is soaking wet. What do you think happened there?" Ellie said.

"Someone is giving Kyle a run for his money. Come on, let's go inside and get ready for the day," Rob said.

"I would not mind if you gave me a run for my money," Ellie said with a smile.

"Ellie, we already made the bed," Rob responded and turned to look at her.

"Well, let's go mess it up. Come on, it's early. Ben is busy with Barb. Kyle is headed to change. The horses are calm with Atlas. And you and I have," Ellie suggested

"Have no excuses," he said, grabbing her hand and running up the stairs.

While lying in bed, Ellie received a text message advising the academy supplies were ready to be picked up at the police academy. She quickly got ready and walked downstairs. Ellie made her way to the barn, looking for Atlas and maybe Kyle.

"Atlas, did you get the text message about our uniforms for the academy? They are ready to pick," she said excitedly.

"Oh no, my phone is not working, and my car is still not working. It doesn't matter that I can't leave since I have not finished here. There is a lot to do to make sure the mustangs are ready," Atlas replied while laying hay in the stall.

"Wow, Atlas, you are really taking this job seriously. I am very glad to see that. Why don't you take a break and we can all ride together? Have you seen Kyle? I am sure he will want to go with us," Ellie replied, looking out the window and searching for him.

"I am not sure if he is at the cabin or maybe he left. He was pretty pissed at me for dumping water on him," Atlas said.

"You two are a mess. Go get ready, and I will find him. He seems like a pretty nice guy. Don't worry. I am sure he will be over it by now," Ellie said, walking outside.

"I am not worried. I don't care if he is mad at me or not," Atlas said, running towards her cabin.

Ellie walked towards the west cabin but stopped when she noticed Kyle walking towards her. "Hey, I was just looking for you. Did you get the text from the academy?" she asked.

"Yes, I guess I need to tell Attie and make sure she is ready to go," he responded.

"No, I just told her. What is up with you two? I thought you were getting along," she asked while they were walking back.

"Don't get me wrong, Ms. Ellie, I just think she is too," he said but caught himself.

"Too impulsive?" she responded.

"Yes, Ma'am," he responded.

"OK, enough. You and I are going to be classmates, and my husband speaks highly of you. So, from now on, it will just be Ellie. No more Ms. or Ma'am, please," Ellie corrected him.

"Yes, Ma... I mean, thank you, Ellie. I just worry about Attie because she is too carefree," he said.

"Well, sometimes being carefree is alright, and maybe it's a bit refreshing. You and I have been taught discipline, but civilians are spontaneous. Can you imagine us being that unpredictable? Think of it as a Marine and Special Forces just winging it?" she said, laughing, and they both laughed for a few minutes. "Can I ask you a question?" Ellie said between chuckles.

"Yes, Ma' am, Ellie, of course my life is an open book," Kyle said, wiping the tears off his eyes.

"Are you transitioning alright back to civilian life? I know it is difficult," she asked.

"I think so. I just want to be normal. It seems like I have not been normal for so long. I guess the first step is always unsteady, but I am sure I will get the hang of it. How about you? Are you ready for this type of life?" Kyle stopped to wait for her answer.

"Well, I am not sure if you know I got injured while out on the battlefield. It took time for me to find my way home and back to Rob. I do have him, Ben, and Ava. They are my people. Do you have people?" Ellie asked while reaching for Kyle's arm.

"To be honest, Ellie," he said with a smile, "I have been alone for so long, and I really cannot recall the last time I had people. That was one reason why I decided to transition to the law enforcement field. I miss the military family, and they were my people," he said.

"What are your plans? I mean, do you have a place to stay while at the academy?" Ellie said while they started walking again.

"I reserved a room in Cheyanne, and I put all my stuff in storage at a place near the academy," he said as they got closer to the main house.

"As you know, Atlas is working here on room and board. I know you have been helping her a lot because, let's be honest, she needs guidance. I would really like it if you would think about staying here. We have plenty of room and space if that is what you are looking for," she asked.

"Amazing, you guys are really nice, but I don't want to intrude. You already took in one stray, and I don't want to impose. Besides, as you can see, Attie and I don't see eye to eye," Kyle replied.

"Why don't we make a deal? You stay a few days and see if it is a good fit, and then make a decision. You know, adapt and overcome," Ellie was just finishing her sentence when she caught Atlas running out of her cabin wearing a crop top, joggers, and white sneakers. "You need to stay. I cannot deal with this girl by myself," she said, looking at Kyle, "Atlas you, I don't mean to be mean, but we are going to the academy. First impressions set the tone for the training. Why don't you come to the main house, and let's see what else you can wear."

Atlas looked, and she was not even wearing matching socks. They all started to laugh as she tried desperately to explain how her clothes were dirty because of the raccoons. Kyle's cell phone rang, and he started to walk towards his car as he answered it. Motioning to them, I will meet them here in a moment.

"Who do you think was calling him? "Atlas asked

"I don't know, maybe his wife or girlfriend," she casually replied.

"He didn't mention he was married, and I did not see a ring," Atlas said, turning to see Kyle sitting inside the vehicle. "But he looks serious. It must be important."

"So you looked to see if he had a ring," she asked while leading Atlas inside of the house.

"Well, you know, just for conversation. I don't," Atlas said in a hurry.

"He is very attractive, rough and all," she said, trying not to smile.

"No, I am not here for that. He is nice, but he is not my type. Besides, I am here to start my career, and I don't have time for such nonsense," Atlas said.

"Alright then. Let's be serious, what are you wearing? I am a bit taller than you so my clothes will look too big for you. Why don't we look though Sabina's stuff? She was about your size? Her clothes should fit better on you until we can clean yours," Ellie said.

"Why are you so nice to me? You and Rob and Kyle? Even Ben is grumpy but still nice. I don't get it," Atlas said, opening the closet and reaching for a pantsuit, "what do you think?"

"Yes, that is perfect. See if there are shoes that will fit you. You cannot go with sneakers." Ellis said, selecting some black pumps. As she reached for them, Ellis remembered Sabina telling her how she had broken her heel and that Bill had to carry her inside the hotel.

"You alright? I don't have to wear them if it bothers you. I am sure I can try some other shoes," Atlas said when she noticed her reaction.

"No, don't be silly. Sabina was the kindest person I knew. She would love for you to enjoy her clothes, heels, and anything else that fits you. I just still have a bit of a hard time dealing with her passing," Ellie said as she helped Atlas change. Then she helped her pull her long brown hair up into a messy ponytail. Atlas watched as Ellie transformed her look to be more mature and professional. "Alright, you don't need much makeup, just some blush and gloss. Walla!"

"Ellie, I really don't know how to thank you. I look so different," Atlas said.

"Great, you just need to become a bit more confident and centered. You will be fine. By the way did you call your father? He must be worried about you by now." she asked, trying not to pry.

"Well my phone is not working. It looks like I am a mess, but I talked to Director Spinelli before I came and he assured me I would be fine. He also mentioned the $5,000.00 bonus sign-on money. I hope they can give me an advance so I can fix my phone and car. We better get going. I really don't want to be late or miss him," Atlas said as she walked outside before Ellie could get a word in. Atlas walked towards Kyle's SUV, and he stepped out, hung up his phone, and reached for the door to help her in.

"Wow, Attie, you look really nice. It suits you," Kyle said, opening the passenger's side door and helping her inside. Kyle then stood outside, waiting for Ellie to join them. A few minutes later, Ellie walked over, and Atlas stepped out to see if she wanted to sit in front of Kyle.

"Hey, do you guys mind riding together? Rob wants to go into town as well to buy some more supplies. Besides, he doesn't like Spinelli, so he wants to make sure he doesn't get fresh or do something like that. So we will meet you guys at the academy?" Ellie said.

"Sure, no problem. We will stop at the auto store and grab the water pump to fix Atlas' car," Kyle responded as he walked around the car once more to help Atlas back into the car. "You ready?" Atlas nodded as he closed the door. It took about 40 minutes to get to the auto shop, but Atlas barely spoke a word during the trip. She simply keeps grabbing her wallet.

As they parked, she asked, "How much do you think the part is going to cost?"

"It should not be that much less than $100.00. Why are you short?" he asked.

"No, I am good. I will put it on my credit card. I can pay it off with my bonus check," she answered with some relief.

Kyle stepped out and opened the door for her once more, saying,

"You know, Attie, that is not a lot of money. You can't just keep counting on it as if it is an endless pot of money."

"I know, but that is all I have until I get my first few paychecks. I will catch up once I start working steadily," Atlas said as she stepped out of the car and made her way into the store. Kyle got in front of her and opened the door. She looked at him with some surprise at his old-fashioned good manners.

"You know Kyle, you don't have to keep doing that. I can open my own doors, but I do appreciate it. It is very nice, and it makes me feel special, like a lady," Atlas said.

"I don't mind because it is the right thing to do. You should feel special like a lady when you are with a man regardless of whether he is with you or just your friend. After all, you are a lady," he said as he opened the shop's door, "let's go in and find your part."

She smiled at him, saying, "Thanks."

Kyle walked up to the counter and asked for the part while Atlas waited at the counter, ready to pay. The man rang up the bill, and she quickly paid again without saying a word. The man handed her the receipt and the part. Kyle reached for the part, "Now, Attie, you don't want to get dirty." Once again, he reached for the door, opening it for her as she walked outside. Kyle quickly placed the part inside of the truck and helped her back into the SUV.

"Thank you," she said.

"We are really close to the academy. Are you getting excited or nervous?" he asked while he drove towards the center.

"I guess a bit of both. You must think I am a baby. This is really my first time away from home and on my own," she confessed.

"I think you are brave. It's OK to be both. To be honest, I am a bit of both as well," he kindly said.

They made their way to the recruitment center and saw that Rob and Ellie were waiting for them near the staircase outside. Atlas looked out of the passenger's side window, mesmerized by the enormity of the building. It was a large three-story brick building with pillars. Just outside, there was a fountain and a statue of a fallen officer. At the very top of the building, the sign read Wyoming's Police Academy. She waited patiently for Kyle to open her door, and as soon the door opened, she stepped out, ready to join the rest of the recruits. Atlas looked down and read the names of officers engraved into the cinder block with the letter EOW. "EOW?" she said out loud.

"End of Watch," Kyle whispered.

There were a number of recruits lining up and waiting to enter. Atlas noticed she was only one of four females in an ocean of men. As they entered the auditorium, each one was handed a large box containing all the necessary equipment. Director Spinelli came out to greet everyone, saying, "Good

Morning, Ladies and Gentlemen. Welcome to Wyoming's Police Academy. Here, you will be taught everything you need to know about law enforcement. We will teach you the fundamentals and skills to survive. It will be up to you to apply it. Allow me to be blunt: some of you, I can already tell, will not be returning on Monday to start. We thank you for coming up, but you will be dismissed. Please don't bother reapplying. We have an expectation of you. If you decide to come dressed today like you are going on a picnic or to the beach, I don't want you in my academy. You were notified to come dressed in a professional manner. Those who made the effort are welcome to stay. Julie Pearson, Joshua Jones, David Mc Donnelly, Julius Walker, you are dismissed."

Atlas watched in horror as the recruits walked out of the building in shame. She looked at her clothes and then at Ellis. She shot her a huge smile and placed her hand over her heart in a circle, singing, "Thank you." Ellie simply nodded as if saying you are welcome. The moment was then interrupted by Spinelli, who continued his speech, "Let me warn you, those of you who have remained don't get cocky. This is going to be the toughest and hardest training you will endure. I understand we have military members who have joined us. Please raise your hand if you have military experience?" Everyone but three, including Atlas, raised their hand. "Alright then, I will say to those who do not have military training, don't be discouraged. Sometimes, it is better to have a clean slate than to have bad habits.

This academy will adhere to strict rules and regulations. There will be no preferential treatment based on gender, age, or disability. You will be expected to pass all examinations with a minimum score of 90 percent. In addition, you are required to pass all fitness skills tests. As a 10-year veteran of the prestigious Atlanta Police Department and SWAT team Commander, I will tell you this will be hell for all of you. The only thing I can compare this to is SEAL training. I designed this new curriculum because I am tired of officers dying in the line of duty. So believe me when I tell you if you are not fit for this challenge, walk out now." Everyone looked around, and one of the guys made his way to the door. "Alright, then good luck recruits. I will see you on Monday."

Atlas opened her box, which was filled with supplies with her name on it. She noticed an invoice for $500.00 taped to the outside of the package, and she stared at it in shock, saying, "What the hell is this?"

"Hi, I am George Adams." he said, extending his hand, "That was crazy. Just like that, we lost four recruits. And what about the last guy just walking out. Five are no longer here." he noticed Atlas was not answering him, she was just looking at the paperwork, "Did you not read the email and text message. You have to put a $500.00 deposit before you can take the equipment."

"Crap, I don't think I can put it on my credit card. I just maxed it out and then some. What the hell am I going to do?" Atlas said, closing her box.

"Come on, Atlas, we will take our boxes to the car and then come back to help you," Ellie said, walking out with Rob.

"I am sorry if you don't have the deposit. They will not allow you to be in the program," George told her.

"You ready?" Kyle asked, "I already put my stuff in the SUV. We can put yours in the backseat."

"I will not be going with you guys. I guess no. I am sure this was a huge mistake," Atlas said as she could feel the tears start gathering in her eyes. "Do you think you can fix my car today? I would like to head home as soon as possible."

"You are going to quit? You have no backup plan?" Kyle asked, pulling her to the side of the room away from everyone else.

"No, I don't know what to do? I am out of money and credit. I cannot ask Ellie to help me. So you are right, I am done," Atlas felt the first tear escaping from her eyes and rolling down her face.

Kyle tenderly wiped it away and said, "I already covered you. Don't quit. I guess what I was trying to say was, "I am your backup plan."

"No, Kyle, I can't take your money," she said, pulling herself together.

"You are not. Besides, it is a deposit. When you graduate, I get it back. Now, come on, wipe your tears. Deputies don't cry. If Spinelli catches you, we will all pay with extra pushups." he said with a smile, taking her box to the car.

"You figured it out?" George said as he walked towards Atlas, "I see your boyfriend helped you out."

"No, he is not my boyfriend. He is my friend," she said, walking behind Kyle. "Sorry, I am Atlas Miller, and that is my friend Kyle Noyes. We will see you on Monday," Atlas said, catching up with Kyle.

Chapter 4

Runaway

Ellie realized Atlas was struggling with money. She did not want to embarrass her but wanted to make sure no one missed a meal. She decided to walk to the barn and invite Atlas to join them for dinner.

"Hey Ellie, I am almost done with the barn. Do you need me to do anything else?" Atlas asked.

"Wow, Atlas, you are really taking this job seriously. The barn looks amazing. Are you getting hungry? I was going to start dinner if you want to come to the house and eat," Ellie asked as she looked around.

"I don't want to be a bother, but I am a bit hungry. Just let me finish up here, and I will help you cook. I want to earn my keep," Atlas responded, tightening up the last few details. The women make it to the house to find Ben in the kitchen, which is already starting with dinner.

"Ben, I thought it was my turn to cook?" Ellie asked, pulling the spoon out of Ben's hand.

"I didn't see you. I assumed you had forgotten," Ben said, sitting at the table.

"No, I didn't. I just wanted to make sure I invited everyone to eat and see how much I needed to prepare," Ellie responded, "Atlas is going to join us. Is Barb in her room?"

"Barb left while you guys went to town. She did tell me to wish you good luck this week and not to worry, and it should be a quick trip," Ben said, standing, trying to grab a cup of coffee.

"Well, why don't you give us a few minutes to figure out what will be served? In the meantime, can you see if Kyle and Rob are ready to eat?" Ellie said as Ben reluctantly left, not wanting to argue with her.

"So Barb just comes and goes?" Atlas asked without thinking, then quickly saying, "Sorry, I need to think before I speak. That is none of my business."

Ellie shot her a smile and then noticed she was quiet, "What's wrong Atlas? Don't you know how to cook?"

"No, it's not that I know my way around a kitchen. In fact, my mom taught me well," she said.

"Are you missing your family?" Ellie asked.

"Yes, I guess I am a bit homesick. It's silly, right?" Atlas responded.

"No, not really. When I was abroad, I missed mine terribly. Can I ask you a question? Did you call your dad?" Ellie asked.

"No, I haven't spoken to my dad. I thought about calling him, but my phone is still messed up," Atlas responded.

"Here, take my phone call and tell him you're all right and where you are. Your family needs to know where you are; they need to know how to get a hold of you, and you should really tell them you're safe. Give him my phone number and the address, just in case. You can use the office for privacy, but you need to call," Ellie told her while handing her the cell phone.

As Atlas was going into the office, Rob and Kyle entered the house." Hey my love, what's for dinner? Rob asked while giving Ellie a big kiss.

"I'm not sure. I was waiting to see what you guys were hungry for. Atlas is in the other room trying to get a hold of her father, but after that, she's going to help me with dinner." Ellie told them.

"I'll go check to see if she's OK," Rob said, but he was quickly stopped by Kyle, who stated, "No, no, you two figure out dinner. I will go check on Attie."

Kyle turned the corner and heard Atlas speaking to someone on the phone. She was saying, *"No, I'm alright. You don't have to do that, I swear. I'm good. I really appreciate it, really, Dad. You don't have to worry. No, no, I don't need your money. I have a job and a place to stay, and I will be starting the Academy soon. No, I'm not sure if I'm staying here. Well, it all depends. Yes, I know it's a long way from home, but you always said I needed to grow up. Yeah, that's fine. Of course, I'll speak to Mom.*

Hey Mom, no, no, I'm good. I know I should have told you, but you always said I should go out and have an adventure here. I am having an adventure. Yes, I do know what I'm doing. No, I'm not taking any chances. Dad has the address and phone number as soon as I get my phone charged. I'll call you love you too. Wait, Mom, did anyone call for me? No, I was just, yeah, I know. I definitely do a lot of distance, all right, Mom. I have to go help with dinner. Oh yes. No, ma'am, you don't have to worry. No, I will not be doing that. No, really, Mom, they're really nice. I hope you can come to visit soon. I had better go. I love you. I will talk to you soon. Bye," Atlas hung up the phone and turned around to notice Kyle's standing in the doorway. Atlas could not stop tears from rolling down her face.

Kyle took a step forward and hugged her saying, "What's the matter? Are you alright?" Kyle wrapped his arms around her.

"Yes, I just called home. I guess I am just a bit homesick. You must think I am silly," she said, pushing herself back and wiping her tears. "Hey are you staying for dinner? I am going to help Ellie cook," Atlas could hear Kyle's cell phone ringing.

"Yeah I hope that's OK Ellie and Rob invited me," he answered his phone call and stepped aside as Atlas walked back to the kitchen.

"Is everything all right with your Dad?" Ellie asked as she was placing the plates on the table

"Yeah, they're good. He wasn't happy, but he understands. I gave him your address and phone number. I hope that is alright," Atlas said.

"Sure, I am sure he feels better knowing you are safe. Did you see the emails from the academy?" Ellie said as she mixed seasons into a pot.

"No, I don't have access until I get my cell phone fixed. Was it something important? I know everything is important, but something I have to complete," she asked, trying to walk around the counter to help.

"Yes, there are several attachments. I got dinner. Why don't you log on to the office and check your email?" Ellie suggested.

Atlas noticed Kyle had walked out of the porch from the office. He seemed to be engaged in a serious call. She wondered who he was talking to, but she decided not to intrude. Atlas logged on and opened the email from Director Spinelli. Kyle walked in, placing his phone inside his back pocket.

"I thought you were helping with dinner," Kyle asked as he entered the office.

"Ellie said we got emails from the Academy. I was signing the paperwork," Atlas said as she tapped on the keys on the keyboard.

"What! Did you read it or just signed it blindly?" Kyle said in a loud tone.

Atlas was surprised at his attitude change," I acknowledged twice and signed. What is the big deal?"

"Did you send it?" he questioned as he walked around to see the monitor.

"Yes again, what is the big deal?" she asked, trying to figure out what he was telling her.

"The big deal is that you signed the commitment contract. You just committed to work five years in exchange for a $5000 sign-on bonus. Do you even know what that means?" he was frustrated at her. "I told you if you don't know something, you need to ask?"

"Yeah, I have a job guaranteed for 5 years," she said in a smartass tone, pushing her chair away from the desk and standing up.

"Well, yes, but did you read the fine print? Of course, you didn't. It says if you fail the academy or any future training, you will have to pay back the cost of the academy, the bonus, and any other money they spent on you. Get it?" Kyle as he pulled up the paperwork.

"Yeah, I do, and I don't care. I am committed, so I guess I better not fail," Atlas said, walking out of the room.

"It is not just failing, and you are stuck here. You limited your choices," Kyle yelled at her.

Atlas stopped dead in her tracks and returned to the office to say, "You know I am getting sick and tired of you treating me like a child. I am not a baby," she then turned around.

"Then stop acting like one. You cannot be so careless with your life. Your decisions affect others. You are selfish," Kyle said, turning his attention back to the computer screen.

"Enough! I am not your child, little sister, or girlfriend. I can make my own decisions. It is my life, after all." she said, turning and facing him.

"Exactly, that is what you are not getting. It is your life, but living the way you are has consequences," Kyle responded.

"I don't care. Besides, Anthony or Tony said he would help me," Atlas said with a huge smile.

"Anthony, who the hell is Anthony or Tony? You mean Spinelli. Director Spinelli, he just wants to get into your pants," Kyle responded.

"No, don't say that he is just nice," Atlas said, crossing her arms around her chest.

"He is a slimy guy. Why do you think Rob went with Ellie? He gives out a bad vibe. You need to stay clear of him, "Kyle said.

"Stop telling me what to do. I can take care of myself," Atlas said, placing her hands on her hips.

"Sure you can, but guys like that can get naive girls like you in bed with just a few cheap words," Kyle said as his cell phone rang again.

"Well I will keep that in mind but let me tell you something I am not a whore. I don't sleep around," Atlas pointed her finger at Kyle.

Kyle was looking at his cell phone and then looked up, saying, "Wait, I never called you a whore, Attie. Please don't put words in my mouth."

"I better go help with dinner before you call me lazy too. And stop calling me Attie!" Atlas said, storming out. Atlas walked into the kitchen and immediately started washing the dirty dishes.

"Everything alright?" Ellie asked

"Yeah, Kyle and I had a difference of opinion," she responded

"Well, that sounded more than just a difference of opinion if you ask me," Rob said, walking inside and taking a peek inside the pot. What's for dinner? "

"Beef stew. I thought that since the weather was getting cooler, it would be nice. Atlas toasted bread. You want to wash up. All we're missing is Ben, "Ellie said, looking around the room.

"No, Ben, he went into town. He said not to wait for him. I guess it's just us," Rob replied.

"Atlas, why don't you tell Kyle to join us?" Atlas reluctantly stopped washing the dishes, and as she turned off the water, Kyle walked in, stating, "it smells delicious."

"Yeah, my Ellie is a hell of a cook. " Rob said, reaching his arm around Ellie.

"Did you make dessert?" Kyle asked, eyeing the fresh fruit on the counter.

"No, I did not," Ellie responded as she made her way to the table.

"Well, I see the oven is warm. I can make us an apple pie if you would like, "Kyle.

"You can bake?" Atlas asked with a smirk on her face, turning to dry her hands with a hand towel.

"Yeah, one of the many things my grandmother taught me, "Kyle said

"How was your call with your Dad?" Ellie asked, hoping to stop the tension between Kyle and Atlas.

"He was super upset, but he got it. Well, the one who gets it is my mom, "Atlas responded as she served the dinner and then sat down.

"Tell us about yourself, Atlas. How many brothers and sisters do you have? Ellie asked.

"We are five all together. My older brother Tim is a fireman, my sister Annie is a teacher, and then it's me and little brothers James and Nick, work with my dad at the Brewery. Lots of people work there in St. Louis or wish they did. It's a good, steady job with benefits, like my father says. My mom is a librarian, and then there is me trying to figure my life out," Atlas said as she served herself a bowl of stew.

"Wow, that is a nice family. My parents died when I was little, and my brother Scott raised me. He joined the Army and met Bill. They were connected at the hip. Until Scott was killed in action, and Bill promised to take care of me. That is how I joined the Young family. Ben took over as my father figure. I tease him a lot, but I respect him and love him like my dad," Ellie explained.

"Well, I guess it is my turn," Rob said, "I lost my dad when I was young, and it was just mom and I for a while. I wandered around a bit, got into the rodeo, and bucked off more times than I cared to admit. Made it back home and found my calling in the Army. I was deployed and captured with Bill. When we were rescued, I met this angel, Ellie, and the rest of our story to write. Kyle Noyes 'Maybe' you're up."

"I have nothing special to share. Oldest of three boys. Brothers both play football at the University of Tennessee. Parents are very proud of all. I don't have a strong connection with them. I joined the Army when they were like 10 and 8. My parents like to travel a lot. Dad worked in marketing, and Mom ran most of the clubhouse charities. They are good people, just not the warm type, if you know what I mean," Kyle said with no expression on his face.

"So guys excited about the academy?" Rob asked while helping to clear the table.

"Yeah, Tony says it's going to be the best time of my life," Atlas said, reaching for a piece of bread.

"Tony? Who is Tony, one of our classmates?" Ellie asked as she grabbed the dishes from Rob's hands and walked towards the sink.

"Stop, Ellie, this is rich, why don't you enlighten Ellie and Rob with more of Tony's wisdom," Kyle said, taking the dishes away from Ellie's hands and taking them to the sink.

"OK, what is the secret? Who is Tony?" Rob asked.

"Tony, you know Anthony," Atlas said, stuffing another piece of bread inside of her mouth.

"No, Atlas, you don't mean that ass Spinelli? Why the hell are you calling him Tony?" Rob said, making a face.

"He said I could in his emails and texts," she said with a mouth full of bread.

"I don't know which is worse. You are talking with your mouth full, or you are calling Spinelli Tony," Rob said, laughing while Ellie shot him a dirty look.

"Like I told her. She should not trust that slimy guy. He is just, wait, why is Peanut out of the barn? Atlas did you forget to coral her," Kyle said as he raced outside to catch the horse, "Damn it! Attie, I told you to be responsible," he yelled while pulling on the horse.

Atlas ran after him, saying, "Kyle, I swear she was the first horse I corralled. Look, the saddle is on. I didn't do that. Really!"

Rob and Ellis ran out after them, waving their arms at them.

"Damn, Kyle, I am sorry it was my fault. I got Peanut ready for Ellie and me to go for a ride. I left her tied to the fence and got side-track by the food and conversation. I am sorry, Atlas. I didn't mean for Kyle to get on you," Rob said.

"It's alright, Rob. He was going to yell at me for something or other," she said, walking back inside the house.

"Yeah, but Atlas, you really should not get too close to Spinelli. He is the director, your boss, your drill instructor. Get it? He cannot be your friend, and you should not be friendly with him. He might be giving you the wrong idea," warning Atlas before she made it inside the house.

"Hey Kyle, how long will it be for that pie to be ready?" Rob asked as he helped Ellie get on Peanut.

"About 45 minutes or so," Kyle replied.

"Great, we should be back by then," Rob said as he got on his horse. Kyle watched them ride away. He then made it inside the house and began prepping to make the pie.

"Attie want to help me make the pie?" Kyle asked as he watched Atlas wash the dishes.

"Yeah, I guess," she said, walking towards him.

"Alright, let's start by grabbing all we need," Kyle said.

"Where are the pie shells?" Atlas asked as she looked around the kitchen and then opened the refrigerator.

"While you are there, grab me the butter, and I will need a cup of ice water," Kyle said as he reached for the all-purpose flour. Kyle then started whisking the flour, butter, and water. He took six apples and a peeler, "can you peel the apples?"

"Are you asking me or telling me? "She snapped back.

"I thought you wanted to learn? If you don't, it's alright," Kyle responded while placing the skillet on top of the burner and melting some butter. He turned to see Atlas was reaching for the apples.

"Do I need to wash them first?" Atlas asked quietly.

"Yes, rinse them, pat them dry, and peel them. Then, I will show you how to score them. Then we slice, alright?" Kyle said with a smile. He added cinnamon and sugar to the pan.

Atlas did as instructed and then said, "Ready to core and slice them."

Kyle reached around Atlas and placed his right hand underneath hers. He then stepped forward a bit and reached for Atlas's right hand, cupping it as she held the knife. "Go slowly. I don't want you to cut yourself while coring the apple." He leaned over her shoulder, and Atlas could feel the warmth of his breath, the beat of his heart, and his commanding strength. She instinctively followed his every move as her body lightly touched him. Atlas was lost in the moment when their dance was interrupted by the aroma of the skillet.

"I will finish this. Why don't you go stir the butter to make sure it doesn't burn," Kyle said, releasing his hold on her.

It took Atlas a few seconds to realize what Kyle was saying. She nodded and did as she was told without saying a word.

"You alright?" he asked.

"Yes, of course. I was just wondering how you learned to bake an apple pie. I mean, is it not a common military skill?"

"My mom is not what you would call a warm and fuzzy person. To say the least, my parents are driven, and they are always striving for excellence. I just didn't really fit in with them, but my grandmother, on the other hand, was my heart. I spent a lot of time at her house, and she was the one who taught me everything that is good in my heart," Kyle said as he started working on the pie crust.

"Well, that is sweet that she taught you so much," Atlas said as she stirred the apples.

"Take the filling out of the skillet, pour it into a bowl, and let it sit for a minute. Then come here, and I will teach you how to knead the dough," Kyle said, calling her over to the counter where he had the paste ready. "You need to make sure you put flour on the counter before you put the dough down. If you don't make sure you have a good base, the paste will stick to the counter."

"Alright, so what do I need to do," she answered as she timidly got to the counter.

Kyle then guided her towards him and had her step in front of him. He placed his hands over hers once more. He reached over Atlas and helped her roll out the dough with the rolling pin. He towered over her as they rolled the pie crust out. At first, they were out of sync, but in no time, they found their rhythm. Their bodies collide together as one. He stopped and lifted the rolling pin, which caused Atlas to jolt forward.

"Is everything alright?" she asked.

He looked at her and then the dough, saying, "Yes, you are doing great. You are a fast learner.

"Or maybe you are a good teacher," Atlas replied.

Kyle then reached over and grabbed the pan, showing her how to place it. Kyle then reached for the salt and handed it to Atlas. He then whispered, "You need to add a pinch of salt at the bottom before you put the apple filling in."

Atlas grabbed the salt shaker, but it slipped. She immediately recovered it, and after adding it, she threw some over the shoulder, striking Kyle in the face. She immediately stopped and looked at him in shock, "I am so sorry," she paused and said, "My mother always does it that way. I guess I got caught up with the memories."

"It's OK. I don't mind a little salt," he said with a huge smile, reaching for the baking pan and walking to the skillet. He then placed the filling into the pan and laid the topping over it. He then showed her how to seal the edges and vent the top.

"It's nice to hear you laugh and smile. You always seem so uptight." Atlas said.

"Well, I tend to always be the one who worries. OK the pie is ready to go in. You do the honors." He said, handing her the pie.

Atlas took it and placed it inside of the oven. She then instinctively grabbed the skillet handle which she had carelessly left over the hot burner, which was still on.

"Hell, that hurts how I could be such an idiot," she yelled.

Kyle ran cold water and walked her to the kitchen sink, allowing the cold water to soothe her injury. She looked at him and became totally confused. Kyle was really two people, one ogre, and a gentle giant. She smiled at him as he dried her hand and wrapped it with ice.

"Let's walk outside and sit on the porch. We need a break from the kitchen. The fresh air will do us both some good," Kyle said.

"You must think I am so stupid?" Atlas said as she took a seat in one of the chairs on the porch.

"I never said you were stupid. It's really irritating when you put words in my mouth," Kyle said, walking towards the rail, "you are careless. That's all not stupid."

"Hey, I don't mean to irritate you with my carelessness. You are not obligated to look out for me. I am not a child," she huffed back.

"Well, someone has to. To be frank, you are a bit of a wrecking ball," Kyle said.

"Seriously! That is what you think of me. You are a tightly-wound jackass," she replied.

"You know what? I am not engaging you in this conversation. I best excuse myself. Besides, we will start the academy tomorrow," Kyle replied.

"Go! I don't need you," Atlas said.

Kyle walked downstairs, yelling," You do. And don't burn my pie. Or yourself, for that matter."

"I..." Atlas said and then stopped her response, so she stomped her feet.

"Good Lord! I thought we heard fireworks," Ellie said, walking up the stairs with Rob.

"The pie is in the oven, and it should be done by now. I was just waiting for you to come home. I am going to head out. Besides, we start the academy in the morning," Atlas said while walking towards her cabin.

Chapter 5

Day One

Kyle walked out of his car and was surprised to find Atlas waiting for him. Kyle could see that she had done her best to be ready, but as he inspected her uniform, he noticed her gig line was off, and her shoes were just not up to standards.

"Good Morning. Aren't you surprised that I am ready on time," Atlas said with a huge grin.

"You are looking pretty good," he said as he unlocked his door and threw his bag into the backseat, "do you have the rest of the gear?"

"No? I just got a book bag and a bottle of water. What else do I need to bring with me?" she asked, trying to pull on the front passenger door.

"Attie, didn't you read the welcome packet inside the gearbox?" he scoffed at her.

"No, I thought it was just an invoice," she responded.

"Alright, let's grab the side-by-side run to your cabin and grab it quickly," Kyle said as he ran towards the barn.

"Seriously! You think I am that dumb. Of course, I read it. My box is right here. I just don't have a gear bag," she said, chuckling. "I got you, didn't I? I got you good."

"I will hand it to you today. You did. Just for that, I will give you my duffle bag for your gear. It is much easier to carry stuff than this big box. Go ahead and grab it in the backseat. Just hop back there and load your stuff while we wait for Ellie," he said.

"Ellie is not joining us this morning. She and Rob left about 30 minutes ago. He wanted to see her off for her first day at the academy. Isn't that sweet?" she said as she jumped into the back.

"Yeah, I think that is very nice. I would have done that too to make sure Spinelli knows she is not an easy target," he responded as they took off.

"Why do you say that about Tony? He is a nice guy," she said as she attempted to transfer gear into the bag when suddenly Kyle slammed on the brakes, causing her to jolt forward. "What the hell? Did something run across the road?"

"Yep!" he responded, clutching the steering wheel.

"What was it? A bear or deer?" she asked, trying to sit back and grab the gear that spilled all over the floor.

"It was my indigestion," he said, putting the car in park.

"What? You're what? Your stomach hurts? Are you nauseous? You can have my water if you like," Atlas said, picking more items up and reaching for her water bottle.

"Thank you, I appreciate it. I just need to ask you for a big favor," Kyle said as he turned towards Atlas, who had her butt lifted as she was stretching to reach her flashlight that rolled into the back seat. "I will wait. I can't talk to you in that position."

"I got it, sorry. I didn't mean to put my ass in your face," she said with a smile.

"Listen, Attie, I really need you not to call Spinelli Tony or Antony, for that matter," he asked.

"Alright, I will stop if it bothers you that much, but only if you answer me one question. Why does that bother you that much?" Atlas said, placing her last item into the bag and jumping into the front seat.

"He is our instructor, and I don't want you to get into trouble for being disrespectful," he struggled to say.

"Nope! You will not lie to me. I don't know you well, but I can tell you are not telling me the truth. So spill it, why don't you want me to call him Tony? I wouldn't say it to his face if that is what you're worried about. It makes you uncomfortable when I say it and more than that, simply talking about him," she insisted.

"Alright, here is my opinion. I think he is slimy and I like you. I mean, I consider you my friend. I have seen what guys like that do to young, naive girls. I am not saying you are like that, but he just seems to have bad intentions. Please, I really don't ask you for much. Can you just do this one thing as a favor to me," Kyle said as he started to drive.

"Since you asked me so nicely, I promise to do my best," she said, putting her seatbelt on, saying, "Safety first," and then smiling.

They reached the parking lot and met with Rob and Ellie, who were saying their goodbyes. Ellie picked up her bag and walked towards Kyle's SUV, saying, "You guys ready to do this?"

"Yes, but Ellie can check Atlas' belt. I am not sure if her gig line is straight. I don't care much about equipment pushups. And then hand me her shoes so I can shine them up really quickly," Kyle instructed Ellie.

Ellie looked at Atlas and had her sit back on the seat, "you heard the man hand over those shoes. Tonight, get with one of us, and we will show you how to get a nice shine on them, alright?"

Atlas did not know how to feel about this, but she knew to trust them, so she did as she was told. She handed Kyle her shoes as Ellie tightened up her hair and fixed her belt. Once all was accomplished, they walked into the front doors of the academy. They were the first cadets to arrive as they followed the signs to the classroom and found their assigned seats.

"Wow, this is a big room," Atlas said, looking at all the seats and nameplates.

"Well, kids, I am in the second to the last row up top. See you at the break. Good luck to all of us. Just remember to always answer with a Sir sandwich. ' Sir, yes Sir, or Sir, no Sir,' my Brother Scott's best advised to survive basic training," Ellie said as she made her way to her seat.

"I get it, thank you. And just in case I forget, thank you, Kyle, for all that you have done for me," Atlas said, finding her seat. She put her gear down and turned to see Kyle sitting right next to her.

"Martin, A. followed by Noyes, K," he said.

"Maybe," she responded, smiling.

A few minutes later, the room began to fill with other cadets who were just as eager as they were to get started. Everyone found their place, and right next to Atlas was a "knockout" female. She was about 5 '8 tall with long blond hair, blue eyes, large breasts, and a tiny waist. Atlas was not sure if those were her real breasts. Atlas also noticed her uniform seemed to be snugged in all the right places to extenuate her body.

"Hey, you know what we are doing today?" she said, looking around.

"No idea. By the way, I am Atlas Martin," she said, extending her hand to shake it.

"Yeah, Atlas, is that really your name? Wow, that is very, very unique. I am Pricilla Lambert. So where are you from Atlas?" Elisa asked, still looking around the room

"Missouri and you?" Atlas answered.

"Seattle, but I just finished my tour with the Coast Guard. Did you serve?" she asked.

Atlas just nodded no and looked around the room to see who was sitting next to Ellie.

"You think these are assigned seats for the entire academy, or can we move them?" Pricilla asked as a tall male entered the room, turning off the lights.

"Good morning, cadets, and welcome to the first day of Hell Week. Today, we will start by accessing each one of you. The ladies' locker room is to your right, and the men's is to the left. You have five minutes to make it out to the field. See you all out there, dismissed," he yelled out.

Atlas, Ellie, and Pricilla ran to change without hesitation while the men struggled to make their way into the locker room.

"Today is a good day to be a girl," Ellie said, quickly changing and helping Atlas hang her uniform, "always take the extra second to hang it up. Believe me, we will change multiple times. We did this basically all the time."

"You Navy?" Pricilla asked as she tied her hair into a ponytail.

"Marines, you?" Ellie said as she looked at Atlas, who was pulling her hair into a ponytail as well. Ellie shook her head, telling her no, "Pull your hair up as much as you can like into a bun."

"Oh I am a Coasty" she said running out.

Ellie pulled Atlas back and whispered, "Don't do what she does. Trust me."

Atlas said nothing and simply followed Ellie's lead. The girls were the first to reach the track where they found Spinelli standing there with a stopwatch.

"Ah I see how this class is going to be always lacking behind the females. Alright ladies it is up to you to set the pace. Give me 12 laps I don't care if it hurts just don't you dare stop," Spinelli yelled out.

The girls took off together but soon enough Pricilla passed them. Atlas started to push herself and race after her, but then she remembered what Ellie told her earlier. She backed off and fell behind Ellie.

"I was wondering if you remembered what I told you," Ellie said with a grin, "pace yourself. This is a three mile run and it's the first one. Let me know if you need me to slow down."

"I am good right now, this is a good speed," Atlas said, keeping up and making it almost through the first lap when she noticed the men running past her.

The rest of the cadets joined in and quickly they were out running them. Atlas could see Kyle running at a fast pace but she concentrated on Ellie. She knew to trust her even though at times she thought they were falling behind the pack. Then suddenly Kyle joined them.

"Hey I made up for lost time, can I tag along? "He asked Ellie who nodded yes. Atlas was losing her breath and began to struggle.

"One more lap you can do it," he said, smiling at her.

They reached the end and Atlas turned to see several cadets still on the track when Spinelli blew a whistle yelling, those of you left in the field failed. He yelled, "Good luck this afternoon you will have a second chance at redemption. Now get the Hell off my track!!"

"That was insane," George said, holding his chest. "I can't believe I failed the first exercise I thought I was in better shape."

"Don't sweat it but we better move and keep up with the group," Ellie replied

Spinelli walked to an obstacle course and started calling out names from a clipboard. George was the first one up Atlas watched as he struggled to make it over the eight foot wall. He jumped up but was unable to pull himself over. He made three attempts when Spinelli yelled go around and finish. Reluctantly George did and the next cadet got started this continued until it was Priscilla's turn. She turned to Atlas saying "watch how this is done!" And she took off.

Pricilla made it seem easy until she got to the wall. She jumped, grabbed the top of the rail and was unable to pull herself over the wall. Running back and trying two additional times until she heard Spinelli yell, "Go around! Next cadet." At the end of the skills test only four cadets had made it over the wall.

"Gather around cadets if you hear your name take a step forward: Callahan, Jones, Noyes, and Stevens congrats you made it through the first assessment. The rest of you need to pull it together and figure out what needs to be done to get over that wall. We are breaking you guys up into four teams and the guys and girls who made it over the wall are now your team leaders. Ladies, I mean female cadets. Let's see who is left alright Martin you are on Callahan's and Lambert you belong to Noyes. Team leaders' expectation is to at least make it over. We will work on speed later. Just in case you are not understanding me it is up to you to ensure everyone makes it over. Dismissed, go grab lunch, shower, and change back into your uniforms. You got one hour. Don't be late!!" Spinelli yelled out walking back towards his office.

"So I belong to you. I guess you will do, for now. You know I slipped, that is what kept me from getting over that wall," Pricilla said as she tapped her hand on Kyle's chest, "Wow what branch of the military did you serve?"

Kyle quickly brushed her hand away from him, "I didn't share anything about me with you or anyone. If you can get over the wall then get over it. Maybe try to wear looser clothing. It might help when you stretch."

"You're an ass," she replied.

"I know but at least I am an honest ass," he said walking away.

"Hey Noyes, you got a sec?" Callahan asked, running towards him, "hey do you mind if we trade girls? No offense but I don't really want to work with Martin."

"Yeah, sure I don't really care, but why did she say something to you?" Kyle asked.

"No, but seriously look at her. She is not, let's say, very athletic. You and Stevens had to baby her through the first run. I just don't have the patience to break in a new girl. I spent a long time working with just men and I am thinking I might just hurt her feelings. I just don't think she has what it takes. So you good if we trade?" he asked.

"Yeah, just get straight with Spinelli and I am good. I will work with Martin to get her in shape," Kyle said and then stopped, "but you do understand you are getting Pricilla and she seems to be a handful."

"Yep, that was what I was hoping for. I can handle her type. Martin on the other hand is like my little sister and I just don't want to see her cry. Besides, I like the way Pricilla handles herself. I get a kick just watching her" he said.

"Well just don't get anything that requires penicillin you know what I mean?" Kyle said with a smile as he walked away. Everyone went their separate ways for lunch. Kyle noticed that Atlas was slumped outside of the classroom by herself.

"What's up? Are you good?" Kyle asked.

"Yep, it's just that everything hurts. I knew it was supposed to be hard, but today was ridiculous," she said barely lifting her head,

Kyle sat next to her and waited a minute or two before telling her, "look Attie I know you can do this, but you need to get your mind straight. We are on day one and not even halfway through today. Here is my advice: take it or leave it. You push yourself one day at the time, one event at the time, one thing at the time. You need to learn one thing at the time so you retain it. Got it?"

"So you're saying I am stupid and I got things the first time around?" Atlas snapped back at him.

"No and I would appreciate it if you did not put words in my mouth. You need to listen and process before you respond. I am really trying to help you, however, I will only help you if you are willing. So get it through your thick head. I am your friend but I can be your friend, you don't necessarily have to be mine. Got it?" Kyle said as he got himself up.

"Wait Kyle I am sorry. I am just scared that I will not make it. I can barely move and you are right we are not even halfway through day one," she said.

"That is alright. Here take my hand, let's get you up and going. Go ahead, take a shower and then meet me in the classroom," he said.

"Alright, but I didn't bring lunch. I really don't mind skipping it," she said as got up.

"I figured you didn't pack one. Ellie and I packed enough for all of us just in case. I will see you in like 10 minutes," Kyle responded as he also got up and headed to the showers. He walked into the locker room to find Callahan walking out.

"Hey I just wanted to let you know I got straight with Spinelli we are straight I got Pricilla and you are stuck Martin," he said as he walked out while Kyle just rolled his eyes.

A few minutes later Kyle and Atlas met up in the classroom as planned. While sharing their lunch he patiently began explaining what needed to be accomplished. Atlas was impressed by his kindness, but she did not want to sound weak. They were joined by Pricilla, who seemed enamored by Kyle's dismissive disposition.

"Hey what are you two love birds doing? I guess it's true what they say you can find love at the academy" Pricilla stated as she walked towards them. "Cute you guys even got the picnic thing going on."

"What are you talking about? Kyle and I are just friends," Atlas responded.

"Well Noyes when are you going to work with me? After all, you are my team leader. So do you want to meet after class and we can get a workout routine?" Pricilla said flirtatiously.

Callahan walked into the class, "hey Lambert I cleared it with Spinelli you are now on my team. Noyes and I traded girls."

"Wait what you traded us? What is he talking about Kyle? Why didn't you tell me?" Atlas said.

"Yeah, sorry, Martin, but I just don't have time or patience to work with you. No offense, you are just really not in shape," Callahan said.

Atlas didn't know what to do; she was both embarrassed and furious. She could feel her tears sneaking up, and she did everything possible to hold them back.

Suddenly, Kyle placed his hand over hers, and he said, "No worries, we got this. I promise I will get you over the wall."

Spinelli walked in and everyone stood at attention. He was an arrogant man, who made sure he was the center of attention in the entire room. He strutted with an air of superiority, belittling trainees with cutting remarks that echoed through the halls of the academy. With a haughty demeanor, they wielded their authority like a weapon, enforcing discipline through humiliation and condescension, failing to recognize the value of encouragement and guidance in molding future officers. The trainees felt the weight of Spinelli's arrogance, a heavyweight overshadowing their eagerness to learn and excel in their training.

Kyle could tell that Spinelli was scoping out the cadets to find the weakest and most vulnerable. He understood Spinelli wanted to weed out the weak, but he was a bully, and Kyle hated bullies. He also understood that Spinelli was at a higher level of authority and could easily use his position to take advantage of inexperienced females like Atlas. As Spinelli gave his speech, which he often did, busting a grand tale of his accomplishments, he would end each statement and give one of the females a wink or look. Kyle watched him even though it made him sick to his stomach.

The group made it to the end of the day, and Spinelli waited in the hallway. He stood tall with a stern gaze as if he were measuring each cadet's exit from the room. Spinelli called Atlas over to him as she walked out of the room. Kyle stood back, watching his demeanor and gaging how Spinelli engaged with her. Atlas stood at attention as it appeared he was berating her, but he immediately stopped when Pricilla walked over to him.

"Go on, get out of here, but I better see some improvement in the morning. Remember, it is up to me whether or not you make it to the end," he shouted at Atlas as he walked with Pricilla to his office.

"You alright?" Kyle said, reaching for her bag.

"No, yes, I guess. Director Spinelli was just telling me that I need to make sure to show improvement or else. He did offer to go over some stuff with me, but then Pricilla walked up. I guess I should ask him about it tomorrow. What do you think? Should I ask him about it later?" Atlas asked as she walked behind Kyle. He immediately stopped and turned to look at her with a cold gaze.

"What did I say something wrong?" she asked.

"Do what you want, but if you ask me to stay clear about Spinelli, he has bad intentions. Why don't you just watch and see how he acts with Lambert, you know, Pricilla?" he said, walking back towards his car. Atlas nodded in agreement, trying to reach for the door handle, but he grabbed it and opened the door for her.

"Let's take you home and we can grab some food. Rest for a bit and then get started with our assignments. Try to keep in mind that most of our days at the academy will be 'Ground Hog Day,' and they will soon mesh into one long day." Kyle told her as they drove back to the ranch.

Chapter 6

Groundhog Days

Kyle was right when he told Atlas her days at the academy would be more like Groundhog Day than anything else. The days started earlier for her than for others. She had morning chores to accomplish before showering and getting ready for the day to come. Atlas half-awake to make her way to the stable, where she had to move the horses out, clean each stall, feed, and brush six mustangs. Some days were easier than others; it all depended on the grueling exercises of the day prior.

Time had flown by easily, and Atlas had been working hard to ensure she made the cut. Ellie noticed that each morning before leaving, Kyle would ensure he had packed enough food for Atlas and himself. He would always ask Ellie if she wanted him to prepare her lunch. Some days, she would say yes, but for the most part, Ellie would rather meet with Rob at the local cafe for a quick bite. Every day, Kyle and Atlas spend time running the course right before they have lunch. Ellie could see Atlas's improvements with Kyle's help; she was confident that Atlas would be successful during the next assessment.

When they returned to class after their lunch break, Ellie made it a point to speak to both Kyle and Atlas, who were already sitting in assigned seats, "Hey, you two, how was your run today?"

"It was great! Today, I made it over the wall. I can't believe I did it. I feel so accomplished," Atlas enthusiastically said and then turned to Kyle, "I know I could not have made it without you. Thank you!"

Kyle simply smiled as he gathered his books and pen for the upcoming lecture. Pricilla then came over and sat next to Kyle. She placed her hand over his, saying, "Hey Noyes, do you always stay here for lunch, or do you ever go out?" Kyle didn't get a chance to respond because Callahan walked over towards them, saying, "Lambert, you need to stay tonight and work with me for a few hours. You need to get your ass over that wall. I will not have Spinelli yelling at me because you have no work ethic."

Pricilla smiled and winked at Kyle, then stood up and placed her hands on her hips. "I don't know who you think you are talking to, but you don't address me in that manner. You don't need to worry about the wall. I got that test in the bag. As a matter of fact, I just talked to Tony about it over lunch. If I am not worried, and he is not either, why are you?"

"You better make it. Man, Noyes, I should have never traded chicks. This one is good to look at, but man, she is a handful. How is your girl? You think your girl is going to make it." Callahan asked, looking as Pricilla wiggled her way to her assigned seat.

"Of course, Martin has been working very hard this week. I am confident she will make it with no issue," Kyle responded without missing a beat.

"Good to hear. I wish I could say the same," he said as he made his way back towards his chair. Kyle looked towards Atlas, who was mumbling, 'thank you' at him.

Within seconds, the laughter and chatter in class came to a halt as Spinelli walked through the door. Everyone stood at attention as he looked around the room, "Cadets, tomorrow we have our next physical assessment. There are several of you who will need to show improvement if you want to remain in this program. I don't want to hear any excuses or whining about it. This one counts, and you can only afford to fail one. So, to be clear, it is imperative that everyone make it over the wall. My best advice is to keep moving and don't stop." Spinelli shouted at the class and continued with, "Are there any questions?" One cadet raised his hand, but Spinelli quickly responded, "There should not be any. I believe I was clear, but since some of you are not clear. Leave your gear. We run."

Everyone lined up in their uniforms and shined shoes, "I know you are not dressed for P.T., but in the real world, you will be in court, at a ceremony, or on your way home, and you will need to respond to something. What are you going to tell the bad guys, 'so sorry I am not dressed for the occasion? GO! I expect at least three laps around the complex," he said as leading the group.

By the end of the day, the cadets found themselves running, jumping, and doing pushups. Atlas was pushing herself to her limits, and she did not want to disappoint Kyle, who had been working so hard with her. Finally, he made it close to her, "don't overdo it. Remember, we have a big day tomorrow. Just enough today to make it look good. This is a trick to get in our heads. Find a rhythm and keep it."

Atlas slowed her pushups, remembering to breathe and push air out of her mouth. She closed her eyes and opened them to hear Ellie on the right side, "you got this girl. Slow and steady, we will do them together."

Spinelli looked and noticed the three of them working together. He smiled as he recalled his days during his academy working in a team to get the task accomplished. He looked around and found several cadets helping one another, all except Pricilla. She was too busy making every effort to be noticed. He noticed her alright, her shorts were tighter and snuggled to her butt. The top button of her shirt was not secured, exposing a bit of her cleavage. He watched her as she squatted to the ground, pretending to do pushups. Spinelli imagined her confidence exuding through each push-up, a playful glint in her eyes as she maintained eye contact with him. Effortlessly flirting with a wink or smile between reps, making an alluring and captivating display of fitness and charm.

Spinelli was lost in his own thoughts, captured by Pricilla's tactics. He finally released his gaze and yelled out, "dismissed," walking away toward his office.

"What the hell was that about?" Adams commented as he got himself up. "Dude, why did Spinelli run us like that? He has some nerve. I hope we all make it tomorrow. I would hate to ruin my birthday."

"Oh, it's your birthday, George? How nice do you have plans?" Atlas asked as they walked back towards the classroom.

"Man, after today, I am getting smashed. I am crushing the skills test and then going out with the boys. Pub crawling, do you know what I mean?" George enthusiastically responded.

"I never heard of pub crawling. What is that?" Atlas asked.

"It's really an English tradition I picked up when I was deployed abroad in Germany. You go with a group of friends to visit multiple bars or pubs in a single night. The intention is to try different drinks and make more friends along the way to join you at the next bar. You want to join us?" he asked,

"No, it sounds fun, but it's expensive. I am saving all my money to go home in a few weeks for our Thanksgiving break. I hope you have a great time, though." she said, reaching her seat.

"Wait, why don't I pay you to drive us around? Think about it, you can use my car. You will be the paid Designated Driver (DD). Really, you will help me out and make a few bucks. What do you say?" he insisted.

"Let me think about it. I have another job to pay for my room and board. I guess as long as I am done with my chores, I can make it. But I will confirm in the morning, alright?" she answered, sitting down.

"I will text you about the details later, but I need your number, " Adams said as he stepped in front of Atlas' desk.

"Sorry, my phone finally died, and I don't have the money to replace it. Why don't we talk about it later, alright?" she said.

"No problem," he said, walking towards his seat.

The instructor walked in and dismissed them for the day, wishing the entire class good luck in the morning.

The morning came upon them quickly, and Atlas found herself once more on the field at the academy. Spinelli stood there stoic with his clipboard, yelling instructions and directions to each one. He then proceeded to explain that the only task scheduled was the obstacle course. Once completed, the cadets will be dismissed for the remainder of the day.

The cadets then lined up behind their team leader and waited for the next announcement. Atlas stood behind Kyle, whose gaze was fixed in the distance. She tried to figure out what he was staring at, but she could not figure it out.

Suddenly, she heard, "Stevens, get your people on the course. You are group number one. Once you complete the course, go to the instructor and take your time. Remember, you will not pass if you don't get over the wall," Spinelli's words echoed throughout the field.

One by one, Ellis' group lined up, and they walked together to the starting line. Atlas heard Ellie telling her team to push through each obstacle and keep moving. She went first, making it look effortless. Atlas was in awe to see how she navigated through each task without slowing down, slipping, or falling. In a matter of seconds, it seemed Ellie was at the finish line. Her group followed her lead, and soon enough, they all made it through the course.

"Next, we have Callahan's group. Come on, come on, guys, we don't have all day for this. Let's go!" Spinelli impatiently yelled out at the group, which was scattered, and slowly made its way to the beginning of the course. This was the total opposite of the first group. Callahan stood in the end, saying nothing to his team. They simply waited for Spinelli to call out their names to go through the test.

The second cadet, Benson, struggled with the wall. He jumped up but could not pull himself over, so he slipped and slid down. He made a second attempt and finally ran around it. Then it was Pricilla's turn; she jumped up but could barely pull herself over the wall, but not without pulling her top down, exposing her breast bone. She slid down, stopping, and then looked down, pretending to be embarrassed, readjusting her top before continuing. All of which cost her precious time off her overall score. The following three cadets made it over. With this display, Atlas could tell Spinelli was not happy.

"Look here, if you are not going to take this seriously, you will be discharged from the program. Do I make myself clear?" he shouted at the top of his lungs.

"Yes, Sir." Everyone responded back.

"Noyes! You are up. I better not see one of your guys fail, you hear. If you do, we all are staying all day and all night working on this wall," Spinelli yelled while looking straight at Atlas. "You go first, and do not waste my time."

"Yes, Sir." Atlas felt all of her confidence slipping out of her body when she felt Kyle reaching and holding her hand.

"You got this. Just remember one thing at a time: run through it, over it, no matter what, you don't stop. I believe in you. Go, do you like how we practiced?" he said. "You got this," encouraging her to make it.

Atlas stood for a second or two looking at the horizon and took off as fast as she could when she heard Spinelli yelling, "Go!"

Atlas navigated through each obstacle with ease until she found herself facing the eight-foot wall; she was holding back her speed until that moment. Using all her strength, she recalled Kyle's words to use her momentum, jump, pull herself upwards, hooking her left leg, and use her ankle to hold her weight. Atlas lost a few seconds of time with this technique, but it was all she needed to get over to the other side.

Ellis watched as Atlas jumped over and ran to the finish line. Ellis and other cadets jumped and cheered while Atlas got the thumbs up from the instructor. Ellis then turned to Kyle saying, "Nice work. She never stopped."

"It was all her," Kyle responded.

"Listen up, people," Spinelli said, "Martin, the shortest and in less shape compared to everyone else, just killed the obstacle course. I don't want to hear any excuses. I have watched her each day with Noyes working and pushing herself while you guys are slacking off, taking lunch breaks, and hanging out. You know what that tells me? She wants to be successful, while you guys are just trying to wing it. If you fail to meet the minimum standards, you simply fail. You will have one more opportunity to make it. You are dismissed!"

Chapter 7

No Inhibitions

The air was getting cooler with each day that went by. Kyle made his way towards Atlas' cabin, carrying several logs of wood. He dropped the wood on the porch, noticing a ruby-red sun parked near the porch. Knocked on the door and waited for Atlas to open the door.

"Hey, what's up? I was not expecting you. Did I miss something? I was sure I completed all my chores for today," Atlas surprisingly said, peeking out the door.

"The weather is clearly turning colder. I wanted to make sure you know how to light the fireplace and have enough wood to keep you warm," he said, looking at the strange vehicle. "I am sorry if I am intruding if you have company."

"I don't have company. Why are you asking me that?" Atlas responded as she stepped outside. "Oh! You are asking about the car. It's Adam's car; it's his birthday, and we are going out tonight."

"Well, that is none of my business. I just wanted to make sure you were ready for the weather changes. I brought you wood, and if you would like, I will show you how to light your fireplace unless you already know how. Will Adams help you?" Kyle said as he started to step away.

Atlas ran behind him, saying, "Wait. I am not dating Adams. If that is what you are implying?"

"No, absolutely not. You do whatever you want," he said.

"Wait," she said, smiling, "I am trying to make extra money. I want to go home for our Thanksgiving break. I have been saving my money from the ranch, but I am still a bit short," Atlas said, rubbing her arms on her shoulders. "You are right. It is getting colder. Come on in," she said, walking into her cabin.

Kyle followed her, carrying some wood into the living room area. Kyle knelt, placing the wood into it. He then waved Atlas over to show her how to get her cabin warm.

"I am sorry, I am running a bit late as usual. I need to get ready. I am driving Adams and some of our classmates on something they call pub crawling. I am like their Uber. Pretty cool, right? I am a paid Designated Driver, a DD," she said with a smile.

"I guess," Kyle said, piling the wood inside of the fireplace.

Atlas walked into her bedroom, leaving her door open. Kyle could see her changing from the reflection of the mirror that was peeking out the side of the doorway. He wanted to look away, but he was captivated by her figure. All he could see was her back as she slipped off her top and put on a black bra. She struggled to reach the claps. It took all he had not to run and help her. Then Kyle watched as she quickly covered herself with a shiny tank top. He turned away as she walked out of the room, saying,

"I just wish my cell phone was working. I am not sure how to get from place to place, and I really don't think the guys will be very helpful after a few shots. Hey, do you want to go with us? I am sure Adams wouldn't mind," Atlas asked.

"No, Attie, that is not my thing. Is that all you are wearing tonight?" he asked.

"Yeah, this and a coat," she looked down at herself, "Why? In St. Louis, this is how we dress to go out bar hopping. I thought it was the same thing, or am I wrong?"

"No, you are right. Pub crawling and bar hopping are the same thing. But..." he said and was interrupted by Atlas, who placed her weight on her right leg and hands on her hips,

"But what? "She snarled at him.

"You are not in a big city like St. Louis. This is Wyoming, and the people here are different. There is one female for every ten or twenty guys. You go out dressed that way. You might be giving out the wrong impression," he responded quickly.

"The wrong impression? Are you saying I look like a whore? Or Easy or something like that? Because I don't appreciate the implication," Atlas said, starting to raise her voice.

"There you go again, putting words in my mouth. All that I am suggesting is for you to cover a bit. Besides, it is going to be cold outside, and you cannot afford to get sick," he responded.

Atlas thought about just walking out, but then she looked at her top, pulling on the sides. "You know what? You are right. This might not be the choice of attire for tonight. I might have to help Adams get into the car, and I don't want him puking all over my favorite shirt. Let me see what else I have that is, like you say, more appropriate." She returned to the bedroom and pulled off her top, flinging it on the bed.

Kyle instinctively turned his head slightly, and he could see her walking around the room in her bra again. From that vantage point, he was able to admire her small waist and figure. The bra tastefully reveals a hint of sun-kissed skin, framing her neckline. Paired with form-fitting jeans that hug her hips and taper down her legs, the ensemble embodied a blend of comfort. Her presence radiated a quiet confidence, making her the embodiment of natural beauty in simplicity.

As she walked out, he quickly turned his head away, a bit embarrassed by his actions. He lit the fire and placed some wood to ensure the room would warm itself. Kyle used the poker and cleaned off the dust so Atlas would not have to worry about it.

"What do you think is better?" Atlas said, turning around to show off her choice of a v neck gray long sleeve top still showing a slight bit of cleavage; she tucked her shirt inside her jeans, a tan belt with large cowboy buckle, and lightweight hooded jacket that draped over her and a pair of tan western boots.

"I guess I should give you your Christmas present early," Kyle said, reaching inside his coat pocket and pulling out a present while he was still kneeling down.

Atlas was looking at him confused, "You don't have to give me anything. You have already done so much," Atlas replied, almost stuttering with embarrassment.

"Take it. You will need it tonight for sure," Kyle said, handing her the package.

Atlas ripped open the paper, dropping it on the floor, and she could see the box revealing a cell phone. She then looked at him, smiling and giving him a huge hug.

"Well, I guess I did well?" he said, hugging her back.

"Oh my God! Kyle, I really should not accept it, but I need it so much. I can't believe you got me a cell phone. You are amazing. Thank you! Thank you!" she said, releasing her hug and holding the cell phone next to her chest.

"I took the liberty to have them set you up with the same number you had before. I hope you don't mind. I figured your family would want to have a way of contacting you," Kyle said and then continued, "I didn't have your contacts, so you will need to go into town and have them transfer your information later."

"Yes, yes, of course. I am just," she said but could not finish.

Kyle reached for her hand, but she was busy fixated on the box," All alright then, you are ready for your hustle. Don't be out too late. Attie, make sure you are careful, alright," he said, pulling her coat closed and then walking out of the cabin. He stood there stoic with his gaze fixed on Atlas as she rushed past him to the driver's seat and pulled away, waving goodbye.

Kyle waited several minutes and then closed her door shut and started walking back to his cabin. His thoughts overtook his senses. He could not understand how he allowed himself to start falling in love with Atlas, *"Attie Attie,"* he said out loud. *"I can't fall in love with you. I simply cannot let that happen."* Kyle stopped at the top of the hill and looked at the orange-grayish sky. He wanted to leave everything behind. He knew Atlas was too young to become tied down to a man like him. He simply had to let her live her life, but she was so careless with it. *"Attie, you are my curse,"* he yelled at the sky and made his way back to his cabin.

Kyle watched the road for hours, waiting to see Adams' car return to the ranch. It was past 10, then 12, and at 2:00 A.M, he began to worry. *"Where was she? Why did she not call? She would have called if she got herself in trouble. Trouble,"* he thought, *"trouble finds her with ease."* He wanted to call her, but he did not want to be bothering her. All Kyle could do at the time was wait and look at the clock as time began to tease him with anxiety.

3:00 A.M. Now he was really worried that the only bar open was at the Reservation, aka the Rez, which was about an hour away. She would not have taken the guys there. It seems so careless, so remiss, and so very dangerous. Then he stopped. It was Atlas. I better start heading that way. Suddenly his phone rang it was Atlas,

"Hello!" he answered

"Hey is this Kyle?" a male voice asked.

"Yes, this is Attie's cellphone. Who is this? What happened to her? Is she alright?" Kyle fired out his questions.

"Well, I am not sure. We are here at the Red Pony on the Rez. She was fine an hour ago, but something happened. Dude, I think someone spiked her drink." he said.

"Wait, she was not supposed to be drinking. What the hell do you mean?" Kyle said, furious, as he walked to his truck. "What are you saying? Where is she?"

"Look, Mister, I am just trying to help. She seems like a nice girl, and I just don't want anything bad to happen to her. Can you come pick her up?" he said.

"I am on my way, but Buddy, can you keep an eye on her, please? I will pay for your time," Kyle pleaded.

"I will do my best, but the bar is pretty busy. I will give her the phone. Maybe you can talk to her while she waits," he suggested, and he handed Atlas the cell phone.

"Attie! Attie, it's Kyle. Can you hear me? Attie! Attie, come on, talk to me. I am on my way. Come on, Attie!" Kyle shouted into the phone as he tried to get her to answer.

"Hello, Kyle, is that you? I am dizzy. I am really dizzy. I just want to lay my head down," Atlas whispered.

Kyle pulled into the parking lot like a bat out of hell, wheels rolling, smoke coming from the breaks. He stopped right next to the building and jumped out. He ran into business seeing his fellow cadets drinking near the dance area. He scanned the area and walked to the bar, not seeing Atlas anywhere. He slammed his hand on the bar, yelling, "Buddy, where is the girl?"

"Man, she was here a minute ago. Wait, Manny, where is the girl who was sitting here?" the bartender yelled at the bar back.

"Oh, I just saw her leaving with two guys. I think they are headed to the back parking lot," he yelled out.

Kyle ran outside to see two guys walking with Atlas between several cars. He ran to them as one guy jumped into a car, and they pushed Attie to the side of the car. Kyle got there on time as the second guy began pulling off Attie's coat. He then began to grope her as he was pulling her top off. Kyle ran towards them and immediately punched the guy in the face. Managing to get him away from Atlas, who was unconscious and slid to the pavement.

Kyle swung at the guy, connecting his fist to the guy's face. Kyle took another step forward, closing the gap between him and the guy. Kyle punched him several more times in the face and body, causing him to fall flat on the pavement. Kyle then turned his attention to Atlas, but he felt a sharp pain on the back of his head, seeing blood gushing from it. He turned to see the other male holding an impact wrench in his hand. Kyle leaped forward on him and strangled him to the ground. They were tangled together, and Kyle held him down when he felt someone kicking him in the ribs. It appeared that the first man had regained his composure and had joined in the beating.

Kyle attempted to fight back but found himself over powered by both men who were taking turns striking him. Kyle knew he needed to stand up and gain some distance, but every time he tried, he was hit harder. He finally grabbed the first guy's legs, which caused him to fall backward and land hard on the pavement. He took advantage of the moment and jumped to his feet. Kyle stood tall, ready to go again.

Kyle was tapped on the shoulder by a group of Native American men standing tall behind him. One of the men looked at the two men and stepped in front of Kyle, saying, "So it looks like these two Wasi Chu, white men do not belong in the Rez."

Kyle then reached down and grabbed Atlas, pulling her to her feet and holding her up. He then said, "Look, we don't want any trouble. These guys drugged her, and they were trying to."

Hush fell over the gathering as one of the men knelt next to Atlas and put his hand on Kyle's shoulder, saying," No need to explain. We know what they have been doing here. We have not been able to catch them, so you changed that. Don't worry. They will never be able to do this to another girl again." Kyle turned his attention to Atlas, who was in and out of consciousness.

"Do you have any idea what they gave her?" he asked.

"Most likely a Molly laced with another hallucinate. She will be alright in a few hours, but you need to keep her hydrated," the man responded.

Kyle lifted Atlas and stood her on her feet, guiding her towards his car. He then noticed one of the men who helped him, clutching firmly in his weathered hand a piece of glowing ember. With a decisive nod, he reached for a branding iron and walked to the two culprits. They were now carried forever the etched letter "R," a stark reminder of accountability for their misstep for the remainder of their lives.

"Like I said, these Wasi Chu will never be able to do this again. Not on the Rez, not anywhere," he responded. Kyle turned to see the men holding one of the attackers down as he was branded with the letter "R" in his hand. The smell of cooked flesh made him recall his days in the Middle East when he witnessed rapists being branded or mutilated for their actions. He quickly shook memories away and concentrated back on getting Atlas away from everyone.

Making it to the car, Kyle could tell Atlas was still in and out of consciousness; he laid her in the backseat so she could rest while he drove them home. He needed to take her to the ranch as fast as possible when the Bar back met him at his door saying, "Dude, don't worry about the rest of your guys. We will make sure someone gets them home. Here is your girl's ID and keys. We require them for anyone inside of the bar, even if they are not drinking. You can come back to the car in the morning or whenever," he said.

"Sorry, do you mind giving the keys back to one of the guys in the group? They can deal with their car on their own. I will have my hands full for a bit," Kyle said, stepping into the driver's seat.

"No problem, I will make sure they get home safe. Take care of your girl. I am so sorry for the situation. It is just hard to look out for the females. You know what I mean?" he said, walking back towards the bar.

Kyle started driving, looking in the backseat every few minutes to make sure Atlas was alright. Approaching the ranch, Atlas sat up and began looking around in confusion.

"Hey, where am I? What the hell is going on? Who the hell are you?" she yelled, trying to open the back door.

"No! No! Attie is me. It's Kyle," he pulled over to the side of the roadway, jumping out and running to the back door where Atlas was trying to run away.

"Leave me alone! Get away from me!" she kicked at him, and as he stepped back, she managed to push her way past him. Atlas took off running into the night, making her way into the National Forest next to the ranch.

Kyle ran behind her, but he did not want to scare her more than necessary. He needed to keep an eye on her, but he also realized she was hallucinating. Somehow, he needed to convince her that she was safe. He decided to stop running and just call out her name, "Attie, Attie, wait. It's me, Kyle. Atlas Martin, stop!"

Kyle lost sight of Atlas, who was running further into the dense foliage. He followed the twisted paths and finally stumbled upon Atlas. Her steps were unsteady, and her laughter floated through the trees like an eerie melody. Concern etched his features as she seemed obliviously lost in her intoxicated haze.

"Attie, it's me, Kyle," he called out, his voice tinged with worry as he approached cautiously, not wanting to startle her.

Atlas' head snapped up, her eyes wide with an unfocused gaze, "Who're you?" she slurred, her words tangled in a drunken stumble. "Gotta find my way back to the bar...lost my friends,' she mumbled, her words trailing off into the night.

Kyle took a step closer, his tone gentle yet urgent, "Attie, it's not safe out here alone. Let me help you get back to the car. I am worried about you.

Atlas squinted, trying to make out his face in the dim light. Suspicion clouded her mind, "You're not one of them, are you? One of them is trying to mess with me," she muttered, her voice waving between mistrust and vulnerability.

"No, Attie, I 'm here to help," Kyle reassured his outstretched hand as a beacon of reassurance. "Let's get you back, okay?" stepping forward.

Atlas was reluctant and tried to run again, but Kyle held her by her shoulders. She pushed and punched, trying to get away while he kept saying, "Attie, you are safe."

"No!" she yelled, "I am not going with you!" she wiggled and pushed some more.

Kyle pulled her into his body and held her for several minutes, whispering, "I am not one of them. It's me, Kyle. Come on, Attie, remember me. Please. Attie, you are safe now. I got you. No one is going to hurt you. I promise. I promise I got you."

Atlas finally looked up and said, "Kyle, is that you. Is that really you? I promised I wouldn't drink. I don't know what happened," as she said those words, she fainted right into Kyle's arms. Totally unconscious, he carried her back to the car. He felt her forehead and noticed she was burning up. They finally made it home, and Kyle quickly rushed Atlas inside. He took her into her cabin and carried her into the shower.

He turned on the cold water and waited a few seconds before trying to get Atlas on her feet. He removed her coat, allowing it to fall on the floor, and walked her, fully clothed, underneath the cold water. With gentle guidance, he steered Atlas, who was struggling to stand. She felt the cold water hitting her like daggers to her body. Atlas leaned against the tile wall, shivering despite the heat.

"You will feel better soon. We just have to get the fever down," Kyle said in a compassionate tone. He grabbed a soft washcloth, damping it before gently placing it on the back of her neck. Atlas then leaned into his comfortable, warm embrace as the water cascaded over them.

"Kyle, the room is spinning," she whispered.

Kyle held her up, and they both were covered with the cold water. He turned off the water, reached for a towel, and wrapped it around her. "Come on, Attie, let's get you out of these wet clothes and put you in bed. Are you feeling better?"

"No, the room is spinning," she said, looking at the light.

"Close your eyes, Attie," he said, turning off the light. He then pushed her body into the wall. As she leaned her on the cold tile, Kyle then pulled off her wet top. He flung the shirt off her shoulders and unbuckled her jeans. He helped her step out of her pants. Atlas stood there for a moment, half-naked, exposed, and vulnerable. All she was wearing now was her black bra and matching panties. He placed his warm hands around her naked waist and led her out of the bathroom.

"Let me help you to the bed, Attie," Kyle said,

"Don't call me Attie," she responded with a smile.

Kyle smiled as he wrapped his arm around Atlas, supporting her weight as they navigated towards the bed. Atlas' breaths were labored, her strength fading with each passing moment. Kyle offered her a sense of security. His steady grip provided her stability during Atlas' desperate time.

As they reached the bed, Kyle guided Atlas down, ensuring she was comfortable and safe. Atlas's eyes then met Kyle's, and she reached for him, saying, "I want you." She then pulled his body over hers and kissed him. The brush of their lips, a gentle meeting that felt like the world had slowed down just for them. The kiss was a soft, lingering sensation speaking volumes without words, a mixture of warmth, passion, and an unspoken promise.

A perfect kiss that was more about the emotional resonance and the genuine affection between Atlas and Kyle. Kyle was caught off guard by Atlas' kiss. He wanted to pull away, but instead his body craved hers. Holding the kiss as long as possible. He knew it was wrong, but even for just this moment, he had to allow himself to get lost in Attie's lips. Kyle released the kiss as Atlas fell asleep. He tucked her in and adjusted the blankets with a tender touch.

He left the door ajar and made his way to the fireplace, *"what was I thinking?"* he asked himself as he removed his wet shirt and fling it over a chair so it would dry. Kyle grabbed a blanket from the couch and sat in front of the fire. He was lost in his thoughts as he laid his body on the floor. He started to imagine what would have taken place if he had not stopped kissing his 'Attie. ' He chuckled a bit at the idea while closing his eyes.

He must have fallen asleep, and he began dreaming of this impossible affair when he felt someone reaching for him. A warm, tender body whose scent was so familiar. Kyle was not sure what was happening. Was he dreaming? But this seemed so real? He tried to raise himself, but he couldn't. Was he giving into temptation as he felt soft hands running up and down his bare chest? The tender sensation of a woman's touch while her hands circled his chest and stomach. Kyle could feel a woman's breast brushing over his bare chest.

The kisses were intoxicating, and Kyle did not want to stop this encounter. He could feel the excitement of the moment when the female's hands reached for his belt buckle and undid his pants. She then reached down and began massaging his groin while using her fingers. She teased him to the point Kyle felt himself beginning to lose control. He reached his hands and caressed her face, opening his eyes and recognizing Atlas. Kyle then pulled Atlas' hands, saying, "No, no, Attie. Stop Attie, Stop Attie! Stop!" He pushed her away.

Atlas was shocked and tried to kiss him once more, saying, "Come on, you know you want to? Don't you want me? I know how you like it. Come on! Why are you turning me down again? Don't you think I'm sexy?" You always do this to me." Atlas then began to cry.

Kyle leaned up and realized Atlas was still under the influence, and she was hallucinating. Kyle reached for her, but she pushed him away, saying, "I'm sick of this. You always do this to me. You always embarrassed me. You get me horny and then turn me down. I hate you! Get away from me! This is why I left."

Kyle looked confused as she yelled at him; he stood up and went to the kitchen, returning with a glass of whiskey.

"Come on, drink this. It will make you feel better soon," Kyle said, handing her the glass.

Atlas reluctantly took it while drinking. Her face cringed as she tried to hand it back to him, saying, "That is so strong. I don't want anymore."

"Please take another drink. You will soon feel chills, and it will help you," Kyle insisted, pushing the drink back to her.

"Alright, but I will only take one more drink," Atlas said.

"Alright, then one more," Kyle said as he waited for her to take a drink. He then grabbed the glass, stood, took the glass to the kitchen, and came back in a few seconds to find Atlas sprawled out on the floor. He grabbed another blanket and placed it over her.

She turned and warmly smiled at him, "Hey Kyle, what happened? How did I get home? Oh, my head is spinning, and I'm so cold."

"Attie, do you know where you are?" he said as he knelt next to her.

"I promise, Kyle, I was not drinking. I had water most of the night until we got to the Rez," Atlas explained.

"Do you remember what happened there?" he asked.

"Yes, well, a little, and some of it is fuzzy. I remember walking in and sitting at the bar. I asked for ginger ale. I had one or two. I think the bar was pretty full. I remember it was like 2:45, and I told the guys we needed to leave at 3:00. They were good with it. I went back to the bar and asked for water, and I got a water bottle. Then, a guy bumped into me, and I dropped my bottle. Another guy handed me my bottle. After I started feeling bad after drinking the water," she said.

"They must have switched the bottles. You were drugged" Kyle said.

"Drugged? With what? Why?" she said, confused.

"I think they were trying to take you or rape you," he said.

"Kyle, I am so cold. How did you find me?" she asked, shivering.

Kyle wrapped the blanket around her and rubbed his hand up and down her shoulders to warm her, "this will pass. I promise you will be alright."

"Why can't I remember? Did they?" she asked in a panic.

"No, no, I promise you. They did not hurt you. I got there in no time. The bartender called, and I got you before anything happened. I promise," Kyle said, pulling Atlas towards him and trying to both calm her down and warm her as she shivered.

Atlas began to feel her body tiring, and before she fell asleep, she turned to Kyle and said, "Thank you, but do you mind staying here with me? I don't want to be alone. I am so cold. You're my hero."

Kyle helped her down to the floor, tucking the blanket around her, but Atlas then pulled the blanket up, inviting him to cuddle with her. Kyle laid his warm body onto hers as he whispered in her ear, "I am not your hero I am the monster you needed tonight to fight evil. You're alright. I got you. Go to sleep, Attie, and I got you."

Then, they both fell asleep and snuggled next to the fire. Kyle woke up with his arms wrapped around Atlas, his fingers tracing her bare arms. He imagined this would be the way they woke up together every morning if there were a couple. Kyle could not help but think deeply about it when it concerned Attie. He kept thinking of the other day getting her up. She was standing there screaming at him. She looked so sexy it was dark, but he could see her perfect curves. He could see her beautiful breasts and her erect nipples. Gorgeous. I just want to touch, caress, suck on them and then work my way down her body, cupping her beautiful butt. "I would work on making her scream with pleasure with every touch of my tongue," he thought to himself.

As his mind continued to wonder, he said to himself, "She is a beautiful and dangerous woman. I shouldn't have these thoughts because she is young and impulsive. She would never be ready for what I can provide. We have the academy to get through. What am I thinking? I can't have feelings. I know this is why I keep riding her ass. I can't let myself get any closer than I am." Holding her tight next to my body has put me in a tailspin.

"She is too damn young" I will just keep pushing her away. "But damn, she is going to be challenging." Kyle wondered if they could make it work, then he stopped and told himself, *"This is crazy. I can't be falling in love with her. She is way too young, and she has so much life to live that I just can't."*

Chapter 8

Misunderstanding

Atlas began to wake up. At first, she looked confused, wondering why she was sleeping on the ground and in Kyle's arms. "What happened last night?" she asked herself; she could feel her head pounding, recalling bits and pieces of the night.

While she shifted her body, Kyle simply asked, "Hey, you are waking up. How are you feeling?"

"Kyle, I'm not sure what's happening. How did I get on the floor?" Atlas asked as she tried to rise up, but Kyle held her down slowly.

"Don't get up too fast," he warned her.

She looked down at herself and realized she was not wearing her clothing.

"Here, take my shirt," he told her while handing her his button-down shirt.

Atlas was confused, and she was exposed and vulnerable underneath the blanket. She immediately grabbed his shirt and put it on. Kyle stood up, turned his back, and walked towards the kitchen.

"Let me get you a cup of coffee, and I will explain everything afterward," Kyle suggested. "Maybe some breakfast?"

Atlas quickly buttoned up his shirt, and she said, "Yes, coffee, that sounds amazing."

Kyle began to open the cabinets and realized there was no food in the cabin, "Attie all you have is coffee, what do you eat?"

"I eat," Atlas replied in a low tone.

"I know we eat breakfast together in the main house and mostly peanut butter and jelly sandwiches for lunch. What about your dinner?" Kyle questioned.

"I normally skipped dinner. I'm trying to save money and maybe shed a few pounds. I want to visit my family for Thanksgiving," she responded, walking towards the kitchen.

"Atlas, that's insane, you need to eat more. We are training your body to not sustain itself without proper nutrition. What have you been eating?" Kyle asked.

"Please don't lecture me. I have a headache; I woke up half naked, and the last thing I need is another talking to," she replied.

"You know, you're right. I just don't understand you," he said while pouring her a cup of coffee.

"What is to understand? How are you confused? I'm saving my money because I wanna go home to see my family, my friends, my people, don't you have people? Don't you have a family? Don't you miss them?" she asked.

"I'm not sure. I've never been close to my family and don't have many friends. The few friends I have are in the military. I guess I just got used to not being with people," he said.

"Kyle, I don't understand how you can get used to being alone? Don't you get lonely?" she asked.

"You're right. We're very different. You and I are so different," Kyle responded, pouring him a cup of coffee.

"Crap! Adam's car! I think I left it at the Rez. I have to give him back his car. Damn it! I really needed that money!" she said, slamming her cup on the counter.

"You don't have to worry. Adams and the guys got home safely. He texted me last night. He was concerned about you. He told me to tell you not to worry. He's gonna pay you anyway," Kyle said, pouring her a refill.

"No, Kyle! I can't take his money, and I didn't finish the job. So I'm thinking I don't have enough money to make it home. I guess I'm just staying here for Thanksgiving, and if it makes you happy, I will use the money I have saved to buy some groceries. I don't think anyone's going to be here for Thanksgiving. Everybody has plans to go somewhere for the holiday. Damn it! I just thought I would make enough money to ride the bus home," she said.

"I'm sorry, you were taking the bus?" he asked.

"Yeah, Greyhound, you know the bus; what, have you never ridden a bus before?" Atlas asked.

"I just can't picture you riding the Greyhound bus, a Greyhound," Kyle said with a smile.

"Well, clearly, my car can't make it, and I don't have enough money for a plane ticket. So the next best option is the bus. Why, what's wrong with the bus?" Atlas responded.

"Nothing's wrong with the bus, and it's just that, have you ever ridden a bus across the country? Do you even know who rides the bus? You are always careless. Failure to prepare. Just careless," Kyle responded.

"Great! All I need right now is another lecture from Kyle Noyes, ' Mr. Maybe' For your information, I can take care of myself. Buses are safe," she said.

"I never said they weren't safe. I just said you were not prepared. Did you even think about the type of people who ride Greyhound buses? No, you didn't because if you did, you would reconsider your plan. Mainly, old people and recently released convicts ride buses. I cannot picture you sitting next to either. Also, it is like 20 hours, if not more," he said.

"It wouldn't take me 20 hours to get to Saint Louis; it's like a 12-hour ride, if that," she responded.

"I am not trying to question your intelligence, but Greyhound makes multiple stops along the way. It will be like 20 or more hours," Kyle said.

"I'm not sure why we're even discussing this. I don't have the money to go, so now I'm stuck here," Atlas said.

"No, you're not. I'll take you, and I will drive you to see your parents if you would like," Kyle said.

"What?" Atlas responded.

"It's on my way to Tennessee. I don't mind stopping and dropping you off and then picking you up on my way home. I mean, here is my current home," Kyle said.

"Really! You would drive me to Saint Louis?" she asked.

"Yeah, I'll take you. I know you're homesick, and you need to see your people. I get it," he said.

Atlas was so happy she walked into her bedroom to change your clothes and returned Kyle's shirt. She entered the room, noticing the shirt she was wearing the previous night ripped. Walked out holding it as she began to feel a panic attack coming over her. She turned around and stood in the doorway. How did my shirt get ripped?"

"Oh! Atlas, I meant to explain that," Kyle said, walking towards her.

"What happened to me last night, Kyle? Why, my shirt all is ripped? Why did I wake up in my underwear? Tell me, tell me the truth. What happened?" she asked.

"I told you some guys drugged you, but I got there on time. I promise nothing will happen to you. Trust me, nothing happened to you," Kyle said softly.

"Did you and I? I mean, did you and I have sex?" she asked.

"No, I would never take advantage of you that way. You know me better than that, or at least I hope you know me better than that," he replied.

"Alright, I must have been hallucinating. I could have sworn we did something, and I'm glad we didn't. I mean not that you; you're my friend, and I don't want to ruin that. You know, sex complicates stuff. Besides, you're like Kyle. Did I hurt your feelings? I didn't mean to hurt your feelings. I'm just saying we're friends. That's all we're friends," she replied.

"I know we're just friends, and that's all. We're going to be there, so there's no need for an explanation. Why don't you go shower, and I will go get you some groceries? You can't keep living like this," Kyle said.

"I don't think I've done that bad for myself. I'm still alive," she replied with a smirk on her face, turning as if she was showing off.

"By the grace of God, you're still alive. I don't know how, but you're right. You're still alive," Kyle said, clearing the cups from the counter.

"You know, sometimes you can be such an Ass," Atlas said, walking towards the bedroom. She walked into her bathroom and turned on the water to shower.

"Get cleaned up, and I will meet you at the main house for breakfast. Then we will do whatever we need to be done around here and go out for dinner," he said as he heard the water running inside the bathroom. "Attie, did you hear me? Do you want to go out with me? Maybe dinner with me tonight?"

As the water was running, Atlas began washing her hair and cleaning her body. All she heard was dinner, and she yelled out, "Ok, dinner out sounds great."

Kyle walked out of the cabin and headed toward his cabin to get ready for the day. He then walked to the main house and started making their breakfast. Atlas bounced in with a huge smile. "I see you are feeling better?" he asked, serving her a plate of food.

"Yeah, I am ready for the day ahead. Where is everyone else?" Atlas asked as she shoved food in her mouth.

"I think they are still out looking for more ponies. I think Ellie went out to help pick them out. I can text them if you need to speak to them," he replied.

"No, I was just wondering if Ellie was prepared for the next series of exams. I was hoping we could study together. I thought maybe some prepping would do us some good," she said.

"Do you want me to go over some stuff with you?" Kyle asked as he sat down with his plate of food.

"Yeah, I would, but I don't want you to think I am dumb," she said, pushing food around with her fork.

"Why do you always put yourself down? You are impulsive, but you are super smart. I don't understand why you do that?" he asked, clearing the plates.

"Well, I will grab my notes and meet you at the barn. We can study and work. Good?" she said, walking out the door.

They spent several hours doing chores and quizzing one another until the evening came upon them.

"Go get ready if you like, and I will finish here. I will meet you at the main house in an hour. Oh, and Attie, wear something nice," Kyle suggested. He watched Atlas bounce out without saying a word.

Atlas looked through her closet and couldn't find 'something nice' to wear to dinner. She wasn't sure why this feeling of excitement and nervousness had taken over her. Atlas told herself it was no big deal. It was just dinner with Kyle. She didn't want to make a fuss about it but also wanted to look nice. Atlas decided to go to the main house and grab something out of Sabina's closet. All the clothes were hers for the taking. What better time than the present?

Atlas looked through all the beautiful outfits that were at her disposal. She meticulously perused the racks, eyeing the array of dresses. With a discerning eye, she thought of the quintessential little black dress. Then, her hand landed on a sleeveless midi dress. She pulled it off the rack to expose the label Versage, "Oh Lord, I have never dreamed of owning something so beautiful," she thought to herself.

Carefully, Atlas slipped into the dress, feeling the luxurious fabric hug her frame in all the right places. As she zipped it up, the dress accentuated her figure flawlessly, the sleeveless design exuding confidence and sophistication. Shoes were next on her agenda. She looked around and found a pair of pumps, Saint Laurent Lee sling-back pumps.

They fit her to perfection; it was as if the pumps were made for her. Atlas rubbed her hand across the croc-embossed patent leather and secured the buckle. She looked down at the pointed toe and stood up in the stiletto heel. The final touch was an appreciated handbag, clearly a no-brainer, and the Veradage Mini shoulder bag. A quilted patent leather with gold and a detachable strap.

Atlas decided to wear little make-up, just blush and lipstick. She focused on her hair, which often drove her crazy. Not today, Atlas pinned it up in half up-do, a sophisticated style alluring her long flowing hair caressing her shoulders. With a final glance in the mirror, Atlas knew she had found the ideal ensemble for the occasion. "This puts something nice to shame," she laughed to herself as she reached for a wrap to keep her warm from the winter breeze.

She heard a light knock on the front door, and for some strange reason, her heart skipped a beat. Atlas ignored it and walked to the door, where she found Kyle dressed in a nice black suit with a purple tie that seemed to enhance the warmth in his eyes. Atlas was shocked to see how handsome he looked and felt speechless. When Kyle broke the silence by saying, "You look real pretty tonight, Attie."

"Thank you "were the only words that Atlas could say. Kyle placed his hand behind her back in the small of her waist and led her to the car. He opened the passenger side door and helped her inside. They drove silently towards Cheyenne. As they got closer to the downtown area, Atlas turned her attention to Kyle, saying, "Kyle, this is my first time coming to Cheyenne. I did not think this place was so metropolitan; it looked like a sleepy little town."

Kyle let out a slight laugh, "You know, Attie, you always make me smile. The restaurant we are going to is The Metropolitan. I really hope you like it." A few seconds later, they reached their destination, and Kyle drove to the valet area and stopped. Atlas instinctively placed her hand on the door lock. Kyle then tapped her left hand, telling her, "Wait, Attie, don't be in a hurry. The attendant will help you out. Just wait for him," She felt a bit embarrassed but followed his instructions. She nodded in agreement as a young man opened the door and helped her out. She watched Kyle intensely while he handed her his keys. Then, he immediately walked next to her, placing his hand on the small of her back and leading her inside.

"Kyle, this place looks super fancy. Are you sure you want to eat here?" she asked nervously.

"Absolutely, come on, relax," he said, throwing her a confident smile to encourage her.

"I am not sure I am dressed appropriately for this type of place," she replied, looking down at her dress.

"You look amazing, don't overthink it. Just enjoy it," he said, again placing his hand on the small of her waist to lead her side of the restaurant.

"Kyle, are you sure?" she said, looking deep into his eyes. He did not respond; just led her inside without missing a beat.

They were led by a very stuffy maître d into a private elevator to the top floor. Stepping out, the couple was escorted to a corner table overlooking the town, where they were seated without waiting. Atlas sat and began gazing around in amazement. She noticed the atmosphere was romantic and classy. The room had warming lights, just enough to illuminate but not too bright. The decor was clean and classy, as she had only experienced it through the magic of television. Each table had white and red linen, along with a candlelight centerpiece. She looked around and noticed the walls were sparking as if they were waterfalls. *"Breathe,"* she thought to herself.

"You alright?" Kyle asked, placing his hand over hers.

"Yep, I mean yes, but I am not sure why we are here," Atlas asked, feeling a bit overwhelmed.

"We are here to eat dinner," Kyle responded nonchalantly.

"Don't be smart. I have never been to a place this fancy," she replied, trying to catch her breath.

"I am surprised I figured one of your boyfriends treated you to a nice dinner," he said, placing his napkin on his lap.

"Dinner, yes, but it was more like Applebee's or Outback. Nothing this fancy," she responded, mimicking his every move.

"Oh, I am a bit shocked you are from Saint Louis. They have really good restaurants there," Kyle could not help but say with a smirk.

"Yes I guess but I have never gone to any of them. I don't even think my mom and dad have either. We are more blue-collar working class people. Not like," she stopped herself because she did not want to start bickering in public.

"Well, that's a shame. No matter where you are now. Enjoy it" he handed her the menu." What do you want to eat?"

"I am not sure. But can I ask you a question," she said after opening the menu and looking at it for a second.

"Sure, you can ask me anything,' he replied.

"Why aren't the prices listed on the menu?" she blurred out.

Kyle smiled, took a breath, and responded, "So you don't choose your meal based on cost. Just pick whatever you want."

"I guess I should be a bit embarrassed to say this, but I don't know how to order," she whispered.

"Well, tell me what you are in the mood for chicken, pork, steak, fish, or maybe you prefer vegetarian style," he suggested.

"Beef sounds good. I haven't had a steak in a while," she replied with a smile.

"Alright, now we can order red wine since we are having beef. Good start. How do you like it cooked rare or well done?" he continued.

"I guess medium. My dad says it is the best tasting," she answered

"He is right. Medium is a wise choice; the meat is not tough. Great, you are doing great," he encouraged her and then asked," We will have both soup and salad and, in the end, dessert."

"That is so much food it's a bit overwhelming," she answered, still looking around the room.

"No worries. If you would like, I will order it for you. Just stop me if I choose something you don't like. Sound good?" he suggested.

"No, it's good I trust you," she said, turning her attention back to Kyle.

The waiter came, and Kyle placed their order, selecting it with ease. Every item sounded delicious. All Atlas could do was smile as he took charge. Then, in minutes, they received their wine and warm bread. Atlas fought the temptation to reach and shove bread into her mouth. Instead, she waited and followed Kyle's lead.

"Atlas, why don't you tell me about your family? How do the Martins celebrate Thanksgiving?" he asked, trying to break the tension.

Atlas looked up, swallowing a huge drink of wine." Oh, I guess traditionally. We have a turkey and fixings, pies, and stuff like that."

"Go on, tell me more, "Kyle asked, sipping his wine slowly.

"Mom cooks all day. She makes her special stuffing and mashed potatoes. Oh, we don't have a green bean casserole. Instead, she makes fresh green beans with toasted almonds. That is my favorite, I guess because we only eat it once a year," Atlas looked and Kyle smiled warmly at her. "Oh God did I say too much? I am sorry did I manipulate the conversation?"

"No, of course not. I am enjoying every word. Are you feeling more comfortable now?" he asked once again, laying his hand over hers.

"Yes, thank you. What about your family? I guess you are looking to spend time at home," Atlas enquired.

"I am not really sure. Your family sounds warm and inviting. Mine, on the other hand, are more on the cold side. My mom does not cook. I don't think I have ever seen her near the stove. When we have dinner, it is more catered style, or we are at a resort. My parents love to travel. One Thanksgiving when I was young, we spent it in Japan. The Japanese do not celebrate Thanksgiving. I think it was the first time I had a duck. I recall my little brothers crying because they thought we were eating Donald Duck or Duffy. To be honest, I don't recall many good memories with my parents. It has all been more about the competition than the love. You know what I mean? Mom is always trying to outdo Dad and vice versa. It has always been too much," he responded, his eyes darkening.

"Oh, that is a shame, but you spoke about your grandmother, right?" she asked, trying to lighten the conversation.

"Yes, my grandmother was a special lady. Going to spend time with her is one of the fondest memories I have. She was a tough and yet warm lady. Gigi, I called her. She loved life and lived it to the fullest. Man, I miss her," he said.

"Oh, Kyle, I am sorry I didn't know she passed away," Atlas said, placing her hand over his.

"Yes, several years back. After I had joined the Army, I received the notification. She died in her sleep. Nothing more than simply going to sleep and just not waking up. I am glad she went peacefully. Gigi loved life. Everything was an adventure for her, and I would never want to see her suffer. You know what I mean?" Kyle said, coupling his hand with Atlas. She quickly moved it out and once again began looking around.

"Wow, I must be losing my mind, but is this place moving or something?" she said with some awkwardness.

"Yes, it rotates slowly so the patrons can enjoy the scenery in a 360-degree experience. I thought you understood that when we entered. I would have explained it to you, but I didn't want you to think I was a smart ass," he said, smiling and enjoying his dessert.

"This has got to be very expensive. Why are you spending so much money on dinner for me?" she asked.

"Let's not talk about the expense. I told you it was my treat. I just wanted you to have a good time. You have been working so hard to make it through the academy. So, like I said before, don't overthink it, and just enjoy it. How about stopping for a drink somewhere after dinner and before heading back to the ranch?" he suggested.

As they left the restaurant, Kyle stopped and purchased a single red rose, handing it to Atlas before she entered the car, which was brought over by the valet. She sat for a second, smelling the rose, and waited for Kyle to take his place in the driver's seat. She mustered the courage to ask, "Where to now?"

"I saw a pretty decent place on our drive over. Do you want to try it?" he replied.

"Sure sounds nice," she said, buckling her seatbelt.

They pulled over just a few miles from the restaurant. Once again, Kyle parked and helped Atlas out of the car. He stretched his hand, and she reached for it without hesitation. They walked inside, looking around for a table. Atlas then focused on a corner table with a couple who were sitting next to one another. Kyle placed his hand on her waist and led her to the other side of the room. Atlas kept trying to figure out who was sitting at that corner table.

"What gives Attie? Do you not like the place?" Kyle asked as he helped her with her seat.

"No, it's not that I just thought I saw someone I know?" Atlas replied, a bit distracted.

"Do you prefer to go? We don't have to stay here if you are uncomfortable," he said, sitting himself down across from her.

"No, I am not. I think this place is fine. I just can't make out who that is. It is a bit dark here, don't you think?" Atlas responded.

"Why don't you look at the menu and pick something out? What about a nice sangria or wine?" he suggested.

"Oh yes, I guess what are you going to ask for a beer? "She asked, staring at the corner table.

"Yes, I guess I will just order whatever is on tap. If I was not driving, I might get a Scotch or Whiskey. Or a glass of goat milk if they had goats here," he rattled on.

"Oh, that sounds good. Milk sounds good," she looked at him for a second, "what milk? Goat milk? That sounds disgusting, "she answered.

"Just wanted to see if you were paying me any attention. You seem awfully curious and distracted at the moment," he said, then placing the order with the waitress who had come over.

"Well, for your information, I think I spotted Pricilla. At least I believe it is her, and I am trying to see who is with her," she said.

"Look, Attie, I don't think you should make an effort to figure out who she is out with. That is her business and not yours," he said, trying to block her view.

"What aren't you curious about? I am. I want to know what her type is. You know she is so high maintenance and all," she replied with a rude tone.

"Stop being so caddy. That is her business, not yours. She is free to date whoever she wants, she is a grown woman," he replied while the waitress brought them over their drinks.

"Excuse me, Miss, do you know who is sitting with that lady over there?" she asked the waitress.

"Please don't answer her. That is none of our business," he interrupted, and the waitress left without saying a word.

"Why did you do that? I was just curious," she answered, sipping her drink.

"I told you that is none of our business," he said while taking a drink.

"Oh my Lord, it's Spinelli. Look around, Tony Spinelli. What a whore?" Atlas could not get the words out fast enough when Kyle stood, dropped cash on the table, and pulled her chair away from the table.

"Let's go! You will not make a scene in this place. Come on, we are done here," Kyle said in a tense tone.

"What are you doing? Why are you so upset?" Atlas said, walking out with Kyle.

They reached the car, and Kyle opened the door for her, but she refused to enter, "what is the matter with you? Do you like Pricilla? I am so sorry to tell you that it seems like she is with Spinelli. I bet in a matter of a few hours, those two will be in his room naked and ready for one long, sex-filled night."

"I don't care about Pricilla or Spinelli. Least of all, what do those two consenting adults do? I just don't want you to talk about it. You sound so childish right now. Lord, how could I have thought you…? Never mind, I will drop you off at home. Come on, get in." Kyle's voice seemed to be more of a roar than a suggestion.

"Alright, I will get in. I just don't understand why you are so upset. I mean, if you don't like Pricilla, why does it bother you so much? Can you tell me? I think I deserve an explanation," Atlas barked back.

"No, you don't. It is all my fault for this moment. I forgot that you are not much older than a child. You can't help it because you are just a kid. You act like a child, you say childish things, and basically, you are just young. Too young to understand," Kyle said, driving in the direction of the ranch.

"Too young. I was not too young a few hours ago. Tell me, Kyle, why did you take me to that fancy restaurant? Did you think you were going to impress me? Are we not dating? Why do you treat me like I am your girl? I am not, you know. I don't belong to you or to anyone. I am independent, and I can take care of myself. As a matter of fact, stop the car. Stop the car!" Atlas said furiously, trying to open the car door.

"What the hell are you doing?" Kyle said, stopping the car.

"I don't want to be an inconvenience for you anymore. I am happy to walk home from here. I don't need you. I don't need your charity or your advice or multiple opinions. Got it. I don't need you or anyone. I can do it all by myself." she said, jumping out of the SUV and started walking away. "And by the way, I think Pricilla is a whore. A whore, I tell you. If she sleeps with Spinelli so she can pass the academy, she is a whore. I don't care if you agree or not. If you find her so attractive, go find her. I think she will be at the nearest Sinner's Paradise local motel with Spinelli giving him head," Atlas said, walking fast towards the front gate of the ranch.

Kyle drove behind her, slowly gathering himself, and waited for her to reach the gate. He took a deep breath, jumped out of the car, and grabbed the gate, "look, Attie, I am sorry. I just wanted you to have a nice night out, that is all?"

"I did, but I still don't understand why it bothers you so much that Spinelli and Pricilla are together."

"It is not that. Tonight was supposed to be just about us. It bothered me because you seem so preoccupied with other people's business. I just simply don't like gossip or drama. Spinelli and Pricilla are train wrecks that we don't have to be part of. Do you get that? I just don't have the energy to deal with that type of chaos. I have seen that story unfold so many times in the military. Young lady, older guy in a position of authority. She falls for him, and he uses her for a good time just in the meantime."

"In the meantime, what do you mean?" she asked, leaning on the gate.

"I mean timepiece. She is disposable and replaceable," Kyle said, extending his hand and trying to get Attie to enter the car once more.

"I get it. I know what you mean, but you still have not told me why you got so upset with me when I pointed it out. Do you have feelings for Pricilla?" she asked as they walked towards the passenger side of the SUV.

"No, I do, but not the way you think. I feel sorry for her if that is the way she runs her life. Girls like her use their outer beauty and forget about their inner one. What will happen to Pricilla once her beauty fades? Will she find herself happy, or will she look for a good plastic surgeon to make her look pretty again? It is all an endless cycle of chasing something you will never achieve," Kyle said as he closed Atlas's door and got into the driver's seat.

"So you do think she is attractive?" Atlas responded, looking out the passenger side window.

"Man, Attie, you just hear what you want to hear. I think this conversation is over. I will drop you off at the main house and go park my car. If you need me to walk you to your cabin, I will," Kyle said, looking straight ahead.

"No, I was planning on sleeping at the main house tonight. I left my regular clothes there. Besides, in a few hours, we need to feed the horses. I will see you in the morning. Good night, and thank you for dinner. I am sorry if I ruined your night," she said, stepping out of the car.

"Attie, you didn't ruin the night. I am not mad at you. I am just frustrated with myself. I will see you in the morning. Have a good night," Kyle said, driving off towards the barn.

Atlas did not think twice about the evening and simply went inside to prepare for the next day. *"One more week, she thought, and they would be heading home for the Thanksgiving break."* She could not wait to get there and see her family. Atlas was not looking forward to the long ride home with Kyle, but they would be fine. In a couple of hours of work, they would fall back into their routine. Kyle would be back to his old self, and she would make him laugh about something or another.

Atlas walked into Sabina's bedroom and changed her clothes. She laid the little black dress on the bed and wondered where else that dress had been. *"Maybe a classy party or event? A nice romantic dinner with Bill or a night about town. Wait what? Was that why Kyle was so upset? Were they on a date? No way! She and Kyle. God No! He was more like an older brother or uncle. What was she thinking, Kyle?"* she laughed. Atlas laid herself in the bed and instantly fell asleep laughing at the thought of her Kyle being an item.

Chapter 9

What Really Matters

Kyle walked into the main house early the next morning to find Atlas had all her notecards spread out over the counter. He could smell a pot of coffee brewing and bread toasting. She walked out of the pantry with grape jelly in one hand and honey in the other.

"Are you ready to hit the books before we go to the barn and feed the horses?" she asked.

"Just coffee for me, thanks. I fed the horses already. I figured you needed to study, so I managed without you," he replied, drinking his coffee in one swallow.

"You alright?" she asked, "do you want to go over some material with me?" she offered.

"No, I am good. I just got a text from Ellie and Rob. I have to meet them at the gate in a few minutes. They are bringing in new ponies. I will help settle them down and then catch up with you," he said, walking out the door.

A few hours later, Atlas, Ellie, and Kyle found themselves at the academy and were done with their first series of examinations. They stood outside in the hallway, waiting for Spinelli to post the results. The doors of his office opened, and he walked down the corridor, arrogant as ever, uniform pressed, hair perfectly still, and a smirk that brought shivers to the troops.

"Class, if you do not see your name on the board because you failed. Remember, if you fail the exams, you will be removed from the program. At this venture, there are no opportunities for retakes. Take a close look at the scores. The top 10 percent will be immediately placed on a sponsored list. Agencies throughout the state are willing to take you on now. They will pay you back for your education and training, give you a job, and provide you with the $5,000.00 bonus check that attracted you here in the first place. Congratulations to those who made it," Spinelli said, pegging the list on the board and walking away.

"I know I don't have anything at all to worry about," Pricilla said out loud while strutting to check the list. "Yes! Like I said, that 5 grand is already in my bank account," she said, walking towards Spinelli office.

Several cadets took their turn looking while Atlas and Ellie waited to be last, "you nervous?" Atlas asked Ellie as they looked at one another.

"I don't like tests," Ellie said, walking closer to the clipboard, "ready?" she said, encouraging Atlas to find her name on the board.

"Oh! I made it, how about you?" Atlas asked looking around, "where is Kyle?"

"He had to head to Cheyanne didn't he tell you?" Ellie responded looking for his score on the list. "Wow! Kyle got a perfect score."

"What is he doing in Cheyanne? Did he say anything to you?" Atlas asked, trying not to sound too curious.

"I think he better be the one to give that news. To be honest, he did not explain it to me. He talked to Rob, and I kind of overheard them. I don't want to get it wrong. Besides, that is his business, you know what I mean. Kyle seems like a very private guy. What is the deal with you two anyway? I didn't think you liked him in that way?" Ellie turned to see Atlas looking out of the window.

"Well, we are just friends. I don't know him well. I just wonder about him at times. You know he is different. Anyways, where did you place?" Atlas asked.

"I am in good standing. What about you? Where did you place?" Ellie asked as they walked outside to rejoin the group.

"It looks like I am good too. I probably will get sponsored by the State Police or local Sheriff's office," she said.

"Well, don't sound so enthused about it. I am there with you. We might even be working for the same department. So who did we lose?" Ellie said out loud, looking around.

"Garcia, Roberts, and Smithy," Adams responded, "Man, they are all good guys, but they partied too hard. We better change and do our PT before Spinelli catches us hanging out.

Four more days of exams and then a week off, "he said, running towards the gym.

The next few days seemed to be the same process. Exams result from anxiety and are followed by physical training. In a blink of an eye, Friday afternoon was upon the cadets. Once again, Spinelli walked towards the bulletin board and posted the following note:

CONGRATULATIONS CLASS YOU HAVE ALL EARNED A WEEK OFF

GO HOME, ENJOY YOUR FAMILY, REST, AND BE SAFE.

REPORT BACK NEXT MONDAY AT 0630 HOURS.

In a matter of minutes, the academy hallways were empty. Ellie and Atlas drove together to the ranch without saying a word. As Ellie parked the car, she looked at Atlas and asked, "What are you doing for the break? Do you want to stay here? Rob and I are going to visit his mom, but. " I am going home to Missouri. Kyle said he would drop me off on his way to Tennessee. I think he is meeting his family there. So I am good, don't worry." she said, hopping out of the car.

"Great! Let me know if things change. Ben is spending time with some friends in town, but he will keep an eye on the ranch. You go and enjoy your family. I am sure you miss them," Ellie said, walking towards the main house.

Atlas ran to her cabin and started packing her bags. She must have packed everything and then rethought the arrangements. Atlas decided she only needed a small bag with essentials since she had left clothes at her parent's house. She only packed the little black dress just in case there was another opportunity to show it off. Time began slipping away as Atlas prepared, and when she looked at her door, Kyle stood there.

"Ready?" he asked.

"Yes, I am. I just have a small travel bag and my book bag. Is that alright?" she asked, dragging her luggage across the room.

"Of course, but you might want to grab a pillow and blanket as well. It is a long drive, and that might make you more comfortable," he suggested, reaching for her bags.

"Oh, right. Do you want me to grab one for you as well? I don't mind. I have an extra pillow," she said, pulling two pillows from her bed, but Kyle did not respond. He simply placed the items in the hatch and made his way to the passenger's door to open it for her.

"Ready?" he said, waiting for her to enter and secure her seatbelt.

"Ready," she replied with a smile, "aren't you excited about going home?" she asked.

He made his way to the driver's side, and they began their trip in silence. A few hours into the trip, Atlas, who had fallen asleep, woke up from her nap and looked around. "Hey, how long was I out?"

"Just a few minutes or so. Maybe a few hundred miles," he replied, looking straight ahead.

"Why didn't you wake me? I guess I am not very good company?" she replied, sitting herself up.

"I don't mind the silence. You looked so peaceful. I thought you might need to sleep," he said, staring forward.

"Hey, can I ask you a question? Did you get sponsored? I know you made it to the top of the list. Did you decide who you are going to go work for?" she asked.

"I have a few offers on the table. What about you? Who picked you up?" he asked.

"I guess Ellie and I are going with the local sheriff's office. It makes sense for her since she will not have to move far. I will be able to stay at the ranch a bit longer. Well, at least until I can find my own place. Other people are looking at places clear across the state. What about you, Kyle?" she asked while her voice cracked a bit.

"I am not sure yet, Attie. I have a few offers across the state and some more local. I know Cheyenne is one of the departments that are interested in me. But to be honest, I have not made up my mind. I think after this trip, I might be more confident in making a decision," he answered.

"Why after this trip? You think your folks will want to move closer to you?" she suggested.

"Oh God no, but let's not talk about them. How about your family? Do you think your parents will be happy to see you? I am sure they are very proud of what you have accomplished so far, and all by yourself?" he said with a smile.

"I hope so. But you and I both know I could not have done it without Ellie, Ben, Rob, and you, of course. I would have been home months ago with my tail between my legs, embarrassed and ashamed," she said, looking out of the window.

"You would not. I am sure you would have found a way to make it," he said without missing a beat and shooting her a smile.

"I am so glad that you have so much confidence in me. You do know I appreciate all that you have done for me, right?" she said.

"Hey, in a few hours, we can stop to get a bite to eat. We can drive straight through and make it to your house by breakfast time unless you feel like stopping and getting some rest. If so, we can make it by lunchtime. It all depends on how much sleep you want to get?" he suggested.

"I am good at doing whatever you want to do. I don't mind helping to drive if you want to take a break. I do have a little money left over if you want to stop. I can pay for a hotel room," she responded.

"No, I am good at driving the entire trip, and I enjoy it. I just want you to be comfortable. Let's play it by ear. If you get tired, let me know, and I will be happy to stop somewhere for either food or rest," he said.

Several hours into the trip, Kyle looked at Atlas, who was sleeping, clutching her pillow while sleeping. He pulled over into a gas station, stopping to fuel up. Atlas woke up for a few minutes and noticed they were only a few hours from their destination. "Hey, do you want me to take over? I don't mind driving for a bit," she suggested.

"No, I am still good. I am going to run in and get a coffee. Do you want something to drink?" Kyle asked as he opened the door.

"I am good for right now. I will walk around to wake up a bit. Like I said, I can take us the rest of the way," she said.

Kyle quickly jumped back into the driver's seat and waited for Atlas to return to the car. He started driving as Atlas nestled herself back between her seat and the door. She then turned to look at him and said, "You are not tired?"

"No, I am good. I drove all over the Middle East. I'd rather drive than ride," he responded.

"Well, I can at least keep you company," she said, snuggling in a bit more and then yawning.

"Don't stay up for me. You will need to be ready to greet your family. They know you are coming, right?" he asked, navigating through the night.

"Yes, I called my mom. She probably has breakfast ready for us. I hope you don't mind, but my Mom loves cooking for other people. She probably went out and bought out the store and then some. Eggs, bacon, sausage, pancakes, coffee, and the works," she said, fighting off her sleep.

"That sounds nice," Kyle said, and as he glanced over, Atlas had fallen asleep once more. She was abruptly awakened when she felt the car stopping. Atlas opened her eyes just as Kyle was pulling the key out of the ignition.

"Hey, we are here," he said

"Oh my God, I can't believe it. The house looks so big. Come on, I want you to meet my Mom," Atlas said, running out towards the side door. Kyle got out of the car and made his way to the hatch. He grabbed Atlas baggage and started making his way to the door. Atlas was way ahead, and he watched her running inside. Then, a short, thin lady came out.

"Kyle, right?" she asked.

"Yes, ma'am, where would you like me to leave Attie's bags?" he asked softly.

"Come inside. We can bring the luggage in a bit," she said, leading him inside the house, "come on, don't be shy. I am sure you are exhausted from driving all night. Let me get you some coffee and a plate."

"Thank you so much, but I don't want to be in any trouble. I am sure you want to catch up with your daughter," he said as she handed him a cup.

"Nonsense. You sit down for a hot homemade meal first," she said.

Kyle could smell the fresh breakfast food inviting him to sit and eat. He was hungry, and he did not want to be rude. So he sat down as Atlas' mom brought him over fresh, warm rolls, "here are cinnamon rolls. I just got them out of the oven," she said.

"They smell amazing, Mrs. Martin. Thank you for all your hospitality, but you should not have gone through so much trouble," he said, serving himself a roll.

She reached into the basket and placed a second one on his plate, "they are small, and one is never really enough. Please, Kyle, you don't have to be so formal. I am Hannah. I have heard a lot about you, Kyle, and it's very nice to finally meet you."

"Thank you, Ms. Hannah. It is very nice to meet you as well. Attie, I mean Atlas, was not lying when she said you made breakfast for an army," he said, shoving another bit inside his mouth," the food is delicious."

"Eat up, son. You are right. I made enough for an army and then some. I was hoping my daughter would join us. But I guess she ran upstairs and forgot about us," Hannah replied.

"Oh, Ma'am, I am so sorry. I think I better get going. I am sure you two want to catch up," he said, starting to stand.

"No, you don't. Finish your breakfast, and then we will discuss it," she said, handing him more food.

"Well, to be honest, I haven't had a home-cooked meal in a while. Don't mind having another plate. Your food is amazing. It reminds me of my grandma's cooking," he said as she handed him homemade white gravy with his biscuits.

"Now that warms my heart, dear. What are you planning for Thanksgiving? Are you headed home to meet with your folks?" she asked as Atlas came to the kitchen, joining them at the table.

"Mom, I told you Kyle is just dropping me off. He is headed to Tennessee for the holiday, and he will pick me up on his way back. Stop giving him the third degree," Atlas said as she reached for food.

"Are you spending time with your family in Tennessee?" Hannah asked, looking at Kyle with that mother, knowing all looks, son or daughter, who had a reaction to her questions.

"Well, to be honest, Ma'am, I mean Ms. Hannah, I am headed to Tennessee but not to meet up with my folks. My parents and brothers are skiing in Aspen, and I did not want to join them. I thought I would meet up with some guys from my old unit," he said.

"Great, it is settled then. You will stay here with us. We have plenty of space and more than enough food. Atlas goes upstairs and makes sure there are clean towels in James' old room. Come on, go on now! You can eat your breakfast after," Hannah said as Atlas stood up and ran up to the third floor.

"Ma'am, Ms. Hannah, I can't stay here, but I appreciate the invitation," Kyle said, pushing his plate away and getting ready to stand.

"No, Sir, there is nothing to discuss. You will stay here with us, and I have no objections. I have raised three boys and two girls in this house. We have four empty bedrooms and to be honest, we will enjoy the company. Atlas tells me you have been more than kind to her. It is the least we can do, and I will not take no for an answer. Now, you eat in peace, and afterward, you can make yourself comfortable on the third floor. You will have the space all to yourself. Go upstairs, take a hot shower, and rest. My husband Thomas will be home by noon. Since today is Saturday, he only has to work a half day," she said without allowing Kyle to object.

"I guess all I can say is thank you so much. But I would feel better if you discuss it with Mr. Martin before asking me to stay," he suggested.

"Nonsense, Thomas and I are more than grateful to you. It will be a pleasure to have you stay here," she said, clearing the table. Kyle tried to help, but Hannah shot him with one of those motherly looks. "Go on and gather your things. Atlas will show you to your room. Now do as I ask, young man," she said as Attie walked into the kitchen again.

"Your mom sure does not take no for an answer," Kyle said, walking out with Atlas and grabbing his bag.

"Yep, it has been like that all my life. Don't worry if my mom says for you to stay, my dad will not object? He should be back in a couple of hours, and you can meet him," Atlas said, grabbing her blanket from the car.

"Where does your dad work?" he asked as they made their way into the house.

"Anheuser Busch Brewery is in charge of distillery and bottling. My brothers, James and Nick, also work there with him. Don't worry, and you will meet the entire family on

Thursday. James and his wife, Sarah. Tim is the fireman here in the city, and his wife, Arleen, and my sister, Annie, and her husband, Larry. You will also meet my nieces and nephews as well as Nick's new girlfriend, but I don't know her name. I am not sure who else my mom invited for dinner. I hope you don't mind. It is always a mad house around here," she said as they walked up the flights of stairs and showed him the bedroom.

"Attie, this is a very nice house. You grew up here," he asked as he placed his bag on the floor.

"Yep, I lived here all my life. I went to school a few blocks from here. I will show you later. Right now, I am beaten, and I am sure you are too," she said, walking out of the room. As she made her way to the stairs, Atlas saw her mom walking up the stairs.

"Is the room alright for you, Kyle? Let me know if you need an extra blanket or more towels. Did Attie show you the room?" she said

"Mom, he is fine. He is just tired. Let him rest for a bit before you shower him with attention," Atlas said, trying to lead her mom down the stairs, "do you know if anyone has called for me?"

"Oh, honey, you know I would tell you if anyone came or called for you. Why are you still wasting your time with that? I was hoping by now you would be over all that," Hannah responded as the ladies made their way downstairs and Kyle closed the bedroom door.

A few hours later, Kyle heard someone tapping on his door. He rolled out of the bed and walked to the door to find Hannah standing just outside in the hallway.

"Kyle, I was not sure if Attie brought you some fresh towels, so here are some. Thomas will be here in a bit. I just brewed some fresh coffee when you come downstairs," Hannah said, handing him a pile of towels.

"Thank you, Ms. Hannah. I will be down in a few minutes," Kyle said as he rushed to get ready. After a quick shower and shave, he ran down to the kitchen just in time to help place the linen on the table.

"Did you rest enough? I know that is a bit of a long trip. Atlas tells me you drove straight through, and you young man did all the driving," she said, handing him a cup of coffee.

"Thank you so much," he replied while taking a drink, "where is Attie? I mean, Atlas?"

"Some things never change. I believe she is sleeping. She will be out for several hours. I don't think an earthquake will wake her up," Hannah said with a smile, looking out the kitchen window. "It looks like Thomas is home."

Minutes later, a tall man walks into the kitchen holding a black metal lunch box, "Hannah, whose SUV is parked outside? Did Atlas make it home safe?" he said, giving his wife a quick kiss on the cheek.

"Mr. Martin, I am Kyle Noyes. I am a classmate of Atlas," Kyle said, extending his hand to shake his hand.

"Thomas Martin, Sir," he said.

"Nice to meet you," Kyle replied.

"Please have a seat. I will join you for a cup of coffee. Where is Atlas? Sleeping?" Thomas asked as he sat across from Kyle.

"What do you think? Of course, Atlas is sleeping. I was just telling Kyle it might be a bit before we see her rise," Hannah responded as she joined the men.

"Kyle, you and Atlas are at the academy together? Please don't take offense, but you look more like an instructor than a cadet. I guess what I am saying is that you are a bit older than Atlas," he said.

"Yes, Sir, I am because I served in the military before starting a new career," he said.

"Oh well, thank you for your service. Army?" he asked

"Yes, Sir. Navy?" Kyle enquired.

He nodded as he reached for some pastries and offered some to Kyle, who picked one.

"I guess you were just not done serving? I am not sure why Atlas decided to join the department. And least of all, so far away? Are you the friend that helped her find a job and a place to stay?" Thomas asked.

"Yes, Sir. I just wanted her to be safe," Kyle added.

"Well, my girl is a hard worker. Just so impulsive, unpredictable, and even careless at times. She gets that from her mother. Right, Hannah? My Hannah was the same as when I met her. At times, I think she still is." he said with a smile.

"Kyle, don't worry. My husband is only joking, but I agree that Atlas is very impulsive," Hannah replied.

"Sir, I was just trying to help. I think your daughter is very spontaneous," Kyle replied.

"We are grateful for your help with Atlas. I am hoping that this experience will help her grow up. My wife tells me you are joining us for Thanksgiving week," Thomas said.

"Sir, I was not planning on it, but it is impossible to turn your wife down," Kyle said while trying not to smile.

"Yes, you are correct. Hannah is not one I would challenge. Make yourself at home. Let me know if you need anything. My boys will be in and out of the house throughout the week. My daughter Annie will come over some time as well. I am not sure of the schedule because she is a school teacher. She talks to her mother all the time, but to be honest, I don't keep up with them. All my kids are a bit unpredictable, except for my son Timothy, Tim, the oldest. I guess he turned out to be more like me," Thomas said, smiling at his wife.

"Now Thomas, you know Tim is on track because he is a fireman here in the city. He has a lovely wife, Arleen, and two beautiful kids. But enough of that, why don't you boys go out or something? I need to clean this house, and you will only be in the way, Thomas," Hannah replied.

"Well, Kyle, that is our cue to make ourselves scarce," Thomas said, placing his cup in the sink, "Come with me, son, we can head to the shop. I will show my project car, a 1968 Shelby GT Mustang. I named her Ruby."

"I would be happy to. How long have you been working on her?" Kyle said, walking behind Thomas.

"Kyle, don't go out there without a coat. Atlas will kill me if you catch yourself with a cold. Here, take one of Thomas' coats right there in that closet," Hannah said in a motherly tone.

"Yes, Ma'am, thank you," Kyle said, grabbing a coat and following Thomas outside.

"You learn quickly; you just don't argue with Hannah," Thomas said, leading the way to the garage but stopping midway, "look at that sky as blue as can be, and just to the west clouds leading our way. You watch. In a few hours, the temperature will drop, and then there will be snow. Missouri weather, if you don't like it, just wait 15 minutes."

Chapter 10

Respect

Kyle followed Thomas into the house, chatting about classic cars. Hannah had placed snacks, fresh coffee, and pastries on the table, along with a note explaining she had gone to the store to buy groceries.

"One of the kids should be here in a few minutes. Hannah only leaves out snacks for the grandchildren," Thomas explained while grabbing a pack of Oreo cookies, "but what she doesn't know wouldn't kill." Kyle laughed, reaching for a pack for himself.

"Hey, if you are not too tired, how about Atlas taking you around town to see some of the sites?" Thomas suggested, watching Atlas coming down the stairs, "I am so glad you made time to see me. You know your old Dad."

Atlas rolled her eyes as she gave him a big hug, "Hi, Dad. I came down earlier, but Mom said you and Kyle were playing with your car."

"Refurbishing," he corrected her and went on to say, "Why don't you take our guest to see some of the sites while your mother gets supper going?"

"Oh, Dad, did you even bother to ask Kyle if he wanted to go? You just want him to see your precious Brewery, right?" Atlas responded.

"That is a wonderful idea. Great, Kyle, go see a little of our beautiful city. When you come back, we can work on Ruby some more," Thomas said, making his way up the stairs.

Atlas stood there, rolling her eyes as her Dad exited the room, "I guess you have to go take a tour. Let's go and get this over with. You want me to drive?" she snipped.

"Wait, Attie," Kyle said, reaching for her hand, "we don't have to go if you don't want to. I am alright staying here, "he pulled his hand back since Atlas put her hands on her hips. "You don't have to feel like you are stuck with me. I am not here to be in your way or to change your plans. I can leave and head to Tennessee. I will just tell your parents that something came up."

Atlas huffed, realizing that she was being rude, "No, I am sorry. I didn't mean to be like that with you. I just hate that my parents always treat me like I am a child."

" Well, you are. You are their child. But don't worry, I will go upstairs and pack my bags. I will just wait for your mom to get back and thank them for their hospitality, "Kyle said, turning away from Atlas and he began walking away.

"No! Wait!" Atlas said, taking a step closer to him, "Listen, you don't have to go. Please, Kyle, my mom will be so upset if you go."

Kyle turned, and they were standing just inches from each other. "Is that the only reason you want me to stay? Is it because of your mom?"

"No," Atlas responded as she took a deep breath, catching a whiff of his cologne, "Kyle," she whispered, "Please, please stay."

"Tell me, Attie, do you want me to stay?" Kyle pressed her.

"Alright, yes, I want you to stay," she took a step backwards, "happy? There I asked you. What else do you want?"

"Nothing more for right now," he turned and started walking back upstairs.

"So? Are you staying?" she demanded to know.

Kyle stopped and just turned his head to say, "Yes, of course, since you asked me so nicely, Attie," he turned back and continued up the stairs.

"Stop calling me Attie. I will get us tickets for the brewery, and we should leave soon. Kyle, did you hear me?" She responded, slightly annoyed.

"Yes, Attie, I will be down in a few minutes. I need to wash up and change my shirt."

Atlas turned and entered the kitchen. She was frustrated by the situation when she noticed her mother opening the back door. Atlas grabbed the door knob and pulled the door open to find her mother, Hannah holding large paper bags filled with groceries.

"Hi, Honey, can you help me with the rest of the groceries," she said, unloading one bag into Atlas' arms," these bags seem to be getting heavier by the minute."

"Mom, what did you buy? We don't need that much food? Why did you get so much?" Atlas asked.

"Oh, Atlas, these are just a few bags. I have several more in the car," Hannah replied.

"Mom, this is crazy. Let me grab my coat, and I will help you unload the car," she said, placing the bag on the counter. Atlas then heard footsteps rushing down to the kitchen as she looked up at Kyle standing in the doorway. "Well, Kyle, I hope you like to eat. My mom just bought out the store and then some. The rest of the store is inside the car, neatly packed in her backseat."

"Great! You ladies stay here. I will be more than happy to get them for you," Kyle responded, walking outside.

"No, Kyle, wait, Atlas will help you, right Honey?" Hannah said, pushing her daughter toward the door.

"Yes, Mom, I will help him. I just need to grab my coat," Atlas replied, rolling her eyes.

"Well, don't stand there, Atlas. Kyle is already outside, and he has his hands full," Hannah said.

"Mom, it's not my fault. Captain America can't wait a second," Atlas responded, walking to the closet.

"Hurry up, Atlas. Kyle is already on his second trip," her mom pushed.

"I am coming," Atlas said, pulling her arm through the sleeve of the coat and trying to reach for the second one. She finally made it to the door to see Kyle holding the last few bags.

"Nice," he said to Atlas as he slid between her and the doorway.

"Crap! Kyle, I swear I was headed to help you," Atlas replied.

"No worries. Where do you want these last bags, Ms. Hannah?" Kyle said, holding the bags in his arms.

"Right here, Kyle. Thank you so much," she said, giving her daughter that motherly look.

"Mom, I said I was going to help. Kyle is just. Well, he is just Kyle," Atlas protested.

"Honey, why don't you help me put all this stuff away?" Hannah suggested.

"I would love to, but I can't. Dad asked me to take Kyle on a tour of the Brewery," Atlas replied, grabbing Kyle's arm and pulling him to her.

"No, Attie, that can wait. We need to help your mom. After all, she spent so much money and time at the store. The least we can do is pitch in," Kyle said, reaching inside one of the bags and starting to pull out fresh vegetables. "If we work together, we can get done a lot faster."

"Don't mind my daughter, Kyle. It is not that she is lazy. She simply does not want me to tell you stories about her. Isn't that right, Atlas?" Hannah teased with a smile.

"Why bother fighting you, Mom? You are going to tell him anyway?" Atlas said, helping to put the groceries away.

Just as they began to empty the next few bags, a small framed woman walked through the back door and into the kitchen, saying, "Hey Mom, who's black SUV is outside?"

"Oh, Arleen, come in and meet Kyle Atlas's boy. I mean, friend, no classmate, right? Did I get that right?" Hannah said hastily.

"Oh, friend?" Arleen responded, reaching out her hand for a handshake.

Kyle reached his hand, and they shook hands while he responded, "Nice to meet you. Kyle Noyes, I am a classmate of Attie's at the police academy. You must be Tim's wife right? And Tim is the firefighter?"

"Yes, Kyle, you got that right. Well, you two are done here for now. Arleen can help me with the groceries. Weren't you two headed out?' Hannah said, looking directly at Atlas.

"Out, you said. Where are you guys heading?" Arleen asked with a half-smile.

"It's not what you think, Arleen. I am just taking Kyle on a tour of the brewery. Why don't you guys join us?" Atlas said, raising her eyes toward Arleen.

"No, we have too much to do here. You kids go out and have a good time. I'm not having a great time. Arleen and I will get everything settled and in its place. Then we will start with dinner. What would you like to eat, Kyle?" Hannah responded.

"Mom, you just purchased too much food, and now you are asking what he likes to eat? Isn't that a bit much?" Atlas protested.

"Hush! Atlas, Kyle is my guest, and I will pamper him if I want to. You don't mind, do you, Kyle?" Hannah said, looking at Kyle, who was almost chuckling, "See Atlas, Kyle likes it. Now Kyle, what do you like to eat?"

"Ms. Hannah, I just got out of the Army, where I ate a lot of dirt. Anything homemade is heaven to me," he said without hesitation.

"Good, then it is settled. Anything except dirt. See, mom Kyle is easygoing. Now, let's get out of here before the two of them start telling you about my childhood," Atlas said, pushing Kyle out the door.

"Baby pictures, that is what I will have ready for you when you get back, Atlas. You will see that Kyle, my Atlas, was a beautiful girl. She was bold as an eagle but still gorgeous. Happy! Oh, Atlas was one happy baby," Hannah said, teasing Atlas as she walked closer to the back door, "I am not sure what happened to her. Now she is all business," she then let out a loud laugh. Everyone began to laugh well except Atlas, who was simply mortified.

"I look forward to seeing those pictures, Miss Hannah. We will be back soon," Kyle yelled out as Atlas kept pushing him down the driveway and into his car.

"I really like this one," Arleen said to Hannah as they stood in the kitchen, watching Kyle and Atlas drive away.

"I do as well. I hope Atlas finally understands how she should be treated. But you know, Arleen, if there is a way to push a man aside, my daughter will find it," Hannah responded as if lamenting the past.

"Mom, I really hope Atlas is happy. She seems happy. Don't worry, Kyle seems to be really nice, and" she stopped herself.

"And what, dear?" Hannah enquired

"Well," Arleen responded, turning her back to Hannah.

"And handsome, right? Kyle is very handsome and rough. A real man, unlike those pieces of rubbish, she is always bringing home, right?" Hannah responded without hesitation.

"Yes, Mom, Kyle is a catch. He might be too much for Atlas. That is a man and not just any man, the whole package and then some. You know what I mean?" Arleen said.

"Yes, Dear, I know exactly what you mean? If I was Atlas' age, I would be all over him and then some," Hannah said, laughing as the words came out of her mouth.

"Mom!" Arleen protested.

"I am still a woman. I know what I like. I know what I want, but who can give it to me?" She stopped and then continued, "I just wished my Atlas knew that as well. I really pray that Kyle can keep her on track."

"Well, so she has not heard from..." Arleen tried to ask but was quickly interrupted by Thomas, who abruptly entered the kitchen.

"And I hope we never do it again. I hope that chapter in our lives, and especially in Atlas' life, is closed," Thomas interjected.

Kyle drove for several blocks until they reached a red light, "you want to tell me what is bothering you?" he asked.

"Nothing," she said, looking out the window.

"Nothing, are you sure?" he insisted.

"No, nothing is bothering me. Why do you ask?" Atlas finally responded, looking at him.

"Because I am sitting at this intersection, and I don't really know where we are going. I see the Arch, and I am driving that way, but I have no clue how to get to the St. Louis Brewery. Do you care to tell me, or should I just keep driving?" Kyle responded by pressing the gas pedal and getting them across the intersection.

"Sorry? I guess I was just daydreaming. You will want to keep going south like you are now. I will tell you when to turn. The building is very old and rustic. You can't miss it," she said, reaching for her cell phone and focusing on it.

"Attie, if you don't want to go we can stop," Kyle suggested.

"No, it's all good. Just keep on straight for like four more miles," she said, staring at the phone.

"You are expecting a call? I can sync your phone to the car if you would like," he asked.

"No, I am good. We are almost there," she said, still glancing at the device.

"Did you get a hold of your friends? You know, after we are done here, you can just drop me off, and you can take the car to see them," he said.

"See who?" Atlas said, finally looking up.

"Your friends, your people. The ones you wanted to see besides your family. Really take the car and go see them if you like. I don't mind hanging out with your dad. He is really nice, and besides, I offered to help him change the carburetor later today," he smiled at her.

"Really, you wouldn't mind if I used the car to see my friends?" She was puzzled at his suggestion.

"Not at all. I will let you use the car under one condition: that you stop moping around. I really want you to have a good time and take full advantage of your time off. Attie, pretty soon, you will be working at an agency, and opportunities like this to get away will be few and far between. It is almost impossible for a Rookie like you like us to go home for the holidays. So this might be one of the few times you will have this opportunity," Kyle told her as they were approaching the entrance to the brewery.

"Kyle, you are so right. Thank you for offering me the car. I know I have been acting a bit funny. I will do better at being present. Let's go inside and take this tour. I am sure you will enjoy it. Saint Louis is filled with all kinds of history and legends since it is one of the oldest cities in the country," Atlas said while they were parking. Once they stopped, Kyle took the key out of the ignition, stepped out, and walked around to open the door for Atlas.

"Why thank you, sir?" she said with a smile. "Now, follow me on the tour. I will be your trusty guide. When I was in high school, I worked here, giving tours over the summer. My dad was so proud he told everyone to come and take a tour with me. It was crazy. We had an overflow of people because my mom and dad would stop and tell strangers about my touring skills."

"That sounds amazing. They seem like they were very proud," Kyle said, opening the glass door that led into the distillery.

"Proud but crazy. My family has always been a bit insane. My dad has worked here all of my life. My brothers, James and Nick, work here with him. I know in his heart he also wanted me to work here, but it just wasn't a good fit for me," she said.

"It sounds like you enjoyed the job while you had it, though," he said.

"Yep, believe it or not, I was really good at it," she said smugly.

"I really don't like it when you do that, Attie," Kyle said, walking away from her and reaching the ticket counter. "Two, please," he said to the lady at the counter.

"What are you talking about?" Atlas asked while following him.

"I don't like that you are constantly putting yourself down. I don't know why you do it? Is it for attention, or do you really believe you are not that smart?" Kyle replied.

"To be honest, I guess it's a little of both. But when you hear you are not good enough for so long, part of you just starts to believe it. Then it's a matter of time, and you know when you look in the mirror, you are not good enough, smart, or even pretty. You simply have transformed into whatever you have been told," Atlas said as she walked next to Kyle.

"Attie," he said, grabbing her by her shoulders, "I don't know who filled your head with those lies. You are one of the bravest, smartest, and prettiest women I know, and so much more. I wish I knew who told you that. I would rip their head off."

"It's alright, Kyle. I have become numb to it, I guess." she pushed him back, "But I appreciate all the nice things you just said about me."

"Attie, I mean them, and I hope you start believing me when I tell you such things," he said, holding on to her arm.

Atlas shook her head, "enough about my past. Let's talk about the history of beer and how it transformed the beautiful city of Saint Louis," she said with a smile. Atlas took Kyle by the hand and led him through the entire distillery. She showed him the tanks, the processing plant, and the laboratory. As they made their way through each section, Atlas took her time explaining how her family influenced the beer industry and all of their contributions. Reaching the last hallway that leads to the bar sampling area, Atlas turned to Kyle and said, "You know, Sir, it has been a most enjoyable experience taking you through this tour. I do hope you come back and meet me in St. Louis," she said with a huge smile showing him the bar.

"Why, Miss, I have truly enjoyed learning about your industry and the time you have taken with me," Kyle responded once again, placing his hand on the small part of her back and leading her into the room.

"Thank you. You can choose a sample of light, flavor, or dark beer," she said, waving her hand in front of the samples.

"I don't know which one you suggest. After all, you are the expert," Kyle coyly replied.

"No, not really. I am not a big beer drinker. I am sure you have more experience in that area than I do. You can choose your favorite or try something from the newer selection. Some of those flavors are not on the mark yet, and they will ask for your opinion. I caution you, though, some are very good, and some will not," she said, twisting her expression.

"Come on, Attie, live a little. Let's try something new and not comfortable. How about this one? It doesn't look too dark, so it can't be top-heavy. It is not too light, and therefore, it should not taste like water down slush." Kyle said as he raised his cup near his nose, "it doesn't smell bad or too strong. What do you say we both take a taste of?"

"Alright, but I warn you, I don't like the taste of beer," she said, taking the cup from his hand and taking a huge sip. Her face twisted as she pressed her lips, trying hard to swallow the liquid. She shook her head in disgust.

Kyle began to laugh while trying to take the cup out of her hand and said, "I guess it smells better than it tastes, ha?"

"What you are not tasting? You're kidding, right? A deal is a deal. I tried it, and now it's your turn," she told him while taking another cup from the counter and pushing it towards him.

"No, Ma'am, if I learned anything in the Army, was never to volunteer for execution. After seeing your reaction, I will not be trying that at all. But thanks for the show," Kyle said, walking out of the beer garden and heading to his car, leaving Atlas in shock for a few seconds.

She quickly followed him, saying, "Coward! I can't believe you set me up. I thought you were one of the good ones."

"I am and I am so glad you are finally realizing that, but I am not dumb so no I am not tasting anything that makes your pretty face turn that way. Now why don't we head across the street and I will buy a pretzel from Gus. Your Dad recommended the place this afternoon. I have not been able to stop thinking about them since we got here. Besides, their aroma has overtaken the entire space." he said while opening the car door for her.

"Alright but you are buying since you pulled that joke on me," she said with a smile.

"Absolutely, it is the least I could do since you have been such great hosts and good sport," he said, closing the door and getting into the SUV.

They entered the establishment, and the smell of freshly baked pretzels was intoxicating. Atlas looked at Kyle, who had the expression of a little kid walking into a candy store. "Why, Kyle Noyes, do you look like you just made it into heaven? This is just Gus Pretzels, and we are not eating caviar," she snapped at him.

"You don't understand, Attie? Places like this bring back memories. Memories of my childhood of better days and times. Smells can trigger the brain to recall a different time and place. Some are good, and some are bad, so you have to be aware of it. Memories can sneak up on you and catch you when you least expect it," Kyle explained, taking a deep whiff of aroma in, "this takes me to a good place. I can go back to many years ago, right after I enlisted. The guys and I were given leave and drove from Fort Leonard Wood to Springfield, here in Missouri. One guy in particular was from Saint Louis, Crawford, and all he could talk about was Gus Pretzels. We didn't have enough time to drive to the city for one, but we found a stand. I recall vividly how happy Keith looked tasting that pretzel and dipping it in mustard. Kyle's eyes seemed to turn to a bright green tone as he talked about his friend.

"Alright then, know you can call your buddy and tell him you had an honest-to-God Gus Pretzel made right before your eyes. You can even ask for extra mustard," she suggested, heading to the counter and placing her order. Kyle patiently waited, watching the staff enthusiastically make his pretzel. Within a matter of a few minutes, Atlas walked to him, holding a brown paper bag containing his treasure. Kyle smiled, giving her a wink. He reached into the bag, grabbed his pretzel, opened the packet of mustard, dripped it on the nice, warm dough, and took a huge bite. Atlas watched Kyle smile as he attempted to consume the entire thing in just a few bites, "Hey, slow down. They can always make us more."

"This is amazing, Attie. Do you want one?" Kyle said, returning the bag to her.

"Well, maybe just a half. They do smell delicious," she replied, taking a bite and, with a mouth full, continued, "You're going to call your buddy Crawford and tell him you are here. I am sure he would love to see you."

"No, Attie, I can't call him," he responded and took another bite.

"Why don't you have his number? Do you know where he lives or where he might be?" she suggested.

"I know where he is, and I will go see him before we go back to Wyoming," he said, closing the bag, "I better not get full. After all, your mom is cooking dinner."

"Do you want to go see your friend now? I don't mind. I can go with you, or you can drop me off at home," she said, walking out with him.

"Attie," he started to say, but she interrupted him,

"If you don't want me to come with you, you can just drop me off at home. That is fine," she responded with a strong, angry tone.

"I am not sure you want to go with me. It is not that I don't want you to come with me," he said, opening the car door for her.

"So if you know where he is, let's go. Mom is going to be cooking for several hours, which means we have plenty of time to look after your friend. What, you don't want him to tell me stories about you?" she said, smiling.

"No, Attie, he will not be able to tell you any stories about me," he said as they drove onto Highway 55 and started heading south.

"Why have you always been boring? No sense of adventure, I bet. Or he might tell me something scandalous about you," she said and then went on, "I got it. He might tell me about how you and your squad went into a house of women to get it on. It was probably your first time. Don't be embarrassed, and I will not laugh. Well, not much, if it was. We all had those sexual encounters that we wished went better. Nothing to be ashamed of," Atlas looked up, and they exited the highway.

Kyle finally stopped the car and walked around to help Atlas out, "Attie, I know you are just being yourself, so I don't take anything you said personally."

"God, Kyle, I was just kidding. If you want to see your friend by yourself, I can just stay in the car," she responded, "I am not going to ask him anything if that's what you would like," Atlas said, stepping out, but Kyle's frame was blocking her view for a few seconds.

He took a deep breath and said, "Attie, you can ask Crawford anything you like, but he will not answer you."

"Why are all your friends rude, or do they simply don't have a good sense of humor like you?" she said, trying to get around him.

"No, I don't think that I have very few friends left. Most of my friends were killed in action or took their own lives because they could not handle the trauma they had experienced during their military careers. Look around you, and this is Jefferson Barracks National Cemetery. Here is the only place I can give my respect to my fallen friend. You are welcome to come with me, or you can stay in the car," Kyle said, stepping aside to expose the multiple graves.

Atlas took a few steps forward and found herself staring at the neatly aligned rows of white headstones that created a solemn and dignified atmosphere. The vast expanse of the cemetery was punctuated by the American flags adorning the graves, evoking a sense of honor and remembrance. The meticulous care given to the grounds reflected the deep respect for those who served, making it a poignant and contemplative space. For a moment, she found herself speechless at the sight and taken back. Then she turned toward Kyle, who was silently lost in thought. Taking his hand tenderly, she looked at him and said, "Let's go pay our respects to your friend Crawford."

They walked hand in hand several yards from the car down a hill to a spot overlooking a small wooded area. Atlas was reading the names of the fallen when she heard something coming from the wood line. She tapped Kyle's hand, and they both looked up to see a beautiful doe walking through the tombstones. Kyle cleared his throat and broke the silence by saying," Now, that is a good sign. Seeing a deer in a cemetery evokes a sense of a spiritual presence. It means that the departed souls are at peace, and the deer are watching over our loved ones." He took two more steps and realized they were standing in front of Crawford's final resting place.

"Kyle are you alright?" she asked, squeezing his hand.

"Yes, I am good," he answered, looking at the tombstone and then turning his attention to Atlas, "but I am glad you did not stay in the car."

"Can I ask you what happened to Crawford? He was very young when he died," she asked almost in a whisper.

"Kevin Crawford, trained to be the best Ordinance Explosive Disposal Technician. He was a master at his craft. Patient, slow, and detailed oriented. There was nothing

Crawford could not take apart. He was good, really good, you know what I mean, but he was not arrogant either. Don't think he got careless or callous. No, he saved our unit because we were careless.

During one of our missions we were looking for two military personnel who had been kidnapped. We received Intel that the insurgents had booby-trapped some caves and abandoned wells to deter us from any rescue efforts. One of our newly appointed officers ordered several of us to run into a cave to search. We knew better, but no one spoke up. Following orders, my unit found itself blocked by a series of landmines. There was no way out unless someone disabled them.

A young soldier started to freak out. He got claustrophobic and ran outside without thinking. Crawford threw himself in front of the danger to protect us from the blast. The deafening roar of the explosion was muffled by Crawford's selfless sacrifice. I can still feel the heat of the explosion as it hung heavily in the air, pushing us backwards. We found ourselves covered in pink dust," Kyle stopped.

"Pink dust? What do you mean pink dust?" Atlas asked, letting go of his hand.

"The detonation furry pulverized Crawford and another soldier's body, and in its aftermath, the air was filled with a haunting pink dust, a stark contrast to the somber surroundings. Sprinkles of pink dust lingered, a poignant testament to the force that abruptly extinguished a life, their lives. This ethereal haze served us as a solemn reminder of the fragility of existence, as it settled gently over the remnants of that tragic event, leaving behind an eerie and melancholic atmosphere," Kyle explained as he reached into his pocket and pulled out a penny, a nickel, a dime and a quarter and laid down over the tombstone. He then turned to Atlas and said, "Alright I paid my respects we can go now."

They walked in silence towards the car, and Atlas stopped looking around, she asked, "Why did you put change on Crawford's grave?"

"Leaving coins on a fellow soldier's tombstone is a long-standing military tradition, symbolizing a gesture of both respect and camaraderie. It signifies that another soldier visited the grave and was there and honor the memory of the fallen comrade. A penny means someone has visited the grave. A nickel signifies that the visitor served with the deceased service member at boot camp. That is why I left them both." Kyle explained as he started to walk to the car.

He opened the door and helped Atlas in before he continued, "I left the dime since we served together at some point. A quarter because I was physically with Crawford when he died. Finally, the silver dollar is the most important coin. The silver dollar is also a token of our shared experience, harking back to a time when a dollar could buy a meal or a drink- a simple reminder of the enduring bond among those who served together. So you see, I left them all, and now I will take this other silver dollar and stop somewhere to have a drink in his memory."

"Kyle, I am speechless. I don't know what to say," Atlas responded as he closed her door. He walked around and sat in the driver's seat for a minute. Then they were on their way out when Atlas said, "Thank you, I mean it. Thank you not only for your service but for teaching me about these traditions and about you. Really, I am grateful."

"That's alright, Attie. I know you are. I want you to understand that police work is very similar to that of the military. You see, all these graves are just a small group of men and women who sacrifice their lives for our country. You would like people who would honor them, but they don't. Vets are often forgotten and neglected. Cops are the same way. No one is happy to see the police. A fireman, yes, people love firefighters but police are only invited to the party when things go wrong. Do you understand? You might think it is all about the glory, but there is no glory here. You get it?" Kyle said, driving towards her house as it started to snow.

Atlas tapped his hand on the steering wheel and said, "I think so. I know you worry about me, but honestly, I am good. I know very well what I signed up for, but I am also grateful that I have you to worry about me. You are very kind to me even when I don't deserve it."

"Everyone deserves to receive kindness," Kyle said as they pulled into her parent's garage and parked. Kyle stepped out and assisted Atlas into the house.

Chapter 11

Compassion

Atlas and Kyle walked into the house to find Hannah cooking while Thomas was sitting in the kitchen. Hannah turned to see something bothering Kyle's face; he was pale and somber. Hannah then glazed at Thomas, who immediately turned his attention to Kyle.

"How was the tour?" Thomas asked.

"It was alright," Atlas responded.

"Where did you go?" Hannah asked as she gave Atlas that motherly glaze.

Kyle stood still for a few seconds and then broke his silence by saying, "It's snowing outside. Here, Attie, let me hang up your coat." he then helped her take her coat off, and he walked to the other room.

"Don't ask what happened because I am not sure. We went to the Brewery and then to Jefferson Barracks Cemetery. He wanted to pay his respects to a fellow soldier," Atlas explained.

Thomas immediately stood, "How many coins did he leave?"

"All of them, Dad, penny, nickel, dime, quarter, and even a silver dollar," Atlas said. Thomas walked towards Kyle, leaving Atlas and Hannah alone in the kitchen.

Atlas started to follow him when her mother said, "No, Honey, stay here. Let your father speak to him. Give them some space. You know Atlas men grieve differently than women. They tend to hide their feelings, and all of a sudden, they sneak up on them. On the other hand," she said while placing plates on the table, "us girls, we handle our emotions differently. We are what you would say upfront. Come on, help me set the table."

"Mom, Kyle was fine until it started to snow. Then he got quiet and weird," Atlas told her as she placed the silverware on the table.

"Come on, help me with supper. Don't worry. Thomas will speak to him and work through it. I must say, Kyle seems to be very nice," Hannah asked her.

"Yes, Mom, he is a very good person," she paused to see her mother smiling, "but you know he is just my friend, that is all," Atlas responded, walking towards the sink.

"I wasn't implying anything except that he is nice, and he seems to be into you," she responded.

Atlas stood in the doorway listening to her father and Kyle while her mother's back was turned.

"You alright, son?" Thomas asked Kyle, who was standing still, holding Atlas' coat in one hand and the door knob to the closet in the other. "You seem almost frozen."

"Yes, Sir," Kyle replied, shaking his head and leaning into the closet, "I was just lost in memories. I guess you would say bad memories of a time long ago in a place that I can only describe as hell."

"I have been there. When I was in the Navy, I was aboard a ship whose boiler room had blown up. The steam emitting from the room melted a man's skin right off. I can still see my captain running in to save a crew member. It was a horrible scene, to say the least. I barely made it inside. My arm was scorched, but I helped pull him and other guys out alive," Thomas said as he waited for Kyle, "to this day, just the faintest smell of flesh burning takes me back to that day."

Kyle walked out, and the two men stood still for a moment, trapped in their thoughts and experiences. "I started to talk about Crawford, and then we went to the cemetery. I was good until it started to snow. Just the first dust took me to a dark place and time. I don't think I have told anyone what happened to Crawford until today."

"Son, you have been through a lot. Your soul is damaged. It's the price we pay for freedom. But you know you are not alone. Now that we know one another, you can reach out to talk or not talk anytime," Thomas said, placing his hand on Kyle's shoulder, "talking to someone who has been there helps. It helped me, and I am more than happy to help you."

"Thank you, Mr. Martin," Kyle responded.

"Anytime, Son, now let's get in there before Hannah gets on to us. You know she spent all day making dinner,"

Thomas told him, leading him to the kitchen, "Hannah's food is amazing. Come eat. It will do you some good."

"Yes, Sir, I will never turn down a home-cooked meal," Kyle said with a smile.

"Great, you boys are back just in time. Come, Kyle, you sit next to me, and Atlas pulls up another chair for Arleen. She should be back any second. She just went to drop off food at the fire station for Tim and the boys," Hannah explained with a smile.

"So, how do you like our little city, Kyle?" Thomas asked while everyone was waiting to start their meal.

"I like it so far from what I have seen. It has a lot of history. I learned a lot from the tour Atlas gave me. The brewery is very nice, and the processes are fascinating." Kyle said.

"Yes, we are very proud of our products. Did Atlas take you to the beer garden? Were you able to taste some of the new products?" Thomas asks as Kyle produces a huge smile and a small laugh.

"I did see the garden, but Attie tasted the beer samples," Kyle stated. "And from her reaction the new line leaves a lot to be desired."

"It was super nasty! Dad really it tastes like feet!" Atlas responded while twisting her face in disgust.

"Feet?" Arleen repeated walking into the house.

"Yes, old smelly feet!" Atlas repeated.

"How do you know what feet taste like?" Hannah asked, holding her laughter in as much as she could.

"You should have seen her face, it was priceless. I have never seen anyone change colors so fast. It must have been horrid," Kyle said in between laughing.

"Do tell more," Arleen said, sitting herself down with a plate of food.

"That is not funny, Kyle. He was a coward and did not taste it," she responded while everyone was laughing. Kyle shot Atlas a wink and a smile, but she had her head down and texted on her cell phone.

"Atlas Marie Martin!" Hannah said at the top of her lungs, "You know better than texting at the dinner table."

Atlas rolled her eyes and put her cell phone away.

"Atlas, you have a guest. You can't just run off gallivanting about town. What about Kyle?" Hannah asked before realizing Thomas was staring at her, "What?" she said, looking at Thomas, "Kyle, my apologies. We did not raise a discourteous child."

"I agree, Atlas. You should stay here and keep Kyle Company," Arleen stated.

"You would," Atlas said, looking at Arleen and then turning to Hannah. "Mom, don't start. Besides, Kyle doesn't mind. He even lent me his car so I could go out. Right, Kyle, you don't care?" Atlas responded, grabbing the bowl with mashed potatoes and serving herself a large helping.

"Great, then you can help me figure out the carburetor for Ruby. I am rebuilding it, and my hands don't seem to want to do what I need them to do. Its hell getting old," Thomas suggested.

"Thomas, that is not what I am saying," Hannah stated.

"Ms. Hannah, I would really prefer to stay here and help with Ruby rather than be a third wheel for Attie and her friends," Kyle interjected.

"See, Mom, Kyle is good with it," Atlas said, picking up her plate, "well I better get ready."

Arleen followed Atlas while she headed up the stairs, "Wait, Atlas, are you sure you know what you are doing? Why are you going out?"

"I am going to see my friends. What do you care about?" she snapped back at her.

"You can't lie to me. I know you are going to go look for that loser," Arleen responded, walking closer to Atlas.

"For your information, I have not heard from him for months. I am going to meet up with Roxanne and Judy, that's all," she said, turning her back to Arleen.

"Where are you going? To Fast Eddies, I bet. You and I both know he hangs out there all the time," Arleen said, holding Atlas's arms and trying to pull her back, "don't go. Stay, please stay. You have a nice, handsome, caring guy downstairs. Why are you so desperate to mess things up?"

"Who? Kyle? You're kidding me, right? You sound just like mom. I am not with Kyle," she said, shaking Arleen's hands off her shoulders.

"Well, I will tell you this. If I had a man like Kyle sitting at my kitchen table, I would not take chances with some immature, drunken loser like Eric. You can do so much better," Arleen said, "you do what you want, but I promise you will regret it." Arleen watched as Atlas ran up the stairs. She returned to the kitchen to find Kyle deep in conversation with Thomas.

"I need you to unbolt the manifold from the intake," Thomas was explaining.

"Don't worry, Mr. Martin, I know how to do that. I've worked on several cars before. Trust me, I am pretty handy with tools," Kyle said

"I hope you are good at dodging," Hannah replied as she began to clear the table.

"Dodging?" Kyle responded with a puzzled look on his face.

"Yes, Sir, Dodging flying tools. My Thomas likes to throw them across the room when he gets frustrated," Hannah explained.

"Oh, I see where Attie gets her temper. I believe she has thrown a flashlight or two at me," Kyle replied while gathering the silverware.

"Leave that Kyle. I will get it. Go with Thomas. I am sure you boys have things to put together. Arleen will help me here," she said, giving Thomas a quick kiss on his cheek, "treat him right."

"Come on, son, that is our cue to exit to the garage," Thomas said, walking out of the house.

As they walked to the garage, Kyle turned to see Atlas running out of the house through the front door and jumping into his SUV.

"There is still time to stop her, you know," Thomas suggested.

"No, she needs to go. It seemed very important to her," Kyle said, "I just hope she is careful."

"Me too, son, me too," Thomas said, walking away from Kyle and into the garage.

Kyle watched as Atlas drove off down the snow street and disappeared in the distance. He took a deep breath and followed Thomas into the garage to begin working on the carburetor. He began by unbolting the manifold when Thomas cautioned him,

"You can use this screwdriver to undo the bolts just to make sure the jets don't fall into the motor. The jets need to be removed before you do anything else," Thomas instructed.

Kyle smiled, imagining his father telling him what to do. However, he never had that experience. Everything Kyle had learned about mechanics came from his time in the Army and not from a father-son bonding experience.

"You know, son, Atlas is a good girl. She simply gives her heart away too fast. Patience is the key to all good things. Take her mother, for instance. It took me over two years to reach her heart. Hannah was wild and carefree. She loved "love," you know what I mean. The idea of love is what I mean. She would invest herself in someone or something and give it all there was to give.

Much like my Atlas. She is so hot-tempered and impulsive. I had Atlas a good job with me. Not to brag, but working at Anheuser Busch is a big deal here. I literally inherited my job slot when my grandfather retired. The tour guide was a starting job for Atlas, but in a few years, I am sure she would have been in charge of the tours. But not my Atlas. She wanted something else. At first, she talked about joining the city's Fire Department, but Tim told her all the requirements, and she changed her mind.

Suddenly, Hannah tells me that Atlas has given up her apartment and is driving to Wyoming for a job. Don't get me wrong, I know my daughter is strong and capable, but never in a million years would I have thought she would move so far away from her family. You know I am the one who chose the name Atlas, strong and stoic. I want my daughter to be independent and self-sufficient, but I also don't want her to struggle. This is all to say to you, her mother, and I am very grateful you are part of her life."

"Mr. Martin, I appreciate your kind words. I have known your daughter for just a few months, and I can honestly tell

you she is all that you have described: stubborn, hard-
headed, and strong, but she is also kind and a hard worker.
And if I might add, I am also very grateful that she is in my
life," Kyle said while crawling underneath the car.

Chapter 12

Suspicion

It was just about 3 AM. Kyle could not fall asleep even though he was lying in bed. His mind was racing. He was not waiting for Atlas, but in reality, he was. Kyle was worried it was late even for her. Getting up and looking out of the window all I saw was snow coming down nonstop. He thought about laying back down but he realized it would be of no use. Kyle decided to walk down stairs and maybe get a drink of water in the kitchen. As he reached for a glass, Kyle heard the car pulling up and parking.

The back door opened slowly, "hey, I didn't think anyone was awake," Atlas said, trying to turn away from Kyle.

"I couldn't sleep," he said, taking a step closer to see her eyes red from crying.

"I didn't realize it was this late," she said, turning away from him, pulling her hair forward, trying to shield her face.

"You've been crying?" he asked.

"No, it was just smoky at the club, that's all. What did you do while I was gone? Something good, I hope," she asked.

Kyle took a step forward. The room was dark, but the street light illuminated the kitchen just enough. He took a step forward, standing in front of Atlas. He moved her hair away, exposing her eyes," please don't lie to me. You don't have to tell me why, but I know you have been crying. All I want to know is, are you ok?" he whispered.

Atlas looked at his eyes and could see the reflection of snowflakes coming down, "Yes, I am fine. I was being silly and sentimental, that is all."

Kyle's hand slipped down her arm, "you want to talk about it?"

"No, not really," she replied, crossing her arms and causing Kyle to pull his hand back, "I am just stupid sometimes. No, that is not true most of the time. I should've stayed home with the family and you. Instead I go out chasing the past and well," she paused, "I got my feelings hurt. Now, I am standing here like a dummy once again, pouring my heart out to you. You must think I am a child."

"Attie, you are not a child. I think you are just tender-hearted, and that is ok. I don't know who or how you got your feelings hurt, but I can assure you watching you like this does not change the way I see you," he said, wrapping his arms around her and pulling her towards him. Atlas' head was tucked nicely into his chest, and she felt his warmth while listening to his heart beat. "Give yourself a break. You are making lots of changes. People, I mean your friends, if they are your friends, they will support you even if they don't agree. True friends will be there for you. It's alright if you feel hurt when you find out that they are not in it for the long haul."

"Oh, Kyle, I was just expecting something different," she said, burying her face into his body.

"Attie, you will learn there are people who are with you for a moment, for a season, and for life. It is tricky to know which is which," he said, holding her tight.

"Kyle, I just regretted going out. You don't understand, I looked desperate. I was never that girl," she said, pushing herself away from him and walking towards the window.

Kyle was confused, but he did not want to push her for information. He walked towards her and stood behind her. Atlas could feel once again the warmth of his body pressing against hers. She felt safe and steady, so she went on," I ran around town catching up with my friends. Ha, my friends, these people don't get me. They don't want to hear what I am doing or how I am improving myself. All they talked about was how I ran away. You know," she turned fast and found herself once again in Kyle's warm embrace, "you are right. They are not my friends. Not anymore. Right now, you are my friend. I guess my only friend."

Kyle held her for a few minutes in silence. He could feel her body relaxing, and she began letting go of his embrace, "why don't you go to bed and get some rest? We can talk about this more in the morning."

Atlas agreed and started walking away from him. She turned and said, "I really want to go back to the ranch. Do you think we can leave on Friday? I just need to get back, and I don't want to be here anymore."

"Sure, Attie, we can leave anytime you want," he replied, staring out the window.

"Thank you, Kyle," she said, running to him and hugging him from behind, "thank you, that makes me happy."

"That's alright," he said, placing his hands over hers.

She pulled away, "I know you have been spending lots of time with Dad. If you like, I can show you more of the city in the morning. Maybe my mom and even my dad will join us. We could go out to lunch. What do you think?"

"Yes, of course. That sounds very nice," Kyle replied.

"Good, then it's settled. I'll see you in the morning. Night!" she said, running up the stairs.

Kyle made his way back to his room. Now more than ever, his mind was wondering. What was happening? Why did he feel such a connection with Atlas? How was this ever going to work out? No! He said to himself he could not be falling in love with Atlas. She was careless and childish. He had to stop thinking about her. Besides, he told himself there was a lot more to those tears than friends and hurt feelings. What was going on? What was happening that Atlas did not tell him about? Why was she in such a rush to go out and then suddenly pack up and go back to the ranch?

Kyle went over each detail in his mind; however, his heart had other plans. Falling asleep in his mind, he was still entangled with more questions. He found himself in the kitchen once more with his arms wrapped around Atlas. She was uncontrollably crying, and he was comforting her. Her face was buried in his chest, and he needed her to know he was there for her. Kyle pushed her face back lightly and raised it towards his. "You are mine, and I will never let anyone hurt you again." bending his head a bit, their lips crushed. It was a passionate kiss seemingly endless.

Their lips were connected as his right hand tenderly caressed her hair, and his left lay on the small of the back, braced her. He needed Atlas to know how he felt through that kiss. Their energy was enchanting and explosive. He could feel her giving herself up to him without protest. Could it be that Atlas wanted him as much as he wanted her? He could feel her hands circling his back and then his chest. She began to unbutton his shirt. Her lips instinctively moved from his lips to his exposed skin. Atlas began kissing his chest while pulling her hair back, exposing her neck, which he began to kiss. Her hands began to linger and wander down. She reached for his belt and started to buckle it. But before she managed to lift her in his arms, he had all intentions of making her his. Taking the first steps up the stairs, he looked down at Atlas, and he heard her saying, "Kyle, Kyle,"

Kyle lifted her closer to his body, and again she called out his name. This time it was different, it was distant, he looked down and he no longer was holding Atlas in his arms. Instead she was standing at the doorway calling his name, "Kyle! Kyle wake up." He shook his head and opened his eyes. It was a dream, just a dream. He managed to focus just in time to find Atlas jumping on top of him on the bed.

"What is it?" he asked.

"Here you left your cell phone downstairs and it's blowing up. Mom thought it might be important. She told me to run it up to you." Atlas said, handing him the cellphone.

"Alright. What time is it?" he said, trying to sit up, but Atlas was over him.

"It's about 7 or so. Mom made breakfast. Are you hungry?" she asked, trying to peek at his cell phone.

"Attie, can you please get off of me? I would not want your parents to get the wrong idea," Kyle said, pushing her body up.

"No way! My parents trust you. Besides, you are just my friend. Why would they think we are doing anything up here?" she snapped but did not move off.

He threw her off, causing her to slide into the side of the bed and almost fall. Kyle reached for her, bringing her back on top of him.

"Come on, Attie, get up. You play too much," Kyle protested.

"Nope, not until you tell me who is calling you?" she demanded to know.

Kyle gave her a stern look, and with a quick swipe, he flipped her over. Now, he found himself on top of her. He was not wearing a shirt, and Atlas could see that he had several scars on his body. Instinctively, she reached and placed her hand over one of them, "what's this from?"

"A gift from the insertions. It is shrapnel that taught me the true meaning of cover and concealment," Kyle responded as he gazed into Atlas' eyes.

"I guess you better learn to duck, ha?" she said without thinking.

"Yeah, I guess. I better take this call. You need to go downstairs before your mom starts wondering about us," he said, stepping up from the bed. She could see that he had several more scars on his back.

Once again, she reached for them and traced her hands over his back, stopping near his waist. "Kyle, honestly, what happened to you?" she asked.

"War. War is what happened to me. I was young when I joined and damaged when I got out. Do you think all this is free? Civilians never understand the cost of freedom. They take it for granted, but us vets we know. Our bodies bear the scars of your nonchalant lifestyle. Hundreds of us are branded like me. War is ugly, and no one wants to talk about it," he said, standing and walking towards the door as if telling her to get out.

"Wait a minute, soldier. How dare you? What gives you the right to assume I know nothing about your pain and suffering? For your information, I never asked you to go and fight for me or for anyone," she said furiously, trying to stand up. When she finally made it to her feet, she said, "Thank you for your service, but as I recall, you were not drafted. You chose to go abroad and fight a war clear across the world."

"You are right, Attie. I chose to serve my country, and if I needed to do that on the moon, I would have. But you would not understand. Do you want to know why? Because you are naive to all that. You have been shielded from combat. You think that because you donate a few bucks a year, you do your part, or you offer to buy us lunch once in a while, that makes up for it. I will tell you, no, and it does not.

All that does is make you feel better." he said, holding the door open.

Atlas walked to the door and stopped, "you know something, Kyle, there are times you can be a real Ass."

"I know, Attie, but you seem to bring it out of me naturally. Tell your mom I will come down in a few minutes, Attie," he said, closing the door behind her.

Atlas turned and yelled at the top of her lungs, "Don't call me Attie!" she came running down to the kitchen to find both her mom and Arleen standing there.

"What's the matter, Honey?" Hannah asked.

"Kyle is such an Ass. I went upstairs to give him the cellphone, and there he stood naked in his smugness, telling me how I don't understand the sacrifice of servicemen."

"Kyle was naked?" Arleen asked with a huge smile, "he sleeps naked?"

"Arleen," Hannah said with a smile.

"Oh, is there anything else that needs to be taken to him? I would love to see that specimen in all its natural beauty," Arleen said, waving her hand over herself as if to cool herself off.

"Arleen!" Hannah repeated.

"Come on, mom, you know we might be married, but we are not dead. Kyle is one gorgeous man. That chest and those broad shoulders are just calling me. And those eyes would be crazy not to get lost in those eyes. Am I right, or am I right?" Arleen said.

"Arleen, you are crazy. Kyle is not all that. Besides, he is not my type," Atlas interjected.

"If I was not married, he would surely be my type," Arleen said with a smile.

"Mine too," Hannah said, laughing, "I might be old, but I am not dead. That upstairs is all man."

"Mom!" Atlas said, "You two, stop that. Kyle will be down any minute."

"You are right, Honey. I don't want him to feel uncomfortable. And you better apologize to him. You don't know what he has been through. He is not only our guest but a hero. I will not have you disrespecting him. If your father hears about this, he will have your head on a platter, young lady," Hannah scolded Atlas.

"I wonder what he would say if he heard you two melting over Kyle," Atlas replied.

"He would say we have good taste. He is a catch." Hannah responded.

"And then some," Arleen agreed.

"Am I interrupting?" Kyle said, peeking his head into the kitchen.

"No, no, come on, Kyle. We were just preparing breakfast for the fire station. Arleen is going to head over there and deliver it," Hannah explained.

"Do you need help?" he asked.

"You can come with me anywhere, "Arleen responded.

"I will go. If it's alright with you," Atlas said, looking at Kyle.

"That would be nice," Kyle answered while pouring himself a cup of coffee.

"Well, did you get to make that phone call?" Atlas asked.

"Yes, thank you, I did," he said, swallowing his coffee and then looking at Arleen, "I am ready to go."

"Great! I have several pans of food, and I would really appreciate it if you could help me carry them to the car," Arleen said with a coy smile.

"Kyle, I will grab your coat," Atlas said, "you probably forgot its cold outside."

"No, Attie, I did not forget. I am just warm-hearted, and my body always runs hot," he responded.

"No way!" Atlas replied.

Kyle then took her hand and placed it on his chest, which was exposed. Atlas could feel the warmth emitting from his body. He then quickly pulled her hand away, saying, "See, I told you so."

"I want to feel too," Arleen said with a huge smile, "what I was just curious about."

"No!" Atlas protested, "The food is getting cold. We better get going. Mom! Right, the breakfast will be cold before we get there."

Kyle grabbed two large foil pans and walked outside. Atlas took the opportunity to chastise Arleen, "What are you thinking? You cannot go around touching Kyle. You are married. Married to my brother. What the hell, Arleen?"

"Look, if a handsome man wants me to measure his body temperature, I will, Atlas. I will not apologize for being curious. You, on the other hand, you better wake up. That man is into you," Arleen responded.

"First of all, that is just Kyle. Second of all, you know I am not looking for a relationship. I am getting over Eric," Atlas explained.

"Eric Noles, that no good piece of sh, "Arleen started to say but stopped before Kyle made it back inside.

"Kyle, there are two more pans. Do you mind?" Hannah said.

"Of course not, Ms. Hannah. The food smells fantastic. Those guys are surely lucky," he said, smiling.

"Well, don't worry. When you get back here, I will have something special for you," Hannah responded.

Kyle walked out, and Hannah looked at Arleen and Atlas, "Listen, you two, you better get along. I don't want to be embarrassed by either one of you. So, no more bickering, you hear. Kyle is a fine man, and thank the Lord, Eric is out of the picture. There, I said it. I never really cared for him, but my opinion does not matter. That was your day yesterday; let's just focus on today. Now, don't you two let my food get cold."

"You are right, Mom, I am sorry. I am sorry to Atlas. I was just kidding with Kyle," Arleen said. "Why don't you follow me out to the station? I am going to hang out there for a bit. I don't want you and Kyle to be stuck."

"Alright, I will just start the car and go tell Kyle the plans," Atlas said, running out to meet Kyle while carrying his coat.

Arleen started to walk out but stopped, "God, Mom, I hope this one works out for her. Kyle seems so good for her, don't you think," Arleen said.

"Oh, honey, from your lip to God's ears. I hope she never gets back with Eric. He really broke her. She finally looks like her old self, "Hannah said, watching out the window as Atlas helped Kyle with his coat. He then walked her to the car and opened her door. "He is good to her, and she needs that. I have prayed so many nights for my Atlas to be alright. Now look at her. She is strong, healthy, and happy. She is no longer holding herself together with tape and glue."

"Yes, Mom, but you know last night she went out looking for Eric," Arleen revealed.

"Well, let's hope she did not find him. I don't want her to go through that again," Hannah said with a worried tone.

"Don't worry, Mom. I already suggested that she just hang out with Kyle. They will only be here a few more days. I doubt she will run into Eric if she didn't find him last night. He is probably messing with some other girl's head," Arleen said, placing her hand over Hannah's shoulder.

"I hope you are right. I don't want Thomas to know Atlas went looking for Eric. He will be so disappointed and upset with her. You know how he feels about Eric. Oh Lord, if Thomas finds out, he will hit the roof, and his blood pressure will skyrocket. No, no, do not say a word to Thomas. We better just wait and see. Now go before Atlas comes in here looking for you, "Hannah said, walking Arleen to the door

Chapter 13

Sparks

Kyle was quiet on the way to the fire station. Atlas again found herself mesmerized by her cell phone. They reached their destination, and he parked when the phone rang. Taking a glance and putting it down without answering it.

"Looks like someone wants to get a hold of you, ha," Atlas said, breaking their silence.

"Let's make a deal, Attie. Let's leave the phones in the car and just enjoy the day off the grid. What do you think?" Kyle suggested

"Alright, I am game if you are," she replied. Kyle then placed his phone inside the center console. He got out of the car and started walking around to open the door for Atlas. She had waited for him since this had become their thing. She started to place her phone with Kyle's but changed her mind, putting it in her pocket instead. Kyle opened the door for Attie and then made his way to help Arleen. She followed Kyle to ensure Arleen did not say something smart to him. Arleen was handing out the heavy pans when Atlas's cell phone fell out of her back pocket and to the ground.

"Geez, I hope you have a good case," Arleen said, picking up the phone and handing it back to Atlas.

"Oh yes, but no, I brought it to see if you could charge it for me," Atlas mumbled.

Kyle didn't say anything; he just grabbed the pans and stood there silently as if waiting for instructions. "Don't give me that look. I know our deal: no cell phones. I just want mine charged for later," Atlas said, handing Arleen her phone and rolling her eyes at Kyle.

"You better wait to charge it since it got wet, just in case. Leave it in the car for now," Arleen suggested. Atlas laid the phone on the seat and joined them. The group walked inside to find a slew of people, kids, and single women having a field day at the station bay. As they made their way through, it was obvious to Atlas that Kyle looked like fresh meat in that environment.

"There you guys are. We were wondering where Mom's food was," a male voice yelled at them.

"Kyle, this is my brother Tim, the superhero of the Martin family," Atlas introduced them.

"Tim, Kyle, it is nice to meet you," he said, shaking his hand. "Wow, I see Mom put you to work as well. Come on, follow me upstairs. The community tours are down here. The ladies brought us food, but the guys prefer moms, you know what I mean."

Walking through the crowd, Atlas could hear the women whispering about Kyle. He was making them go nuts. "Horney old women," she thought to herself.

Finally, upstairs, Atlas asked, "Why are there so many women downstairs? I mean, I didn't see any men. Are all those women single?"

"Fire Bunnies!" Tim replied, "You know Atlas women who fantasize about men in uniforms. Hot men like me," Tim responded, trying hard not to break out into laughter.

"Don't look so shocked, Atlas. You might be one too. There are some hot guys here, and you put them in a uniform and look out. Why do you think I always come to these things? I need to keep an eye on mine, and you should keep yours at arm's length," Arleen smugly interjected.

"Arleen, I swear!" Atlas responded by shooting her a killer look.

"Come on, little sister, why don't you give me a hug? You know Arleen is just kidding," Tim said, sliding between the two women.

"Let's set the food up before the guys come in here." Arleen then turned to Kyle, continuing, "Would you be a dear and get the rest of the food."

"Absolutely," Kyle said without hesitation.

"I will go with you," Atlas said, not wanting Kyle to get trampled by the mob of women. They made it to the car, and Atlas was tempted to grab her cell phone when she heard a strange woman's voice talking to Kyle. Atlas pulled the pan from the back seat, which caused her cell phone to fall to the floorboard. She looked up to see this strange woman walking next to him. Atlas hustled after Kyle, and she caught up to them, placing herself between the couple, "it's a mad house, right?" she managed to ask. The woman walked ahead and then turned to give Atlas a dirty look.

"I think it's a nice idea for the community to come out and see what the guys do. You know, once we join our departments, this will be part of the job," Kyle said, following Atlas inside.

"Really? Why?" Atlas asked, trying to keep Kyle distracted from all the female visitors.

"To stay engaged. It's important for the community to know us, and it helps us when we learn who they are and vice-versa. That is how we build trust," Kyle explained.

"You would think these women would have something else to do but stand at a fire station crunching on the men here. What did Tim call them Bunnies? You think there are cop bunnies, too?" Atlas asked.

"I don't know, I am sure there are," Kyle responded, then continued, "You know military service men see them all the time."

"Really, how do you handle it?" Atlas asked, trying not to seem jealous.

"I ignore them, I don't see them, and move on," Kyle said immediately, "they are like a breeze that just runs through you. I'd rather not waste my time with those types of women."

"But some of them are gorgeous. Didn't you see them? I mean, they are very attractive," Atlas responded, looking around at the women who were wearing makeup and nice clothes and were overall well put together.

"Really, I didn't notice. Which one?" he laughed, "Come on, let's go check it out and take a look." Kyle stopped when he noticed Atlas pressing her lips tight, "Just kidding, Attie, I don't have time to waste. Life is too short, and you only get one chance to make today a good day. Are you coming?"

"Yep, let's see if we can go upstairs and help serve the food, "Atlas responded.

"No way! I want to see if I can parallel park the fire truck," Kyle said, laughing.

"Well, there is only one way to find out. Let's go get the keys from Tim," Atlas responded as they went inside and placed the pans on the table. Then, off they went to run through the firehouse like a couple of kids. Kyle helped the children climb into the fire truck, run with the hose, and sound off the siren. Atlas watched in amazement how easily he adapted to this role. He sure was good with kids. She could not help but stare at him. However, she found herself so confused as to why watching all the women go bunkers over him infuriated her. What was happening? She thought it was just Kyle, but those women were like Cougars sizing up their prey? Enough, she told herself when she watched some woman coming on to him.

"Let's go, Kyle," she said, interrupting the advances of a woman who had placed her hand over Kyle's biceps and proceeded to squeeze them.

Kyle strangely looked at her, "What gives? Aren't you having a good time?"

"We need to go upstairs and grab our stuff. It's late. We lost track of the time," Atlas explained, looking at her watch.

"Oh yes, sorry, excuse me, I have been summoned." Kyle excused himself and then followed Atlas up the circle staircase. They had just reached the top level when a fire alarm went off. The fire crew, almost in one move, collectively moved. They geared up, and out the door, they drove away. Atlas looked down and noticed everyone had gone. They were the only two left in the entire station.

"That is some response. They waste no time at all," Kyle said, looking at the bottom floor. "Man, they even cleared out the visitors."

"Yes, they are amazing," Atlas responded, "they always blow me away when they run out of here."

"You want to see what we need to grab and take back to your parent's house? "Kyle asked, walking toward the counter.

"Not really, to be honest. It was just an excuse to get away from the crowd," Atlas admitted, finding herself a bit embarrassed.

"I get it. I am still getting used to people and crowds," Kyle said kindly, walking back to Atlas, "you want to get out of here? I recall something about some sites?"

"Yeah, let's go before they get back," Atlas replied and began walking down the stairs, "wait, we are blocked. Who the hell moved the truck in front of the staircase? We are trapped here until they get back."

Kyle looked around and suggested, "Or we could slide down the fireman's pole," Kyle said with a wicked smile

"No way! I hate heights," Atlas replied.

"OK, I will slide down and see if I can move the rig. Maybe they left the keys," Kyle suggested.

"You and your bright ideas. If I had my cell phone, we could have called for help," Atlas responded, tapping her toe on the floor and crossing her arms.

"Woo! Even if I had my cell, I would have been too embarrassed to call anyone. How would that sound like? Here I am, trapped on the second floor of the fire station. Help! No way! Not this soldier," he replied, reaching for the pole and straddling himself to it.

"I could call Tim, "she suggested, walking closer to the pole and looking down.

"Yes, Tim, stop whatever emergency you are going to and come back. That sounds rich. We are future cops. We don't call for help. We are the help," Kyle responded, reaching his arm out for Atlas to join him.

"Crap! I hate it when you are right," she responded, reaching for his hand.

"Don't worry, I got you. Just grab a hold of me, and we will slide down together," Kyle said, but Atlas hesitated and let go. Kyle then slides down by himself, landing on the floor and looking up.

"Now, what do I do, Kyle?" Atlas asked, looking down.

"Don't hesitate with me next time. You need to learn to trust me and more yourself. Come on now, we can stay here and look like a bunch of idiots when the crew get back, or you can muster the strength to conquer your fear. Either way I am here for the long haul," Kyle said, smiling at her. Atlas shook her head, and in no quick move, she reached for the pole, closed her eyes, and slid down into Kyle's arms.

"Holy shit Kyle I did it!" she said, smiling at him.

"Of course you did. You are invincible; always remember that" Kyle said while still holding on to her.

"Now I just wish the truck wasn't in the way. I kinda want to do it again," she said, stepping back and a few inches away from Kyle's grasp.

"Rethinking your career?" he said, looking up through the hole to the second floor.

"No, I am good. Come on, let's get out of here before we have to explain how we got ourselves in this mess," Atlas said walking out of the station.

Arleen arrived back at Hannah's house carrying a handful of pans. She opened the door and was happy to see Hannah waiting for her.

"How did the boys like my cooking?" she asked.

"Outstanding as usual," she said, trying to place the pans back into the cupboard.

"Where are Atlas and Kyle? Are they on their way?" Hannah asked, trying to figure out what Arleen was up to.

"No, I think they are busy," Arleen responded with a snarky tone.

"What do you mean busy? Did you leave them to clean? Honestly, Arleen." Hannah began to school her.

"No, not clean, but they were left upstairs," Arleen responded with a Devilish smile.

"What did you do, Arleen?" Hannah questioned.

"I might have mistakenly blocked their path out with the rig. I mean, if someone moved the truck in front of the staircase by accident, they might have to wait together for a bit," Arleen said.

"Kyle is a smart man. All he needed to do was slide down the pole and move it," Hannah said, "even I can figure that one out."

"Not if the keys are not left inside of the engine," she said, holding the keys and swinging them in her hand.

"Arleen, you didn't?" Hannah looks at her.

"Well, you know how careless Atlas is. I like Kyle, and he is good for her. I figured what bad could come out of it. So they spend more time together and maybe get to know one another better. After all, they are all alone." Arleen explained.

"Arleen, I don't think we should meddle. It is Atlas life. But to be honest, I like Kyle, and I like Kyle for her," Hannah responded.

"See, you are on team Kyle too. Great, what is the harm of giving them a bit of a push? Atlas needs it. She has to get over Eric, that useless idiot" Arleen said, holding the pans up.

"Why are you in such a hurry to put the pans away? What else did you do Arleen?" she answered.

"I might have accidentally found Atlas' cell phone and it got misplaced between the pans. I am not sure how that happened," Arleen responded with a half-smile.

"Arleen, that is a bit too much," she said.

"I don't, Eric has been texting her. I know it is him. The screen is foggy because she dropped it in the snow. I couldn't tell but I know it is him or one of his friends trying to find her," Arleen said looking into the pan.

"Well, I would not mind if you took those pans to the basement. After all, we don't need them until Thursday. I think they were talking about heading out on Friday. Atlas might want to get another suitcase from downstairs. So I guess it would not do any harm," Hannah replied as she smiled at Arleen.

"Awesome, now we both are on team Kyle. I can't wait to hear how they got themselves out of the fire station. One day it will be such a romantic story to recount," Arleen said.

"Well missy I hope this does not come back to bite us in the ass. And for all that is holy don't tell Thomas," Hannah told her while opening the door leading to the basement.

"Kyle you ready to head back soon it's starting to get dark," Atlas suggested.

Kyle agreed and soon enough they found themselves sitting in front of the house. "You know Kyle, this has been a really nice day. I had a great time with you. I really didn't know how funny you are," Atlas said, taking her seatbelt off.

"Thank you, I think. I had a great time as well. I really enjoyed going to the Art Museum and the St. Louis Zoo. It was crazy cold but it's so nice to see the winter animals having a blast. I still cannot believe the polar bear and penguin enclosure. I swear that penguin with the orange top had the hots for you. He followed you all over. I better look to see he didn't stowed away in here and is just waiting to take me out, "the words just slipped out of Kyle's mouth with ease.

Atlas was laughing and taking it all in when she heard Kyle's phone going off. Her face got stirred as she asked, "Kyle who is calling you so much? I swear your phone is ringing off the hook."

"Attie, can we please just stay in the moment? We are having such a good time. I just want to enjoy this for a bit more. Can we? I don't want to answer the phone and before you ask no I don't want to talk about it," Kyle said without missing a beat.

"But Kyle why?" she insisted.

"No, I don't need to give any explanations. I believe we had a deal and I still have several hours left today. Just leave it alone. Please just for now stop asking," Kyle said, getting out of the car and opening her door.

Atlas felt bad for pushing him, but her curiosity was killing her. What was he hiding? Why didn't he want to talk about it? Why was he getting so worked up about it? These questions and more kept running through her head as she watched him tenderly reach for her hand.

"Don't forget to look in the backseat for my stalker Mr. P. He might be there after all," she said and they both busted out laughing as they made their way into the house.

Chapter 14

Chances

"Hey you two, where have you been?" Hannah asked.

"We went to Forest Park and Kyle got to enjoy our free museum and zoo," Atlas responded with some pride.

"I still cannot wrap my head around Ms. Hannah. I have been all over the world and I have never seen a place that provides an experience like that for free. How can the city manage it?" Kyle asked.

"Oh son, St. Louis is the only place in the country that believes in exposing everyone to the arts, music, science, and even the zoo for everyone to enjoy. They believe price should not be a deterrence. My job contributes like many other companies in the city. Some of the expenses come from tax dollars but mostly they get their money from donations," Thomas said while walking into the kitchen.

"I am so happy you are enjoying our little city Kyle. We are sure glad you decided to join us for the holiday. Maybe next break you kids get you can come back. I would love to take you to Scott Joplin's house and Muny and the Old Cathedral downtown," Hannah said but was interrupted by Atlas,

"And the mighty Mississippi, Eagles Nest, Busch Stadium and," Atlas rattled off.

"I'm sorry Honey, I just get so excited with new blood," Hannah said pulling out a chair for Kyle to sit on, "what about a nice hot coffee?" Kyle sat and Hannah placed her hands on his shoulders tapping them twice, "and maybe a slice of homemade cake?"

Kyle placed his hand over Hannah's turned and smiled, "A lady after my own heart. I would never turn you down for cake." He then turned to Thomas smiling, "Your wife is an amazing lady."

"Don't I know it. Can I have another slice of that cake Dear and a cup of coffee?" Thomas said, joining Kyle at the table.

"Sure," Kyle tried to stand but Hannah pushed him back, "No Kyle you enjoy I will get it for you."

"Mom, did Arleen drop something off for me this afternoon?" Atlas asked in a nonchalant way.

"No, I don't think so. Why don't you check your bedroom, maybe she left it there," Hannah responded, turning quickly away from Thomas.

Atlas ran off upstairs while Thomas gave her a strange look and said, "What is she looking for?"

"Oh you know Atlas she would lose her head if it was not attached," Hannah yelled up the staircase and turned to Thomas, "you two planning on working on Ruby a bit before supper?"

"Yep Kyle, if that is not a hint I would not know one. Come on, let's escape the kitchen soon enough. My daughter will be here and Hannah and the girls will start preparing for tomorrow's festivities," Thomas said, getting ready to walk out.

"Wait, don't forget..." Hannah said.

"No I didn't forget," he said walking to her and giving her a peck on the lips, "we are on standby in case you need something from the store." Then they quickly walked out while Atlas came running down to the kitchen.

"Mom, I am going to kill Arleen. My cell phone is not in my room. Seriously, do you know where it is?" Atlas belted out.

"I am not responsible for your things. Besides you don't have time to be on the phone, we have a lot to prepare for Thanksgiving. Come on, you know you do not eat for free in this house. Everyone does their part," Hannah told her handing her a cutting board and knife.

"Mom, I am your guest. I should not be chopping onions," she replied.

"You are not a guest young lady, you are our daughter and today the cook's assistant," she said, handing her a 10-pound bag of potatoes and 5 pounds of onions.

"Mom, this is ridiculous. What about Kyle? Why isn't Kyle on kitchen duty?" she protested running her hands over the bags.

"Kyle is your guest and he has a job," Hannah said with a smile, "he is keeping your father out of my hair. Now come on, don't be lazy when you chop and lift up the knife like I taught you."

"This is going to take hours," Atlas said, opening the bag of potatoes.

"It would take longer if you were texting. Now remember to wash them first, pat them dry, and put them to boil," Hannah instructed, pointing to the potatoes.

A few minutes into the task, Atlas looked at the clock and said, "Mom, when are Arleen and Annie getting here?" turning her nose at the potatoes as she began the tasking job of washing each one.

"They will get here when they get here. Besides, I told them you were home, so do not hurry. Now you and I can spend this time together. Mother-daughter time, right?" Hannah suggested.

"More like Chef and Servant," she said, then looked at her mom, "I meant to say yes, it's a wonderful idea for me to do all the prepping."

"Hey, it's not that bad, and you escaped last year. As I recall, you just came to eat," Hannah said while striking her with a towel on the butt.

"Yes, but I had plans. Remember, I had to go to Eric's house for their meal," she replied while trying to lift the heavy pot of water.

Hannah rolled her eyes moving Atlas away from the sink and emptying the pot, "You are cooking lazy today. I guess we go back to basics. Empty the pot on the stove with potatoes, salt, and spices, and then pour the water. It might take a few trips to the faucet, but you don't kill yourself."

"Yes, ma'am but that will take forever," she said as she watched the backdoor open and Kyle came into the house. "Are you here to help? Mom Kyle loves to cook, and he makes an excellent apple pie. Right Kyle, you don't mind helping," pointing to the onions, "those need to be peeled and chopped."

Kyle looked at Hannah, who was shaking her head. He then began saying, "Nope, nope. You will not get me in the middle of this. Your Dad already warned me even though I know that look," he walked toward Atlas, reached for her hand, and gave her the knife. "I am sure your mom told you not to be lazy and lift the blade when you cut. Watch out for those juices that can make you cry. I would suggest biting a towel or piece of bread. Either way, I am out. Ms. Hannah, Mr. Martin wanted me to ask you if you needed anything from the store. We are heading to get more motor oil."

"No, dear, I will call him if I am missing anything. Thank you for checking, though," she said, walking up to him and buttoning his coat, "Bundle up. The weather here is funny. I would not want you to catch a cold."

"Let me just run upstairs and grab my coat," Atlas said, springing up and throwing the towel to the counter.

"Atlas, you were not invited. Let the boys, I mean men. Go do their thing. You already have a job. Get to chopping those onions. They will not cut themselves up," she said.

"Come on, Kyle, won't you help?" Atlas said, giving him a pitiful look.

Kyle shook his head, "Nope!' he pulled the chair from the table forward, "but you might want to take a seat. Those are a lot of onions." He looked at Hannah, and they both laughed as he walked out.

The hours had gone by once Hannah and Atlas got into the rhythm of cooking. They spent the time telling jokes and stories and explaining recipes. Hannah and Atlas then began the tedious task of cleaning the kitchen after the prepping was completed. Atlas looked at the clock in amazement, "Mom, I cannot believe we have been doing this for hours."

"It's not easy cooking for this entire family. What did you think?" she responded, handing her a plate to dry.

"Mom, do you think all this work is worth it? Don't get me wrong, your food is amazing, but it's a lot of work," Atlas said, finishing up.

"Yes, Atlas, it is. I am glad you got to experience it. Remember anything worth doing takes work. It goes for everything in life, not just cooking." Hannah turned to assess what else needed to be cleaned, washed, or put away. "I enjoy doing all this work because it is my way of showing the family how much I love them. I take pride in my cooking and I want it done well because it's for you. You all are my heart. Do you understand?"

"I think so," Atlas responded with some hesitation.

"No you don't but one day you will. I know I worked you hard today, but when I am good and gone this will be a nice memory," Hannah said hugging her daughter.

"Mom, you are crazy," Atlas responded, looking out of the window and noticing Annie parking the car. "Great look, who finally decided to show up? She prances here after all the work is done."

"Why don't you go outside and greet your sister? Then, tell Kyle and Thomas to come inside. Annie brought sandwiches for supper. Be nice to your sister, and I will let you and Kyle go out clubbing tonight," Hannah instructed.

Atlas rolled her eyes and ran out to meet Annie, who was already surrounded by Thomas and Kyle. After a few pleasantries, the group started to head in, but Atlas held Kyle back, "Wait, Kyle, after dinner, do you want to go and hang out a bit? You know, get to know the nightlife of St. Louis?"

"Sure, if that is what you want to do," Kyle responded, taking a step forward over the fresh snow.

"I would call my friends to see if they will meet us, but I still cannot find my cell phone," she could not get the words out when her legs began to slip, and Atlas found herself falling towards Kyle "Oh Crap!" she yelled.

"What?" turning instinctively simply to have Atlas fall on him, causing both of them to the ground. They were tangled up in each other's arms and legs. "I forgot there was ice underneath the snow," he began to laugh. Kyle then brushed the snow out of Atlas' hair and face, "I guess we both forgot. Are you alright?"

She was hypnotized by his eyes, which seemed to be piercing through her heart. She could feel her pulse racing, and her mouth was dry, making it impossible to speak. All Atlas could do was nod and continue to gaze at Kyle's deep hazel-green eyes. It took a few seconds and several deep breaths when she mumbled, "Green? Your eyes are green?"

He smiled, answering, "Maybe." Then he laughed, attempting to stand up, but he could not gain his footing and fell back into the snow. "It might be a bit before I try that again."

Atlas then made her own effort with no success, "I think we are done for a bit,' she started to laugh.

"So what do we city girls do to wait for the search party?" he said.

Atlas began to laugh as she rolled on top of him, "No, silly, we are cops, remember? We don't call for help, and we are the help." She startled over his hips, placed her hands on his chest, and bent forward. They were now face to face. As their lips came close together, Atlas could almost taste his breath. Once again she was mesmerized by his scent, his manliness, and those damn deep green eyes. Getting a bit closer Atlas closed her eyes and catapulted herself up and away from such temptation. She finally made it to her feet standing over him.

Atlas gazed down at Kyle, a muscular and handsome man exuding rugged charm, a mix of admiration and intrigue flickered in her eyes, captivated by his robust presence. What was going on she asked herself. Wait no this is Kyle just Kyle her friend. She extended her hand to help him but he instead pulled her back down. Atlas landed over him once more and found herself on the verge of kissing him. Closing her eyes as if to accept her fate when suddenly Kyle rolled over her. She could feel his weight over her body and could feel his muscles tightening up.

He looked deep into her eyes as she tried desperately to look away, catching a huge smile and his famous wink. "Let's make some snow angels," he said, rolling across her, landing on his back, and making the first snow angel. Atlas lay there for a few seconds and then joined him. They were enjoying the moment when they noticed a car pulling up to them.

"Oh look, Kyle, its Arleen. We better go inside before she yells at us." Atlas suggested standing up and running to the house. Kyle was not far behind her as they both ran for the door, "I win! I win!"

"You cheated!" he yelled out, taking both of his hands, rubbing his hair, and covering her with the snow from his head and shoulders.

"Hey that is not fair you're so much taller than I am," she said smacking him on the chest with an open hand. They were both laughing while walking inside.

Arleen made her way behind them, saying, "You two look like a couple of kids rolling around in the yard. You better go take a shower and change before you two get sick."

Atlas started to bolt when she stopped and turned to Arleen, "Hey, by the way, when you get a chance, can you get my cell phone from your car?" She didn't wait for a response and followed Kyle upstairs.

He waited for her on the second level near her bedroom. She made it up the stairs to see him holding out his phone. "Do you want to use mine since yours is misplaced?"

"No, that's alright. I am sure it will turn up. I just want it charged before we head back on Friday," she said, sliding past him and into her bedroom. He walked upstairs and started to undress when he heard a quick tap on the door. Opening the door, Kyle found Atlas standing in his doorway, not wearing a shirt and his pants unbuckled.

"You good?" he asked, puzzled to see her.

"Yeah, I," she stopped herself, "I just wanted to make sure you had clean towels."

"I am sure your mom hooked me up," he said, looking around, "unless you want to come in and check."

Atlas bit her lip, contemplating the idea. She wondered what would happen if she stepped into this room. Feelings of conflict overcame her. After all, it was just Kyle, Kyle, her friend. She shook her head and started to walk away, turning quickly, admiring the man standing just a few feet away from her.

"You alright?" he asked,

"Yeah, but I need to make sure we're friends, right?" she asked almost in a whisper.

Kyle stepped out of the room, walked to her and grabbed her by the arms pulling her to him, "Atlas I need you to know I will always be your friend even if you are not mine. I will always be yours, got it?" he said, pulling her away making sure he looked into her eyes.

"Got it," she replied, stepping out of his grasp, "well, I guess we better shower before they send a search party for us. Then we can go out later if you would like."

"Up to you," he smiled as he watched her going down the stairs.

Kyle walked downstairs to find Atlas and Hannah sitting at the kitchen table, along with Arleen and Thomas. He could see several sandwiches, potato chips, and other snacks along with drinks. Hannah handed Kyle a plate so he could choose whatever he wanted. She asked, "Where are you guys headed tonight?"

"Or are you two staying in," Arleen interjected.

"I think Atlas wanted to show me some of the nightlife in the Show Me state," Kyle said while in the middle of bites from his sandwich.

"Do you think it's a good idea?" Arleen asked, "I mean, the weather's turning, and it might be bad tonight.

Atlas got up and looked out the window, "well, I am not sure if we should go. Maybe we should stay in tonight. What do you think Kyle? Maybe Arleen is right, and the weather might be bad."

"It is totally up to you, Attie. I am happy either way," Kyle responded.

"So you are staying," Arleen stated with a huge smile.

Atlas turned and caught Arleen smiling at Hannah, "No, I think we are good to go. Kyle should be able to enjoy the last night here in the city. We are heading out back to Wyoming Friday morning. Are you ready to go?"

"Sure, I guess we are going," Kyle said, placing his plate down. Atlas grabbed their coats and opened the back door.

Chapter 15

Spinning

They got into the car and started making their way west. Kyle followed Atlas's directions until they reached their destination, an establishment well-known for their music and entertainment.

"You will like this place, Kyle; as I recall, you like country music. I think tonight is line dancing, cowboy hats, and stuff like that," she said, giggling.

"Sounds good. You are right. I am a sucker for country music," he said, holding open the door.

They walked in and were barely through the door when Atlas was swarmed by a group of females. They were all smiling and holding drinks. One said, "OMG Atlas, you look fantastic. I heard you were back in town. Are you here just for the holiday, or are you back?" she asked.

"Hi Emma, no, I am just visiting. What are you guys doing here? I mean, it's county night? I thought you guys just hung out at Fast Eddies or Rush," Atlas said, trying not to look annoyed.

"Who is this beefcake with you?" she said, walking to Kyle.

"Ma'am," he said.

"Ma'am!? I am 27 years old. I am not a ma'am. But that's OK, handsome. I forgive you, it's the lighting. So, who are you? Are you Atlas date? Driver?" Emma asked, rubbing his shoulder and arm.

"No," Atlas said, pushing her hand off of Kyle, "this is Kyle. And honestly, that is all you need to know."

"Well, don't get your number up your butt. I am just a little tipsy. Come on, Atlas, don't make that face. I just wanted to see who brought you here," she said, taking a sip of her drink. "Join us; we've got a spot in the VIP area. Come on, it will be fun. We can catch up. Can you tell us all about your adventure in Utah?" Emma said, grabbing Atlas' arm and dragging her to their table. The other women took advantage, grabbing Kyle and escorting him as well.

Once at the table, Kyle made it a point to sit next to Atlas; he turned to her, whispering in her ear, "Just grab my hand, and I will know it is time to run for the exit."

She nodded and held his hand for a few seconds underneath the table. The women had several drinks on the table, as well as two bottles of liquor.

"Toast to Atlas and Kyle, who so gracefully joined us," Emma yelled across the table, pouring everyone a shot of tequila. "Shot! Shot! Shot!" she continued, instructing everyone to drink.

Kyle took his drink turning to Atlas, "You good?"

"Yes," they chugged the drink and simultaneously slammed the glasses on the table. Atlas poured salt on her hand, which she licked, and ended the ritual by sucking on a lime wedge.

Kyle smiled as he watched her endure the bitterness of the liquor, "What, no salt or lime for you?" she asked.

"Nope, if I wanted a Margarita, I would have ordered one. I like my liquor like I like my women, clear and simple, in other words, straight," Kyle replied.

"Atlas, aren't you rude here? Allow me to introduce to you the rest of the party," Emma said, "This is Elsa, Amanda, and Katy."

Kyle smiled kindly and shook each one's hand. Then he felt Emma's hand sliding on his thigh. Atlas noticed Emma's public display of flirtation, and she could feel her blood boiling. She immediately turned to Kyle, who gave her a wink and a nod. Atlas watched as Emma placed her hand near his crotch, and her fingers began to linger over his belt buckle. She slammed her hands on the table, took two more shots of tequila then announced, "I love this song."

"Great, me too; you want to dance?" he said, standing up. Atlas took the opportunity to push Kyle away from the table and dragged him to the dance floor, all while he was laughing.

"Hey, you know Emma lacks self-control. Didn't you see she was putting her hands on you? I mean, I don't care if you like that sort of thing, but we are in public, and you two just met," Atlas rambled on.

"Sorry, I didn't notice. What did she do?" Kyle said with a smirk on his face.

"You are impossible, Kyle. You should just say thank you. You would need penicillin if you hooked up with Emma, "Atlas replied.

"I got the GI benefits antibiotics I am covered with," he said, enjoying her rant of jealousy.

"Never mind that. Can you even dance? This is a two-step, you know," she said, turning her back to him

"I know. I also know you are jealous, and I can assure you, your friend Emma or any girl at the table is not my type. So why don't you relax and let me lead?" he placed his arm around her back, took her left arm, and extended it over his chest. "Hold on tight, Attie. I love to spin and turn my partner."

Off they went into the crowd, making their way around the dance floor. They danced several songs and Atlas found herself once more staring at Kyle. She could not understand why he was so nice to her. He would spin her around, and she found herself almost floating. She realized she was smiling like she had not smiled in a long time. During one turn, he asked, "Are you happy?"

"I am thankful. What about you?" she asked as the music turned to a slow dance, and Atlas found herself with both hands on Kyle's chest. "Sorry," she whispered.

"No worries," he said, pulling her arms up and placing them on his shoulders. "Here they are good here.' He stopped. "...unless you are not comfortable. I mean, if you want to take a break."

She found herself unable to answer for a second but managed to say, "I really like this song."

"I will take that as we keep going," Kyle responded, pulling Atlas' body closer to his frame. "Will you still love me," he said as they moved together. Atlas looked up with a strange gaze. "Chicago Will You Still Love" is the name of the song. It is one of my favorites of all time."

"Oh yeah, right, Chicago. Will you still love me? Right the song," Atlas responded. Her head began to spin, and she found herself lost again. Atlas could not help but lay her head on his chest. She closed her eyes and began to inhale his scent, which was simply addicting.

What was happening? She asked herself. It was just Kyle. Kyle was her friend; they were just friends. No, she told herself, he was just being nice with the holidays and all the time they had been spending together. That was it. They were just both lonely. Of course, that was it. She was confusing his kindness with attraction. Attraction, you have got to be kidding; it was the tequila that didn't sit well. They were just dancing and the song lyrics were just getting in her head.

The music changed to another two-step kind of song, but Kyle and Atlas were still holding on to one another in the middle of the floor. He stood still, giving her time to open her eyes and look up.

"You good? You want to try another dance or maybe grab a seat?" Kyle suggested.

Atlas felt embarrassed; she was mainly mad at herself for daydreaming, shaking her head. She responded with a definite, "Let's go back to the table. I could use a drink."

"Alright then," he placed his arm on the small of her back as they made their way through the crowded dance floor.

"You two seem cozy on the dance floor. You can teach me two steps anyway, Cowboy," Emma said, taking a shot.

"I'll take one of those," Atlas said, slamming the liquid down. "One more, please. I am very thirsty."

"I think we should order you some water to help with that, not tequila," Kyle said, sitting down.

"Sure, I will grab us a bottle on my way back from the bathroom," Atlas said, turning and almost stumbling. Kyle immediately stood up and caught her, "No, I am good, I promise. I just need to go to the bathroom. Don't worry."

"Are you sure? I can walk you," Kyle suggested.

"No, I am a big girl. I can go by myself," Atlas insisted, starting to walk away.

"Wait up, Atlas, I will go with you," Amanda said, standing up, leaning to Kyle and saying, "Don't worry, I only had one drink. I will watch her for you." She then walked to her. Kyle watched as the two women made their way across the room.

Kyle found himself once more with Emma's hands all over him. He grabbed them and pushed them down, saying,

"You are drunk, Emma. You need to knock it off. I will go to the bar and get everyone some water."

Atlas came out of the bathroom, and she could not find her friend Amanda. She was a bit tipsy and in need of fresh air. She stepped out to the outside patio and held herself up with the help of the bar top table.

"Are my eyes deceiving me? Is that you, Atlas?" a man's raspy voice said.

"Eric?" she said, forcing her head to look up to see a male figure standing inches in front of her.

"Let me take a look at you. You look hot, Atlas. What have you been doing?" he said, running his hands down her torso, tracing her figure and ending up on her butt. Eric patted her on the butt two or three times, leaving his hand on her. "Man, Atlas, a few months away from me, and you turned all your flab into sexiness."

"What are you talking about, Eric? I left to go to the police academy, not to get sexier for you," Atlas said as she began feeling dizzy.

"Look at you, Atlas, now you are up to par to hang out with me. Amazing," he said, wetting his lips.

"I have friends inside, Eric. I need to get back inside," Atlas responded, looking around.

"Do you really want to go back inside or go hang out with me somewhere quieter?" Eric suggested, "We can go inside the car for a few minutes. Come on, Atlas, just like old times but better since you are in better shape." He ran away toward the parking lot. Atlas started going with him but then suddenly stopped.

"Wait! I can't go with you. I am with Ky..." she stopped and then continued, "I have friends inside."

"I saw you inside with some people. Nothing special there. Come on, Atlas, how about a quickie? I will even let you give me a blow job. I am sure you can do it better than the last time," he insisted, pulling her to the parking lot. Atlas could see his car, an old beat-up Chevy Cobalt with a huge dent in the door.

"What happened to your car?" she asked, stumbling with him.

"Don't worry about that now. My dad is going to buy me a new car any day now. Now that you got yourself in shape, we can make this baby rock," Eric said, cupping his hand around her waist and moving her to the passenger's side. He pushed her against the car and began kissing on her neck. His hands slipped inside her blouse, trying to get into her bra without any success.

"Damn, girl, even your breasts got hard. Well, I can feel they are aching for me." Eric's hand then moved down and made its way into her pants. He managed to put his hand into her butt and could feel bare skin. "Oh, I see you are no longer a thick kind of girl. I mean woman. Atlas, you are all women, hard, sexy, and soon enough wet."

"Wait, wait," she protested. "Wait, Eric, I am not sure about this. I got people inside. I have friends, and Ky..."

Eric kissed her trying to get her excited while moving his hand to unbutton her jeans. "Let's get comfortable. You can do some of this out here, and then we can get busy inside the car." He unbuttoned her jeans and unzipped his pants.

"No! Eric, I am not going to be doing this," she said, pushing him away. "I am not that girl anymore," she said, buttoning herself up, shaking her head, and pushing Eric away from her.

"You know you want me!" Eric said. "When you are ready, you will call me. You can't live without me. You can't control yourself, and you will call me," he said, stepping inside his car and driving off, leaving Atlas standing in the parking lot.

Atlas looked around, trying to figure out how to get back into the nightclub. She was turned around and did not seem to find her bearings. She felt a bit sick to her stomach, feeling like she was about to throw up. Atlas closed her eyes and took a deep breath. When she opened her eyes, Kyle was standing in front of her.

"There you are. You feel like you are going to barf. Come on, let's go over there by the trash can. Here is your water," Kyle said, handing her a water bottle.

"Kyle, I think I'm going to be sick," Atlas said, holding her stomach.

Kyle grabbed her by the arm and walked her to the trash can. She bent her head over the can and threw up while Kyle tenderly held her hair away from her face. He then handed her a bandana so she could wipe her mouth. "Done? Alright, raise yourself up slowly."

"Sorry, Kyle. I am not sure why I was thinking this was a bad idea," she said with tears in her eyes, "I am such an idiot."

"You don't have to apologize for it. Tequila sneaks up on you, no shame on that. I have seen bigger men knocked on their asses with fewer shots," Kyle said. "Come on, I have some mouthwash in my go bag. You think you can make it to the car." Kyle said as he led her to the SUV. He helped her get in and assisted her in moving the seat backward so she could lie down. "I will get you home soon, and you can get some rest once we get there."

Kyle drove slowly, making their way back to the Martin's home. He parked the car in the driveway and walked around to help Atlas out, who was still a bit woozy. Kyle helped her step out of the car. He stood next to her, allowing her to pull herself together. Kyle watched as she was still dizzy. He then held her up and assisted her in walking inside the house. He then aided her in going upstairs and opening her bedroom door.

"Kyle, I need to lay down for a minute," she said.

"OK, but I need you to get hydrated and take some aspirin or something so you don't get a bad hangover," he said.

"Go in there, and I will be right back with water and aspirin, alright," Kyle said, helping her to sit on the edge of the bed.

Kyle ran downstairs and then upstairs with the supplies. He walked into her bedroom and noticed Atlas was in the bathroom. He could hear the shower water going, so he tapped on the door, saying, "Attie, are you alright?"

She came out wearing just a towel wrapped around her, "Yes, I just wanted to brush my teeth. I didn't want to stink. I smelled really bad, don't you think?"

"No, it's alright. We can talk about it in the morning," Kyle said, helping her to the bed and in between the covers. Kyle grabbed her T-shirt and turned off the light. He extended her arms over her head and helped her change from the wet towel to something more suitable. He managed to dress her without exposing anything. "Here, take the water and swallow these pills. Trust me, it will help you feel better in the morning." He said while caressing her hair and then pulling the blanket over her. "You good now? I will see you in a couple of hours," Kyle said, walking out of Atlas's bedroom and making his way quietly upstairs.

Kyle took a minute and then changed into his pajama pants and lay in bed. He recalled the events of the day and then the evening. He smiled as he recounted each moment he spent with Attie, his Attie. Kyle sat up in bed, saying to himself, "I can't help it, but I am falling in love with her. What am I going to do? How do I tell her she has gotten into my heart, and now what?" He dropped like a rock onto the pillow, and his mind took over, and he began to dream of his Attie as he drifted off to sleep.

Once again, Kyle found himself rolling in the snow with Atlas. They were caught behind a large mound, but they were not at the Martin's home; instead, they were in a clearing near his cabin at the ranch. There was no one around them, and Kyle knew they were definitely all alone. Kyle felt Atlas' body on top of him. She was covered in snow, and her hair was messy, falling over her face. He tenderly pushed it aside, exposing her lips, and began to kiss her.

Kyle lifted her up in his arms, carrying her inside to the blanket that seemed to be waiting for them in front of his fireplace. The warmth of the fire was welcoming, and he could see the reflection of the ambers in her eyes. He stood her up and watched as she began to unbutton her top. Kneeling in front of her, Kyle reached for her pants, undoing her belt and button and lowering her zipper slowly. He then used one hand to caress her breast as she slipped off her bra. He wanted her and needed to be inside of this woman, but in order to make it a perfect experience, Kyle knew he needed to wait.

His mission was to pleasure her in ways she had never experienced before. Kyle slowly slid off her panties, and now Atlas was standing before him naked. She was everything he had ever desired in a woman: strong, curvaceous, and tender-hearted. Atlas started to shy away and almost step back, but he wrapped his arms around her hips, guiding her towards him or, rather, his mouth. He wanted to pleasure her first. He needed her to know he was not a selfish lover. Kyle knew she had never had such an experience and he rejoiced at the idea this would be his gift to her.

He kissed the inside of her thighs, and he could feel her legs shaking with each touch of his tongue. Circling and making his way closer to his intended target is the source of her pleasure. Getting closer and closer with each kiss, Kyle could tell Atlas was both enjoying the process as well as becoming more anxious with anticipation. Finally, his mouth found her center, and he continued to use his tongue to pleasure her. Atlas felt her heart racing, wanting to lose all control, but Kyle slowed down, giving her time to catch her breath.

Atlas's body bent backward with each touch, and she found herself arching with ecstasy. She had never experienced this type of foreplay. Kyle was driving her to the edge of insanity with each seductive move. She wanted to scream with pleasure but held on, knowing this was just the beginning. Managing to reposition her body forward, she looked down and could see Kyle working his magic between her legs. She reached down and moved one of his hands to her breast. Kyle insensibly began to rub her breast, teasing her nipples.

Her hard, erect nipples showed her excitement. Kyle's lips made their way to her breast le,aving a trace of passionate kisses from her stomach to her breast. Once there, he kissed each one while gently squeezing and fondling them slowly. Kissing her chest bone and neck, then in one quick move, his mouth made contact with her right breast. He traced her nipple with his tongue and pressed his lips over her nipple to suckle on it. Atlas could feel herself once again about to lose control when Kyle assisted her to the floor.

He continued to fondle her breast and suck on her nipples taking turns moving from the right to the left. Instinctively Atlas reached for his right hand and began sucking on each finger. Kyle took advantage of the situation, moving his left hand, teasing her upper thigh, and slowly placing his fingers inside her wet womanhood. She was definitely losing this battle, and he took the opportunity to move, and now they were kissing. Guiding her body over his and making himself ready to take her.

Abruptly, he stopped kissing her and asked, "Are you sure you are ready for this?"

She looked in shock but then managed to yell, "Yes! Yes!" as she was straddling him. He was in her, and their bodies began to move in an erotic rhythm as waves crashed into the shores of the beach. He could feel her coming as they reached climax together. Once again, he did not want to be selfish, and he needed to know she was satisfied. He gazed at her and could tell she was experiencing exquisite passion. Tracing her sides as he cradled her body, he also gave in to the temptation and exploded inside of her body, releasing himself and moaning out loud in an animal pleasure.

They were exhausted from their lovemaking, but Kyle, although satisfied, wanted more and more. He looked at Atlas, who seemed to be in need of a quick nap. Holding her close to his body, he laid her head on his chest, and their warm bodies continued to be connected. Kyle's arms were wrapped around her as Atlas pulled the blankets over them, falling asleep instantly.

Kyle began to catch a distinctive odor of vanilla lingering in the air. Vanilla thought to himself as he continued to sleep. He started to rub his nose but could feel something or someone pressing over him. While keeping his eyes closed, he tried to figure out what was happening. He could feel soft hair and soft skin cascading over his naked shoulder. It was a woman who was sleeping with him on the bed. Who was that? Did he dare bring someone home from the bar? How or who? He was only with Attie. Wait! Attie! He opened his eyes; maybe it was part of his dream. Yes, maybe he was still dreaming, he told himself.

Kyle could feel the person moving and readjusting themselves. Moving minimally, he looked down and found Atlas sleeping on him. He then scanned the room to ensure he was in his assigned room and he had not fallen asleep on her bed. It was the third floor of Martin's house and not

Attie's bedroom; he was sure of it. But how was this possible? He had put Attie into her bed.

He began to caress her hair as Atlas was slowly waking up. She held on and pulled his body closer to hers as if he were her pillow. Kyle decided not to wake her, but he started to get worried. He did not want the Martins to become upset with him.

Atlas opened her eyes, and he could feel her body tensing up.

"Hey there," Kyle said softly.

"Hi," she said, sliding her hand over his chest. She could feel the warmth of his body. "You are so warm," she said, keeping the palm of her hand on him.

"Are you hurting?" he asked.

"No, I'm good. I think your remedy worked. "She responded, trying to push herself up.

"Take your time," he suggested.

"No, I am good," she said, starting to move a bit.

"Can I ask you something, Attie? Do you remember how you made it up here? I mean, I left you in your bed," he started to ask.

"I am not sure. I believe I started having nightmares, and I guess I didn't want to be alone." she stood with some embarrassment, "I am sorry. I really didn't mean to bother you."

"You are not bothering me, but I don't want your parents to get upset. I don't want to be explaining to your dad how we were disrespectful in his house," Kyle said, sitting up and making his way to the edge of the bed. "I will turn my back just in case you're not dressed."

"You're crazy? I am wearing clothes," she said, "I think I am wearing clothes. Didn't you help me with a t-shirt after I showered," she stated looking at herself underneath the covers,

"Not sure, but you are wearing something," he said smiling, turning his face to peak.

"Stop, Kyle, you are making me blush. I feel bad enough about the situation," she said, getting out of bed and wrapping herself in his blanket.

He stood up and walked to open the door for her, "You better go before we are caught."

"Don't worry so much; my parents left really early this morning to drop off the extra food mom makes for the homeless shelter. Then, after dinner, she will go again and drop off more food. You know the extra dishes made by Annie and Arleen. I used to go with them. Maybe you will want to join us tonight," she suggested, standing in the doorway.

"Sure thing, Attie. I still feel funny here in my bedroom like this. I think you better make your way downstairs just in case," Kyle insisted.

Atlas did not respond; she simply ran out and made her way down to the second floor.

Chapter 16

Tangled

As her mind was caught in a daydream, Atlas took the last step onto the second floor to find her sister Annie waiting for her.

"Good Morning, or should I ask why the big smile," Annie said with a cheesy smile.

"What are you talking about?" Atlas responded, trying to wrap herself more with Kyle's blanket.

"Well, it looks to me like you spent the night in the wrong room, or maybe it was the right one?" Annie said, tugging at the blanket.

"Stop that. It is nothing like that. I was just asking Kyle if he needed..." Atlas responded.

"If he needed a little morning love..." Annie laughed, "Nothing wrong with that; I mean, after all, you are two consenting adults."

"No, Annie, nothing like that. Kyle and I are just friends," Atlas protested.

"Friends with benefits," Annie suggested.

"No, Annie," Atlas protested and turned around, trying to make it to her door and get away from her sister.

"Don't get upset, Atlas. I think Kyle is a good guy. I am really happy for you, "Annie said.

Atlas just shook her head, opening her bedroom door. "Whatever, Annie, I don't need to give you any explanations."

"Oh, Atlas, I found your cell phone in the basement among the pans. Here you go. I thought you might want it back, although your man is upstairs," Annie said, chuckling.

"Shut up, Annie!" Atlas said, grabbing the phone, going inside, and closing the door. She immediately regretted it, quickly cracked open the door, and called out," Annie! Annie! Can you please not say anything to Mom or Dad?"

"Sure thing, I like Kyle, and Dad would be so upset at you, not him, "she said, laughing while going to the banister.

Great Atlas said to herself. But she had no time to worry about what Annie implied. What the hell was happening to her? Why was she becoming so confused with Kyle? She felt her heart racing and her head spinning. Atlas dismissed all of her feelings, believing it had been a combination of the alcohol and all the time she and Kyle had been spending together. She sat on the edge of the bed, consumed by his scent from the blanket. It almost felt as if Kyle had his arms around her. She fell on the bed, trying to figure it all out.

Atlas took a quick shower and went downstairs to meet with family and Kyle, who had gathered in the kitchen. "There you are, Darling. You dressed for the festivities of the day?" James asked her.

"What are you guys up to?" Atlas said, looking around and noticing everyone was already at the house.

"We were trying to figure out how to split the teams. What do you think, girls vs boys or Martins against the others?"

"Oh no, you are talking about Martin's annual football game. Mom, do you? We have to do that again this year. We are not little kids anymore," Atlas protested.

"Come on, Atlas, you know how much your dad and brothers enjoy it. Besides, it is tradition," Hannah said, handing her a hot cup of coffee.

Atlas looked around, looking for Kyle, who was standing in the back of the room staring at her. "Alright, but as I recall, this year, I am one of the team captains. So I got the first choice. I choose Kyle as my first teammate."

"No, dear, it is not your year. You were the team captain last year. Remember, this year is Mom and Dad's turn. Since Dad is not here yet, I am stepping in for him," Tim shouted across the room.

"Great, then I go first," Hannah responded. "Kyle, would you like to be on my team?"

"Mom, you don't have to ask. You just..." Atlas started to say. "Well, Kyle, you are on Mom's team."

"I will take James," Tim said as Thomas walked into the kitchen.

"Dad, where have you been?" Atlas asked.

"I got the field ready for the friendly game. I am so glad everyone is ready to go. How far did we get with the teams?" Thomas said, pouring himself a cup of coffee.

"Well, Mom selected Kyle, and you ended up with Atlas. I guess we will file in line from that. Our spouses will be with Mom, and the Martins will team up with Dad." James explained.

"That is so not fair, Dad. I don't want to block Kyle; you all know he was all American. I expected to stand a chance against him. Besides, if I do a lousy job, everyone will blame me," Atlas protested.

"You will do a lousy job anyway, Atlas. I am not sure why you are worried," Tim interjected. "I, on the other hand, love the idea of blocking and chasing my girl around the field. So suck it up, Atlas."

"Wait!" James yelled, looking at his father, "Kyle was all American. Where?"

"Oh, that was years ago," Kyle replied modestly.

"What was your last name?" James insisted.

"Noyes, Kyle Noyes," Atlas said, walking to her mother's side and crossing her arms.

"Wait a minute! Dad, we watched him. Kyle Noyes from Tennessee. You were picked up by the University of Tennessee to be their number one draft for quarterback. Dad and I watched you play some time ago," he said, walking to Kyle and tapping him on the shoulder, "Man, you were on fire. Remember, Dad, that was a perfect game."

"Yes, I remember," Thomas responded and walked towards his wife, handing her the football. He then gave her a kiss on the lips.

"Dad I don't think it is fair you know all about Kyle and his football talents," Atlas attempted to protest once more.

"Look, Atlas, it is all settled. You need to block Kyle, and that is all," Thomas said, "OK, let's huddle and get this game going. Remember, the loser has to pull out the Christmas trees from the attic."

"That's right, Atlas, don't cost us the game," Tim shouted.

Kyle walked over to his team and immediately recognized Hannah as the captain, "Alright, Ma'am, what's the plan?"

"Look, Kyle, for the first time in years, we have a shot at winning. Mainly, it's bragging rights, but today, I like my odds. How about you give us a good strategy, and we will simply execute it." Hannah responded enthusiastically.

"Well, that is easy. In order to win we must play our strengths so we match our counterparts. Let me hold on to the ball as much as I can, and I will send it downfield to whoever is closer. Sounds good?" Kyle asked.

"Sounds perfect. Besides, I know my limitations, but I doubt Atlas does," Arleen said and then continued, "She has to block you."

Everyone took their spots on the makeshift field when the game kicked off, with Thomas kicking the ball clear across the backyard and Kyle catching it, yelling, "Fair Catch!" but Atlas was already in midflight, attempting to tackle him and missing. Atlas fell straight into a huge pile of snow and became covered from head to toe in the white powder.

"Are you alright, Attie?" Kyle asked, extending his hand to help her up.

Atlas stood up furious as she watched her family laughing at her, "I don't need any help. I would have taken you down if you hadn't called out," she said while trying to dust herself off.

"Not really, Attie, but OK, whatever you have to tell yourself," Kyle said, trying not to join in the laughter.

"Stop calling me Attie," Atlas said, walking away.

Kyle then set the team up, and in a matter of seconds, his team had scored. Kyle looked around and noticed the person celebrating with the most passion was Hannah, who kept jumping up and down in front of her husband. Kyle had a huge smile on his face when Atlas approached.

"Why are you so happy that it is just one touchdown?" Atlas asked.

"No, it's never about the win, Attie. It's about the game, the people, and the simple joy something like this gives. You are so lucky."

"Lucky? You are kidding me, right? This is a nightmare. If we don't win, Mom and the spouses will never let up. Oh!

And Dad and his boys will blame me the entire year. This really sucks," she protested.

"You are nuts. It is not a Super Bowl; it's a game. Don't think you can come here and sweet talk me into letting you score. No way, Attie, you are going down!" Kyle said, ripping the ball out of Attire's grip and tossing it over to Larry, who was just waiting for his opportunity.

Atlas stood there with her mouth open and her hands on her hips as Kyle smiled and winked at her with his wicked smile.

"Man, Atlas, that is one handsome man if I do say so myself," Arleen commented, walking past her.

"Shut up, Arleen; Kyle is just an ass," Atlas responded, making her way toward her group.

"And what an ass he has," Arleen replied.

"I kinda have to agree," Hannah added.

"Mom! That is not appropriate," Atlas protested.

"The truth always hurts, baby," Hannah responded, walking towards Thomas.

"Mom, what are you doing?" Arleen asked Hannah as the two lined up to block for the next play. "Cheating just a bit. I figure if I keep Atlas' mind wondering she might like Kyle for more than her friend. He likes her, you know, and I think she likes him back."

"My love, what are you doing?" Thomas asked, watching his wife's plot. "Are you meddling?"

"No, I am not, but I am prospecting. I like Kyle, and I like Kyle for Atlas. If he joined the family, we would always kick your butts," she said with sparks in her eyes, and then Hannah broke out into laughter.

"Well," Thomas said, stepping close to his wife and whispering in her ear. "I am team Kyle all the way."

Taking advantage of everyone's distractions, Atlas attempted to run past them and score for her team. Kyle watched as she tucked the ball underneath her arm and ran straight for the goal. He took three steps to his left and immediately snatched her up. Kyle then threw her over his shoulder and ran to the opposite side, crossing the goal line and scoring for his team.

"No, Kyle, that is not right. You cannot carry me across the goal line. I had the ball in my hands the entire time," Atlas protested as he started to put her down.

"All is fair in love and football. Sorry, Attie, you should've passed the ball," Kyle said, lowering her feet and yet holding her close to his body. They stood there, standing toe to toe, trapped in one another's eyes.

"It's over; you guys win," Thomas said, grabbing his wife's hand, and the group began to walk to the house. "Atlas, you and Kyle clean up here. We will see you inside in a bit."

Kyle's gaze was piercing right through Atlas as he continued to hold her close to him. At that very moment, he did not want to let her go. His mouth opened, and his lips were aching to touch hers, if just for a brief second. He moved his hand to cradle the back of her head, gently stroking her hair. She felt frozen as if his stare had immobilized her, making her feel like a statue. She instinctively wanted to kiss him back as their lips started to connect, and they heard Arleen calling for them.

"I am sorry," Atlas said, pushing him back. "I guess I got caught in the moment." She quickly turned and headed into the house. Kyle followed a few steps behind her. She walked in to find her dad standing in the doorway.

"Alright, if you would head upstairs to the attic and start bringing down the Christmas boxes. I will get the boys to help move the furniture," Thomas instructed.

"What about Annie? Why can't she help? Atlas protested while Kyle stood still behind her as Atlas started to head up the stairs.

"Don't fuss, Atlas; Annie is helping Mom with dinner," Thomas said, looking at Kyle. "She has a lot to learn when it comes to losing. Why don't you relax and enjoy the win."

"Thank you, Sir, I prefer to help. I will head to the attic and give Attie a hand," Kyle didn't wait for his response, running up flights of stairs. Kyle opened the door and found Atlas looking at the top shelf.

"Why the Hell do they put things up so damn high? I am not sure how they want me to bring them down?" Atlas stretched as far as she could, her fingertips barely making contact with the box. Kyle stepped directly behind her naturally grabbing the box and bringing it down and placing it by the doorway. When he turned around once again, he stood toe-to-toe with her.

He bent down just enough and whispered, "Attie." He brushed the hair away from her face and pushed some of her hair strands behind her ear tenderly. His lips found her and in a long, passionate kiss. Atlas could feel her legs shaking while her entire body begged for more. Her mind started to race with all the possibilities and exchanges. She could not wrap her head around what was happening. Kyle? This was real; Kyle was kissing her. More than kissing her, he was consuming her mind and, if he wanted, at that very moment, her body as well.

She started to freak out a bit. Atlas had never experienced such conflict between satisfying pleasure and true surrender. How was this happening? Her mind was not clear, but her body was all his for the taken. As the kiss continued, her arms rubbed up and down his shoulders. She stepped closer to get her body in the right spot for him, and the small of her back began to curve. Atlas thought if she were a cat, she could see herself purring.

Suddenly, the cell phone in her pocket began to vibrate, and she pushed Kyle away. Instinctively, she looked, and it was a message from Eric, "HEY BABE U @ UR FOLKS?"

"I see you are busy," Kyle said. "I guess this is not the right time to talk."

"Talk?" Atlas replied, barely looking up at the screen, "Is that what you call it?"

"Sorry, Attie, I just couldn't wait one more second. I wanted to kiss you, and I needed to kiss you. I guess I misunderstood." he said, taking a giant step back.

"Wait," she said, putting the phone back in her pocket, "I just need a second."

Kyle stepped forward and grabbed her forcefully, pulling her body onto his; he then whispered in her ear, "If you hesitate, don't pick me."

Her phone started to ring, and Kyle reached for her cell phone from her back pocket and handed it to her. He stepped away from her, giving her his famous gaze. She gave the phone a quick glance, then looked up to see Kyle pick up a box and head down the stairs. She started to say, "Wait," but then heard a voice on the phone, and she began to speak to them while walking down with an additional box.

"Dinner! Atlas, come on, Kyle is already sitting," Hannah said. "Put that cell phone away. You know how your dad feels about them during dinner."

Atlas sat next to Kyle and gave him a look, but he barely acknowledged her.

"Let's pray," Thomas suggested, "Kyle, would you care to do the honors."

"If it's alright with you, Sir, I would defer the honor. God and I are not on speaking terms at the moment." Kyle replied, bowing his head.

"I understand. I get mad at the old man myself from time to time," Thomas said. "There was this one time."

"Thomas, hold the war story till we are done with grace. The food is getting cold," Hannah scolded him.

"Oh yes, dear," Thomas laughed, "like I said, sometimes I get mad at him too. Sorry, My Love. Lord thank you for the food we are about to receive made with loving hands. We thank you for our health, family, and good friends you brought to our house. We ask you to keep our family safe, healthy, and happy in the years ahead. Amen."

While the food began to be served, Atlas had a dead gaze fixated on Kyle.

"Everything alright, Atlas?" Hannah said, handing her a plate with food.

"Yes, I am just wondering if we are headed to the shelter after dinner," Atlas asked.

"Oh yes, it is tradition. Kyle, would you care to join us? We take dinner to the shelter for those who are less fortunate," Thomas explained

"Absolutely, it would be my pleasure," Kyle responded

"Kyle," Hannah tenderly said as she reached and tapped Kyle's arm, "I just wanted to make sure you will be alright," she took a breath, "You know there are a number of Vets at the shelter."

"Yes, we live in a society that perpetuates the idea of helping homeless veterans but does nothing to solve the problem. What a system! We call on our sons and daughters to give up their youth, their safety, their souls, and even their humanity in the name of our country. These kids have no idea what is happening to them. Little by little, they are exposed to the worst of mankind. Then, after they are put in through the ringer, they are dumped with a thank you for your service and nothing more." Kyle responded while his eyes became dark.

"Yeah, it upset us as all, son. All the sacrifice for what? A phone number to the VA?" Thomas interjected, "That is why Mom and I always try to do something for them."

"Come on, Atlas, if you are done with dinner, let's help Mom get the food ready," Annie said, standing up and walking into the kitchen.

Atlas slapped her hands on the table, saying, "Yeah, I am so done."

"Kyle, if you don't mind, you can follow behind us or jump in with Mom and me," Thomas said, walking toward the kitchen.

Kyle then felt his cell phone vibrating, "Mr. Thomas, I can go warm up your car if you would like. I need to return this call."

"Sure, son, go ahead. The keys are over by the front door," Thomas replied.

"Where is Kyle?" Atlas said casually to Thomas.

"He got a phone call and he is taking it outside," Thomas responded.

"I am sure it is his parents just wanting to wish him a happy Thanksgiving. Don't worry, Atlas." Hannah responded.

"I am not worried, but it's not his parents. He got an email from them this morning. I guess they forgot they were in the same country. It must be his girlfriend or wife." Atlas said candidly.

"What wife?" Hannah asked, stopping dead in her tracks.

"I don't know, maybe he has a wife. He is so secretive I don't really know him." Atlas responded,

"You stop talking nonsense. Kyle is a good man. He does not seem like the type to be playing around," Hannah scolded her.

Thomas walked close to Atlas, "Listen, I don't ask for much from you, but I need a favor," he stopped and then continued, "I need you to please stay close to Kyle. He just got home, and seeing some of the Vets might be too much for him."

"He is fine. I haven't seen anything like that. I don't understand why you guys are babying him so much," Atlas protested, heading to the door.

"Honey, this is serious," Hannah said, "listen to your father."

"What?" she answered.

"Kyle might not realize his mind is still fighting a war a thousand miles away. You get that, right? A part of him is still fighting. He is struggling to understand that not everyone is out to hurt him. Seeing guys like him homeless, hungry, uncared for might trigger an inner voice," Thomas explained.

"A voice?" Atlas asked,

"His voice tells him that no one cares. Soon, if you are not careful, that voice gets louder, and it teaches you are helpless. Isolation can take over, and that is the danger zone. Soldiers who feel their country has broken every promise made to them will feel helpless, hopeless, and isolated. Once they go dark, if they are not brought back, they will die," Thomas stated.

"Die! No way, Dad, are you exaggerating? Kyle is fine." Atlas said

"How do you know he is fine? Because he said so," Hannah added.

Atlas looked at her mother, "Yes, and because I know him."

"Wait a moment ago, we went on and on about how you didn't know him," Annie said.

"Well, I do. I guess. No, I do; maybe," Atlas could not find the right answer.

"If you are his friend, you will trust me. Stay close to him while we are at the shelter. He needs a friend to stand with him," Thomas walked close to her and put his hand on her shoulder.

"Alright. I am sure he is fine, but I will do as you said. Can we please go now?" Atlas said, walking out.

Hannah and Thomas walked slowly behind her. "That daughter of yours will be the death of me yet," Thomas said, smiling at his wife.

Don't look at me. I didn't make her by myself," Hannah said, laughing while they made it to the car to meet Kyle.

Chapter 17

Red

"Why don't you drive, dear? I would love to sit back here with my girls and the winning team," Hannah said, hopping into the back seat.

"Sure, Ms. Hannah, you are the boss," Kyle said with a smile as he helped her into the back seat. Kyle then felt his phone alerting once more, and Atlas noticed he was looking at it. He entered the car to hear Atlas from the rear seat shout, "Everything alright? I noticed you've been on your phone more than usual."

Atlas then attempted to hand Kyle the keys to his SUV, but he waved her off. She secured them in her pocket, and they all entered the vehicle.

"Yes, thank you. Where is Mr. Thomas?" Kyle asked, trying to change the subject.

"The GPS has the address; just follow it. We are maybe 25 minutes away. The city made the old Famous and Barr building into a Veteran's shelter. It is a pretty nice place that was converted from a warehouse to a multifunctional building. The shelter provides healthcare, job placement, and permanent housing assistance. The upper area is the living quarters. They are able to provide a safe space for them to get a good night's sleep," Thomas explained as they moved forward.

Approaching the building, Kyle could see a large number of people lined up outside. He estimated over two hundred, mainly males, but he could see a couple of women among the masses. He noticed one woman in particular was standing at the top of the stairs, making a point to welcome each individual. Looking at the female, he thought to himself, "I know her."

"Kyle, you can park around back, and they will send someone to help us unload the food and all the other stuff, Hannah added," he said, looking at his wife.

"Mr. Thomas, who is the woman standing in front?" Kyle asked as he parked the SUV.

"You mean Luna? Luna Le Grand is the foundation that runs the shelter. She was married to…" Thomas started to say but was quickly cut off by Kyle.

"Luna Le Grand, I knew her back in the day. Luna is here. What a small world," he said and stopped, placing the car in park. "What a small world," he repeated.

"So who is she?" Atlas asked, jumping out of the car and meeting him at the driver's side door.

Kyle took a long, deep breath and then said, "Luna was my buddy's girl. Man, Teddy was so lucky she was a sweetheart. We lost Teddy a few years back, and I lost track of them. Wow, Luna, I just can't believe my luck."

"What? You got like a crush on her or something? I mean, the way you are talking about her, you would think she is a model or saint or something," Atlas protested, noticing everyone had gone inside. "Come, let's get in there before they think we are missing."

"Yeah," he said, checking himself once in the side mirror.

"What the hell, Kyle?" Atlas shouted.

"Luna always notices if you are not together," Kyle said with that killer smile as they made their way into the building.

Walking in, Kyle noticed all the attention to detail, the pictures of soldiers, flags, and tons of challenge coins adorning the upper walls. Since the building was made of brick, he also found a makeshift memorial with the names of fallen servicemen and women. As they navigated through the corridor, Kyle started to hear the voices becoming louder, and soon, they walked into a large ballroom filled with laughter.

"Welcome to Le Grand Veterans Hall," a female voice said.

"Luna Le Grand," Kyle responded.

"Kyle Noyes. Oh, my love, is that really you? Come here and give me a hug. I missed you, how have you been? Tell me everything," she said

Kyle stepped into her arms, and they embraced for several minutes. Atlas stood there watching them, feeling her blood boiling. "Who the hell was this woman? Why was

Kyle so taken in by her? If she was so special, why did he never talk about her?"

"Hi, I am Atlas Martin. I am not sure if we've met before," Atlas said, extending her hand.

"Oh, I am sorry, dear," she said, releasing her hug but still holding Kyle's arm,   "Kyle... Maybe..." she winked and shot him a huge grin, "he graduated from Basic Training with my boyfriend and then husband, Theodore Le Grand."

"I was sorry to hear that we lost Teddy... Luna, I wanted to call, but..." Kyle said, taking her hand.

"What could you say, Kyle? Teddy struggled with all the darkness of war. Lord, if I couldn't get through to him, who could? But come on, let's get this party started, and then maybe we can catch up. I mean, if that is alright with your girl," Luna said, taking Kyle by the arm.

"I am not his girl. We are not together. Kyle and I just go to the police academy together," Atlas said in a stoic, nonchalant kind of way.

"Great, then I can keep him all night," Luna said, leading him inside to meet and greet people, leaving Atlas standing alone in the hall. Atlas watched as she moved with a grace that seemed effortless; her presence was commanding, almost intimidating, without the need to utter any words. Her eyes, like two pools of emerald, held a mesmerizing depth, drawing you in yet hinting at a mystery untold. Each delicate feature of her face seemed perfectly crafted as if sculpted by the hands of an artist. When she smiled, her radiance and enchantment lit up the room, casting a shadow of doubt and insecurity over Atlas.

Her allure was not just in her physical appearance but in her confidence; she exuded a magnetic charm that captivated those around her. At this moment, enslaving Kyle, a beast to her pry. With every glance and every gesture, she seemed to effortlessly capture the attention of others, leaving an indelible impression in his mind.

As Luna moved through the room, she carried an aura of undeniable allure, a presence that lingered long after she was gone, much like that hint of perfume making its way through the atmosphere. Atlas thought, though her beauty may inspire admiration, it also stirred a gnawing sense of unease, a fear of losing the affection of those who fall under her spell.

Atlas could feel every part of her body heating up until she was on fire. She was furious at herself for not making it clear that Kyle was not available. Well, at least not to Luna. Luna Le Grand is a tall, slender woman with a curvy and fit body. Atlas's eyes were piercing at Luna while wondering where she was from Brazilian, Dominican Republic, or Africa. No matter, Kyle could not be interested. The feeling of jealousy was intense and overwhelming; it triggered anger, insecurity, possessiveness, and resentment. Atlas was steaming and did not understand Kyle's response to this other woman. She shook her head and told herself, "Luna is not his type, or was she?" Feeling intrigued by his behavior, Atlas quickly followed them into the dining hall.

"So glad you could join us," Luna said to Atlas, who was still enamored by her beauty. "I was just telling Kyle about our annual fundraiser. It is a ball. It would be lovely if you two could make it."

"Luna, I think you are getting ahead of yourself. Atlas and I are just visiting for the holiday. I am not sure if … well, it's hard to make plans so far ahead with the academy schedule." Kyle responded.

Thomas walked towards them, "What are you guys handing out here? Come on, let me introduce you to a couple of people," Thomas said, grabbing Kyle and moving him to the other side of the room.

"What do you think, Atlas? You think you guys can make it?" Luna insisted.

"Well, Kyle is correct. Our schedule is difficult; that is why we came over for Thanksgiving." Atlas responded, looking around the room for Kyle.

"I know you, right? We met before, didn't we?" Luna asked while scanning the room.

"I don't think so," Atlas responded while taking her phone out to see who was messaging her.

"Atlas is such an unusual name. I am sure I heard it before. Wait! You are Eric Noles' plus one from last year's gala. You guys didn't make it. I recall the Noles had two empty spaces at their table. We ended up auctioning them off. Yes, that is it. You are Eric's plus one." Luna said.

"No, I am not. I am not anyone's plus one," Atlas responded furiously walking away from her. Atlas began to receive text messages from Eric as she was scrolling down as her sister-in-law Arlene walked towards her.

"Why are you just standing around? You need to put the cell phone away; who is texting you anyway? Is it Eric?" Arlene demanded. Just as she spoke, Annie walked towards them, asking, "What gives why you guys are just standing here? We need to get busy before Mom or Luna gets on to us."

"It looks like Eric is back in the picture," Arlene said with some sarcasm.

"Oh, is he? I like Eric. I guess I'm team Eric, huh?" Annie responded.

"What the hell are you guys talking about?" Atlas said, looking up. "There are no teams."

Arlene gave her a dirty look. "The hell they're not, and I am so team Kyle."

"My money," Annie said, "is with Eric. Besides, he is loaded. He comes from a good family very affluent. Don't get me wrong, I like Kyle. Kyle's nice, handsome, educated with a hot body, well-mannered all around, and a nice guy, but we all know Atlas doesn't like nice people. Atlas prefers bad boys. So, like I said, I am team Eric all the way."

"You guys are ridiculous," Atlas responded. "Why do I bother even talking to you."

"You weren't really talking to us," Arlene said. "We just added our two cents because you're never going to ask us, but to be honest at least you are never going to do better than Kyle and Honey if you can pull it together because if not, Luna will keep him for herself." Arlene then started looking for Kyle in the crowd and spotted him right next to Luna," see what did I tell you there she is putting her hands all over your man and here you are playing on that stupid cell phone with a guy who didn't even bother to come see you."

"Honestly, Arlene, I think you're making too much of a big deal out of it. Eric's a good guy. He just likes to party. Pretty soon, he will get it all out of his system. We will be attending a wedding," Annie said as she began to laugh. Atlas put her phone in her backpack and walked away from the door, making her way straight to Kyle.

"Oh good, my love, you decided to join us," Luna said to Atlas. "Are you done with all your telephone communications?"

"Telephone communications? What are you talking about? "Atlas responded in a snooty tone.

"Yes, of course, I forget what Americans call hand phones. Mobile phone? OH yes, cell phones," Luna said with a smile and then continued, "I left my American slang book at home, and I am a bit off."

"Well, I am glad to hear you have not lost your exotic accent," Kyle replied

"My love will never go away. I will always be exotic that's what makes me fun and mysterious." She let out a giggle while Kyle gazed at her and smiled.

"Maybe you two need to be alone," Atlas interjected with a bitter tone.

"My love, I am so sorry. I forgot you were standing there where my manners are?" Luna said she didn't turn and continued looking at Kyle." It is so good to see you, my dear friend. It has been too long, way too long."

"You are right, Luna. It has been too long," Kyle replied

"Well, nothing like the present to make up for a lost time," Luna replied, then turned her attention to Atlas, "I do hope you can join us for the gala."

Atlas was about to respond when her phone rang. Atlas took it out of her pocket allowing Luna to see the caller was Eric. Luna took the opportunity to say out loud, "It's Eric. Please give him my warmest regards." She then put her arm around Kyle, and they walked away. Atlas again was furious; all she could see was red. She couldn't stand the idea of Luna and Kyle. Ignoring Eric's call she caught up to them once more and heard Luna inviting Kyle to participate in her fundraiser.

"So, will you make an effort to try to come, Kyle? You will have an amazing time," Luna said

"What are you two plotting?" Atlas asked.

"My love, we are talking about the gala. I wish you and Eric would have made it last year so you could convince Kyle to join us" Luna insisted.

"Join us; what are you two together now?" Atlas was furious as she asked the question with her arms on her hips and pressing her lips tight while her gaze was focused on their every move and gesture.

"My love, I figured you would come with Eric this year, and Kyle will be mine, and it's all settled," Luna proclaimed, "Oh dear, it looks like Mrs. Martin is calling me over. There must be an issue with the food. Great, I will see you two in a jiffy."

Once Atlas's cell phone rang, she pulled it out of her pocket, and before she could say anything, Kyle said, "You should answer it. I am sure Eric wants to speak to you," and he began to walk away.

In a range of emotions, Atlas answered the phone, *"Hello, what do you want? Why are you calling me?"* as she was speaking, she noticed Luna heading towards Kyle. Atlas was confused; she didn't know what she was feeling or going through. Her head began to spin, and she felt like she could not focus. She shook her head and focused on the voice on the cell phone," *What are you asking me? You know I'm leaving in the morning? Yeah early. I am at the shelter like we do every year. You should know that. No, you can't come here. Why? Because my father will kill you. Alright, alright, I will figure something out. Yes, yes, I'll see you tonight. I'll text you now please stop calling me.* Atlas finally got rid of Eric temporarily and now she could try to figure out the Kyle situation.

"Everything alright, dear?" Hannah asked Atlas, "You were shouting into the cell phone. Are you alright? Is everything alright?"

"No, Mom, everything is not. Everything is a mess," Atlas explained while trying to scope out Kyle's location.

"Well, you know what I say about messes. If you make it, you gotta clean it up. If you didn't make it, you need to walk away. So dear, which one is it, Atlas? Did you make it, or are you simply walking away?" Hannah asked with a stern voice.

"No, Mom, you don't understand. It is not that simple. My life is complicated, don't you get that? Atlas responded.

"Honey, life is not complicated; it's messy, and it's messy because you make it messy," Hannah said, walking away.

"Miss Hannah, do you need me to start carrying the dishes back to the car? It looks like people are starting to clear out?' Kyle asked as Atlas was walking behind him.

"Yes, dear, if you do not mind. I'll show you; come on, we're going to the kitchen," Hannah responded, wrapping her arm around Kyle's arm and walking away. Once in the kitchen, Hannah handed Kyle a pile of pans and pots. "Oh, sorry, that might be too much."

"No, Mom, it's OK. I will help him. Don't worry." Atlas took the opportunity to jump in and take some items before anyone could protest.

They walked to the car in silence. Kyle opened the hatch and began piling the pots inside when Atlas came behind him, "I guess I owe you an explanation."

"No, you don't," Kyle responded.

"I went to Wyoming trying to get away from... well, my past. I wanted to prove that I could do things on my own. I guess I was both running from my past and trying to find myself," Atlas said while handing him her parcels.

"And you did well, at least I thought you did. You are straight. You worked hard, studied like no other, and passed all your skills. You did it. No one did that for you. You should be pretty proud of yourself. I know I am of you," Kyle said while packing her items into the vehicle.

"I'm not so sure," she said.

Kyle turned and took her by both arms and said in a stern tone, "You don't ever let anyone tell you are not good enough. You are! You can do anything. You have a lot of heart. Don't ever let anyone tell you what to do, not even me, you got that?"

"Yes, I got it," Atlas said with confidence, giving him a hug.

As he held her body close to his, "Why didn't you tell me about Eric? You know, if I knew he was in the picture, I would have never told you about my feelings," Kyle said almost in a whisper.

"It's complicated. Kyle, I don't want to hurt you. That was never my intention. Please believe me," Atlas said as she felt Kyle's body stiffening up and pushing her back. He gazed into her eyes and he could see tears starting to flow down her face. Reaching and tenderly caressing her face he brushed her tears away. He pulled her in close to his body once more; Atlas could feel his strength as his muscles cradled her. She was intoxicated by his aroma. He released her slowly and said, "It's alright as long as you are happy, Attie."

Atlas could not speak for several seconds when she managed to say, "I'm sorry, it is just complicated."

"No, Atlas, you are just young. Love is never complicated. It is simple and pure. Either you love me, or you love him. I get it. It's Eric you want, and I am not Eric," Kyle then reached for her, placing his hands on her face, pulling her close, and pressing his lips into hers. Atlas closed her eyes and could feel his soul entering her body, and the powerful gesture was almost too much for her to stand. Her legs became weak and she began to shiver. The passion of this one kiss was enough to send her into a tailspin. She could no longer think or argue. All she wanted was for this feeling never to end. Her arms braced his broad shoulders; holding onto him, she craved more. She felt as if she was floating in a cloud.

Suddenly, Kyle released his kiss, and she could see his eyes turning dark once more. She thought to herself, is this goodbye? Atlas began to panic, "No, Kyle, I don't want you to go. You are important to me."

"Here, take the keys, Atlas," Kyle said, handing her the keys, "I am going to hang out here for a bit."

"What are you serious? You are staying here because of Luna, aren't you? What the hell was I thinking?" she yelled at him as he turned his back and entered the facility.

"What is going on Atlas?" Arleen asked as she walked ahead of the rest of the group.

"Kyle, your team, Kyle, he is a jerk. He is staying here because he wants to catch up with Luna."

"Are you sure? He doesn't seem the type. I mean, if it was Eric, I would say yes, but not Kyle," Arleen said.

"I just spoke to Kyle. I guess you are driving us home. He seemed pretty quiet. Did something happen?" Hannah responded.

"No, nothing, Mom. Just do me a favor and stay out of it. Where is Dad? I really want to go home. I have things to do before we leave in the morning." Atlas said, entering the vehicle.

"Your father is just checking on Kyle. I thought we had asked you to do that. You don't seem to understand how hard it is for servicemen to come back home. They are constantly struggling with the war they left behind. Their scars never heal, and places like this can bring back a lot," Hannah scolded Atlas.

"Kyle is a big boy. Besides, he has Luna to care for him if he stumbles," Atlas said, starting the engine, "Mom, why don't you call him so we can go, please."

"I will not hurry your father because his spoiled, selfish daughter will not provide a serviceman a few moments of kindness. I swear, Atlas, you worry me. Now we will sit here and wait as long as it takes," Hannah responded.

"Yes, Ma'am, but" Atlas protested.

"But nothing," Hannah snapped back.

"Here he comes; you can relax now," Arleen said while Thomas made it into the car.

"How is Kyle?" Hannah inquired.

"He is quiet but in good hands," Thomas replied

"I bet," Atlas responded.

"What?" Thomas asked

"Never mind her. Thomas, are you sure he will be alright? You remember the first time you went into that facility," Hannah said.

"Kyle is good. He has a couple of buddies there. I told him to call me when he was ready to come home, and I would come back to get him. I guess a few of the fellows are going to catch up." He tapped Hannah's hand, saying, "Trust me, he is alright."

"I just wish Atlas would have stayed with him," Hannah said.

"No way!" Atlas responded, "He has Luna for that anyway."

"No, Hannah Atlas does not belong there. She cannot relate, and it would just make everyone uncomfortable. You know what I mean. Those guys need to tell war stories and relive their times together. It helps them come home," Thomas explained.

"How does Luna fit in the mix?" Atlas asked.

"She was an Army wife. It was as if she served right next to her spouse. She lived every terrifying moment, but worst, she did not know if he was coming home. It is brave to be a military spouse. They give up more than anyone else. They give up peace of mind," Thomas said, giving his wife a kiss on her cheek.

"I never knew, but what was the story with Luna's husband?" Arleen asked.

"Teddy never really came home. He served one too many tours without realizing the war had taken over his body, mind, and soul. During his time, he led several combat missions, and several of his men died. Teddy might as well have died with them. He came home and tried to make it, but life was never normal for him. Unfortunately for him, the battle in his mind won. One day, Luna woke up to a loud, familiar sound in her backyard. She walked out to find Teddy slumped over on the ground near her rose bushes. He was dressed in full formal military uniform with his service weapon next to his lifeless body. No note, no goodbye, just simply gone. " Thomas said.

"What killed himself? That is such a cowardly move," Atlas said, pulling into their driveway.

"Atlas, you don't know how much pain he must have been in to end it all that way," Hannah said.

"Please, Mom. Only a coward goes out that way. I would never even think about it," Atlas interjected.

"You know, dear, I hope you never do. But if you do I hope you remember your harsh words," Thomas said, getting out of the car and making it inside of his house.

"I don't know what the big deal is. If Luna was such a good wife she would have seen it coming," Atlas said to Hannah as she started walking to the house.

"No one sees that coming," Hannah said and took a deep breath. "Why don't you come in and makeup with your Dad."

"I have some errands to run. I don't think he wants to talk to me anyway." Atlas said, looking at the keys while Hannah walked away.

"Where the hell are you going? To hook up with Eric, I bet. Are you so selfish and inconsiderate that you are actually going to take Kyle's car to hook up with another man?" Arleen said, holding Atlas back from going into the SUV.

"He doesn't care. He is with Luna and he made it clear I can go with Eric," Atlas said, jumping into the driver's seat.

"Atlas, you are making a huge mistake. HUGE! You hear me, Huge! Kyle is a good man. He loves you, and you know it. If he didn't love you, he would not set you free to make this big mistake. But listen to me, Kyle is too much of a man to watch you or stay with you. He set you free; don't you dare think you can go back to him after you are done having fun with Eric," Arleen cautioned her.

"Let me go, Arleen; I know what I am doing," she said, slamming the door.

"I hope so. I really do hope so," Arleen said.

Atlas rolled down the window and said, "Tell Kyle I hope he and Luna had fun playing catch up!"

"You are so dumb, Atlas," Arleen yelled as Atlas drove away.

Chapter 18

Turbulence

Atlas drove back to her parent's house in disbelief that she had spent the night with Eric. He had reminded her of good times, and they needed so much to get straightened out. She mainly wanted to get Kyle out of her system. "Idiot!" she yelled at herself, turning the engine off and looking at the clock, "How the hell is it 4 AM? I am going to need to pack in a hurry. Crap! Kyle, he is going to kill me. Oh, who cares? He probably spent the night with Luna." She walked into the kitchen to find her mother sitting at the kitchen table.

"Where have you been?" Hannah said with a stern look on her face.

"I am not a child; I don't need to ask permission to be out," Atlas responded.

"I went to your room, and you were not there," Hannah started to say, but Atlas cut her off, "I am here now."

"We called you several times," Hannah explained.

"What is going on? Why are you being so weird?" Atlas said, reaching for a cup of coffee.

"Kyle is gone," Hannah said with tears in her eyes.

"What do you mean he is gone?" Atlas said, putting the cup down.

"He is no longer here. We looked for you, but as usual, you disappeared," Hannah began to scold her.

"Wait, Mom, what are you telling me? Kyle is gone. What does that mean?" panic began to take over Atlas' body. "Please, Mom, tell me," Atlas pleaded.

"He came home looking for you, but you were gone, and so was his car," Hannah explained.

"Wait all this because I took his car?" Atlas said.

"No, he received a call from his mother. I guess his father suffered a heart attack while they were skiing. They were not sure if he was going to make it. Kyle needed you, Atlas. Your father and Luna took him to the airport. Kyle wanted you to go with him, and here you are, walking into the house like a thief in the night," Hannah stated.

"Wait, what? His Dad? Luna? Kyle never speaks of his family. How long ago did they leave?" Atlas replied.

"About two hours ago. Your dad took him to Scott Air Force Base to hop on a military flight to Colorado. Thanks to Luna and her connections, he did not have to wait for military approval," Hannah said, getting up from the table.

"What about his car? I guess he wants me to drive to Wyoming or Colorado I guess. Did he say that?" Atlas asked.

"Unbelievable! Selfish! You are only thinking about you. Kyle might lose his father or could have lost him waiting on you," Hannah said, shaking her head. "No Kyle is a very dissent man who worries about you even if you don't. He told me he had purchased an open plane ticket. It is at the Delta boarding desk waiting for you at Lambert International Airport. Kyle asked your dad to leave the car here, and he will arrange for it to be shipped sometime later. So you have a way to get back to Wyoming or Colorado, or anywhere you want to go; it is an open ticket. You just need to pick the destination," Hannah started going up the stairs.

"Mom, what do I do?" Atlas asked.

"Clean up your mess," Hannah said as she took a step. "I love you, dear, and I will always love you, but that does not stop me from feeling disappointed in your actions. I beg you to take your time before you book your flight," Hannah said, taking two steps.

"Mom, do you know if Luna left with Kyle to see his father?" Atlas asked.

Hannah took a deep breath before saying, "God, I hope so." She then continued up the stairs and went into her bedroom.

Atlas took one more drink of her coffee as her mind began to wonder if Kyle was with Luna. Was she comforting him during their fight in Colorado? "Kyle comes from money," she said out loud. I am sure his mom would prefer a woman like Luna over her. What was I thinking? Kyle is with Luna, and I am with Eric, and the rest is nothing.

Slamming the cup into the sink and shattering it she imagined that a sign that her daydreams of being with Kyle were gone. Atlas cleaned up the shards and threw them into the trash. She ran upstairs and began to pack quickly. Her plan was to make it to the airport before her father returned. She did not need him to confirm her worst fear that Kyle was with Luna. At this moment she simply knew in her heart Kyle had left without her.

Atlas tapped on her mother's door to say goodbye but no one answered the door. Making her way downstairs, she ran into Arleen, who was walking in through the back door. "Oh, so you finally made it home, and once more, you are fleeing without saying goodbye."

"Arleen, I am not in the mood. I called an Uber. I'm heading to the airport," Atlas responded.

"You finally came to your senses. Are you going to meet up with Kyle in Colorado? Mom told me what happened," Arleen said with a half-smile. "That is really nice of you to go be by his side."

"No, I haven't decided what I am going to do yet. I figured I would go to the airport and make a decision there," Atlas said, texting for her ride.

"I can take you if you like," Arleen said kindly.

"No, I am good. I don't want you to talk me into what you want me to do," Atlas snapped back

"Atlas! I would not do that. You need to make that decision. After all, it is your life, and you will be the one to live with the consequences of your choices," Arleen responded.

"Sorry, I guess I am a bit on edge. But I would rather be alone for a bit. I need to clear my head. Honestly I am scared to ask your opinion. I just need to do this by myself. You are right. It is all on me, and I will live with my decision," Atlas responded.

"Alright, do you want me to say anything to the family?" Arleen asked, pouring herself a cup of coffee.

"No, I will call them later," she responded, looking at her cell phone.

"I can sit with you and wait for your ride if you like," Arleen said, pulling out the chair away from the kitchen table.

"That would be nice, Arleen, but my ride's here. I promise to call and let you know how things go OK." Atlas said, grabbing her gear and walking outside. She hopped in the backseat and leaned back. While making their way to the airport, her mind once again began to wonder about Kyle. She held back her tears as long as she could. However, as they made their way to the terminal, Atlas could feel tears flowing down her face.

"Lady, are you alright?" the driver asked.

"Yes, thank you. Life is just complicated, you know?" Atlas responded, trying to wipe her tears away.

"Life is not complicated; it's those who make it so. Surround yourself with good people with no complications. Bad folks, on the other hand, will kill you with challenges. We are here, which airline?" the driver asked.

"A Delta, I think," Atlas hesitated to respond.

"Delta, and what is your destination?" the driver asked, pulling to the drop-off section.

Atlas opened the door quickly and jumped out without answering him. She turned to thank him, but the car was clearing the drop zone and speeding away.

She walked through the terminal in a daze, making it to the customer service desk without a decision in mind.

"May I help you?" the receptionist asked.

"I think I am Atlas Martin. I believe you are holding a ticket for me?" she said.

"Yes, Ma'am, you must be a pretty special lady," the receptionist stated.

"Why? Whatever do you mean?" Atlas was puzzled at the comment.

"These types of tickets are really expensive. We have to accommodate you anywhere you would like to go, so the airline places a high dollar hold on the account until the destination is settled. This is like what you would call a golden ticket to any of Delta's destinations worldwide. So where are you headed?" she asked with a huge smile.

"Am not sure. Can you please check when the next flight to Aspen, Colorado, is?" Atlas asked.

"Absolutely, Aspen is beautiful this time of year. Are you going skiing perhaps?" she said while typing rapidly on her keyboard.

Atlas began receiving text messages and her cell phone was alerting non-stop.

"Miss, the next flight to Aspen is in four hours. Would you like me to make a reservation for you?"

"Yes, please," she said, looking at the messages; then she looked up and said, "Wait, can you check for Cheyenne, Wyoming? When is that flight?"

"Ma'am there is one in two hours to Cheyenne and another one in five hours. But I can always get you a connection through Aspen if you would like?" she replied.

"Yes, can you do that flight? How long will I be in Aspen for the layover?" Atlas asked again, looking at her cell phone.

"Since you have an open ticket, it will be up to you. I will tentatively book you a connection flight with a three-hour layover, but you will need to confirm it. You can always change it to another time. Will that work for you, Miss?"

Atlas was distracted by her cell phone and simply nodded yes in agreement. Then, taking her tickets and walked through the lobby. She took the escalator upstairs and was just heading to security when her cell phone rang.

"Hello," she said, stopping in her tracks, "Eric, I am at the airport, and I am getting ready to go through security. What do you mean you are here? Why? Where are you?" Atlas demanded to know. Turning around, she spotted him walking towards her.

"Well, I guess you got your wish. You made me chase you all the way here," Eric stated.

"You were clear this morning we are better apart than together isn't that what you said," Atlas stated.

"No, I said I didn't say that. I merely said it did not look like we were ready for anything serious. I thought you wanted to establish yourself in Utah," he said, taking her bag and rolling it towards him, "why don't we grab something to drink and talk about it?"

"Eric, I am heading out in a bit. I really don't think we have time for this. Besides, I have somewhere to be." Atlas responded.

"Seriously, I think you have time for one drink. You always say I never want to talk, and now that I make an effort, this is how you respond," Eric insisted

"Alright, but I just want a coffee, nothing more," she said, walking toward the cafe.

"Come on, let's sit at the bar. I will have a beer, and she will have water," he told the bartender.

"Look, first of all, I am heading to Wyoming, not Utah. Secondly, I want coffee, not water. I so wish you would listen when I speak," she said, pointing to the coffee pot to the bartender.

"Well, I promise to do better once we get married. Alright?" Eric said with a deviant smile.

"We are not getting married. You made that very clear that my family is blue-collar and yours, well, one of the wealthiest in Saint Louis. Remember? That was your argument before I left for Wyoming, ' Atlas said, looking at her ticket.

"Old news, Babe, that was like our last fight before you dropped off the face of the earth and decided to relocate to Montana," Eric said, taking a long drink of his beer.

"Wyoming!" she responded, standing up.

"Sit down; I was just playing with you. You are always so dramatic. It doesn't matter where you went. You are here now. So once you get back to Wyoming, you can finish there, and I will make my plans to settle there," Eric said, asking for another beer.

"Eric, you have not asked me to marry you. You are just planning all this without my say, so…" she said, grabbing her bag.

"Here, take this as a promise ring," Eric said, placing the ring in her hand.

"This is my grandmother's ring. I thought I lost it. Why do you have it?" Atlas said, holding it in the palm of her hand.

"You left it at my place when you left a few months ago. I figure you wanted me to have it. Then I thought you were just looking for an excuse to come back to me that is why you left it behind. Finally, it hit me: you wanted me to ask you to marry you. So here we are. I haven't spoken to my parents yet but after we will make it official. I will have my mother start looking for venues and whatever else is needed for the wedding here once you are done with the academy. Your parents will not have to stress about the expenses. Then I can get a job up there in Wyoming while you work as a Cop. I am a great salesman. I can score a job anywhere," Eric said, finishing his beer.

"Eric, I am not sure about any of this. I am not done with the academy. I am living in a place where I work for room and board. It is complicated," she started to answer when he got up and walked away. She started to follow him when she noticed he had not paid for the drinks, "Eric Eric!" she called out, but he simply just waved her goodbye as he walked away. Atlas slammed money on the counter and headed to security to get to the departure terminal.

Now, her head was seriously spinning, and confusion took over. She leaned on the rail while moving through the airport. Finding her flight, Atlas wondered what was waiting for her in Aspen. It took only a few seconds for her to find her seat; Atlas stared out the window, trying hard to hold her tears in when the flight attendant came over to her. Tapping her on the shoulder, "Excuse me, Miss, you are not in the right seat?"

She wiped her tears away, "I am so sorry. I thought this was my assigned seat. Let me just get my bag, and I will move."

"No problem, Miss," the attendant said, taking her bag from her hands.

"See, this is my seat C3?" Atlas said, holding up her ticket.

"Sorry, Miss, this section is 2 C3. Please follow me as you are in First Class 1C3. Here you are; this is your seat. First

Class is pretty empty, but I will make sure someone takes good care of you during our trip. Would you like something to drink?"

"Sir, I am confused. Are you sure this is my seat?" Atlas said, looking around.

"Yes, Miss, this is your seat. Are you alright?" he asked.

"You must think I am silly, but I have never been in First Class. I am in a bit of a shock. The ticket was a gift, and I did not expect all this," she responded.

"Well, Miss, enjoy it; someone must think a lot of you. I am sure they would want you to enjoy the best. Since this is your first trip in First Class, I will personally ensure you are well taken care of," he said with a kind smile.

Atlas settled in as the attendants pampered her all the way to Aspen. Throughout the flight, she felt torn between her feelings for Eric and the possibilities with Kyle. She was just trying to figure it all out when she heard the pilot announcing their descent. Alright, pull it together, she told herself. I am here to check on Kyle because, after all, we are friends. As soon as we land, I will contact my dad. He should know where they are. OK, that is the plan.

Chapter 19

Murky

Planning at the airport, Atlas managed to figure out a destination and made her way to the hospital. She told herself this was just a friend checking on a friend. No matter what was happening between them, she needed to make sure Kyle was alright. Walking through the main entrance of the hospital, she noticed that the lobby was particularly empty. This must be a very exclusive private hospital, she thought. Atlas explained to the receptionist that she was a friend of the Noyes family who needed to provide them with some important information and would not be visiting the patient. Under that rouge, the staff was extremely helpful in directing her to the Cardiac Unit.

Taking a few deep breaths, she got into the elevator and made her way to the cardiac waiting area. Standing just outside the small room with dim lighting, Atlas could see through the glass walls one person sitting alongside the wall. It was clear it was Kyle holding his head down, bent over, looking overwhelmed and defeated. She put on her best fake smile and walked in. He did not move or acknowledge her entrance. Atlas sat next to him and grabbed his hand, which he had buried in his face.

"Hi," she whispered.

"Attie? He responded.

"How is your Dad?" she asked.

"He will be alright. They took him to surgery, and my mother decided to take my brother back to the resort. They were exhausted, and there was no need for them to wait here," Kyle responded.

"That is good news, isn't it?" Atlas said.

"Yeah, he is very lucky," he said, caressing her hand.

"How are you? Did you make up with your family? I mean, are you guys good?" she asked, trying not to be too pushy.

Kyle looked up at her and gazed into her eyes. "We were never bad, Attie, and we are just different. My family is not like yours, but that does not mean we don't love one another. We simply love differently."

"Oh, I am sorry. I guess I misunderstood what you were telling me," she said, pulling her hand away.

"Attie, why are you here?" Kyle asked.

"Because you are my friend, and we are friends, right?" she replied, standing.

He stood behind her, grabbing her shoulders and leaning into her to whisper in her ear, "Yes, we will always be friends, but why are you here?"

She turned and found herself once more wrapped in Kyle's arms, and she could feel his energy transferring into her body. His broad shoulders, muscular chest, and piercing eyes made her melt into him. Closing her eyes, she stepped in for a passionate kiss. Atlas wanted his lips on hers. As they got closer, Kyle's presence became all-consuming. Atlas' body shivered. Her legs failed her once more, and she held on to him. He went over, and she could feel his lips lingering over hers. Atlas was prepared for his kiss, but suddenly, she felt him tense up and pull himself away.

Shaking her head, she asked, "What's wrong?"

Grabbing her left hand and exposing the promise ring she is sporting, "I see you and Eric have moved forward into a commitment. I am sorry this time. I am the one who misunderstood," he said, taking a step back.

"No, you don't understand. All this is just a big mess," she started to explain, trying to get closer to him.

"You are right, and we are just friends. I need to come to terms with that. I hope you and Eric are very happy together," Kyle replied.

"What?' she demanded to know, "you are not going to give me a chance to explain myself."

"No need. I trust in actions, not words. It is clear that you and Eric have made promises to one another. And although it might be difficult, I will support you as your friend." he took a deep breath, "I appreciate that you came to be with me. I do."

Atlas did not know how to respond. She stared at her grandmother's ring, trying to find the right words. She could feel the tears filling up in her eyes; this was not how she had pictured this moment. She needed to clear the air once and for all. Kyle made his way to the window, and she could see the reflection of his deep gaze staring at nothing. Atlas took two steps towards him when the door flung open,

"All I could get was black coffee and a pastry that has seen better days," Luna said, walking to the room and carrying a small paper tray with two cups of hot coffee.

"Luna! I did not know you were here." Atlas replied, looking at her and then Kyle, who had turned around.

"My love, I did not want Kyle to be by himself. I did not know you were coming. Are you hungry? I was going to send for some proper food. Would you like me to order you something?" Luna asked, placing the tray on the table.

"No, I will not be staying long. I just came over because I had a layover. I wanted to ensure Kyle was alright," she said, trying not to lose control.

"Of course, my love, I would not let him be alone in moments like this. You need to be surrounded by people who love you or are friends, right?" Luna said, walking to the door, "I will let you two catch up for a bit. Excuse me, I will give your mother a call and see if she is on her way back, "Luna walked halfway out the door, stopped, and turned, "I guess congratulations are in order, Atlas. Eric's mom told me the news, but this is not the time for that conversation. See you all in a jiffy," she said walking out.

"I am an idiot! Here I am trying to clarify myself, and you have Luna here at your beck and call," Atlas scolded Kyle.

"First of all, Attie, I did not ask you or Luna to come here. I am not with Luna, and she is not at my beck and call. Luna has her own motives for being here," Kyle began to explain but was quickly cut off.

"I bet she has her own motives, and it all involves you," Atlas responded.

"Unreal! Attie, you cannot possibly be jealous," he responded.

"Stop calling me Attie. You know it drives me insane," Atlas said furiously.

"You don't think the idea of you and Eric drives me crazy. I am not made of stone, Attie," Kyle said, walking closer to her.

"Well, this is rich. Here I think you were all alone," she started to walk to the door, "And you are in the warm, loving arms of your beautiful Luna. I better head out. I really don't want to be in your way," Atlas responded.

"Stop, Attie! Just stop being so immature. I am not interested in Luna, and she is not my type," Kyle said, walking towards Atlas. He stood behind her, "You are my type, but you know that. What do you want me to do? You are with Eric, but do you love him?"

"Being with Eric is all that I have ever thought of? I wanted to marry him from the first time we met," she replied.

He spun her around. "But do you love him?" Kyle insisted.

"He is good for me, and I love being with him. We don't argue. He makes a decision, and I kinda go with it," Atlas began to explain.

"It seems to me Eric is not making you worth the effort. You deserve someone who makes you feel like you are worth the effort," Kyle said, reaching for her. "You are worth my effort. Tell me, Attie if you don't love him I will fight for you, but I need you to tell me."

"Kyle I don't know what to say?" Atlas turned towards him.

"Just remember, if you hesitate, don't choose me," Kyle said, realizing his grasp and gently laying his hands on her shoulders.

"My love, you are still here. Perfect, I just ordered some food. Kyle Darling, I just spoke to your mother. She will be returning shortly," Luna said, walking into the room, grabbing a hold of Kyle's arm, and brushing his hair with her caressing hand. "My love, you look exhausted. As soon as we get word from your surgeon about your father, we should go back to the hotel."

"Thank you, Luna. I will not be joining you two. I am sure Kyle is in good hands with you," Atlas said, pushing her way out.

"Attie!" Kyle yelled out but could not move because Luna was holding on to him. Breaking free, he made it in time to catch Atlas inside the elevator. "Attie!" he yelled once more.

"Stop calling me Attie!" she managed to say before the doors closed.

"Kyle," Luna came running to him with the cell phone, "it's the surgeon."

Atlas walked out of the hospital, made her way to the corner, and called for the nearest Uber. "Idiot, that is what I am an idiot. I just need to focus on the academy and, hell, my wedding. If Eric's mom wants to pay for it, she can do so. I am done playing mind games. No hesitation at all. This ends with Kyle today. He is with Luna, and then I am with Eric; that's it."

Atlas got to the airport and made her way to her flight. She kept turning back to see if Kyle had followed her, but there was no sign of him. Settling into her First Class seat, Atlas allowed all her emotions to take over. The section was practically empty, and no one noticed she was crying. Atlas felt her heart breaking. She could not understand why or how she had fallen in love with Kyle. "Kyle," she whispered, was unattainable for her now. He had a lover, and it was Luna and not her. How could she compete with such a beautiful, talented, and compassionate woman?

Atlas shoved her face into the airplane pillow to hide her feelings. "I have to get him out of my system," she closed her eyes. She was exhausted from the output of emotions and fell fast asleep.

Atlas found herself laying on a large bed, naked covered by a silk blanket. Sitting up, she could see the large room with a beautiful balcony overlooking the mountains. The scenery was picturesque, with snow-covered peaks and burnt orange sky as the sun was barely making its first appearance. The clouds in the sky looked like shooting stars burning away with the sun's rays. It was simply breathtaking losing herself in the moment Atlas felt happy, content, and, most of all safe.

"Good Morning," he said.

"Hi," Atlas replied, turning away from the window and finding Kyle standing in the doorway. He was wearing simply long jogging pants and his chest was exposed. The natural light in the room accentuated the contours of his physique, showcasing a muscular, well-shaped man standing confidently in front of her. Kyle's bare chest revealed his defined pecs and chiseled abs. Atlas examined his broad shoulders tapering down to strong arms, veins subtlety tracing their definition. She was lost looking at his body and began aching for him.

Tapping lightly on the bed, Atlas called for him to come near her. Her back began to arch as she waited anxiously with each step Kyle moved forward. Soon, there he was with that piercing gaze and warm smile, melting her into his loving arms.

"Excuse me, Miss," a female voice said to Atlas, "Miss you need to wake up. We landed, and it's time for you to board the plane."

Atlas woke up to find herself all alone in the plane," I'm sorry, I must have fallen asleep."

"Must have been a great dream. I hated to wake you up," the flight attendant stated.

"Yes, it was a great dream, but sadly, it was just a dream," Atlas said, gathering her items.

"Well, I hope you get along with Kyle. Right, that was the name you called out," she said.

"Sadly, no, it was just part of the dream. Now, it's time for me to face reality. Thank you for everything," Atlas said, walking out of the plane. She turned around once more and told herself, "Yeah, that was a hell of a dream. Goodbye, Kyle I hope you and Luna are very happy," taking a deep breath, "enough with the sentimental crap," she scolded herself and made her way back to the ranch. After a long day of travel and an emotional roller coaster Atlas thought best to rest up and make all the necessary explanations to Ellie and Ben.

Atlas woke up bright and early to get to the horses. Her plan was to avoid Kyle at all costs. Walking into the barn she found Ben already cleaning the stalls, and washing the horses.

"Good Morning, my child. How was your trip back home?" Ben asked in between tasks.

"It was very revealing," she said, standing next to him and taking over brushing the horses. "How was your vacation?"

"Ah, it was nice, but you seem sad. Did something happen while you were away?" Ben asked.

"Nothing. Well, nothing of importance," she replied, trying to get the horse to stand still.

"Something of importance took place. Your energy is not centered. The horses are feeling your sadness my child," Ben insisted, taking the lead of the horse and walking it away from Atlas.

"Sorry, I guess I am a bit off. Maybe I am just tired from the travel," she said, walking away from the horses," Did you hear from Kyle? How is his dad doing?"

"He spoke to Rob a few hours ago. I believe his father is stable enough and on his way to a full recovery. Kyle should be joining us in a day or so. Is that what is worrying you?" Ben asked. Atlas placed her hand on the door frame to steady herself, and Ben noticed the ring on her finger. "Oh, I see you made a decision about your future. Are you having second thoughts?"

Atlas was shocked at his directness and turned to look at him in amazement, "No, why are you asking me that?"

"You don't seem happy wearing that ring. It seems more like a heavy chain than a promise," he said, turning away and walking the horse out to the corral.

"I am not feeling well. I better not be near the horses today. I can do something else if that is alright," she said.

"No, you need to clear that heavy burden you are carrying. Why don't you concentrate on that today? Come back tomorrow if you feel free," Ben said, jumping on the horse and riding away.

Atlas rolled her eyes at his words and made her way to the main house.

"Welcome back, Atlas, how was your visit? Did your mom miss you and spoil you?" Ellie asked with enthusiasm.

"It was nice. Ben said for me not to work in the barn today. I am not sure what you need me to do before the academy starts," Atlas replied.

"Relax, why don't you just sit and have a cup of coffee with me? We can head to the academy together in a bit," Ellie suggested as she watched Atlas pour herself a cup of coffee. "Something you want to share with me?"

"No, not really. I was just worried about Kyle. I mean his dad," she said, sipping her coffee.

"I see," Ellie said," I understand now how that trip really went."

"What do you mean?" Atlas said, sitting down.

"Atlas, you got engaged, and it doesn't seem to be Kyle. What is going on?" Ellie asked, reaching over and placing her hand over Atlas' ring.

"This," she said, waving her hand, "this is nothing. It is just my grandmother's ring."

"No, there is a lot more to that story, and you know it. You would not be wearing it on that finger if it was just a family heirloom," Ellie started looking at her with contempt.

"You are right. Eric, my ex-boyfriend. I mean, I guess my boyfriend found my grandmother's ring. The rest got complicated, and it is just a mess," Atlas said with tears in her eyes.

"It all makes sense now. Why don't you tell me what happened, and I can try to help you figure it all out if you would like?" Ellie suggested.

"Thank you. I just need some time to wrap my head around it all. Maybe then we can talk. Right now, I think it would be best to concentrate on the last few weeks of the academy. Then the state exam, and we still need to figure out where to work," Atlas stated with some determination.

"You are right. There is a lot we need to figure out. I just want you to know you can always count on me," Ellie stated, taking a deep breath and looking at the table.

"What is it? There is something else, right? Is it Kyle? Did something happen?" Atlas could feel panic taking over.

"I need to tell you that Kyle is not coming back to the ranch or to the academy with us," Ellie started to say

"What?" Atlas said, slamming her cup on the table.

"Kyle spoke to Rob this morning. His father is stable and will be alright. It is not that," Ellie said,

"Then what is it? He decided to stay with Luna and just drop everything. He is a jerk. I thought we were friends. I never thought he would be such a coward," Atlas said, standing up and taking her cup to sink.

"Atlas, Kyle got fast-tracked. He is done with the academy. From what I understand, he tried to stay and graduate with us, but Spinelli did not allow it. Did you not see him on the phone trying to work it out with Spinelli? God, he pushed as much as he could to stay with us. Mainly for you. Kyle didn't want you to struggle with the academy or the state exam. Who the hell is Luna? Ellie asked.

"What do you mean he got fast-tracked?" Atlas asked as she looked out the window.

"He got sponsored by Cheyenne, and they want him to start right away. Kyle is taking the state exam tomorrow in Cheyenne and hitting the streets immediately. He is the only one that got taken by that department or fast-tracked. Kyle has very special skills that they want and need. So I am sorry to say we will not see much of him for a while." Ellie said, looking at the clock, "grab your gear. We don't want to be late on our first day back." Atlas felt numb but followed Ellis's direction, and the two women headed to the academy.

Chapter 20

Alpha

Walking into the academy, Atlas felt like her world had changed over a few hours. The place did not have the same energy, and she felt a bit lost without Kyle. It was not as if they were attached at the hip, but it was rather comforting to know he was there and always had her back.

"Welcome back, Recruit Martin. I will need you to drop off your gear and meet me in my office in five minutes," Spinelli barked at her.

"Yes, Sir," Atlas said, dropping off her gear and running into the locker room to ensure her uniform was straight. A few seconds later, Atlas found herself knocking on his door,

"Enter," Spinelli yelled out.

"Sir, Recruit Martin reporting as requested," she said.

"Relax, Martin, I need to speak to you about your improvement here at the academy. You have demonstrated that you have a heart and a passion for this line of work. Unlike most of the recruits here, you do not have military experience, and yet you have been able to adapt to this paramilitary environment. I would have guessed by now you would have packed your bags and gone back home to work at the nearest Waffle House. However, you have proven me wrong," Spinelli said with no emotion in his voice.

"Thank you, sir, I think," she responded without hesitation. Then, he gave her the best fake smile as he got closer to her.

"Look, Martin, the jury is still out on you. I know you relied on Recruit Noyes to inspire you. I watched you guys training, studying, and spending every second together. He dedicated a lot of his time and effort to get you through these last few months. This was the reason I pushed so hard to get him fast-tracked." Spinelli continued as Atlas's effect on her face changed, and she could feel her blood starting to boil, but she did not respond.

"Noyes is a gifted individual, natural at anything he does. You, on the other hand, have to work hard at your craft. Don't get me wrong, I can see your drive and determination. I fear that you are not ready to see it. It's not that I need to provide you with any explanations, but I want you to know I separated you two for your sake. You young lady need to find your fire. Noyes showed you have it, and now it is up to you to use it."

"Yes, Sir, I understand," Atlas replied.

"Alright, then, you are now in charge of the Noyes' group. I expect you to inspire them, lead them, and teach them. No one in your group fails because if they do, you will fail as well. Do I make myself clear?" Spinelli shouted at her once more.

"Yes, Sir," Atlas replied, trying not to let her fear show. Her mind began to wonder if she was ready for this responsibility. Could she get the group into shape? How? Why her?

"Recruit Martin, I need you to focus and get out of your head. I gave you this responsibility because soon you will be making life-and-death decisions. Split-second decisions that require you to rely solely on your training. You will have to enter a room and be the calm voice in the chaos. If you are not up to the challenge of leading a group in a controlled environment, then what makes you think you can patrol my streets?" Spinelli asked once again, walking up to her face.

"Sir, I appreciate the confidence you have in me. It will be my honor to lead the group. Thank you for the opportunity," she mustered the strength to reply, looking Spinelli straight in the eyes.

"Alright then, you are dismissed. Get the Hell out of my office and make sure your group is ready for PT. We will run for the next hour," he shouted again, walking to his desk.

"Yes, Sir," she said, turning to the door.

"Oh, Martin, I guess congratulations are in order as well," he said.

"Sir?" she replied

"I see you are sporting an engagement ring. You went home single and came back engaged?" he asked, making his way to the back of his desk and sitting down.

"No, Sir," she started to answer but held back and continued, "It's a promise ring. Nothing definite yet."

"Alright, but here's a piece of advice, Martin: this is not the time or place for big changes in your life. You need to concentrate on completing this task ahead of time and getting certified. I have seen several recruits, both men and women, who become distracted with planning their futures without even securing their present. I would hate to see all your hard work go to waste because you are planning a wedding and starting a family," Spinelli said without missing a beat.

"Thank you, Sir. I will keep that in mind," she replied, opening the office door.

"One more thing, Martin, you and Stevens have been selected to stay here in this area. Congratulations, not everyone has been picked up. You should be happy at this news," he said, looking down and shuffling papers.

"Yes, Sir," she said with a huge smile.

"Once you settle into your department, if you are successful in my training and the state examination, both you and Stevens will be allowed to return to the academy to help train. I believe the recruits can learn from shared experiences. You are dismissed," he said nonchalantly.

Atlas walked out of the office and into the courtyard as a feeling of joy took over her body. She was ecstatic at the news. Atlas was dying to tell Kyle all about her news. She ran to the track to look for him when sadness took over as she realized he was no longer there. Looking at the track and the picnic area, she recalled all the hours they had spent together. If not for him believing in her, she would have never made it through these past months. Atlas thought about calling him, but she then told herself, "Kyle is training, and I better not distract him. Spinelli is right when he says we need to stay clear and focused."

Turning around and walking back into the gym, she found herself among her group. All the eager smiles of her classmates recanting their home and vacation adventures.

"Alright, recruits," Atlas announced with a stern tone, "Director Spinelli wanted me to share that Recruit Noyes was selected to be fast track and he is now training in Cheyenne. I was selected to be the team leader. We will continue with the same training regimen that Noyes showed us. His discipline and work ethic have gotten us through so far, and I don't think there is anything we need to change."

"Noyes was a fast track," Adams commented, "good for him. Kyle is a good guy. I would walk through a door with him any day."

"Great! We are good, then. Let's get into our PT clothes and show the rest of the recruits we are the best. No man left behind, remember? We are a team, as Spinelli reminds us all of the time. He will make us run for the next hour. Do you all know what that means?" she stated.

"Two hours," Adams replied.

"Yep, so grab your water, hydrate, and look out for one another. Adams, you will set our pace for today. Keep steady; we have all been out this week, and I am sure no one thought of working out. Slow but steady. You guys realize Spinelli is a beast, and we will go through the obstacle course as well. No need to panic. Go over the techniques in your head, visualize each part, and go for it. We have survived it in the past. We will do it again today," Atlas encouraged her group to take the lead. "See you in three minutes."

Atlas entered the locker room to find Ellie and Pricilla changing into their PT gear.

"Hey, what did Spinelli want with you?" Ellie asked as she continued to change.

"Nothing," Atlas said, biting her lower lip.

"Don't lie to me. What did he want?" Ellie insisted.

"We have been sponsored and are staying right here. The sheriff's department picked us up officially," she said with a huge smile.

"That is such good news. I did not want to commute to another part of the state. I mean we could but I like our home," Ellie said with a huge smile.

"And Director Spinelli gave me the lead in my group," Atlas said, changing out of her uniform.

"Oh, Atlas, that is amazing. You will be a great leader for the guys. I am so proud of you," Ellie said, hugging her.

"Did you get engaged? "Pricilla asked, grabbing Atlas' hand.

"No, it's just a promise ring, that is all," she said, pulling away from Ellie and turning her back.

"Oh wow, I can appreciate the hesitation. I mean, I would have thought that if Kyle had proposed, he would have given you at least a better-looking ring. That looks like it came out of a claw machine at Chuck E Cheese," Pricilla said, half laughing.

"For your information, it is my grandmother's ring. And I am not with Kyle. He has nothing to do with this at all," Atlas replied, slamming her locker door closed.

"Oh! Well, to me, he is a bit of a nice piece of arm candy. I heard his family is loaded, and I just thought, what a cheap ass. But I guess you know other cheap asses," Pricilla said, starting to walk out.

"Not that it is any of your business, but Eric Noles comes from a very prestigious and affluent family in Saint Louis. He has a lot of class and money to go along with it," Atlas responded with indignation.

"Noles, Noles, wait, isn't his father Donald Noles co-owner of the Saint Louis hockey team? I read about him in Forbes Magazine. He is one of the richest men in the Midwest, and you say you are dating his son, Eric? No way!" Pricilla teased.

"Yes, as a matter of fact, he is planning our wedding, but you know, Pricilla, I don't have the time to discuss this right now. We need to be at the track immediately, and you need to join your teams," Atlas said walking tall out of the locker room.

Ellie waited for Pricilla to pass them, grabbed Atlas by the arm, and said, "You and I need to have a serious discussion tonight."

Atlas nodded in agreement and walked to her group. The day was grueling with all the physical challenges Spinelli had put into play. Between the running and jumping jacks, Atlas tried to stay present; however, during every break, they took her mind back to Kyle. She wondered if he was all alright and if he missed her. By the end of the day, Atlas felt accomplished; none of her teammates missed the mark. She wanted to call or text Kyle, yet her pride got in the way. Everything in her told her to call, but then she thought of Luna. She was no competition next to Luna, and it was best if she tried to forget him.

Walking to the parking lot, Atlas did not feel the conversation she was about to have with Ellie. Things needed to be said, but she simply was not in the mood for another argument.

"Ready?" Ellie asked.

"Yep," Atlas said quickly, taking her cell phone out.

"Listen, Atlas, I am not your mom or sister, but we are friends. I believe that gives a bit of a leg to tell you what I am about to tell you," Ellie stated.

"I am sure as soon as we graduate, I will be able to move out. If you want me to go earlier, I guess I can ask one of the guys if I can crash with them," Atlas said.

"No, of course not. Atlas, you are always welcome to stay with us. You are family, and that cabin will always be available to you. That is not what we need to talk about, "Ellie said.

"It has been a very long day, and I just thought since Kyle is gone, you would want me to move out. I can, but just not today or tomorrow," Atlas began to explain.

"No, silly, you are not going anywhere. Not until you are ready to move out, alright? Please put that out of your mind. I do want to speak to you about this." Ellie said, grabbing her hand.

"Oh, you mean my grandmother's ring?" Atlas said.

"Well, if it's just your grandmother's ring, why are you wearing it on this finger?" Ellie asked.

"I thought I had lost it but it appears that Eric had it. We had been together just before I came to the academy. We were pretty hot and heavy for about six months. No, maybe more like three or four. It's not important. We were inseparable and started making plans." Atlas explained.

"Ok," Ellie said in amazement.

"Yes, plans about our future. Eric would tell me things like when we are married, we will live in Creve Coeur, which is a very exclusive area in Saint Louis. Then he would say Mom will get you with ladies at the country club. Or don't worry about money, my family is loaded. So I started believing that is where we were heading, "Atlas explained.

"So what happened?" Ellie replied as they continued to drive to the ranch.

"I was spending the night when his mother called Eric, and he told her he was not dating anyone seriously. When I confronted him, Eric told me it was all pillow talk. We were not that serious besides my family, who are working-class folks and not high society," Atlas said.

"Wow!" Ellie said.

"Yep, I stormed out. I was furious I had made a fool of myself at work telling everyone I was getting married to Eric," Atlas said, looking out the window.

"You didn't?" Ellie said with a stern look.

"I did worst of all, and he told all our mutual friends. I pursued him. He had me under his spell, and I would do anything he asked. Eric made me sound easy and cheap," Atlas explained.

"So what did you do?" Ellie asked.

"I went for a drive. I blasted the music and drove west. A few miles out of the city, I saw the announcement for law enforcement officers in Wyoming. I thought it was the answer to my prayers. I quit my job, emptied my savings account, packed and headed here," Atlas said.

"So you were running away?" Ellie asked.

"I guess, but then somehow I found myself. You know what I mean. I found my voice and my strength. I thought I could go back home and face everything with this new me," Atlas continued.

"Alright?" Ellie said as they were pulling into the ranch.

"Home was great. Kyle was there, and he centered me, I guess. Things started moving so fast with him. He is so different. Kyle is decisive, confident, and kind. He gets me so angry, too, but it doesn't last. We argued, and the next day, we got along like nothing," Atlas said, looking around and noticing the horses prancing around the corral.

"You miss Kyle?" Ellie asked.

"Yes, he gets me, you know what I mean. I know I am repeating myself, but somethings are worth repeating. When we were in St Louis, things got complicated. Well, no even before, but things got real at home. I bumped into Eric, and I thought I would naturally get back with him, but not really," Atlas responded.

"Ha," Ellie said as they parked by the barn.

"I was out clubbing, and Eric wanted me to ditch my friends, but I didn't. Man, I felt so in control that day. At that moment, I was on top of the world," Atlas said, getting out of the car.

"Kyle was with you that night, right?" Ellie asked, catching up to Atlas, who had made her way to the corral and was watching the horses running around.

"Yes, he was inside the bar, and I didn't want him to think badly of me. I don't know why, but it was important. So I sent Eric packing," Atlas said, looking forward.

"What happened? Ellie asked, standing next to Atlas.

"Luna Le Crowe happened," Atlas said, turning around and leaning on the wooden rail.

"Who?" Ellie asked, looking at Atlas

"A drop-dead gorgeous widow who was friends with Kyle. He was smitten with her, and I lost my shit. He was telling me how he had feelings for me, but then he was worried about how he looked in front of her. Clearly, she had him under a spell," Atlas replied, turning her face away from Ellie.

"Are you sure she is with Kyle?" Ellie asked, gazing straight at Atlas' eyes.

"Yes, she made it abundantly clear they are together. I saw them together in Aspen when Kyle's dad had a heart attack," Atlas stated.

"OK," Ellie acknowledged.

"Luna had the nerve to say Kyle would be her date for the annual fundraiser gala," Atlas said, turning her back to Ellie so she would not see the tears in her eyes.

"A gala?" Ellie asked, trying not to make Atlas uncomfortable.

"That is not important. I took a good look at myself and realized I had no chance with Kyle. Luna is all that and more. I was beside myself, and I did what I always did. I ran. I ran right into Eric's grasp. Here I am trying to clear up this mess," Atlas explained.

"What are you going to do?" Ellie said lightly, placing her hand on Atlas' arm.

"I don't know," Atlas responded.

"Well, what is the hurry? Why don't you slow yourself down? Take your time before walking down the aisle," Ellie suggested.

"I am going back home for Christmas and tell Eric we need to slow down. Maybe a long engagement to see how things go," Atlas said, taking a deep breath.

"That sounds like a good plan," Ellie said, trying to comfort her a bit.

"Yeah, Spinelli told me I needed to focus on the academy and my career," Atlas said, whipping her tears away from her face.

"Seriously, that is good advice," Ellie responded.

"I just really wish Kyle was here," Atlas said.

"Because you need him or want him?" Ellie asked in a half-like whisper.

"I don't know, but at least I would like to know he was alright. Have you heard from him?" Atlas asked.

Ellie continued, "No, and I don't think we will. Cheyenne's program is really hard, and they will probably switch him around. I know they are moving him through the Field Training Program pretty quickly. The day he spoke to Rob, he told him he would be out of contact for the next few weeks. Don't worry, Kyle is a survivor. He is intense, but he always makes it out alive."

"I know. I guess I just got used to him being around," Atlas said, pushing herself away from the rail and starting to walk towards the house.

"Yeah, I get it. Now you have to swim by yourself, but you know you were pretty amazing today," Ellie said enthusiastically.

"Thank you," Atlas stated.

"Alright, why don't you sleep in the main house tonight?" Ellie asked as they started walking towards the house.

"Sounds like a plan," Atlas replied as they made their way to the porch of the main house.

The girls sat on the porch for a few minutes when the front door opened abruptly, and Ben walked to the rail—taking in the beautiful scenery of rolling hills, the pasture, horses, and mountains in his background.

"You know Mother Earth has given us a gift. Look at this land, the land of my father's and their father's before that. Man forgets that before, we were tied down to industry and technology life, and this was all we had here. We worked the land alongside animals. We were grateful for every day because those were hard times. Look at those clouds moving across the blue sky, warning that snow will be coming soon. Soon, this will all be a white blanket," Ben said and as he turned around, he noticed both ladies giggling.

"I am sorry, Ben," Ellie said between laughter, "I am still not used to your predictions."

"I am trying to tell you both that life is never easy. You can't just sit there and wait for things to happen. You need to make the effort every day," Ben scolded them.

Atlas looked at Ellie and then to Ben, "We must have forgotten something."

"Yes, you two did," Ben said in a huff.

"Goodness, when is Barb getting back? You are in a better mood when she is here," Ellie replied.

"Yeah, she can keep you warm and content," Atlas said, trying not to laugh.

"Forget it! You two are hopeless," Ben said, walking back inside, "dinner is ready for you two hyenas. Oh, by the way, you received a package in the mail, Atlas. I assumed you would be spending the night here. I placed it upstairs in your bedroom."

"A package? I wonder who sent you a gift." Ellie said while Atlas was sitting still, "Aren't you curious?"

"I am scared, to be honest," Atlas admitted reluctantly, standing up and making her way inside the house.

"It is just a package. Who knows, it could be from your parents or Kyle?" Ellie suggested walking Atlas to the staircase, "Go check it out, and then we can have dinner."

Atlas took in Ellie's words, and suddenly, she imagined it was something from Kyle. She ran up to the room, and there it was, a brown box wrapped with no returned address. She sat on the bed and lifted the parcel. Lifting it, she could tell the item or items inside were well hidden. With some hesitation, she peeled open the layers to uncover a small note that read:

Congratulations to you, my Dear, and welcome to the family. Eric has just notified us of your engagement. His father and I could not be more content with his decision. I have taken the liberty to start the preparations for the nuptials. I included the engagement announcements which have already been sent. I also made the Post-Dispatch and other news outlets aware. We will need to stay on top of the media posting since this will be the wedding of the year here in Saint Louis. After all, it is not every day a Noles marries a local girl. I have provided you with a proper engagement ring that is more per your up-and-coming social status.

I will notify you of all future events since you will need to travel.

Regards,

Mrs. Dana Noles

Peeling open the package, Atlas found a huge square-shaped diamond with large triangle-shaped yellow stones on either side. She was taken back for a few seconds, stunned somewhere between shock and admiration. What had she gotten herself into? What a mess! And yet she was captivated by the size of the diamond and all the possibilities her life would be alongside Eric. Immediately, she replaced the rings, telling herself, "Wow, I can't wait to show this off to Pricilla!"

Chapter 21

Resolute

Just as Atlas replaced her ring with this massive, luxurious, glamorous ring, her cell phone rang, and out of habit, she instinctively answered.

"Hello, yes, Mom," Atlas said.

"I just was innovated with calls about your engagement. You can imagine our surprise Atlas" Hannah told her.

"I don't know what you want me to say, Mom," Atlas replied.

"I want you to answer me, is this the way you are cleaning up your mess?" Hannah demanded.

"Well things got out of control but I am sure it will be alright" Atlas stated.

"Seriously Atlas this is a very immature way of dealing with things. You disappoint me, dear. How can you not possibly see how your carefree decisions affect others?" Hannah urged her.

"Mom, you always encourage me to be adventurous," Atlas began.

Hannah cut her off, "This is not an adventurous, this is careless. How can you be so narrow-minded not to see the path you are on and now have dragged your entire family on your adventure? You are not on an island just because you are far away?"

"Mom enough I love you but you should trust me I know what I am doing," Atlas said.

"I hope so, Atlas. I pray you didn't just jump and didn't gauge the depth of your fall," Hannah cautioned.

"It is all good I would hope you would just be happy for me," Atlas replied.

"I love you Atlas but you worry your Father and me, we will support you after all you are an adult and it's your life. I just want you to consider everything" Hannah asked.

"I have," Atlas replied

"What about your career in Wyoming?" Hannah asked.

"It's fine. Eric is willing to relocate," Atlas stated

"Oh did you think of Kyle and his," Hannah started to state.

"Stop Mom! Kyle is just my friend and classmate that is all. Anything else was just your imagination. Besides he is in good hands with his precious Luna," Atlas replied.

"I see. You need to speak to your Dad. Please call him as soon as possible. You know Atlas I love you. If this is what you want and you are sure, we will support you," Hannah stated.

"Thank you. Mom I have to go but tell Dad I will call soon," she reluctantly responded.

"Love you" and with that said Hannah hung-up.

Atlas walked out of the bedroom sporting her new huge rock. Every time she looked at the ring it became more beautiful as well as heavy. She decided a nice long walk would do her some good to clear her head and then maybe just maybe try to call her Dad. She was truly dreading that call which would be filled with disappointments and questions.

"Lord, I have more questions than anyone else can imagine," she said out loud.

"Why don't you unburden yourself with the moon and the stars?" Ben said, coming out of the shadows.

"You startle me," she said, holding her breath and tapping on her heart.

"My child you look like your troubles are drowning you. I am told I lack listening skills, but my wife Willow is the best. I know you think my Willow is gone, but she is not. Her spirit is hanging out in the trees, in the wind, and even in the snow. Go on, my child, go out into the forest and talk to her. I promise you will feel better," Ben suggested with a very kind tone.

"I don't know how," Atlas said reluctantly.

"Go to the hot springs there and you can see Willow. She will help you in many ways even to learn how to speak to her. Trust the land, my child, it has been here and will be here a lot longer then we will," Ben said pointing the way, "I took the liberty of saddling a horse for you as well. It is waiting for you in the barn."

Atlas looked at the barn and began walking with purpose. She thought the idea was crazy, but who was she to judge? Ben was right she needed to speak to someone even if it was Ben's dead wife. She jumped onto the horse without hesitation and soon found herself surrounded by trees. The path was a bit steep but the horse seemed to know the way. Reaching the hot springs Atlas could see the nice warm milky steam calling her in. Taking a quick look around before she disrobed and walked in slowly. The hot water initially stung but as she continued stepping forward into the water her body temperature got acclimated to the water. .

Once totally inside the hot spring water took over all of her senses. Atlas leaned back and began experiencing herself drifting and losing herself in the water. Looking up she found the only light came from the milky moon dimming as the clouds crossed its path. "I can finally breathe," she said out loud. Closing her eyes there was nothing left but to surrender to the elements and hope for the best.

"What do I know? Tell me how I can clean up this mess. I want...Lord, I don't know what I want. I guess all I want to be is happy, but I am so worried about the expense. I want to be free of this burden. I need someone or something to help me. Can you help me?" Atlas submerged into the water and when she pushed herself out a shadow seemed to appear over the water.

"Who is that? Is that Eric or Kyle? What am I going to do? It simply cannot be Kyle. Kyle is gone and he has already forgotten me. I just need to get over him. He needs to be just a memory. I need to focus on Eric. Eric is my future and besides I cannot embarrass my family. Mrs. Noles has already sent out the announcements. I am expected to be Mrs. Eric Noles. I just wish I had forgotten Kyle as quickly as he forgot me. I wish I didn't have to think about him anymore," with that, the image disappears and Atlas took that as a sign of all the gods agreeing her destiny was with Eric. Standing up and allowing all the water to run down her body Atlas felt she had finally cleansed her body, mind, and soul of Kyle. She wished him the best as she walked out of the spring dressed and returned to the main house.

"Atlas you are soaked! Where have you been?" Ellie asked.

"I went to the hot springs," she replied

"Whatever for?" Ellie asked while helping her get inside the house," You should have told me. I would have at least given you a blanket. Now you might catch a cold,"

"I am alright Ellie. I just needed to find some answers," Atlas smiled, "I first thought it was crazy, but I'm good now. I am good."

"Good you sound numb. What did you decide?" Ellie asked as she helped her to the bedroom.

"I'm getting married to Eric. Plain and simple it is all I ever wanted and now my wish is coming true," Atlas replied.

"I guess. Are you sure? Don't get me wrong you sure don't seem happy," Ellie said walking into the bathroom and turning on the water in the shower.

"I am you will see the wedding will be beautiful. You and Rob will come, right?" Atlas said walking into the shower.

"We will try. Remember we are still in the academy and then training. I am not sure if the agency will let us both go. Don't worry we will try to be there for you, but if not you will come here," Ellie said, turning her back to Atlas so she would not see the tears in her eyes and then continued," You and Eric can stay in the cabin as long as you would like. This will always be your home Atlas. Take a nice hot shower and I will get you some tea."

Atlas must have been in the shower for a while. She walked out to find the tea on the nightstand. The covers of the bed were pulled down welcoming her to rest. She no longer had the strength to fight or think anymore. Atlas slipped into her bed and fell asleep as soon as she placed her head on the pillow. Soon her dreams deceived her by taking her back to the hot springs. Finding herself in Kyle's warm arms.

Chapter 22

Spellbound

Atlas awoke from a restless but passionate dream. She contributed to her decision and moved on with her day. She made her way downstairs to find several packages in the front room. Looking around there were packages of all shapes and sizes throughout the house.

"Oh, glad you are here, Atlas. All these are for you. I ran out of room in the spare bedroom down the hall. I started putting them in the office, but Rob is going to kill me if he can't get in there. So, I moved them to the living room, dining room, and kitchen. And...And there is more outside. The poor UPS guy was dying unloading them."

"What are all these?" Atlas looked around in astonishment.

"Girl, they are your engagement and wedding gifts. Welcome to high society. Now, I am going to need you to decide where you want them." Ellie said.

"All for me! Are you sure?" Atlas said, picking one of the boxes up.

"Yes, and your mother-in-law left a word for you to sort them. You will need to send her pictures along with the sender's name and address. She will take care of the thank cards since let me see how she put it, 'You are too busy at the moment to deal with your social obligations.' I guess she doesn't want her family to look like they are not grateful" Ellie replied.

"My mother-in-law. When did you talk to her?" Atlas said, grabbing another box and shaking it.

"Mrs. Noles texted me. I am not sure how she got my phone number, but she surely took the liberty to provide me with a list of dos and don'ts I needed to share with you." Ellie said, walking into the kitchen. "Well, since it looks like we are in wedding mode now, what do you think if we take some of these packages to your cabin? You can start taking pictures and sending them out. Then come back for some more until you are done or you get more. Atlas smiled and said, "Sounds good. Do you mind if I use the truck? It would make it so much easier."

"Sure you know where the keys are. Take it and use it as long as you would like. Just remember we need to study sometime tonight Kyle will kill me if you get behind," Ellie responded, trying to help her load presets into the cab and bed of the truck.

"I won't get behind, don't you worry," Atlas said, carrying her first load to the cabin. Although the drive was short her mind kept deceiving her and began wondering about Kyle. She was dying to call and check on him, but he didn't call for her. "No! No!" she yelled at herself, "I am with Eric. Kyle is fine and I am marrying Eric."

The day was filled with multiple trips back and forth from the cabin to the main house. Atlas finally made her last trip and made her way back to the house to drop off the truck. Walking up the stairs she noticed more packages on the floor of the wrap-around porch. She was exhausted and fell right into a chair gazing into the mountains then closing her eyes.

The banging of the front door opened and Atlas barely could open her eyes to see Rob standing in front of her.

"Hey, I guess congratulations are in order?" he said.

"Oh, thank you. I would get up, but I am beat, "Atlas replied, trying to stand.

"No, don't. Just rest. You seem to have a lot going on. I just wanted to let you know if you ever need us, we are here," he said, walking down the stairs and heading to the barn.

Atlas wanted so badly to ask about Kyle, but she felt funny about it. So she simply stood up and dragged herself into the house. To her surprise, more packages had arrived, and she could not imagine what had arrived now.

"Well, so it looks like your mother-in-law thought of everything. She even selected your wedding gown," Ellie replied while pointing to a large box in the corner. "I just got off the phone with her. She told me to tell you to try it on and to make sure you show her first. Mrs. Noles wants you to put it on to see if it needs to be tailored, but she hopes not because, as she put it, 'it's one of a kind, and the designer went through a lot of trouble making it; however, you might have to shred a few pounds so it drapes better. Holy Crap! Atlas, are you sure this is what you want? Remember, you are not only marrying the son, you are also becoming part of the family."

Atlas smiled and ran up to the box. She noticed the enormity of it. The brown box was almost as tall as she was and super heavy. Walking around it she did not know how to open it or even where to start.

"Rob had to help bring it in, but don't ask me how to unpack something like that because I have no clue," Ellie stated.

"It does look super fancy, right?'" Atlas replied with an enthusiastic look, grabbing the scissors from the table, "There is only one way to know what it looks like. We need to bust this open" she said, starting to reach for the top of the box. She could feel her hands shaking.

"Stop Child you don't know what you are doing," Ben yelled walking into the room. "You better ask for a blessing first and then you show off your dress."

"No way I am not waiting," she pulled herself together, steadying her nerves and opening the box to reveal her wedding dress.

"Impulsive my Child, you should try to remember you are living in the land of our ancestors. I understand you don't follow our traditions but you should respect them. Now all I can do is ask the spirits to keep you safe. Safe even from yourself, "shaking his head, Ben walked out of the house.

Ellie could tell that Atlas was not fazed by Ben's warnings. She simply was hypothesized by the glamor and fuss of all the preparations. Nothing could deter her from proceeding forward and Ellie decided all she could do for Atlas was support her. Ellie then helped Atlas carry the enormous dress into the master bedroom. Atlas quickly went to the bathroom and took a shower. She was careful not to get the dress damaged in any way shape or form.

Slipping into the dress Atlas could feel the weight of the dress on her shoulders and back. Ellie put the white gloves on as pre-instructed by Mrs. Noles to help zip her up. The dress was rich and delicate. She zipped it up and then proceeded to tighten the laces across her back.

"Well, how do I look, Ellie?" Atlas asked with a big smile on her face.

"You look gorgeous, simply gorgeous. I just wished you also looked happy. I am sorry it is your life, I know, but in these few months, I have come to love you like a sister. I worry about you," Ellie responded.

"I am alright. This is all I ever wanted, Ellie, and now that it is here, I am out of my mind," Atlas responded.

"If you don't want me to keep asking you I will stop, but I just want you to follow your heart," Ellie warned.

"Ellie my heart always gets me in trouble," she said looking at herself in the mirror, "soon I will be Mrs. Noyes," she whispered to herself and then shaking her head, "No! No! I mean soon I will be Mrs. Eric Noles."

"Well, the wedding dress fits you like a glove. I will give your mother-in-law a great eye," Ellie responded, fluffing up the dress as she admired the design. "This is a very glamorous dress. You know mine was very simple, but I truly loved it. I loved my entire wedding. The day was wonderful and Rob looked so handsome. He had that yearning in his eyes. I could see it as I walked down the aisle," she stopped and then continued, "Listen to me going on about my day when we need to focus on your nuptials. What is next on the list?"

"I honestly don't know. I don't have the vail because Mrs. Noles has not decided how I am to wear my hair yet. I guess it will either arrive or I just will get it when I gotta do my hair and make-up," Atlas said, taking one last spin and saying, "Wow this dress is getting a bit heavy. Can you help me out of it?"

"Sure. I guess since it fits we send it back like Mrs. Noles asked?" Ellie said, helping Atlas step out of the dress. Both women struggled but finally, they managed to get the dress into the box and ready for shipment.

"Okay, now I am beat. Could you see if Rob can help me load the box into the truck? I will need to drop it off first thing in the morning before we start our day at the academy," Atlas suggested.

"No, I will not allow you to have such an expensive dress just sitting outside. It could snow or rain. Besides, don't you remember the issue you had with the raccoons? I can still hear Kyle yelling at you," Ellie said with a smile and then realized Atlas was not ready to speak about Kyle, "Atlas I didn't mean to bring him up."

"No problem Kyle will always be my friend even if at times I am not his favorite person," Atlas replied, "you think Rob or Ben can take the dress into town for me?"

"It is the least he can do. You work on dinner and I will ask Rob," she said heading out to find him at the barn.

Atlas headed up the stairs skipping dinner and heading straight to bed. The morning light woke up before her alarm. She got ready and made her way to the kitchen for the first cup of coffee of the day. Looking outside she noticed the fresh snow that covered the entire field like a blanket. Part of her was happy she listened to Ellie while on the other hand, Atlas wondered if the dress had been ruined would the wedding be called off? Shaking her head she told herself it was time for her not to be so impulsive the date was set, the invitations out, and everyone was expecting her at the ceremony.

"A penny for your thought," Rob said walking in through the backdoor.

"I'm good. How bad is it outside?" Are the horses alright? Do you want some help?" Atlas said, slamming the coffee down.

"Whoa! The snow is light but I am glad you did not leave anything outside. The horses are fine and no I don't need help. You and Ellie have your final exams today. Go and get her up so you guys are not late."

"Alright thank you," Atlas said running up the stairs.

"Hey I am up and ready, where did you send Atlas?" Ellie said, walking into the kitchen from the front room.

"She is all over the place. I sent her up to get you and maybe run off some of the extra energy. When is she heading back home?" Rob asked.

"I am taking her to the airport right after we take our state exam. I know the wedding is that same week but on Thursday. Something like two weeks. God, who gets married on a Thursday, but the place sounds super exclusive."

"There's your answer. People with money get married whenever they want," he said, laughing.

"I feel so bad for her. She doesn't seem happy. You and I both know she has been miserable without Kyle. I tried to tell her, but she keeps avoiding the topic," Ellie replied

"You, my dear, need to stay clear from that. She will need you if things don't work out. Atlas will need a safe space and you cannot do that if you tell her she is wrong," Rob warned.

"I know you are right, just as much as I know she is wrong," Ellie said, kissing Rob. "Well after the wedding she and Eric might be here for a few days while they find a place of their own. I hope you don't mind. I told her it was alright."

"There you are, Ellie, we cannot be late. You know how Spinelli says if we are less than 30 minutes early we are late," Atlas replied.

"I got it if we are late we run," Ellie replied walking out the door following Atlas.

Arriving at the academy Ellie walked into the class to find Spinelli looking at his watch.

"Good Morning Director," Ellie said, dropping her gear.

"Yes," Spinelli replied with a smug look.

"Oh, good morning, Director," Atlas said, following behind Ellie's lead.

"Ah yes, Martin I got wind that you are getting married right after the exam is that correct?" he questioned.

"Yes Sir. I received the notice from local sheriff's office. Myself and Stevens will be starting here," Atlas said with a confused look on her face.

"Director Spinelli you gave us the news that we were selected to be here a few weeks ago. Did something change?" Ellie asked.

"No, I just don't understand where my training failed you, Martin. I explicitly advised not to make any life changes for at least one year after graduation. Did I not explain myself well? Tell me when did you and Noyes decide it was a good idea to get hitched after I advised against that?" Spinelli shouted at Atlas from across the room.

Atlas swallowed and then replied, "Sir first of all that was simply advice and not an order. Secondly, I am not marrying Noyes. My fiancé is in Saint Louis and he will be relocating with me soon. This will not interfere with any training at all. Finally, with all due respect Sir, my personal life is none of your business and I would appreciate it if you maintain it that way."

Spinelli walked up to Atlas and stood inches from her face, "Well I didn't think you had it in you, Martin. I guess I was wrong and I am the type of person who will admit when he is wrong. It does not happen often but today I was wrong. You will make a hell of a good cop. You are still green way green but there is fire inside of you. However, I am not wrong about the marriage thing if at least it was with Noyes you might have had a chance. Alright, early birds since you two will soon be partners."

"We were not late, Sir," Ellie replied, walking to the door.

"Yes but I didn't like Martin's tone." reaching for her hand, "I also don't like this enormous ring. Make sure you don't wear it, we will not be responsible for it." Letting her hand go, "So you run until the others get here and then run some more," Spinelli said, turning his back to the women.

"Sorry Ellie," Atlas said, bowing her head.

"No worries, that was amazing, so worth the run. It will give us time to quiz one another for the test. Come on, let's set the pace and get started." Ellis replied.

The last two weeks of the academy flew by in the blink of an eye between the academy and wedding preparations. Atlas found herself in a state of pure exhaustion. During the state's exam she could barely keep her eyes open. She felt like the walking dead moving at a snail's pace to the examination room. Walking in she noticed all the seats in the auditorium.

"Here we go the last step before we are certified. Are you excited?" Ellis said standing next to her.

"I am too exhausted to even think about it Ellie, what am I going to do if I fail?" Atlas looked around the room.

"Failure is not an option for Cadet Martin. You will be fine because I was your instructor. You just push through each question like you did this academy. One question at a time. Pace yourself as you run around my court. Now go find your seat. You two cadet Stevens," Spinelli told them while he continued to check names.

"Director Spinelli, why are there so many seats? I thought it was just our class taking the examination," Atlas said looking around.

"Cadet Martin, this academy is becoming the best in the state. We now offer to proctor the state exam and several future law enforcement officers from the entire state of Wyoming will be joining us. My expectations are high, especially from you two," Spinelli responded as he watched Pricilla enter the room.

"Do you know if Cadet Noyes will be joining us?" Atlas stopped and then took a breath continuing, "I mean he is a member of our class after all."

"No, he is not. I thought you understood he got fast-tracked. Noyes is already on the street," Pricilla responded.

"How do you know that?" Atlas asked while Pricilla walked around them

"Well, it's good to know people," she said while smiling at Spinelli.

"Take your seats, cadets!" Spinelli yelled.

Sitting in her seat Atlas recalled all the times she sat next to Kyle studying, training, working, and laughing. They argued most of the time, but then quickly made up. She wondered if he was alright and safe. Hating to admit it, but she missed him. Closing her eyes she found herself drifting away to those first days when she could not even make it over the wall. "Kyle, what happened? Why are there so many miles between us? Why aren't you here?" she took a breath and pushed the air out, "no I need to concentrate on the exam. Failure is not an option, not after all I have been through to make it this far."

The lights were turned on and off to get everyone's attention. The announcement of four hours to complete the exam was made and Atlas watched as everyone started in unison. Atlas was scared but pushed all her fears down. Making her way through each page one question at a time. It seemed like time was flying by as she read the next question and then the following one. Finally, the last page and the last three questions. Placing her pencil down and looking around she noticed Ellie had finished and so did Pricilla. Atlas handed in her test and walked out of the room leaving all the tension and stress behind.

"How do you think you did?" Ellie asked with a huge smile.

"I don't know, but I hate to say Spinelli was right. I knew most of the answers. How about you?" Atlas responded.

"I am pretty sure we did fine," Ellie replied.

"What are you guys doing now, you want to go for a drink?" Pricilla asked.

"You never hang out with us, what's up?" Atlas asked with a strange look on her face.

"Well, I am going to the next county over. I just thought since my friend is busy, maybe you guys wanted to kill some time. I know I have been a bit of a bitch to you guys, but that is just my personality. You guys never really gave me any crap and I respect that," Pricilla responded.

"I have to take Atlas to the airport. She is headed home tonight," Ellie responded, "you are welcome to send her off with me."

"Send her off, why is she not coming back?" Pricilla asked.

"No, I am getting married on Thursday," Atlas replied.

"Married? Who gets married on a Thursday?" Pricilla smiled, "I mean, congratulations, I knew you got engaged, but getting married so soon to Noy,"

Ellie bumped her, giving her a look, "Eric Noles, she is soon to be Mrs. Eric Noles from Saint Louis,"

Pricilla looked at Ellis and then at Atlas, "Yeah, right, great. I hope you are very happy. I can drive if you like."

"No, we got everything in the car already. Why don't you ride with us and then I will bring you back to the academy," Ellis replied.

"That is a great idea then you can hook up with your friend after the test," Atlas replied with a cheesy smile.

"Nice Martin, but that sounds like a plan," Pricilla said.

It seemed like a blink in the eye and the plane was landing at Lambert International Airport. Atlas walked through baggage claim to find Arleen waiting for her.

"Here comes the bride," Arleen said, "you look beat."

"Yeah, it has been crazy busy. Everything is going so fast that I haven't even had time to think," Atlas replied, grabbing her bag.

"Why don't you?" Arleen asked,

"Why don't I do what?" Atlas said, following her to the garage.

"Why don't you take the time to think things through," Arleen clarified while they made it to her car.

"I knew it. I told Mom it was a bad idea for you to come to get me at the airport," Atlas said, tossing her bag in the backseat, sitting down, and slamming the passenger's side door.

"Hey don't be that way. I was just making a suggestion," Arleen replied.

"Don't. Alright here I am and I am getting married to Eric whether anyone likes it or not," she said crossing her arms.

"Well you are right. It is your decision and I will support you. But do not ask me not to point out the obvious. You are rushing into a marriage without bothering to know the groom. You are in love with the idea, but lack the understanding of the commitment," Arleen said taking a deep breath, " I know we are not really close, but I guess what I am trying to say is if you need me I will always be here for you."

"Thank you, I do appreciate it. I just want to get home and try to shake off this jetlag. I honestly don't mean to be bitchy really. I just want to," Atlas stopped, "I really don't know what I want, except I don't want to talk about it either. You know what I mean?"

"I can respect that. Don't worry you will always have us on your side alright. Now we are home. Why don't you go in and I will bring your bags inside."

Atlas ran into the house, up the stairs like she did when she was a child, and flopped into her bed. The darkness of the room was welcoming but short-lived as her mom looked in on her,

"How was your trip honey?"

"Good Mom. I am just very tired?" Atlas replied, trying for her mom not to see her crying.

"I will bring you something up to eat in a few minutes if you would like," Hannah said.

"No Mom, I am good. I just need a few hours of sleep and then I will be fine," Atlas replied, turning her back to her mom.

"Alright, we can talk in the morning before our very busy day. Remember, we have the wedding rehearsal in the morning, then the brunch, the dance lessons, the last fittings, and then the dinner. You are so right. I think we all should get some rest," she said, starting to close the door when Atlas asked,

"Mom, did anyone call for me?"

"No dear. I assumed you have been speaking to Eric. Why would he call here?"

"Yes, no I mean. I was asking for Ky.. Never mind I am just really exhausted," Atlas said.

"Sure dear, we can talk in the morning. By the way, how was your test? Did you do well?" Hannah asked.

"I think so. I am sure I will be alright with that," Atlas replied.

"Sleep well then," Hannah said, closing the door and she could hear her husband walking up to greet her.

"So that adventurous daughter of yours is home. I want to speak to her. I still cannot imagine what she is thinking. In two days she is getting married and that boy, what is his name? Yes, Eric is yet to ask me. Who the hell does he think he is?" Thomas said in a loud tone.

"Now Thomas, you and I know that is not going to work with your daughter. She has made up her mind. Eric will be her husband and they are relocating to Wyoming whether we approve or not. She chose him," Hannah said, trying to calm him down.

"I still don't understand how that miserable waste of a human being is now going to join the Martin family. It was just a few weeks ago I saw Atlas with Kyle " he took in air through his nose and it looked like steam was coming out of his eyes, "Kyle is perfect for her, not that Mama's boy. What does he do anyway besides take up the air?"

"Thomas, calm down. Atlas just got home a few minutes ago. She needs to rest. It has been a long trip for her, along with taking her exams. Come on, let's go downstairs and get you some coffee, and we both can calm down," Hannah said, pushing or pulling him away from Atlas' room

"No, Hannah, I want to know what Eric has to offer my daughter. At least Kyle had manners, class, education, and a future. All Eric Noles has is a name. A name doesn't mean beans if you cannot support your family," he turned around and said, "I swear, Hannah, for all that is holy, if that idiot tries to hurt my daughter, I will,"

"You will do nothing. You're going to give yourself a heart attack. Come on down stairs and take a baby aspirin. I will get you a nice cool glass of water and then we will figure it all out. Were you able to get a few days off for the wedding?" she asked while walking him down.

"It was not easy, but I managed. Crazy to tell the crew that my only daughter was getting married this Thursday and no one was invited. I barely got an invitation. Then that woman kept calling me about the rehearsal dinner, and expenses," he said, finally making it into the kitchen.

"Don't feel bad I got multiple calls, emails, and text messages as well. I am so glad I am a Christian woman because I was about to tell her to go to hell several times," Hannah said, handing him the aspirin.

"Here babe you might need one too. Come on, why don't you sit down? I will get us our coffee," Thomas said, standing up and pouring each one a cup of coffee.

"Top right side of the cabinet," Hannah said pointing, "Yes behind the sugar there. Yep, bring down the brandy. I need my coffee to be lucky as the Irish say   so we can get through this one."

Thomas did as he was told and they both finally let out a huge laugh.

Chapter 23

Fumble

Atlas stood looking in the mirror, wondering what her life would be like in a few hours. The room was filled with lovely flowers, and the last two nights, she did not have time to stop or think. Now, finally, she had found just a few minutes to review the events of the recent days. She held her cell phone and managed to muster the courage to see the recent text from Ellie,

"Congratulations, I just received your test results. DON'T STRESS YOU PASSED!!! We all made it some higher on the list, some lower, but no matter, you made it. I am so sorry I will not be there for your big day, but I will see you soon. Sending lots of good thoughts to your friends from Wyoming, Ellie,"

Atlas was very happy at the news, "well, everything seems to be in the right place for the first time in my life," she thought to herself, "As crazy as I have lived, I am starting in a good place. I have a great career ahead of me, a strong family, and good friends and now I am getting married. But why don't I feel happier or blessed or something? Lately I am just feeling either empty or like I'm drowning. What the hell Atlas, pull yourself together? No doubt you gave your word?

Did I? No! No, no hesitation. I chose Eric, and in a few hours, after all the I do's, I will be Mrs. Eric Noles. This is all I ever wanted. Right," shaking her head," this is all I wanted for so long. Get it together. "

Atlas closed her eyes taking in a few deep breaths and then she heard a knock on the door. She didn't open her eyes or even say "Come in " when she heard and felt the vibration of strong steps coming behind her. She immediately felt her heart skipping a beat and while placing her hand on her heart making a final wish, "please please let it be," opening her eyes Atlas found her Dad standing in front of her.

"You ready?" he asked almost in a whisper.

She nodded yes trying to hold back her tears and putting on her best fake smile.

"You know Baby no one will blame you if you want to take a few more minutes, hours, or simply run," he said with a wicked smile.

"Dad I can't," Atlas replied in shock.

"I can walk you outside, you turn left instead of going straight and you can simply take off. I left the car running. I'll back you up either way," Thomas said, reaching his hand to her.

Atlas turned to see herself once more in the mirror and then said, "I gave my word. I need to follow through with this decision."

"Honey, we love you always. Don't do this for us. This is a huge leap and I need you to be sure. This could be forever you understand you need to be certain," he insisted.

"Yes no hesitation," Atlas replied as those words took her back to Kyle, "I just wished... Well, never mind we better go before the wedding planner comes in a panic."

"Fine but I did leave the car running if you want a bolt," he said as they walked towards the chapel.

The wedding was held in the beautiful and breath-taking Saint Louis Jewel Box in the historic Forest Park area. Walking through the garden Atlas could see the entire area covered in white tents and candles giving off that Gaspy feeling of elegance and glamor. Each detail had been overseen carefully by Mrs. Noles, each flower arrangement, matching vase, and glitter. The soft inviting music was courtesy of the St. Louis symphony since the family had been long time contributors to the arts. The entire event has simply blew Atlas away. How was all this possible in such a short amount of time? Why was this so much? She felt so out of place much like Cinderella at the ball, and yet she missed the excitement of seeing her Prince Charming. It was just nerves she told herself as she kept taking steps forward.

Reaching the doors Atlas felt the enormity of the moment part of her wanted to run in and get over with. She needed to start a new chapter in her life while on the other hand she was uncertain. Caught in the turmoil the large wooden doors opened exposing the grandeur of the chapel.

The glass ceilings glitter and sparkle while the entire room stood up and stared at her. Atlas looked at her father, then she looked upwards seeing what could only be described as tears from heaven as the lights bounced and cascaded over the altar. Her legs felt weak and she needed to gain her composure while standing still looking down the aisle at her destiny.

"Ready?" her Dad asked, making sure she was steady on her feet.

"Yes," Atlas replied, taking a step forward and thinking there was no going back.

Making it to Eric seemed like an eternity with each step closer she felt more and more distant from the person she was just a few days prior. Now she would have to conform to a new reality where she no longer would be carefree and careless. This was the responsible thing to do, she insisted to herself as the ceremony took shape. It was just a blur to her lots of noise and words she could not make out. Then when Eric kissed her she could taste the bitter mixture of tobacco and alcohol coming from his breath into her body. Atlas was shocked but not surprised Eric always liked the taste of alcohol; she simply did not expect him to be so intoxicated at their wedding.

Right after the ceremony the couple Mr. and Mrs. Eric Noles were escorted for photos as the party guests were moved to the reception area. Atlas felt more like a prop rather than a bride. Everyone coming up to them ignored her and spoke only to Eric or his mother. She so wanted to see her family, but was informed they were already seated and if they came over it would slow the flow of the event. She was not in the mood to argue and simply wanted the formality to be over.

Walking into the reception, Atlas assumed she would feel different about her decision but nothing had changed. She looked at Eric who barely said a word to her but somehow managed to get another drink or two in him.

"Why are you so drunk?' she whispered.

"Just cause we are married, don't you think you have the right to tell me what to do? It is my wedding as well. So I'm going to enjoy myself. Loosen up it might do you some good," he said walking away and leaving her standing near the doorway after their grand entrance.

"Come on you two. I need the bride and groom at the wedding table. Dinner will be served, then the groom's toast, the father of the groom's toast, and the first dance," the wedding coordinator explained.

"Wait, what about my parents or maid of honor?" Atlas protested as she was being pushed to the table.

"Mrs. Noles was very specific about the details. She informed me since the family was paying for everything she had the last word. But don't stress we did manage to get the dollar dance in. I guess it was some tradition your mother insisted on. After the dinner and the couple's dance, then the mother of the bride with the groom, the father of the bride then we will transition to that. It's a bit jejune, but your mother insisted and Mrs. Noles gave in," the wedding planner stated while rolling her eyes, "we always can edit later if it changes the atmosphere of the event. Now come on, happy faces are great!"

Atlas took it all in and made her best effort to ignore the jabs and snotty looks she was getting from Eric's family and so called friends. Looking at her groom struggling to cut his steak seemed all too painful as a vision of her new life. Finally, the tension was broken when the D.J announced it was time for the party to begin. All the guests were ushered once more to the grand ballroom just as breathtaking as the chapel. The lights were dimmed and alluring. The music was inviting and tasteful, clearly selected by Mrs. Noles and her goons.

The first few dances were nothing like Atlas had imagined. Eric stumbled trying to stand in his state. He was led off by his groom's man to get it "together" possibly get more liquored up. But the show went on as the DJ announced the Father and Bride dance. She loved dancing with her father, what a great memory and the moment she needed to pull herself together.

"Atlas, I have something to tell you," Thomas said.

"I know you are proud of me. Dad, you don't have to say it," she replied.

"No honey," he said, stopping, "I am proud of you. You really pushed through and made all your dreams come true.

I am happy if you are happy. But I need to tell you. No, I better show you. I don't want that wicked witch of Noles to see. Kyle is here."

Atlas almost stopped dancing, but her father held her up, and they continued, "What? Where? Why?"

"He came for you. I mean because of you. I really like that young man. I just wished you had chosen him over all this. But I respect your choices. What do you want me to say to him? I can send him away if you wish," Thomas suggested.

Atlas did not get an opportunity to say anything because the music stopped and the DJ announced it was time for the "Dollar Dance with the Bride," men lined up and began spinning her around like a rag doll. In between twirls and moves, Atlas managed to spot Kyle standing next to her mom. Her heart skipped a beat, and she could barely catch her breath. All kinds of questions ran through her head: why was he there? Why didn't he come earlier? Why didn't he stop her madness?

Someone spun her so hard that Atlas felt as if she was going to crash into a wall when she felt a strong arm wrapping around her waist and catching her. Looking up her eyes met with those piercing, deep hazel-green gaze that reached the most intimate part of her soul.

She managed to whisper, "Kyle."

"I got you," Kyle replied, handing her a $2.00 bill, "I believe this gets me two dances with the most beautiful bride I have ever laid my eyes on."

"Kyle, how? I mean, why are you here? How did you know? I thought you forgot all about me," Atlas replied, trying to catch her breath.

"You're kidding right? How could I ever forget you? You are like a wild fire always burning and leaving its mark behind," Kyle said while placing his hand around her waist, holding her tightly close to his body.

"I didn't think you would be here or want to be here. What about your job? I was told you had to start right away" she said gazing into his eyes as they sparkled with the lights and the entire world disappeared while they danced. Atlas could feel his warm body next to hers and all she wanted to do was kiss him staring at his lips.

"Attie, Attie," he gently whispered in her ear, "I so wanted you to choose me over Eric. I wish I could give you everything you ever wanted to be happy. I had to come to make sure you were happy. I guess it was just a bit selfish on my part. I am so sorry. I guess I don't need to be here," Kyle said as he stopped momentarily and took a step away from her, but Atlas held on to his back and waist. She managed to pull him back close to her before anyone noticed.

"Sir, you paid for two dances, remember?" she said with a smile.

"You are right, and I will enjoy our last dance together," he said, moving with the slow music in the background.

"Why are you here, Kyle?" Atlas insisted.

"I guess I needed to see for myself that you did not choose me. I learned a long time ago never to force anyone to choose me. I needed to give you time to see if you can find something better elsewhere. Don't worry; I am not going to hold you back. But remember, Attie's life is too short to hold on to someone who is not sure if they want to stay. If you had chosen me, it would have been because your heart told you I am the one, and we belong to one another. It is all your decision, Attie. I never wanted you to stay with me simply because I asked you. I wanted to be your choice, not just someone safe or comfortable. I deserve someone who sees my value and who is not with me out of fear of loneliness or habit. I wanted you to stay because you cannot imagine life without me. My heart will always be open for you, Attie. Clearly, you did not hesitate with Eric and here we are now saying goodbye. I will not stand in your way. Go on and be happy."

"Kyle, you don't understand. All I needed was to be someone's first choice," she said, holding her tears back as she noticed Eric stumbling towards them.

"You are. You will always be my first choice" he stopped dancing brushing her hair away from her face and then saying," Just remember there is a difference between someone who wants you and someone who would do anything to keep you" he leaned over and kissed her gently on the cheek placing her hand in Eric's and walking away.

Atlas could feel her heart breaking as Kyle walked away from the dance floor and the reception room and faded away into the night.

Kyle made it out to the garden, and the crisp air pierced his body like a sword in his chest. He needed to catch his breath and pull all his strength together, stop himself from running inside and grab his Attie, the love of his life, and take off. Looking into the sky and praying for a sign he heard,

"Son, are you alright?" Thomas said, standing next to him and placing his hand on Kyles's shoulder.

"Mr. Martin, I love her, and I didn't come here to tell her I can't live without her, but it is taking all I have not to get back in there. I fell in love with your daughter, but she didn't. What am I going to do? What am I going to be if I just become a memory? Sir, this hurts like Hell," Kyle said, staring straight ahead.

"Atlas might not love you yet, but I know she will. If she only felt half of what you feel for her she would be the one running outside to look for you. Go now and don't give up on her. Keep the space in your heart you have for her safe. Today my daughter has broken your heart and I know you are wishing her nothing but the best. Atlas has lost a good guy, but I hope one day she will understand her mistake and make it up to you. Kyle, my prayer will be for one day my Atlas will find you and plug that hole in your heart," Thomas said, patting Kyle on his back. Kyle raised his hand in a gesture to shake Thomas' but instead Thomas wrapped his arms around him giving out a huge bear hug.

"I am going to head back tonight. There is nothing else to do here. If you don't mind, can you please give my apologies to your family? I do appreciate you all very much," Kyle replied, walking away into the darkness of the park surrounded by the cold winter breeze of Saint Louis.

Hannah walked up to Thomas, "Is Kyle gone? I really think he should spend the night at our house."

"Dear, one night will not change what happened here today. Kyle left with a broken heart but his head high," Thomas replied, holding his wife's hand.

"Well, the party is about over. Do you think they will mind if we sneak out soon. Lord forgive me, but I am so tired of the Noles and their fan-fare. I know we are not rich, but this is just too much. What kind of mess did Atlas get herself into?" Hannah replied.

"I am not sure. I think this is it and they leave for Wyoming in the morning. She starts her new job on Monday. I believe they are driving his car to their new place right somewhere near her station," Thomas explained as the couple started to head back into the reception.

"Wait what new place? She didn't tell me anything about this," Hannah stopped in her tracks to reply.

"Yes, she told Arleen who then had the courtesy to share it with me. I am only her father. Why would there be a need to tell me anything? Your daughter and new spouse feel that living on a working ranch is beneath them. The Noles family rented a fully furnished home for the lovely couple and paid for the first six months. Mrs. Noles did not want her baby to struggle while he relocated his business out west," he explained.

"What business is that?" she asked with a puzzled look of disgust on her face.

"Oh, from what Arleen explained, Eric sells Solar Panels. I don't know how successful he is, but I guess his parents subsidized his income. And apparently, the family wants the newly-weds to have a presentable place more on their high standard he is used to," Thomas said.

"Sweet Lord Atlas stepped on it," she replied.

Chapter 24

Condemnation

Looking in the mirror Atlas felt as if the past three years were only a dream or more like a horrible nightmare. But now it was time to untangle the mess she had made of her life. Splashing water on her face to wake herself up hit her, today was the first day in a long time she found herself lost and all alone. "What the hell did I do to myself? I cannot believe that I am going to have to start over once more. Damn it this fucken sucks.

Slamming the door shut she turned to see the large orange eviction notice posted on the door. "Great, add another embarrassment to the badge. I have got to be the only deputy sheriff lawfully evicted for non-payment because my useless ex-husband decided to gamble the money away. Idiot! That is why I am an idiot," she said, reaching inside the mailbox to find a handful of mail, "bills and more bills, all collection notices, I bet."

Throwing them into her old car, she drove away with several boxes bouncing in her backseat.

"Hey, what are you doing out here all by yourself, Babe?" Rob asked Ellie, who was sitting quietly at the ranch on her front porch.

"Wait," she said with a coy smile, "just waiting for a good time."

Rob looked puzzled and sat next to her holding her hand for a few moments as they both seemed to be admiring the sunset as it brushed over their green pasture.

"You alright?" he asked, trying to figure out why his wife was just sitting so still and calm, " do you want me to get you something to drink, coffee or wine?"

Ellie stood up but felt a bit dizzy and decided it was best not to try it again. Rob became alarmed and jumped into action, "Ellie are you alright? Do you need to go into town to the clinic? Or maybe I should call someone to come over?" he asked in a panic.

"No, it will pass, they always do. Just let me sit here for a second and it will pass," she replied almost in a whisper.

"Here take some water," he said reaching for a glass and as she sipped it he went on to ask, "What do you mean? Have you been getting dizzy often?"

"I am sure it is very common in my condition," she replied smiling, "see it is all over for now."

"Ellis Francis Walker if you are keeping something from me about your health I will not be happy with you. What are you referring to? I thought the doctor said you had recovered from all your injuries. So what conditions are we talking about? What did the doctor say? Or have you ever seen one and didn't tell me?" Rob demanded to know.

"Robert Stevens first of all I am Mrs. Ellie Francis Stevens and soon this will be all over," she said with a huge smile.

"Are you sick? Is it something terminal?" he asked, trying not to spin out of control, "because you know I love you and I will be by your side in this world and the next. No matter what?"

"I know and I am sure you will stick around to see your son or daughter being born," Ellie replied.

"What are you serious about? Are you sure? Oh Lord, I love you Ellie. I love you!" he said, grabbing her and picking her up.

"Alright Rob I am happy too, but please put me down. The morning sickness is kicking my ass," she stopped, "I guess I should stop cursing so much with the baby and all." She then started to laugh as they gave one another a hug. Rob then looked up to see a motorcycle flying up the road kicking up dust.

"Is that Barb flying up here like a bat out of hell?" Rob said as Ellie looked at the cloud of dust heading their way.

"Something is wrong Rob, Barb never drives that fast," Ellie said, taking a step off the porch.

"Ellie, wait, don't let your crazy take over. Let's see what she is up to before you panic. Remember you need to take it easy, you are now living for two. Well more like three because you know I can't live without you," Rob said holding Ellie's hand.

Barb stopped, parked, and immediately jumped off her brand new Harley, "Man this Hog's roll-on is so smooth I didn't even feel the throttle. Hell of a ride. Take my advice kids don't waste your money on anything else Harley is it and a hell of a beast."

"Barb, Ben did not tell us you were coming today," Ellie said, walking to her and giving her a huge hug.

"Doll, I didn't tell Ben or anyone that I was coming, but I had to make it here in a hurry. So here I am I need your help and it's pretty important," Barb said as they walked up to the porch.

"Why don't you come into the house and we can talk about it. It looks serious," Rob said,

"Is it?" Ellie asked.

Leaning on the porch Barb took a deep breath as Ben approached on his horse, "Now that is a sight for sore eyes, and a tall drink of water for this gal," Barb said.

As Ben got closer Barb noted how majestic, and elegant the horse's hair had carefully been braided and was sporting different beads that attracted as well as reflected the light. Ben looked like a great warrior returning home from the battlefield. She noticed his white Mustang was spotting the saddle she gave him during her last visit. Ben had snorted at her because he claimed it was too extravagant. "Too extravagant my ass" she thought, "it was perfect for him."

"I felt the Earth shake, the song of the eagle, and I knew here she was the thunder and the storm," Ben said, dismounting from his horse.

"You old devil you know I would have called if I had the time," Barb replied.

"Let's not lie to one another Barb, you like to make an entrance. And an entrance you always make, much like a hail storm. You come down from the skies and strike the earth hard," Ben replied as he walked up the stairs to Barb.

"Doll you know when I have the opportunity to make an entrance I do. If I had the time I would make sure your world would shake and have you asking for more," Barb said as she ran her hand over Ben's chest.

"Well Barb and Ben we have news as well," Rob said gently placing his arm around Ellie's waist.

"Oh, Ellie are you expecting? What a blessing! I am so happy for you both. This is your time," Barb responded.

"Thank you Barb I am not sure we would be together if you would not have been our guardian angel," Rob replied.

Barb looked a bit concerned when Ellie reached for her arm, "Barb what is the matter? You came for help. Of course, we will help you with anything you need. Why don't you come and we can talk about what is going on."

"Doll don't get me wrong I am very excited for you both. I know Bill and Sabina are looking down on you," Ben said stepping behind Barb, "But there is a dark cloud lingering around."

"I don't believe or disbelieve in your superstitions but I just chill and go with it. No judgement," Ellie said walking towards the door.

Ben stood still for a second or two while the others were eager to walk into the house. He gazed down the road towards the front gate and he said, taking a breath, then he continued to ask," Who could be coming down the road? Whoever it is they are driving like the devil himself is on their heels"

"It can't be. Is that Atlas in her old car?" Ellie asked, making her way back to the porch's rail.

Atlas drove her aging and unreliable car up the dirt road, clouds of dust billowed behind her, obstructing the path she had left behind. Her grip on the steering wheel was tight, knuckles white with determination, as she wrestled with the weight of her decision to start her life anew. Despite the bumps and twists in the road ahead, she pressed on, fueled by a fierce resolve to leave the past behind and embarrass whatever lay ahead.

Atlas made her way up to the main house as she did so many months ago but this time she brought more than just a few bags with clothes and hope. Today she was coming back to the ranch to ask for shelter and forgiveness. She looked at the front seat covered in past due bills and collection notices. "This fucken day," she said to herself, "the only ray of hope is that they will take me once more." Parking her car near the front steps Atlas stepped out to the wondrous view of the mountains, green pastures, and open fields. She felt safe and at home for the first time in a long time. Finally, she no longer saw herself as a lost ship at sea.

"Atlas! Atlas! I am so happy to see you. Where have you been?" Ellie said, running towards her.

"Ellie, it is so nice to see you and all these friendly faces," Atlas said, giving her a long hug.

"Oh my God Atlas you have come at the perfect time. We have wonderful news," Ellie said, almost crying.

"Atlas welcome home," Ben said, walking to greet her.

"You knew I was coming Ben?" Atlas asked, puzzled.

"I felt it and I hoped. I have been dreaming about you. And the hawk seemed to be crying out your name. I worried you were not safe," he replied.

"Get out of my way you old goat," Barb said pushing him aside, "come here girl let me look at you. Don't scare the girl with your dreams Ben. She is a Midwestern girl and not accustomed to your sayings."

"I don't scare easy Barb you know that," Atlas replied with a huge smile, "it is good to see not much has changed here."

"Atlas why don't you hand me the keys and I will drive your car to the barn in your old spot while you all catch up," Rob said, taking her keys, "it looks like you are losing fluid somewhere. Don't worry I will fix it for you later."

"Thanks, Rob. I appreciate your kindness as always," Atlas said, trying not to tear up.

"Come on in and we can have some tea or coffee or something. It looks like we all have a lot to talk about," Ellie said, leading everyone inside the house.

Gathering at the kitchen table Ellie pulls her mixture of nerves and excitement together. She gently cradled her belly, "I have something important to share with you," she began, her voice trembling slightly with emotion. Revealing the news of her pregnancy shed a wave of emotions over Alta's face, surprise, joy, and perhaps even a hint of concern. Ellie's eyes sparkled with anticipation as she explained her plans for the future and how she envisioned this new chapter unfolding. In that moment, surrounded by the supportive embrace of Rob, Ellie felt a sense of reassurance and love that filled her with hope for the journey ahead.

"I am so happy for you Ellie," Atlas jumped across the room to hug her and then turned, "And you too Rob. I am truly happy for you guys."

Ellie then noticed Atlas' face change and she felt her getting quiet, "What is wrong Atlas?"

"I am happy for you two, but it seems like I came at the wrong time. I just need a few days to gather everything together and I will make my way back to Missouri," Atlas replied.

"Are you crazy? Why would you go back to the Midwest? You have a job and husband and life here?" Ellie protested.

"Well a job and somewhat of a life, but as of recently no husband," she turned away so no one would see the tear rolling down her face, "Eric left and don't get me wrong it is for the best."

"Oh Doll I am so sorry you are going through this," Barb said.

"Don't worry Atlas, you can stay here. That cabin of yours is still just the way you left it," Ben added.

"I don't want to impose. You guys are starting a new chapter in your life," Atlas responded.

"And nothing. We promise one another that night at the bonfire you are family. So you are stuck with us. Besides I will need all the extra hands possible to help Ellie stay put," Rob said, shooting her a warm smile.

"What about work Rob? I need to tell them at work. I don't want my squad to be short. By the way, where are you working today? It seems like forever since I saw you at the station," Ellie said.

"It should be more like where I haven't been working. I have taken every assignment there is to make extra money. The only thing Eric liked about Wyoming was the accessibility to casinos. He gambled all his money and mine as well. Eric did not like the idea of living in your cabin so we could save money. His parents had paid for the house in advance, but Eric only paid the deposit, pocketing the rest of the money," Atlas said.

"Oh Doll I am so sorry," Barb said.

"Barb, it has been such a nightmare. I started getting calls from the credit cards and the casinos telling me Eric owed them money. When I confronted him Eric told me he was waiting for his commission on his sales. I thought I was helping by trying to pay off as much as possible. I started working extra duties, moonlighting to catch up with bills. The more I worked the more Eric spent. It was insane. I worked on any assignment but all my earnings disappeared," Atlas stopped, "a few days ago after 15 days of double shifts I came home to an empty house. Eric was gone and so was my engagement ring and all my savings. After the shock wore off, I got a notification that my checking account had been closed. It was nuts. My entire paycheck was gone. So I found myself broke and all alone. I called Eric's phone and it was disconnected so was mine. I had to use the agency's phone to call Mrs. Noles. She immediately informed me Eric had returned home. Moreover, she was extremely disappointed in my behavior. It appears Eric told her I was the one who was gambling and he was tired of paying off my debts."

"That is horrible," Ellie said.

"I could not believe it. I tried to tell her what happened, but she would not even allow me to talk to Eric. She said Eric, the saint had enough and he did not want to speak to me ever again. Then she told me I was responsible for all the outstanding things since I caused this mess and they had filed for divorce. After she hung up I received a call from the landlord who informed me the rent had not been paid. I was told the eviction process had already been served and I had 24 hours to leave the premises. I grabbed my stuff and the stack of bills I found in the house. I loaded my car and headed here, I am sorry. It was the only safe place I could think of," Atlas said.

"Of course, this is your home and it will always be your home," Ellie stated.

"But my timing stinks," Atlas responded.

"No actually it is pretty good," Barb stated, "I came here because I need to send someone in for an extraction and recovery mission."

"What?" Atlas replied looking confused.

"Well, I am not sure if you remember I work in the Pentagon which allows for several missions both at the local, state, federal, and international levels. I have an undercover officer, (UC) infiltrated a militia that has been recruiting locals. The intelligence we received pointed to this particular group as former military members. They were off the radar until the new leader emerged, Dante. Dante's stock piled explosives and weapons. He turned the group into a private paramilitary group that presents a threat to public safety. All intelligence points to Dante and his followers trying to overtake the government. Dante continues to recruit and his group is getting larger each day. Once we were able to flip one of his followers the UC was introduced and immediately recruited. It has been over 15 months and we were receiving good Intel, but recently we lost contact," Barb explained.

"Barb, that is a big ask," Rob interjected.

"Well I came to ask Ellie since she has a military background, but she is pregnant. I can't ask you to put yourself in that position. However, Atlas if you are willing to go in I would be grateful?" Barb asked.

"I am in," Atlas said.

"I want to make sure you know what you are signing up to do. You will be dropped in a location where we know the group is actively recruiting. I have someone inside the bar who will introduce you to the recruiter. You will be given a cover story that you were a contractor who was fired for selling ammunition. You've been bouncing from place to place trying to stay off the grid. I cannot guarantee how long you will be gone. You will have no direct communication with anyone. There is no backup except for your target who I cannot guarantee he is alive," Barb explained.

"I understand," Atlas said.

"Alright Atlas if you decide to do this you will be fully compensated and your agency will transfer you to this task force," Barb said, "I want you to think about it before you decide," Barb warned.

"Barb, I don't have to think about it. I need something, you know what I mean? I need to do something that gives me meaning and puts me back on course. I have been in auto mode for so long I feel as if I am still lost in a fog," Atlas replied.

"Not a fog my child in a dark rain cloud. Don't worry after the rain the darkness is cleansed and the earth is revived. I am sure you will come out of this victorious. You will grow like the grass and move across like the wind," Ben said, placing his hand on Atlas' shoulder while giving Barb a look of confidence.

"It seems like it is all settled then," Barb said, "I will get your cover story ready and make all the arrangements to get you in contact with someone who will introduce you to the group. I need to make sure you understand once you are in with Dante you are on your own. There is no backup nearby, no one is coming for you. If the UC is alive and not brainwashed or compromised we will extract you both."

"What if I cannot make contact? What if he is not there or dead? What then?" Atlas asked.

"You will need to buy yourself time. I promise we will find you and get you out," Barb replied.

"I better prepare some sage to protect you in your journey," Ben said walking out to the field.

"When you return we will have your cabin all set up and waiting for you," Ellie said.

"And I will work on your car. Don't worry about anything, just be careful. I remember all the missions Bill told me about. His advice always was once they give your cover story make sure you believe it. If you believe it they will too. Don't falter or deviate. Remember you are strong and you will stay alive," Rob told Atlas.

Atlas looked at Rob and Ellie who were holding one and another, "I will. I promise. I will always make it home safe."

Chapter 25

Clandestine

Within a matter of hours, Atlas found herself in the back of a van being coached by Barb, destination unknown. Once again self-doubt started gripping into her body and panic began to set in. Taking a few breaths she knew this was the best course of action to get her back or not. Maybe it was just a way to clean up the mess she made of her life and start fresh. No matter it was too late to turn back and tell Barb she was too scared to face the unknown.

"You good Doll?" Barb said, bringing Atlas out of her head.

"Yep, tell me what I need to know. Who am I and what am I doing or where am I going?" Atlas perked up with the main questions that came to mind.

"You are a nobody, a drifter, and an under-the-radar kind of survivor. It is easier for women than men because we blend. Great right, we don't have to be noticed unless we want to. See how it works. We are the real chameleons and are always so underestimated. Many of my UCs are females, they are thrown much like you will be and have to adapt quickly. My advice is don't overthink and don't speak too much. No one there is your friend and even the UC might burn you to save their ass," Barb warned.

"How will I know who I am meeting?" Atlas looked at her with a puzzled look.

"The first contact is easy, the bartender will introduce you to a handler. After that, you will travel somewhere and he will grill you. You give him nothing but your nickname. They will fingerprint you and run you through the system. Your cover is solid, your prints are in the system. You are Laura Johnson, a former military contractor who worked with Blackwater. Recruited right after college because of your vast computer knowledge. You my dear are now a graduate of MIT congratulations," Barb explained.

"MIT? I know my way around a computer but I am not that proficient," Atlas protested.

"No worries they will never get you in front of one. First, they don't know you or trust you. Secondly as a "hacker" they will be too cautious you might go rogue. Besides, every hacker has a signature and they will not want the heat you could bring," Barb said.

"Alright I get it," Atlas said, feeling better.

"Good, you Johnson got yourself in a jam because of your man. He had you selling off weapons from your base. With your skills, it was as if they were never there. He got caught and you are on the run. No family, no friends, no loyalties got it?" Barb emphasized.

"Got it!" Atlas replied.

"Like I said, women are perfect for this job because they blend well. Sometimes too well. Remember your only mission is to confirm whether or not our UC is dead or alive. I need to know if he flipped sides. You will be the only one to determine that," Barb explained. Atlas looked confused and before she was able to ask Barb went on to say," I have followed your career and you have good instincts. Don't doubt yourself now. You can do anything. Remember that always. Alright Doll we are almost there, this is the time for questions or to go back."

"No, I am straight except how do I contact you? What if I need to get pulled out?" Atlas asked, taking a deep breath.

"Here is your only contact," Barb handed her a rabbit's foot.

"What is this? You have got to be kidding right? Luck or Lucky you are wishing me luck," Atlas felt as if she was just losing her mind and rage began taking over.

"Slow down Doll. The charm is more than what it appears to be. It has a tracking device inside of it. They will scan you for bugs and the rabbit foot will be examined. The tracking is not inside it is it? You are the only one who can activate it and once it is on if they examine it then you will be in danger. There is no explaining this type of innovative technology," Barb took the rabbit foot and placed it in her hand.

"Got it," Atlas replied.

"Hold it tight to your heart for 30 seconds and then pull it away. Go on, we need to program your heart rhythm. No one else can turn it on because no one else has your heart rhythm. Once it is on I will know where you are and that you are alive. We will find you and bring you home," Barb placed her hand over Atlas'

"What are you not telling me?" Atlas asked.

"There are two ways to get in with the gang and you are welcome to back out after I tell you this. There is no shame," Barb said holding onto Atlas' hands, "You can get beat in or sexed in. I cannot tell you which to choose, but you will be less useful if they use you for sex. You understand what I'm saying? If the guys come to sleep with you just to satisfy an urge and they will not be willing to talk to you. On the other hand, if you take the beating you will prove that you are trusted. Not quite an equal but not disposable. I need you to understand men are not asked to take this in consideration but we are women and we need to go in with your eyes wide open."

"I understand I work in a male-oriented field. Women can't afford to do what the guys do. A man can sleep around and he is a stud but a woman is a whore. I guess things never change no matter what side of the world you are on," Atlas replied, moving her hands over Barb's "Don't worry I can take a good beating and still stand. I got lots of practice at the academy and my recent life. Right now I would not even feel it. It might even do me some good to get punched back into life."

"Doll no one deserves to get beaten but I know you will be able to stand it," Barb barely got the words out when the van stopped, "We are here. The plane will drop you off three miles from the bar. You will need to hike to it. Once there the bartender will recognize the backpack and start the introductions. Last-second questions or hesitations, this is the time for it."

"Nope. I will see you on the other side of this. Don't worry I will bring your boy home," Atlas said, jumping out of the van.

"Don't ask me not to worry, I always worry. Make it home safe always! God speed my Doll," Barb said, closing the door and watching her walk to the plane as her van drove away.

The plane ride was quick and to the point. Their landing was hard and the airstrip was just a dirt road on the other side of a mountain ridge. The plane's wheels had barely stopped spinning when Atlas was handed an envelope, the rabbit foot, and a backpack. She jumped off and walked away feeling the turbulence of the plane once again taking off. Turning she noted the tan plane had no markings or numbers. Truly a covert mission where no one knew one another. Just as quick as it landed it was off into the blue sky leaving no sign behind that it had even been there.

"Atlas you got this," she told herself as she took a look around and found herself in the middle of nowhere America. Standing in a desolate area she noticed a dirt road leading west. She took her time and made sure her path to the bar could not be tracked. It took her over four hours to reach her destination, a cabin made into a bar. Walking closer she saw the name, The Mission. There were no cars outside and it almost appeared to be closed, but it wasn't. She could hear country music coming from the jukebox and the sound of male voices as well as laughter. Atlas remembered the warnings not to let her guard down taking the first steps into the dark cabin.

"What do you want?" the bartender called out to her.

"Beer or a shot. I have been on the trail for a bit so I will even take water if that is all you got," Atlas replied, dropping her dusty bag on the counter.

"Whiskey or are you more of a Vodka kind of girl soldier?" he asked.

"Not a soldier but I will take whatever you have on tap and I will go from there," Atlas said, trying not to let him see her hands shake.

"You didn't serve or you don't want to say?" he insisted.

"I don't know you but I wouldn't lie about serving. Those who serve deserve honor and I am not one of them. How is that beer coming?" Atlas replied as she grabbed her bag and placed herself in the corner waiting to see if her contact would show or not.

"Hey, is that lucky or just for show?" a voice asked coming from the shadows.

"It depends on the day and moment," she replied, taking a sip of her beer.

The male then reached for her bag and tried to pull it towards him when Atlas held on to it saying, "Man what is your problem? This is just a pit stop, I was just thirsty and needed rest," pulling her bag out of his hands and back at her side. "I don't need to be hustled or robbed. I will just go!"

Once again he pulled the bag towards him and now this time he grabbed her hand dragging her outside," You are not going anywhere who the hell do you think you are?"

"Get your filthy hands off me. I will not be handled! Who the fuck do you think you are?" Atlas shouted.

"You are the person I need to introduce to Dante and his group?" he said, tossing her bag to the ground and pushing her away.

"What are you talking about? Who is Dante? I just walked up to get a drink and maybe a few hours of rest before I moved on," Atlas replied, remembering she was not to let anything slip. She focused on the plan as she picked up her bag and started walking to the road. He reached for her arm and this time Atlas slapped away, "Mister I don't know you, but I do know I will kick your ass if you try to lay a hand on me again. Got it?"

"Maybe you are the one, maybe you are not," he said walking behind the bar," either way you cannot stay here. I will drive you to the camp and you go from there. If you are trying to stay off the grid the people there will help you. You can either move with them or they will help you get to the other side of the state. From there you can become a ghost if you would like."

Atlas stood still but she didn't hesitate and followed him to his truck, an old beat-up truck that surely had seen better days. She had to yank on the handle and the heavy door slammed into her. She jumped into the front seat, placing her body as far away from him as possible. Looking out the window, Atlas noticed they were heading up a side road and towards the top of the mountain. Several miles away from the road, the man turned into the woods and they drove for about an hour when he stopped suddenly.

"From here we need to hike to the next ridge, don't make me regret the introduction. If you are the mole they will come after me as well. Don't fuck this up," he said jumping out of the truck.

"Look, no one asked you to do anything for me. I was good at the bar so I am not sure why you are freaking out," Atlas said standing still.

"Alright then I will let me figure you out either way don't come back to the bar. The Mission is only for service men and women, we both know you did not do that. Don't even try to lie about it, you ain't got the look," he said as he kept walking.

"The look? What do you mean?" Atlas asked as she followed him

"Only don't have a skin full of scars. Your eyes don't tell the story of your darkness. You have not been to the desert where you become just another grain of sand and you are covered with your buddy's blood. You are not soaked to your soul in pain and it changes you and boom! There is that look," he explained as he moved towards a camp. "I hope you are ready for this girl. There is hell on the other side of this camp. You will need to get through this checkpoint. I hope they tell you every step of the way you will be tested. Go on this is where I turn back. God's speed," he turned and started walking away.

"Wait, I thought you were going to make some type of introduction. Where the hell did you bring me? Who is out here?" Atlas called out to him.

"The wolves are here and I am just a shepherd and you are the sheep. My advice is don't get eaten," he said as he walked away then he turned, "Don't fuck it up."

"What the hell?" Atlas said looking around and it started to get dark. The sun was drifting over the mountains and the last rays of sunshine were burning off like the embers of an orange fire. Once the sun set, Atlas knew the temperature would drop like a rock and she was not quite prepared to survive the elements. All she could do now was make her way to that camp and figure it out from there. Taking the last few steps she noticed a man leaning on a tree. He wore camo from head to toe as if he wanted to blend in, but for some reason, he revealed himself to her.

"Who are you?" he asked.

"I was at The Mission and the bartender told me I wasn't safe there. He led me up here, but I am not feeling safe here either. If you let me hang out here for a few hours to rest I will take off at first light and you will never have to see me again," Atlas said.

"They call me Peter, what do they call you?" Peter asked.

"I haven't been called anything in a while. I usually stay out of sight and away from people," Atlas responded, getting closer to the fire.

"Are you hungry?" Peter asked.

"I could eat, but I would appreciate a hot cup of coffee," she said, noting the pot on the fire.

"Sit and I will get you a mug. Where are you from?" Peter asked, handing her a metal cup and plate.

"I could not tell you. I've been traveling for so long I don't even know where I am," Atlas said, pouring herself some coffee.

"You are at the crossroads. This ridge stands between Colorado and Wyoming. So if it is on your bucket list, you are currently standing in two states at the same time," he replied lifting the lid of a small pot that he was heating over the fire.

"What is that?" she asked,

"Beans are just beans, nothing weird. They are hot, why don't you have some? It looks like you have not eaten in a while," Peter said, extending his hand for her plate.

"Thank you, it has been a while. I don't recall the last time I ate something warm," she responded, watching him serve her food and then himself.

"So is that rabbit foot you have with you?" he said looking at her keychain.

"Yep I picked it up some time ago and I guess it has been lucky from time to time," she said, trying not to make too much of it.

"Lucky, I like that. Come on eat and we will get you up to the camp Lucky," Peter said.

"Camp I thought this was the camp. I am not sure if I want to go further. I think I will be heading back at first light," Atlas stated.

"This is not the camp, it is more like the gates to hell and I am the gatekeeper. Listen, you are not trapped. You will be able to return to society if you wish, but you cannot go back the same way you came. By now someone has seen the bartender returning without you. They will either assume he killed you or sold you to some pervert. Going back will bring us too much heat. So I will help you get to Colorado or Wyoming but not The Mission. Got it?" Peter clearly stated.

"Alright I got it," Atlas said, trying to get her bearings.

"Don't waste your time, you will not be able to find your North here. This place is a black hole. There is no way to have a sense of direction here, especially at night. Keep close to the fire and try to get a few hours of rest. We will move right before sunrise and make it to camp in a few hours," Peter told her.

"Aren't you going to sleep?" she asked.

"I don't sleep, I watch the gates beside the nightmares haunt me either way. Don't worry you are safe go on close your eyes I got your six," Peter stated.

"My what?" Atlas pretended not to know what he was talking about.

"I mean I got your back. Look I know you don't know me and if I were you I would not trust me either. I am just a stranger you met along the way. However, right now I am the only one standing between you and the dangers you left behind and whatever hunts us at night," Peter said.

"Bears right, bears hunt us in this part of the country. I had a friend who taught me to never turn down help from someone willing to fight a bear. So yes, Peter you are right I don't know you but right now I trust you enough to close my eyes. And by the way, thank you," Atlas replied, lying on the ground using her bag as a pillow. A few minutes later she felt a blanket being thrown over her.

A few hours later Atlas felt Peter shaking her arm to wake her up. He handed her a cup of coffee and allowed her to have a few swallows before they started their hike. Several hours into the woods Peter finally broke their silence, "So Lucky why are you here?"

"I couldn't tell you. I have wondered so much for so long I can't even recall how I made such a mess of my life," she replied, stopping for a quick break, "how about you? I know your name is not Peter. No one says they call me Peter, who are you?"

"I am just another good guy who got off course. I like that they call me Peter. Peter guards the gates to heaven and ensures only the righteous gain entry," he responded. "You seem to be looking for something or someone. Am I wrong?" he asked.

"I don't know. As I said, my life has been a bit of a series of unfortunate mistakes that created one huge mess. I don't think I am looking for a particular person more like a purpose," Atlas replied.

"Be careful what you wish for. The people in this group might make you regret that wish," he cautioned her.

"What is your deal? I thought you wanted me to go and now you're asking me to check these people out and more than that. Now you are telling me if I like what I see you want me to do what? To stay?" Atlas said standing giving the signal she was ready to continue.

"Look," he said, grabbing her arm. "These people are dangerous, period. I can't tell you to stay or go. But I fear you don't belong with them. Once you get to the camp watch out for the hyenas and wolves," he pulled her close to him and almost in a whisper went on. "The hyenas are a pack of women. They are not true members and have no loyalties.

They are disposable there for one purpose: to serve the males. You get it?"

"I understand they are whores," Atlas replied.

Peter tensed up his grip on her, "they are more than whores. These women are pure evil; they will eat their own. Don't get with them if you want to survive. They will surround you and you will need to fight your way out. Watch out they don't fight, fare, or clean. You will be told they will stop their beating if you have sex with one of the guys. No matter how hard they hit you, don't give in. Got it?"

"Yeah I got it," she said, trying to pull away from his grip, "what about the wolves?"

"The wolves are former servicemen and women. They too came looking for a new mission. Some are disappointed with their government, others are just damaged from the years they served. It always shocks me to say this but it is true, this is the number one country in the world. I love my country but not so much the leaders. Somehow or other our leaders have managed to brainwash our citizens to believe that it was more economically sound to worship our veterans than to care for them. So the wolves came out. Some of them think they are sheepdogs but the reality is they are just wolves. Remember I am one of the good guys but once you are in I cannot get you out," Peter warned, "So stay alive and make it home safe always."

Atlas finally managed to pull herself away from Peter's grip and push him away. She turned to see at the bottom of the hill several small cabins, trucks, a large building, and a few tents. She could see people moving around somewhere exercising, others were chopping wood, and others were just hanging out. Taking it all in she turned back to Peter and asked, "What is this place?"

"Hell this is Hell and here comes your welcoming committee. Remember what I told you, just don't stop fighting" Peter replied.

"Peter, you brought us fresh meat," one of the women yelled out as they surrounded Atlas. Peter held on to Atlas' bag and her lucky rabbit's foot. Atlas took a deep breath as she bladed her body in a boxer's stance and raised her hands to protect herself as much as possible. The lead woman threw the first punch but it did not connect to Atlas' face making it easy to dodge her attack. However, another hyena jumped on her back and managed to get her on the ground. Atlas' knew she needed to wait for the lead woman to start kicking her. Just like she was taught at the academy the leader took her shot. Atlas regressed back to her training and pulled her down to ground.

"What the fuck fresh meat? You have skills but you are also outnumbered. Charge!" the woman yelled at her crew of five to jump and start kicking. Atlas was prepared and used the woman as a human shield as much as possible until the woman lost consciousness. Stoning the crew and giving Atlas enough time to roll and get back on her feet and stand up to them once more.

"Man, that girl has no quit in her. Watch her, she is getting back up and has more swing in her," Virgil said out loud.

"You fucken whore!" another one yelled at her and squared off hands up ready to fight. Atlas knew it was a setup and she swept her feet knocking her to the ground. Once again Atlas wrapped herself with the woman's body and twisted her in the way as the other stomped and kicked at them.

"Stop that! Knock it off," a man came over and began pushing and peeling the women off Atlas who now was at the bottom of a pile. Atlas kicked at him as he reached for her hair and pulled her up to her feet, "I said knock it the fuck off."

"I want another shot at her," the first female yelled out after regaining her senses.

"Shut the fuck up. This girl put you in a chokehold and kicked your ass. Those are the rules you lost, walk away" he said looking at the woman, "and take your hyenas with you" he said as he released Atlas tossing her like a ragdoll to the side.

Atlas stood and put her hands in front of her ready to fight more if she needed to, "Bring it!" she yelled at him.

"Peter, who is this? She is filled with piss and vinegar. Stand down! I said," yelling at Atlas," the man stated.

"She was dropped off at the gates and in need of passage. I call her Lucky," Peter said walking towards Atlas and handing her bag along with her rabbit foot. He then hugged and whispered in her ear, "Don't fuck this up. God's speed. Make it home safe always." He released his embrace giving her items and walked back in the direction they had come from.

"Where is Peter going?" Atlas managed to ask.

"Back to his post, that is where Peter belongs. I am Virgil and I will be your guide through the gates of Hell. So lucky, what is your deal?" Virgil asked.

"No deal Virgil you said you're called Virgil right? I have no deal. I just need to keep moving forward," Atlas replied, trying to get a sense of where she was.

"Well, Lucky the hyenas will not bother you anymore. You surely fought them off. Now we just need to figure out if you want to join our little group or just pass through. Come on, follow me. I will get you first aid and maybe some food. I am sure all you have been eating is granola bars and beans. Peter probably only gave you beans. He loves those things, but don't worry we have real food at the chow hall. Just follow me and we will hook you up," he said while leading her into the dining hall.

Entering the chow hall felt a bit surreal for Atlas the white walls, and tables seemed to be perfectly aligned. Looking around she noticed one man standing behind an opening or window leading into the kitchen. She recognized the inviting aroma of freshly cooked bacon, eggs, and toast taking her back to her mother's kitchen if just for a few seconds.

"Welcome home," the cook told her as she approached the chow line.

"Thank you," she said with some hesitation.

"First home-cooked meal in a while?" he replied, handing her a loaded plate with eggs, potatoes, bacon, and buttered toast.

"Yeah!' she said with a huge smile.

"This is our way of making you feel at home and relax. You are safe with us and especially here," Virgil told her as he looked at the cook signaling for coffee.

"What is this place? Where am I? Don't get me wrong I am grateful for the food and hospitality," she said sitting down ready to dig into the plate.

"That will be up to you to determine. Aren't you going to eat?" Virgil asked, placing the cup of coffee in front of her.

"Well, first I need to clean up and then give grace. So if you will show me to a place where I can clean up a bit I would be much appreciative," she said remembering everything was a test.

"Of course, Cookie keeps her food warm. Around the corner is a washroom. Take your time. Your food will be warm when you get back," Virgil said, returning her food through the window.

Chapter 26

Justified

Atlas walked into the restroom and caught her reflection in the mirror. What a difference a few days had made! Looking back at her was this beat-up face covered in dirt and blood. She took the bar of soap and without blinking an eye started to wash out the grim from her most recent altercation. The cold water was a reminder that she could not let her guard down, not even for a second. "Who were these people? Was Virgil the UC or maybe the cook? She needed to gain their trust but didn't want to appear over eager. "OK, Atlas, you need to slow down and be patient. Trust your instincts and for God's sake keep it together," she gave herself one last pep talk before emerging back to the dining hall.

"Welcome to the party," a male voice said coming out of the shadows, "if my Intel is correct you fought off the hyenas, but you did not serve."

"Yeah, that is right. I did not serve, not because I didn't want to, but because I had the opportunity to go straight to college," she replied walking straight to her table and sitting down looking at the plate of food she bowed her head and prayed. Atlas wanted to pretend, but she thought if anything happened to me I better be right with Jesus."

"Well, I see you at least believe in something more than yourself. They call me Dante and I lead this team. We have only one mission to get this country back on course. We only ask for loyalty to God, country, and family," he explained.

"I have no family, but I honor God and love my country," she replied, hoping that would satisfy him enough to get by.

"Good. You are welcome to stay as long as you like. Understand this we will not keep you if you choose to leave, however, if you decide to stay it is for the long haul," Dante said walking away.

"After you are done eating I will get you settled in and assign you a spot. You can rest for a few hours and then join us for the church," Virgil stated.

"Church?" Atlas said, looking up at him.

"Or not but it might give you a better sense of what we do here. If you are done follow me," he said walking her through a series of tunnels underground.

"This place is a maze," she said, trying to keep up with him.

"Well, we figured underground was safer from the drones, spy planes, and whatever else the government sends our way. We are about 15 feet underground, with no cell service, no signaling devices, and nothing works down here. You are literally submerged within the earth," Virgil explained, opening a doorway leading to a small room, one bed, one small table, and a footlocker.

"You shouldn't have," Atlas said sarcastically.

"This is not permanent. We need to check you out," pulling her bag off her shoulder and taking her rabbit's foot as well," so consider this holdover. The bathroom is around the corner. There is a private shower and restroom. It is yours for the using. Believe me, everyone has orders to let you be. I will come get you in a few hours. If I were you I would try to rest for a bit," he said walking back into the dark corridors.

Atlas decided there was nothing she could do at the moment, but wait for them to come back. She hoped Barb had followed through and her cover story was solid. There was no time to worry she needed an escape plan in case something went wrong. "What the hell? Atlas thought What am I going to do? Okay, calm down, think," she told herself as she opened the footlocker and found a t-shirt, fatigues, socks, and a belt. "Alright let's start by cleaning off this funk and rest. If they discover who I am I will need to run like hell, but if they don't I will need to figure out who the UC is. Was it Peter or maybe Virgil?"

After the nice hot shower, Atlas decided to lay on top of the bed and wait. She made every effort not to let her mind wonder which would lead her to panic. Closing her eyes she recalled her carefree days of hanging out with her friends and watching the football games with her dad. She was just falling into a deep sleep when she felt someone walking into the room. She froze for a second as someone's hand was on her shoulder,

"Come on wake up" she heard a voice telling her and slamming her bag over her. Atlas looked and her rabbit foot was among her stuff.

"What is going on? Did you come to get me for the church?" she asked, looking around but the room was dark.

"No, they are not having a meeting today. Most of the guys are gone, but the Scout wants to see you," he said.

"I was told by Virgil to stay here until church. I don't think I should go anywhere," she replied, trying to adjust her eyes to the darkness.

"Look, it makes me no never mind. I just follow orders here and the Scout wants to see you. I am not going back to tell him you are refusing to see him because Virgil told you to wait," he said.

"Wait, who is the Scout and what the hell does he want with me?" she demanded to know.

"You are new and no one has told you how things work around here. Dante is in charge period. He relies heavily on Virgil and the Scout. All I know is Dante and Virgil served together. I think Peter and Scout served together in the Army I think. The cook and I were brought in a few months ago once the compound was ready. I am not sure what your role is here but Scout wants to talk to you," he said.

"Fine I will go with you," Atlas said, grabbing her backpack and rabbit foot. She clipped her rabbit foot to her belt and put her bag on her back. Following the man out of the compound and back above ground. Atlas noticed the sun was starting to set and the temperature was dropping fast. They began making their way up to the canyon and then they crossed a small flimsy bridge with wooden planks. Halfway across it, Atlas stopped dead in the tracks turning and saying, "This is crazy I don't think this is safe. Where are we going?"

"About three more clicks and you will be in Scout's camp. You need to step it up because it is getting dark. Here take this flashlight. You will need it for the rest of your journey. I will see you back at camp, "he said, turning around.

"Wait! You are not going with me," she asked.

"Nope, the Scout asked for you, not me. Besides if I was completely honest with you that guy scares the crap out of me. Good luck, don't piss him off. I have seen him beat up three without a second thought," he said quickly turning back and he yelled out, "Don't get lost making your way back."

"Crap!" Atlas yelled out as she turned herself back to try to figure out which direction to take. She stopped, but ultimately, she decided to go forward in meeting with Scout. All she could think was that everything was a test and this was part of it. Placing one foot in front of the other she made her way off the bridge. Noticing the smoke coming from the other side of the ridge. With each step forward, Atlas started making out the campfire, which was located at the heart of the rugged mountain terrain. The flames danced vividly, lighting up the night sky with an ominous glow. The crackling of the burning embers echoed through the land while billows of smoke spiraled upwards blending with the stars. She was trying hard not to trip but she felt her feet were betraying her. Feeling unconfident as the dirt and gravel were falling and making things slippery. Finally, she reached the flat platform and in its center, there was a nice warm fire.

"Why am I here?" she said out loud.

"You tell me?" a male voice echoed from a bit of a distance.

"Who are you?" she asked.

"I should ask you the same question, but I rather know what you want?" he said.

"You called for me?" she said, tossing her bag in his direction, "go ahead and inspect my bag. I ain't carrying anything that will interest you."

"I don't care what you are carrying. I want to know why you are here," he demanded.

"You tell me. I was told to stay in the room by Virgil" she paused and then went on," and Peter told me I didn't have to join the group. I just needed to ask for safe passage," Atlas replied, sitting by the fire to warm up.

"Is that what you want for safe passage or are you looking for someone?" He asked.

Atlas turned her back away from the male, not that it mattered because she could not see him and his voice was distant, "I have not decided if I want to stay or go. I thought the ass-kicking I took gave me time to make up my mind. I don't even know what you guys are all about. Why don't you tell me why there are ex-military guys hanging out in the woods? What are you guys planning or should I say plotting?

"You better keep your questions to yourself. Better yet grab your shit and go! You don't belong here," he said, throwing her bag next to her.

"I heard they call you Scout, why do they call you that? I get Peter, he stands at the gate and Virgil is the guide. Dante leads this pack, but who are you?" she asked while staring at the fire.

"I said you need to leave," he shouted.

"Listen, I am not a dog or hyena. I don't move at your command. Besides, you asked me to be here and so here I am. This was a courtesy just that," Atlas said standing.

"A courtesy more like curiosity? What is your mission? What are your orders?" he asked, taking a few steps closer to her.

She could feel him standing behind her. Still far enough away, giving her a few feet of distance between them. As the wind blew Atlas got a whiff of his scent and she thought to herself that the fragrance was familiar "I have smelled that cologne before. No, it couldn't be," she was tired, hungry, and even a bit scared it must be her mind playing games and making stuff up. Atlas was sure this guy was going to attack her from behind like a coward. She calmed her nerves and tried to come up with a fast plan. There was no time to flee, no way would she freeze, so all she had left was to fight. Fight like hell! Atlas she told herself as she heard him closing the gap between them since he took a step closer to her.

"Don't square off on me," he warned, "I don't care if you are a girl or not. If you act like a man I will punch you like one. On the other hand, if you relax I will not harm you. I am asking you to go, next I will tell you but if you decide to disregard my orders I will be forced to make you. Do you understand?" he told Atlas.

"As I said before, I don't take orders from anyone. If I want to stay I will stay. If I decide to go I will go. You don't tell me what to do," she replied, crossing her hand so he would not see them shaking. Taking a deep breath she told him, "If you don't want to be here with me why don't you go?" She could feel him getting closer to her until she felt his breath in the back of her neck.

He leaned in and asked, "Do I scare you?" while he just barely caressed her shoulders.

"No," she lied.

"It is natural to be scared and you should be scared. I can become a monster and have lived that type of life for a long time. You have the ability not to choose fear that as my advice to you. Answer me why does Peter call you, Lucky?

Never mind ...Well Lucky be scared but don't choose fear," he said, taking a step back away from her.

"I told you I don't need your help or your advice," Atlas replied, trying to stay strong.

"You are a stubborn soul. I said Go! I will show you safe passage to Colorado, but you cannot and will not stay here. Got it?" he said, reaching for her.

Atlas felt his move and took a giant step forward, "you don't get to make that choice."

"Fine, but you sleep here tonight. Stay close to the fire and do not remove your boots. Tuck your pants into them and use that duct tape to tape them shut. There is a blanket over there you can lay over not under you hear me," he instructed.

"Why all these rules?" she asked as she bent over and grabbed the roll of tape.

"I see you have not learned a thing about this area," he paused, turning his back to her and walking away, "you need to tape your pants small snakes and insects don't crawl up your legs. I will not be able to see if a larger snake decides to snuggle with you if you are covered. Take those two sticks and strike them several times before you go to sleep," he said.

"Seriously?" she said, staring at them.

"Or not. You might be mighty tasty to a bear," he replied, getting further away.

Atlas turned to try to see who was talking to her, but it was too dark. She sat on the ground and taped her pants tight. Then reaching into her bag she grabbed a granola bar and some water. Placing the blanket near the fire she thought I would rest with my back to the fire in case he returns. Exhaustion kicked in and a few minutes later she was sound asleep when suddenly the noise of cracking brush and branches woke her up. Rising up quickly the fire was almost out and the only thing to do was to grab the two sticks hitting them together and make as much noise as possible. Her heart began to race as she noticed something coming at her. Atlas recalled that she needed to stand and make herself big if it was a bear, but she could not stand her legs were tangled in the blanket.

"Holy Crap! Go Away Bear!" she yelled out hitting the sticks together over and over. Then she heard Scout laughing at her as he approached, but she could still not make up his face.

"I never thought you would fall for that," he said laughing out loud.

"You are such an Asshole!" she yelled," I thought you were a bear," she said, still trying to stand.

"Man that is one of the funniest things I have seen in a while. You were hitting those sticks like a madwoman" he said, still laughing.

"That is not funny," she insisted.

"I am so glad not much has changed," he said, turning his back to her and speaking to her while he walked away, "Except your hair, I like your hair that way. It looks nice."

"What did you say?" she yelled out but he did not answer her just disappearing again into the night.

Atlas was furious and she could not figure out why. She could not afford to lose focus of the mission at hand she told herself, "I hate that guy. I hope Barb nails him to the wall." Dismissing all he told her, Atlas decided to take off her hiking boots and lay underneath the blanket. "The hell with that guy and his bad advice," she said, turning to face the fire and falling asleep.

She was awakened by dirt being kicked all over her and then hearing wood dropping to the ground with such impact that it shocked her. Atlas tried to rise up but again her feet were tangled in the blanket.

"What the hell did I tell you? Careless and dangerous" Scout yelled at her as he grabbed a piece of wood and began striking her blanket.

"What the fuck?" she said raising her hands to protect her head," I can get up just give me a minute."

"Don't move, I need to stun it or kill it!" he yelled.

She then heard a chilling sound of rattle and hissing coming from underneath her cover, "What the?"

"Don't move, don't panic, and don't even breathe. If you are scared it will attack, look at me. Don't move," he said, trying to raise the blanket enough to pull it. "Alright, I will tell you when to move. Look at me, I need you to focus on me and not the rattlesnake."

Atlas opened her eyes and in the dim light she knew those eyes gazing at her, but all she could do was softly nod her head.

"Deep breathe in and out. On the count of three, I will grab the snake and pull it out tossing it with the cover. I need you to move your feet out of the way. If it launches at you have your boots on so that will protect you. Ready?" he instructed, then nodded, "One, two" pulling the snake which was wrapped in the cover, turning his body away from her and tossing it as far as he could, "three."

Atlas stared at his profile for a second and the most excruciating pain took over her body and she yelled out, "Ouch!"

He turned to see she was not wearing her boots and the snake managed to strike just as he was removing it, "why didn't you say something?"

Atlas could feel all her strength spilling out of her body and she was about to faint but managed to say, "You didn't say three." She felt lightheaded and began having difficulty breathing.

"Hang on, I got you," he said, grabbing her and lifting her body in his arms, "don't faint. I need you to fight alright, just keep breathing in and out. I will take care of you. I promise."

Atlas felt as if she was floating in mid-air and tried to keep her eyes open. He lifted her and took her to a cave laying her on a cot. She felt him over her legs quickly cutting the tape and then working on pulling down her pants. Instinctively, Atlas tried to fight him off but didn't have the strength.

"Stop fighting me! I need to remove your pants and take care of your wound. I am not going to hurt you," he told her.

"I will not get sexed in," she yelled at him trying to raise herself.

"You are injured. No one is going to rape you. I am not going to hurt you, but I need you to calm down," he said.

She looked around and noticed the cave was a makeshift room. There was a footlocker and a small table, and she could hear the sound of water running. On the other side of the bed, she noticed a stack of books, a camping bag, and a folding chair. "You live here?"

"It's temporary," he responded, "this is going to sting, but I am sure you can take it," pouring alcohol over her right foot. She tried not to scream as tears began rolling down her face. "That snake barely got you, but it did. I am not sure if any of the venom got in you. I need to scrub your foot to make sure and this part is not going to be pretty." He got up and brought over a pan with water and a bar of soap that smelled like Canfor. Placing her foot in the tub he began vigorously washing and scrubbing her foot. Atlas thought her skin was being pulled away from her body.

"Stop!" she yelled

"This would not have happened if you would have just listened to me. You should have left when I told you," he scolded her.

"Please stop that really hurts," she pleaded, feeling lightheaded again and trying hard not to lose consciousness.

"Hang in there I am almost done," he said softly, "but why didn't you go."

"I needed to find you," she whispered.

"Me? Why me? Don't answer that you just need to go back and tell them I am alive," he said, placing her foot on the bed, and the tub on the ground.

"You need to get out, and I am here to get you out," she finally responded.

"No, you need to go back and let me stay. I will show you safe passage to Colorado, but you cannot stay here," he said walking to the opening of the cave.

Atlas was in and out of consciousness for several hours. She could feel someone touching her forehead, and placing wet clothes on her body. Then she heard another man's voice talking to Scout.

"What happened?" the male asked.

"Rattler got her," Scout responded.

"Damn, Dante will be upset when he finds out," he cautioned.

"I don't give a shit about Dante. He shouldn't allow women to be here in the first place unless they saw action.

Why did you lead her to the camp Peter?" Scout demanded to know.

"She is your way out. You need to take it. Go home you are the one that does not belong here," Peter responded.

"What are you talking about? I am not done here and now I have to worry about her. No way! In the morning I am taking her to the ridge and she can get with her people on the other side of the mountain," he responded.

"Look, Dante is going to want to know what happened to her. I think he is sweet on her and I am sure he will not be happy to know you have taken her," Peter explained.

"You don't understand. She is not that type of girl," Scout responded, taking a pause, and then went on, "I will take her to the path period. I will deal with Dante if I need to."

"You know her don't you?" Peter asked, walking closer to Atlas who was pretending to be asleep.

"I knew her some time ago and I can tell you she is over her head here," Scout replied.

"Someone sent her here. This is no accident. I am sure she has come to take you home. Go home brother there is nothing more for you to do here," Peter said walking back towards the entrance.

"Peter, our mission is not complete," he replied.

"Your portion is. Leave the rest to me. Take your girl and go. That is all I am saying. I need to go back to the gate before someone decides to check on me. Here take this it will help her fight off whatever she picked up," Peter said handing him some medicine. "Don't worry I used it in Afghanistan, back in the days when I was a medic and you were my team leader. Man has times changed. Make it home safe always brother but make it home."

Scout walked towards Atlas, lifted her head, placed two pills in her mouth, and gave her water to drink. "You have a fever, take this, it will help you. I promise I will get you through this."

Atlas opened her eyes saying, "I know you will Kyle I know you will." Then she closed her eyes and fell asleep.

Chapter 27

Wolves

Kyle watched silently for hours, his gaze fixed upon Atlas, who lay peacefully asleep, bathed in the soft glow of the moonlight filtering through the entrance. The small cavern was often quiet, however, this night more than ever it was filled with a tranquil stillness, disturbed occasionally by the rustling of leaves outside. As Kyle watched, a sense of wonder and reverence filled him, realizing the profound beauty of this moment amidst the stones and the love of his life. "Why are you here?" he said, tucking her in with his blanket. She looked even more beautiful than he recalled. "I have never forgotten you, Attie," he said, stroking her hair and checking to see if she had spiked a fever.

Kyle needed some air and he decided to stand at the entrance. Trying to get his mind straight he heard Atlas' restless she must be having a nightmare. She startled herself awake before he made it back to her side. Looking around in a panic Atlas was a bit confused and her memory fuzzy from the medication.

"What is going on?" she almost yelled out.

"You did not listen and got yourself bitten by a snake," he replied.

She started to rise when the horrible pain crept over her head forcing her to lay back down.

"Don't push yourself," he said walking to her with a canteen, "take this and drink some water. You are extremely dehydrated, that is why you have such a bad headache."

After taking a huge chug of water she could feel some relief, but she felt as if she was hungover after a night of partying," what is going on?"

"Are you asking because you don't remember or because you are curious?' he snapped at her.

"I guess a bit of both," she said, taking another drink and sitting up on the bed.

Kyle sat across from her staring at her with his deep hazel eyes taking her breath away. He finally broke their silence and said, "You need to recover soon. I will get you to the ridge on the other side of the mountain. You can make it easily across and signal for help."

"I am not leaving," she protested.

"This is not a negotiation. You are going, that is it. You are not prepared for this type of mission," he responded, walking towards her and snatching the canteen out of her hand.

"It is not up to you. I have my orders and they do not include walking away without you," she responded, pulling herself up and swinging her legs over the cot preparing to stand.

"Man Attie, you have not changed a bit, "he said, turning his back to her and taking a drink from the can.

"Maybe I have, but you are just not giving me a chance," she said standing up, but her balance was off and she swayed almost falling.

Kyle quickly reacted and grabbed her before she lost her footing, "Nope not much has changed. You still push yourself too hard without thinking. Careless and dangerous. Look, you need to rest for several more hours. The venom did not get you but the meds are extremely strong. Listen to me please lay down and rest. We will talk about it in the morning," he then laid her back in the bed but she would not let go of him. Atlas held on to his body tightly and pulled him next to her. There was nothing more to be done but give in. Kyle placed his body underneath hers and allowed himself to sleep for several hours till morning.

The bright sun rays danced on Atlas' face until the warmth woke her up. She was disoriented but came to her senses quickly looking around trying to figure out where she was and who was around her. Bits and pieces were missing from the past few hours, all she figured was the combination of the medication and exhaustion. Finally, she rose up from the bed and found herself all alone. Where was Kyle? Did he abandon her or is this his way of making her go? These were the questions running through her head.

Anticipating the pain Atlas mentally prepared to put some weight on her injured foot and investigate her surroundings. Managing to get to her feet was not easy, but once she was standing things seemed different. In the corner of the room, there was her bag, the plan was simple: get her bag, look for food and water. Grab her stuff and make her way back to the main camp.

Swallowing her last few drops of water and crunching down a granola bar Atlas changed her clothes. She did not forget the last lesson learned and she taped her pants with the duct tape. Moving forward slowly she made her way out of the dark cave and into the morning light.

"Where are you headed?" she heard Kyle asking.

"Back to camp," she replied, taking a step forward.

"I don't think it is a good idea. Why don't you turn around and go in the other direction? You can make it over the ridge in a few hours," he recommended.

"Are you going with me?" she asked for a second.

"Nope," Kyle replied.

"Then I am not going either," she said, moving forward again.

"Stop! You have no idea who these people are and what they are capable of. Trust me you need to go! I mean it Attie you need to return to your family," he shouted.

"I am not going without you. As I recall one time you told me we were family. So here I am to take you home," she said taking a few more steps, "whenever you are ready to go come find me at the main camp."

"Attie, you are simply madding. You still don't get it. You think this is a game. People's lives are at stake. I just can't walk out," he said angrily.

"Why not? You are so good at it," Atlas whispered, walking further away from Kyle.

Walking down to the camp Atlas's mind took her back to those academy days when it seemed to be just Kyle and her. He was so kind and gentle with her, but today he is harsh and impatient. What happened to us? She thought getting lost in her thoughts Atlas did not notice the ATV that came up on her left side.

"There you are?' Virgil asked, "What were you doing with the Scout?"

"Getting bitten by a rattlesnake it appears, and now I am ready to move on," she replied, getting back into character.

"Dante wants you to come back to the camp. We are preparing the church and he would like you to join us and see if you want to stay," he responded.

"Sure I have nothing to lose but a little time. Who knows I might like it here and make this my new home," she replied leaning on the ATV.

"Where do you think you are going?" Kyle appeared with an angry glaze over his eyes.

"Dante is asking for her," Virgil replied.

"No! She is not going with you," Kyle replied, reaching for her hand.

"Listen, you know the rules, we don't fight over broads. Not the other ones and not this one. I think he wants to interview her and check her out for himself," Virgil replied.

"I said no. I have a claim and I don't want her to go," Kyle insisted.

"What? I don't belong to anyone. I go where I please," Atlas replied, giving Kyle a puzzled look. "I will go and speak to Dante. If I want to stay there I will if not I will go. As I recall this is still America and I am free to choose."

"Great hop on I will give you a ride to see Dante," he said, helping her get on the ATV, "Dante is at the gates with Peter."

"I'll see you later alright?" she said to Kyle as they took off.

"Hang on Lucky I wouldn't want to drop you," Virgil said driving away while all Kyle could do was watch them heading down the trail.

"That girl loves to push me to the edge," Kyle told himself, "have mercy."

The terrain was rough and rugged dirt and rocks bounced off Atlas' arms and she could not help but hang on to Virgil. She turned her head and noticed Kyle watching her as they made their way down the mountain. "Why was he so worried about her? Could he still have feelings for her" she wondered, "No way that was years ago," she told herself, "Focus on the mission."

Just as she turned her head there they were standing at the gates Virgil stopped abruptly and almost swung her off the ATV. "One Lucky girl as you ordered," he shouted, taking off just as fast as he drove them.

"Welcome back, Lucky," Peter said, reaching his hand to grab Atlas' bag.

"Thank you, Peter," she said, tucking her lucky charm into her front pocket.

"I am glad you are feeling better," he said, pulling him close to his side.

"Yes, much better," she stumbled to respond.

"Peter tells me you had a misfortune encounter with a Prairie rattlesnake," Dante said walking in front of her.

"Yes I did, but I am much better now," Atlas replied, trying not to allow her nerves to get the best of her. This guy was a beast, to say the least. His 6-foot-plus statue was impressive. He had a natural tan and deep dark eyes. Dante's body was well-defined by his muscularity and intensity. Taking a step he closed the gap between them and Atlas could see his beard covered scars. Gazing up and down her body she felt as if he could see her soul. Atlas worried her face would give her away. He was truly a wolf and she did not want to be his pry.

"Lucky that name suits you well. I am hoping a woman like you will join our community," he said lightly brushing her hair back and placing it behind her ear.

"I appreciate it, but I still have not made up my mind," she replied.

"No pressure. I just want to give the grand tour and then you can make up your mind. We have time here, no clocks, no schedules, no real obligations you know what I mean," he explained.

"So if I want to go there will not be a problem," Atlas questioned.

"No problem, we will show you to the path and you can continue your journey. Just remember Lucky that is a lonely path. Here we are offering you family, stability, and safety." Dante explained bending his face and right now his lips were almost over hers.

Atlas swallowed slowly, feeling her heart racing and pushing like it wanted to jump out of her chest. Finally, she managed to ask, "in exchange for what?"

"Loyalty. I demand it. You decide to stay, you are one of us forever. There is no going back or getting out," Dante said, reaching for her back as if he was going to pull her in for a kiss.

Atlas raised her hands forward to block him and she could feel his defined chest. He was strong and stoic.

"Dante!" Peter yelled out, "Scout has placed a claim over her."

Dante released his embrace and turned towards Peter, "I will speak to him about that."

"Wait what does that mean? I am no one's property. No one will put a claim over me," Atlas protested.

"Calm down Lucky. It is not like you are someone's property. It's just a soldier code. If Scout wants to try to win you over then I have to step out of the way," Dante explained, "but if you decide he is not your type then any of us can give it a try."

"What if I am simply not interested in getting with anyone?" she asked.

"Then nothing," Peter said, handing Atlas her bag and forcing her to get a few steps away from Dante.

"Good to know," she said, taking a deep breath.

"So how about a tour of the area," Dante said, walking to his motorcycle and straddling it.

"Sure, I would love to," she said, putting her bag on her back, hopping on the bike and wrapping her arms around Dante's waist. Peter mumbled to her not to go, but she did not listen.

"I guess you got people watching over you, Lucky," Dante said before starting the bike.

"Your team is very kind. It must be part of your military training," she barely said before feeling the strength of the bike as it launched off. Feeling the vibrations and throttle Atlas could hardly think as her body was overtaken by the intensity of both freedom and thrill with each vibrating second. While Atlas straddled the bike Dante rev the engine, and she could feel the power beneath her. The wind rushed past her as they accelerated and the world became a blur with each edge of the road unfolding right in front of her eyes.

Every turn required focus and balance making Atlas believe Dante had become one with the machine. The open road offered them a sense of adventure filled with possibilities, where each ride could become a journey, and the rhythmic hum of the engine. The sensation of leaning into curves created an unparalleled sense of liberation which blew Atlas' mind. At the heart of the valley, encircled by towering peaks, lies a clandestine paramilitary fortress. Surrounded by the ruggedness, their position was perfectly hidden from prying eyes. A special oasis for the renegades to gather, plot, and live peacefully. Their presence is ultimately just another whisper amidst the echoes of the mountains.

They made it to the edge of a precipice, high in the craggy embrace of the mountains, giving them an overview of the impressive compound several hundred feet below. Dante drove the bike just to the edge, forcing Atlas to hold on to him tighter. He stopped and turned off the engine, placing his hand over hers. She could feel his palm tenderly stroking her grip before Atlas managed to pull her hand away. Dismounting with ease, Dante walked right to the edge while Atlas sat on the bike for a few minutes. She could hear the dirt dropping and giving away where Dante stood. She took a deep breath, putting her nerves in check before making her way and standing next to him. Settling her nerves, she quietly asked, "Why do you call yourselves wolves?"

"Why do we call ourselves wolves?" Dante repeated. Atlas looked puzzled and silent while he continued, "it goes beyond the pack mentality. This is our way of life. Wolves never eat carrion. Rather, we hunt for our meals. You will never see a wolf performing in a circus, not our style period. Although women like you are extremely alluring, we wolves stick to the code we don't mate with our mothers, sisters, or other members of females. You see, once a wolf selects a mate is a lifetime commitment. If, sadly, their spouse dies, they will mourn them for at least a year. Finally, wolves are righteous sons because we honor their parents. If the elderly can no longer hunt, the parents will remain in the den while the younger ones provide for them."

"I understand," Atlas replied, tuning her body, and now she was facing him.

"Do you?" he asked, turning in a swift move reaching and grabbing her face with both hands pulling her towards him. His piercing gaze gave her chills," You need to be clear and decisive in your decision. Once you join this pack, it is for life. We will take care of you, and you will be expected to care for us. The wolf pack lifestyle is not for everyone, and you will constantly be both challenged and tested." He released her and turned away, looking down below, "We are here with a greater sense of purpose. Our way of life is being destroyed and weakened. Forcing us to fight for survival. The valley below is our claim for right now, but we are expanding. Our vision is for our territory to grow."

"What do you mean? Are there more camps like this one?" Atlas asked, hoping to gain more intelligence.

Her question caused him to look up and notice someone looking at them across the mountain. "Aren't you lucky, Lucky? Like I said, if you join this pack, you better be willing to make a choice in mates. It looks to me like someone already selected you and is waiting for an answer." Atlas could tell it was Kyle who was watching them, but she was not sure why.

"I don't know what you mean?" she said, trying to play coy.

Dante grabbed her arms and forcibly pulled her body next to his, then pushed her away. Atlas found herself almost dangling over the edge, "I don't take kindly to women who play around with my mate's hearts. There are few rules here, but there are rules. You will not drive a wedge and create a gouge between us. Scout is my guy, my brother, my friend, and although you are tempting as you are alluring, we follow a code of honor here. I would rather explain why I dropped you here than fight over you. I want you to be crystal clear about what I am telling you. You are beautiful and charming yet not worth it."

Atlas could feel her heart beating faster and panic began to take over as looked down below. She reached her hand and grabbed onto his forearms trying hard not to be dropped. Her feet were no longer on the ground all she could do at this point was kick air. He then pulled her back in and now Atlas found herself in the middle of his chest in a bear hug. Dante held on to her for several seconds before releasing his embrace. She looked around to see if Kyle was still there but he had disappeared.

"What the hell?" she said pushing Dante, "I don't need anyone scaring me to death. I am not here looking for any type of romance. So stop playing games. I would rather get away from you guys. I don't do crazy things and dangling me over a cliff falls under psycho wouldn't you agree?"

"You ask too many questions," Dante said with a wicked smile," hop on it's time to go to church."

Atlas hesitated for a split second but decided it would be in her best interest to find out what this "church" was all about. She hopped on the back of the bike but did not hold on to him. Things began to become clearer for her and it seems Dante is making a play for her. Once again she told herself, "Don't worry this is a test and I think I did well."

Chapter 28

Calisse

Late afternoon just before the sun set, Peter found Kyle sitting at the top of the cliff's edge. He looked distracted and defeated. It looked as if his troubles were a boulder over his shoulders," What troubles you brother?" He asked sitting next to Kyle who turned and looked intently with a lingering gaze.

"Why are you here and not watching the gate or at church with the others?" Kyle replied

"Church was canceled Dante was let's say preoccupied. I came to check on the status of the mission and to be truthful to you," Peter responded, looking down at the long drop.

"I am good," Kyle replied almost robotically.

"Seriously man you are sitting on the edge of a hundred-foot drop and you are trying to sell me' I am good.' Man, that girl has really messed you up," Peter replied.

"Leave it alone Peter she is just another obstacle. I have got to get her to go back," Kyle said without flinching.

"I don't think that is her purpose here. She also has a mission. You need to take her seriously, her orders are solid," Peter warned.

"The problem is that she is not prepared to be here. Man, that girl is careless and dangerous," Kyle replied, "all this time and she still has not learned a thing."

"Sounds to me she got a hold of you. Not sure if it happened in this place or where you came from, but either way she is here," Peter said, throwing a rock and watching it make its way down." You need to deal with her. ``

"Not for long I need her gone. I can't focus or think knowing she is in with Dante," Kyle finally confessed.

"Oh I see now," Peter said as he began to stand up, "brother you are jealous. Well, shake that shit off. This is bigger than you or I."

"You are crazy, we were never like that. Besides that was ages ago and she made her choice." He stood, "I was not her choice. The mission prevails but she needs to go!"

"Brother you need to get unstuck and detach from your emotions. If you get her to go good but at the end of the day if she stays, she stays. And if Lucky, your former lover or whatever her name is, can get close to Dante then we should consider it. After you both complete your part then I suggest you both move on and let me do my thing, Remember I have a mission as well that is beyond all of us," Peter said before walking away

Kyle turned looking down once at the long drop and yelled out, "Damn you Atlas! And damn my stubborn heart that will simply not let you go." He kicked some dirt and rocks over the edge before walking back to his cave. Laying on his hard bed Kyle could no longer control his thoughts. He imagined Dante holding on his Attie while they were riding across the prairie on his bike. He could see Dante's filthy hands caressing her hands until he managed to get her to slide over his lap and now they would be facing one another. What the hell Kyle stops Attie is not that type of girl or maybe she thinks she is playing a role? He tried to think of something else but his mind betrayed him.

Once more his thoughts drifted and he could see Dante on a bike with Attie straddling him. Popping a wheelie as Atlas smiled and held on tighter to him. Soon he would take her to a secluded part of the valley where they could be alone and no one would disturb them. Kyle felt fury building in the pit of his stomach as he continued to daydream of Dante and Attie making love in the field. He felt sick but his mind would not stop showing flashes of them entangled between each other's arms. Dante kissed Attie as she peeled off his shirt and rubbed his chest with her delicate hands. Then using her soft lips to kiss his body made every part of Kyle's blood boil over.

Kyle could feel his heart racing each beat another step closer to a full blown explosion. Taking a few deep breaths Kyle wondered, "What was going on? Why could he not stop those thoughts?" he did not feel this way when Attie was with Eric. "Why does this feel like hell?" He had resigned to the idea of Attie being with Eric, but he would be damned if Dante was going to take her away.

Kyle, no longer willing to live through this agony, allowed his fury to take over and now he ran on pure impulse without thought and much less care. He ventured into the moonlit sky, fueled by the belief Attie was betraying him with Dante. Determined and enraged, he ventured into the night, his footsteps echoing his resolve as he sought out the truth amidst the shadows. The sound of footsteps approaching broke his stride and brought him back to reality.

"Who goes there?" Kyle yelled out.

"It's me, Atlas or should I say Lucky," she replied.

"What the hell are you doing here?" he said walking closer to her.

"Well church was canceled and the camp is practically empty. I found Peter walking the trail and he told me you were up here." Atlas replied trying to catch her breath, "wow this trail ain't no joke. I think it's kicking my tail."

"I see you are feeling strong enough to walk. I guess you can take a rest and I will show you to the other side of the ridge. Once you get across the river you will find a spot to signal so they can come retrieve you," Kyle said, grabbing her bag from her back.

"Are you crazy? I am not returning empty-handed," she said, turning towards him.

"What do you think your boyfriend Dante will miss you? Let me tell you something Dante is just using you," Kyle snarled at her.

"What? Have you gone mad? I am not with Dante or with anyone for that matter. I have orders and I intend on following them," she said, pulling her bag away from Kyle and swinging it to the ground.

Kyle reached for her arms pulling her into him, "Dante will not have you hear me. You are mine."

Atlas was in shock she had never seen this side of Kyle, he was angry and hurt. Looking into his eyes she could tell he was not in his right mind, "Stop it! I don't belong to anyone! Not even you Kyle Noyes."

"You disgust me! I can still smell Dante all over your body. How could you? I didn't get you and Eric but I respected it," he said, pushing away like a rag doll, "Dante? Dante is a maniac and you are sleeping with him why?"

"What? I did not sleep with Dante," she replied.

"So you use him and tease him like you did me. First a damsel in distress and the moment I fall for you," he said and turned his back to her, "you stab me. Is that what you are like? You like to use men and then dispose of them?" Kyle turned to look at her with a cold gaze that pierced Atlas' heart.

"Is that what you think of me Kyle?" she replied as one tear betrayed her strictness rolling slowly down her cheek.

"I don't know who you are anymore, but you surely aren't the Attie from three years ago," he got closer to her, "or maybe it was me and blinders who wanted to believe you were the girl for me."

"You are right, you no longer know me. I am not that helpless, confused, unconfident girl you left behind. I made my bed and laid in it. Trying to make things work until they didn't, but that was my cross to bear. What is your excuse? Or were you always this egotistical ass you are right now?" she said standing toe-to-toe with Kyle.

"Attie, I don't know what to believe. You are slick, deceiving, and so treacherous. Undercover work really suits you my dear," getting close to her and touching the tips of her hair. Looking straight into her eyes with one quick move he pushed her backwards. "You are alluring, sexy, and all-consuming at the same time," he grabbed her once again forcefully causing her back to arch. "With just one look and you drive a man crazy. No! You need to go and return to your family. Leave!"

"No," she answered, feeling his grip tightening on her arms and lifting her off the ground.

Kyle then dropped her, walked away, but immediately returning planting a huge long kiss on her lips, "please Attie I beg you please go," he whispered once their lips separated, Then catching another whiff of Dante's cologne on her he pulled her away from him saying, "why are you so damn stubborn? You need to return to your place and your place is not here. GO!!"

"You gave up the right to tell me what to do a long time ago," she replied, trying to figure out what had turned Kyle so bitter.

"I don't care if I have to carry or kick you all the way to the other side of the ridge, but one way or the other you are going. Move!" Kyle yelled.

"Fuck you Kyle," Atlas responded reaching for her bag.

Snatching the bag away from her and tossing it several yards away Kyle then turned gazing at her and said, "Enough of this game. I watched you three years ago sell yourself to a man for money, position, and social status. Dante is not that type of man. He is plainly dangerous and deranged."

"Looks like I have a type then. He sounds just like you are acting right now," she said walking to retrieve her bag. Picking it up and turning to see Kyle right behind her.

"You wanna stay really? You wanna stay here with me. Me a lunatic is that what you just call me," Kyle responded.

"Yeah you are a lunatic and I am not easily scared remember?" Atlas replied. Suddenly, Kyle's eyes became darker and Attie could sense he was not really himself. She tried to take a step back but he took hold of her pulling on her with one hand and ripping open her blouse, "what are you doing Kyle?"

"I hope Dante didn't wear you out too much. I am going to show you how much of a lunatic you have made me," he said as his hands began to pull her shirt out of her pants exposing her bra. Kyle reached down and began angrily kissing her exposed skin forcefully. Then reach for her belt buckle and undid it while still holding her with one arm.

Atlas felt each touch, kiss, and caress. Her body was moaning and asking for his but she did not imagine it would be like this there first time. Kyle was like a crazy man trying to kiss each portion of her as if to consume her. He lifted her in midair with ease and carried her into his cave. Throwing her down on the bed and then pulling down her pants. Atlas could not move, feeling his hands caressing the tops of her legs. Up and down as he proceeded to kiss her neck and breast. She instinctively arched her back waiting for him. He placed his hand over her panties and slowly made circular motion on the top. Teasing her with each circle more and more while making his way to her womanhood.

Losing her mind with emotions Atlas wanted him. She needed him inside of her. He had lit a fire and now she had to have him. Atlas waited for the perfect movement while Kyle used his tongue to lure her breast. Pushing away the silky material and exposing her nipples. Kissing them gently and then sucking hard while switching from one to the other.

Kyle lifted his head for a second focusing on her panties. He kissed her belly and made it down to the top of her panties. Atlas thought this was the perfect time to reach for him and undo his pants. Her movements caused Kyle to turn and look at her. It was as if she had broken a spell. He immediately stopped and stood up.

"I am so sorry Attie. I don't know what came over me. Please forgive me. I don't want you to think of me that way.

I would never do anything to hurt you," he said, taking steps away from her.

"There you go again telling me what to do, think and feel. I don't belong to you," Atlas said.

"You are right. You are married. Why are you trying to seduce me? Is this what you do with men?" Kyle demanded to know.

"This again. A few seconds ago you were all over me and now you don't trust me. You are crazy!" she said, reaching for a blanket to cover herself up.

"Why do you bother? You have shown yourself to so many times. Why be embarrassed with me," he said.

"Fuck you Kyle. I don't know if it's the altitude or these people you are around, but you will not be disrespectful to me. I don't deserve it and I do wish I could just leave. Go like you order and leaving your stupid jealous ass behind but I have orders and I gave my word," she said sitting up looking for something to wear.

"Your words are funny. You gave your word to Eric and yet I saw you with Dante and a few hours later here you are in my bed," Kyle said tossing her a shirt.

"Well you brought me here remember?" she said standing putting on the shirt and looking for her pants.

"You are right, I apologize," he said, handing her the pants, "I am sorry Attie."

"Sorry for kissing me? Bringing me here? Not completing your mission so I have to come and save your ass," she said trying to put one leg into her trousers.

"I am sorry I fell in love with you not knowing you were with someone else," he began to explain, "but honestly had you told me from the start I would have walked away. I would have helped you, but I would have never thought we had a shot," he said, turning from her.

"Kyle, that was ages ago. We both made terrible mistakes," she started to say.

"You broke my heart. I walked into that church willing to take you away and you were already married. What was I supposed to do? Now you are here and it's like I am back in that dance hall and all I want to do is take you away. I know you said you didn't belong to anyone, but my heart will not accept it. I saw you and it was like waking up a sleeping giant who longs to be with you. Do you understand?" Kyle said.

Atlas walked behind him placing her hands on his shoulders, "I am here. That was a long time ago and yes I chose poorly. But I am here now."

"I can't afford to lose focus on the mission. This is too important for too many. Stay here tonight and rest. I will watch over the camp. We can talk in the morning," Kyle said walking away into the night.

Chapter 29

Tennessee

Kyle needed to clear his head and walked towards the cliff he noticed Peter already sitting there waiting for him. Kyle sat down and they did not exchange words for several minutes. Finally, Peter reached around and handed Kyle a bottle saying, "I thought you could use a belt."

Kyle took a huge chug and as the clear liquid hit his lips he could tell it was moonshine, "Man Peter this stuff is liquid fire," and then he chugged down another large gulp.

"Slow down brother, it will sneak up on you," Peter warned.

"I messed up and I am not sure if there is any coming back from this one," Kyle admitted.

"There is always hope. Don't lose that. It might be pretty but the ailment has a cure," Peter said, reaching for the jar and taking a drink.

"I think I crossed the line with her. I almost took her by force. I don't know what came over me," Kyle then started looking up, "I swear that girl brings it out of me."

"You can lie to yourself, but not to me. It's not the girl, but rather the idea of Dante sleeping with her. Brother, you are jealous of just that. Once you admit that you might be able to tame it," Peter responded.

"No, it's more than that. I worry about her and she is all I can think about," he said reaching for the bottle, "I just don't get it why would she fall for someone who will never treat her right?"

"Maybe she thinks that is all she deserves and you will need to show her otherwise," stopping him from taking another sip," Wait before you take another shot of courage. I need to tell you Tennessee is back," Peter explained.

"That cannot be good. Why is she here?" Kyle asked, grabbing the jar.

"Not sure, but you know how she feels about you. It will not be pretty to see how she responds to your new interest," Peter said, pouring the rest of the liquid over the edge of the mountain.

"You know Tennessee is Dante's woman," Kyle said.

"Does she know that? Last I recall she had her eye on you. I better head back." Peter said standing.

"Tennessee might be the last step in Dante's plan. We need to figure out why she is here?" Kyle said.

"Well I am going to get me some popcorn for the show," Peter said between laughing.

"What are you talking about? I told you I was never with Tennessee," Kyle said trying to stand.

"Tennessee and Lucky now that there will be some showdown," Peter said as he laughed," And all over you," he began to walk away.

"Knock it off! We need to figure out what they are up to before moving forward," Kyle said looking back at the cave.

"That is what I thought. So brewed the last batch," Peter said waiting for Kyle to catch up, "You know that means she cannot leave."

"Yeah I know. Come on we don't have time to lose," Kyle said, taking off in a sprint following Peter down the mountain towards the compound.

Atlas waited as long as she could for Kyle to return, but exhaustion overtook her body, not her mind. She began to dream about making love to Kyle and all the pleasure he would give her. Her mind took her to a seductive place underneath the moonlight and stars where they were isolated from everything. Standing over her Kyle looked down at her devouring her with one single touch causing her to melt and quiver for his body to be inside of her. She dreamed of Kyle being a patient and delicate lover but their passion was wild and feral.

Watching him bend towards her she unbuckled his pants. Atlas started to kiss every portion of his skin. His hard rock abs, muscular chest, and tan skin were all she needed to survive. Atlas pulled him over her showing her lust, but he slowed her down. Arching her back over his hip he began slowly and carefully undressing her. Kyle's hand traveled up and down her torso as if playing a fine guitar. His fingers moved underneath her tank top tenderly awaking her nipples.

Laying her on the ground over a blanket Atlas found herself at Kyle's mercy. He watched her while massaging her breast and moving his hand closer each time to her waistline. With each movement, Atlas could feel her body aching and yearning for him. The anticipation became part of the ritual as he teased more and more. Watching her body crave him while then moving in closer to her. She could feel the warm heat emanating from Kyle. His eyes fixed on her body as the stars danced across them.

With a final stroke, Kyle's hand made it underneath her garments and into her most secret passionate spot. The movement of each fingertip called her to give in to him. She could feel her body betraying her with the desire for him. Reaching for him Atlas found herself straddling his body and he swiftly moved his hand from inside of her allowing himself to enter. It was exquisite, finally, her thirst for him could start to be satisfied. They were moving as one Atlas rode Kyle like a rider to a Mustang. Each time searching for a climax but his control was divine. He waited for her to explode before allowing himself the pleasure.

Atlas was hooked and in her mind, no one would ever satisfy her the way Kyle could. She sat over him and did not want to dismount, telling herself "Just hold on to me for a few more seconds." Kyle gently stroked her hair giving her that great smile and piercing gaze that crept deep into her soul. He gently moved her and now they both spooned in silence.

"Wake up!" Atlas heard as she felt someone pushing her shoulder, "Come on wake up and swipe that stupid smile off your face."

Atlas was half asleep but she could tell a strange woman was yelling at her while holding a large Rambo-looking hunting knife. Instinctively Atlas covered her face, "who the hell are you?"

"So you are the new thing driving the men crazy. What do they call you? Lucky is it?" the woman asked.

"Yeah, Peter named me Lucky. Who are you?" Atlas responded by trying to sit up.

"Tennessee but no one in this camp named me. I am just Tennessee but you might not be as Lucky as Peter thinks," she responded putting her knife inside a sheath strapped to her left thigh.

"I was just passing through and waiting for passage to the other side of the mountain," Atlas replied, "I am not looking for any trouble."

"Well, Lucky it seems like the choice has been made for you. The path is closed. I should know I closed it. I will determine whether or not you are trouble," Tennessee replied walking to the doorway.

"Where is Ky Scout?" Atlas asked, causing her to turn herself back around.

"Yes, where is Scout? He isn't here lying next to you. I see you are fully dressed even wearing boots. What let me guess, you threw yourself at him and he turned you down?" she teased Atlas.

"No, I got bitten by a snake and he allowed me to rest for a while. I am not sure how long I was out," Atlas replied.

"You sure that was it," Tennessee said, placing her hand on her hip over the knife and walking closer to Atlas.

"Yeah, I am sure. Like I said, I don't want any trouble. If Scout is your man there is nothing for you to worry about. I will be gone in a few hours. As soon as the sun comes out I will find my way out," Atlas said, reaching for her bag.

"We'll see about that for right now stay put. I would hate to hunt you down and bring you back, but I will. Got it?" Tennessee said, turning around and walking into the darkness.

Atlas sat there for a few seconds confused and dazed from the day's events, "what the hell was Kyle doing here? What was his mission? Why did Barb send her to rescue him? Was Kyle involved with Tennessee and maybe did not want to leave her behind? Crap I can't stay here I need to find Kyle or Peter. She grabbed her bag and took off in the opposite direction from where she last saw Tennessee take off. Guided by the light of moonlight Atlas found her stride between stealth and speed. She needed to be fast but cautious enough not to be heard. Each step was like walking to a landmine. Any small noise would echo through the trees and give away her position.

Finally, she managed to make it to the valley where she believed Peter was stationed. However, she was turned around and her eyes were playing tricks on her. Everything looked so familiar yet different in this dim light. Atlas thought about calling out his name but she did not dare in case Tennessee was tracking her. Taking a few steps forward she felt someone's arm around her waist startling her but she contained her scream.

"Well aren't I the lucky one to find you here in the forest? Like a lost sheep looking for a shepherd or a wolf?" Virgil said, pulling her close to him.

"Virgil let me go. What are you doing here? Where is Peter? Isn't this his post?" she said, pushing away from him.

"Now you want Peter. This afternoon you were riding around with Dante and if I am not mistaken you just came out of Scout's nest. Why are you looking for Peter?" Virgil asked, looking her straight in the eyes.

Panic began to sit in and all she could think of was to run, but Atlas stood her ground and said, "That is none of your business. I don't feel like being moved around like a pawn from guy to guy. I don't want trouble and Tennessee made it clear she thought I was messing with her man. So I find it best to leave. Peter told me he would point me in the right direction to get out of this camp. Unless you can help me out and I can take off before I piss anyone else off."

"Oh girl, you already did that. I can see why though," Virgil stated walking close to her and caressing her cheek. "You are very seductive."

Atlas stood still trying to figure out her next move. He reached for the tips of her hair and she took a step back looking at his bag, "What you got there?"

"This," he said, reaching for the backpack and showing off several computer chips, "drone sensors. They arm like mini-explosives once we activate them."

"Activate them where? What are you guys up to?" she questioned.

"We are here for the revolution. Soon this little device will be released to the power grid and boom!" Virgil said as his eyes widened like a madman," then we will control the western grid. Can you imagine the power? We will control everything: communications, energy, everything society depends on."

"Wait! If you shut off the power grid their hospitals will not function, the water system will not work, and no one will even be able to call 911. It will be total mayhem," she said in shock.

"Now that is the idea Lucky. We will have total domination of the western region," he said standing behind her.

"Why would you want that? What will you accomplish with that?" Atlas asked, slipping her bag off of her shoulders, and continued, "Is that what Dante wants?"

"Dante is weak. He wants to sell these babies to the North Koreans, Russians, or anyone with the highest bid. Dante is greedy, all he is looking for is a payday," Virgil said, placing the bag down and running his hands over Atlas' shoulders and arms.

Atlas felt a chill and a bit nauseous as he tried to touch her. He turned her around and planted a huge kiss on her lips. All she could do was bite his lip causing him to bleed. He reacted by throwing her down several feet away from him yelling, "Bitch! You bit my lip."

"I don't like men thinking they can just take whatever they want. I am not something or someone you can use and toss away. I am not a hyena," she said standing reaching inside her bag. He stepped closer to her and his large stature was shadowing over her.

"You will do whatever I tell you to do. Dante, Scout, or Peter aren't here to save you. Tonight you will be mine anyway I want you," Virgil said as he clenched his fist pulling it back and Atlas took the opportunity to pull out her bear spray and blast him straight in the face. Quickly dropping her bag and securing the other one.

Virgil was temporarily stunned, he shouted in pain as his eyes began to swell. He stomped his feet several times and then wrapped his arms around Atlas, "you think you got me. I've been sprayed over and over. This just burns my eyes, but it will not stop me." Atlas tried to peel herself away from him, but his massive build was too much for her. He pushed her to the ground and pinned her down with one arm. Virgil rubbed his face on her shirt trying to get some of the spray off.

Atlas squirmed trying to recall her police training. She twisted her body as much as possible making it difficult for him to take her pants off. Then raising her right leg she started kicking him trying to strike his groin. Getting one good knee in the right spot caused him to release pressure on her arms and she managed to pull one out of his grasp. Reaching for anything she felt a large rock near, pulling it, grabbing it and striking the side of his head with all of her might. Virgil's head busted open like a watermelon as blood spattered all over. He appeared disoriented and confused which gave her enough time to get out from underneath his hold.

Kicking, pulling, and sliding Atlas was almost out of this monster's reach when she felt pressure on her leg. He was holding on to her ankle pulling her back towards him. Once again, Atlas tapped into her police training and kicked him hard in the face. Causing his head to swing back, but in seconds, he had her again, "You really think you can get away from me. What do you think this is my first rodeo?"

Atlas found herself again underneath him, but this time her hand was free. She recalled he carried a similar Rambo-hunting knife like Tennessee. Virgil laid his weight over her body trying to bite her neck. Atlas managed to search and locate the knife while he was busy trying to kiss her neckline.

Pulling the knife out of the sheath Atlas stabbed the knife hard in his back just below his shoulder blade.

Virgil froze as the pain traveled over his body. Then looking behind and seeing the knife sticking out he began to laugh, "You will need something more than a knife to stop me."

Suddenly out of nowhere, Atlas saw a foot striking Virgil in the face. The force was enough to move him across the field. Looking around she saw Dante standing there next to her saying, "Are you alright? Did he hurt you?"

"No," she replied in shock.

"Virgil! What the fuck? You know she was asked by Scout what were you thinking," Dante demanded to know as he slowly walked towards Virgil.

"Fuck you Dante and Fuck your code of honor crap. You know I am a mercenary: we don't play by any rules and least of all follow any damn code of honor. I will take whatever I want," Virgil said, standing up reaching for his knife, and pulling it out.

"Do you have the nerve to challenge me?" Dante replied.

"You are no longer in charge. Your woman Tennessee changed the plans. I guess you were too busy playing tourist guide to get the memo," Virgil said, squatting down in a position of attack.

Dante looked at Atlas yelling, "Run! Run! Go find Peter or Scout."

Atlas stood up frozen for a second as she watched Dante charging Virgil, the men were tangled rolling around on the ground. Dante places Virgil in a choke hold trying to strangle him. Dante then yelled, "Run Lucky! Run and tell Barb I am sorry." Atlas watched both men roll to the edge of the cliff and then disappear into the abyss of the drop.

Taking off running down the mountain Atlas had no idea where she was headed, she no longer worried about making noise or giving up her position. Her mission was to find Peter or Kyle and get the hell out of that God forsaken mountain. Making it back to the compound and looking around Atlas found herself all alone. "Where are they?" Think Atlas. She then made it to the dining hall and looked for the entrance to the tunnels.

Placing her hand on the handle she felt someone standing behind her, "So you are Lucky too?" Peter said.

Turning around Atlas saw both Peter and Kyle standing behind her. She ran into Kyle's arms for relief and comfort. She almost collapsed on him, "hey what happened?" he whispered, holding her tight.

"Dante and Virgil are dead. They were fighting on the edge of the mountain and fell off the cliff," she finally said.

"That is a misfortune," Peter replied, "now we don't know the grand plan."

"Drones. I have the sensors here in this bag," she said, pulling away from Kyle and handing the bag to Peter. "Virgil talked about taking out the power grid."

"The power grid, are you sure?" Kyle asked.

"That is what he claimed before he tried to attack me," she said.

"Oh Attie, are you alright?" Kyle said, pulling her back into his embrace.

"Yes, I was able to fight him off. I even sprayed him with my bear repellent, but he kept coming. I thought he was going to rape me when Dante came and fought him off me," Atlas said, catching her breath, "but Dante said something strange."

"What was that Attie?" Peter asked.

"He said tell Barb I am sorry," she replied.

"Now that makes sense. I bet Dante was the agent that was brainwashed," Peter replied.

"What? I thought it was Kyle?" Atlas said.

"No, I thought it was you Peter," Kyle explained.

"I was placed here by the Department of Justice," Peter said, "I was tracking the sensors."

"I came to save you brother," Kyle replied.

"I was told to get you out Kyle I had no other mission but to extract you," Atlas said.

"Well, I wish we had time to clear all this mess up, but my hunt continues," Peter said, "I have to catch Tennessee."

"I don't know what to say, brother. Please make it home safe." Kyle said, extending his hand.

Peter shook it and held on for several seconds, "Your mission is complete here. Go home and work this mess out between you. I will be expecting an invitation soon."

"Peter, are you sure? Why don't you come back with us and regroup?" Atlas suggested.

"I can't. She is truly evil and needs to be stopped. Take your girl through the tunnels. Take the sensors with you and give them to Ms. Anderson she will have them analyzed. Tell her I will be in touch with a location as soon as I find Tennessee. Kyle, I would wait until daylight to move across. The place is deserted and you two will be all alone" Peter said with a huge smile.

"Safe travels my brother," Kyle said as they watched Peter disappear into the night.

Chapter 30

Does it have to be over?

Kyle and Atlas made their way through a series of tunnels ending up at an area that resembled a locker room. Looking around, Atlas recalled the storage room where she was given clothes and allowed to shower during the first time she made it to the compound.

"We can rest here for the night and take off at first light, what do you think? You good hunkering down tonight?" Kyle suggested.

"Sounds good," she said looking for a place to sit, "hey do you think there is a chance I could take a shower? I really would like to get cleaned up and take these clothes off," she said looking exhausted.

"Absolutely, I know there are showers just on the other side of the wall. Why don't you head that way? I will look for something for you to wear among the supplies. Here is where all the gear was kept and extra supplies. I am sure there is soap and other toiletries near the showers," Kyle said, offering her a hand and helping her stand.

"Thank you, I just want to get the smell of Virgil out of my hair and skin," she said, starting to break down a bit.

"Did he hurt you?" Kyle whispered as he walked with her a few steps.

"No, but he did come close. I don't know what I would have done if Dante didn't show up," Atlas said, taking a deep breath.

"I am so sorry Attie. I wish you were never in that position. I feel so responsible for all that has happened to you," Kyle said, stopping dead in tracks.

"It is not your fault. I am a big girl and I knew what I was getting into when I signed up for this mission," she said smiling at him, "shower is over there?"

"Yes, I will get you some clothes," he replied.

"And maybe take a shower too. You are looking kind of rough," she said with a huge smile.

Kyle shot her one of those great smiles, "You're right I am feeling pretty disgusting I can't imagine how bad I smell?"

"Well I wasn't going to say anything, but I think the horses back at the ranch smell sweeter," Atlas said walking away.

"Message heard," he said laughing while grabbing her bag.

Atlas walked into a large room with several showers similar to one that would be found in the school's gym. There was absolutely no privacy, just a shower head and two knobs hot and cold. She could not afford to be particular at this point. Grabbing two towels and hanging them nearby she turned on the hot water and then the cold. The hot water hitting her skin felt like a revival. Losing track of time Atlas allowed the clear water and soap to cover her body. Sticking her head underneath the shower head she felt the pressure of the water penetrating her pores. Atlas remained under the cascade until she felt her skin free of any reminisce of Virgil.

She walked out of the shower room feeling as if she was a new woman. Wrapped in the towel Atlas made her way down one corridor and into another room which looked to be a small dining room. Looking around she noticed clothes on a small table laid out for her. A pair of trousers, a tank top, boy style panties, t-shirt and long sleeve button down shirt. Throwing on the shirt and panties then dropping the wet towel seemed to be all Atlas could manage because she left exhausted.

"How was that shower? Are you feeling better?" Kyle said walking into the room wearing only his jeans and carrying over a tray with food which included coffee.

"Is that coffee?" Atlas replied, seeming to come back to life.

"Yep, a sign of a good soldier is to always know where the coffee is located," he said, giving her once more that sexy smile that made her heart skip a beat. As she sat down at the table Kyle handed her the cup with coffee and he began looking around.

"Are you looking for something?" she asked, taking a sip.

"I had laid out a shirt for me, but as long as you are comfortable," he said, smiling and walking to another room coming back wearing a tank top.

"Do you want it back," she teased, starting to unbutton it.

"No I can get it from you later," he said looking around the room.

"What are you doing now?" she asked, trying not to allow the exhaustion to take over her.

"Blanket, we need to bundle up soon. Your body is warm now from the hot shower, but remember we are underground. Heat rises, the tunnels will become cool and we will need to preserve our heat," he said, dragging in several blankets and sleeping bags.

"Are you planning on sleeping?" She looked at him as he made a bed with the supplies. Getting up and walking towards him.

"Listen, you need to rest for a few hours at least. You had a long, trying day, and you are not used to it," he said, signaling her to come closer to him.

"I'm alright," she replied, kneeling on the covers.

"Trust me for once please, your body has been through a traumatic event. You are running on pure adrenaline. Even though Virgil was unsuccessful in his attack, your mind needs to process what took place. Right now if you allow me to, I will make sure you feel safe," he said, wrapping her with a blanket, "please Attie, it is the least I can do for you."

"Alright, I do trust you, Kyle. I will always trust you," she said, not fighting her sleep any longer. While she slept Kyle held her close to him, keeping and chasing all her bad thoughts away.

A few hours later, Atlas woke up to find Kyle still holding her tight and watching her sleep, "did you get a good nap?"

"How long was I out?" she asked, looking around.

"About two hours, your body needed it. How are you feeling?" he said, loosening his grip.

"Am alright Kyle but I am worried about you. You haven't slept in days, why don't I take guard and you close your eyes," Atlas suggested.

"I can't Attie even if I wanted to," he said pulling her close to him, "I am worried if I do I will lose you again. I am not sure my heart can take it."

"You won't, I will be here when you wake," she insisted.

"I am alright Attie the nightmares chase me and I wouldn't get any sleep," Kyle admitted.

"What is worrying you? Tennessee is gone and Peter is behind her? Dante and Virgil are dead, and their mission was neutralized," she started to say.

"I know right now we are just Lucky and Scout. Tomorrow, you will go back to being Mrs. Atlas Noles, and I will be looking for another mission to forget you," he said.

"What! Are you crazy? You are not going on another mission. I will not allow it" she said furiously.

"Seriously? You wanna pick a fight now?" he said, holding her tighter.

"I am not picking a fight but I cannot imagine you purposely looking for danger. That would kill me," she said.

"You have no right to tell me how to deal with a broken heart when you were the one responsible for breaking it," Kyle huffed.

"Kyle look at me," she said, pulling away from him," I am not ever leaving you again. You are too important to me," she replied.

"Something about your words makes me think you are telling me the truth. But the truth is right now while we are here, while we are playing these roles. You are Lucky and I am Scout without a care in the world. I want you so bad, but I can't have you," he said gazing straight into her eyes, "you are not Lucky you are Attie, my Attie, my girl. Well, you were my girl until you weren't and now you are Mrs. Noles. I cannot ask you to betray Eric and sleep with me. It kills me because you are all I ever think of. I prayed for you to be mine and now I pray you were not here because I can barely contain myself," Kyle admitted.

"I need to explain," Atlas whispered.

"There is nothing you can say. You are beautiful and sensual; you belong to another man. Everything inside of me is screaming, does it have to be over? We could delay our extraction and make love for hours. No one would be the wiser; it would be just part of the undercover assignment. I could live with that just having you even though it was as Scout and not Kyle. Believe me Attie I would kill for that, but then I know you would regret it and I could not live with that. I cannot be the reason you end up resenting me or at worst hating me," he said.

"Kyle are you done?" she said again, sounding extremely agitated, "Eric and I got divorced several months ago. He in fact left me leaving me with piles of debt, self-doubt, and loss. I ended up back at the ranch with Ellie and Rob. Every day after I said yes to Eric I regretted it. I knew I should have ran away with you or after you. But my stubbornness and pride got in the way. I married Eric because of a childish whim that instead of a dream became a nightmare. We tried to make it work, or maybe I tried or didn't. It was like making a square fit into a circle. I thought since I had lost you, I deserved to be unhappy. Telling myself it didn't matter if I hurt forever as long as he stayed happy. Little did I know he was just as miserable as I was, maybe even more?

I thought there were days we would make it work and things would be alright. What a mistake! I came home to an empty house with an eviction notice, a pile of outstanding bills, and calls to my job. My sergeant even told me if I didn't take care of things at home I could face disciplinary action which lead to termination. After three years I had nothing, but a broken soul. Don't get me wrong I know I did it to myself and I deserve it. I know I was childish, greedy, and materialistic" she said, taking a breath, "I didn't understand what you had to offer me. I didn't know you were the one. I was blind and naive. I was careless and thoughtless. For all that and more Kyle I am truly sorry."

Kyle could not help but pull her towards him and give her a long passionate kiss, "no Attie I am the one who is sorry. I should have taken you with me. I should have fought for you harder. I should have loved you better" he whispered in her ear.

"Love me now," she replied, placing her hand over his heart and feeling it beat as if it was going to break through his chest. Kyle reached for her and his lips quickly found hers. He caressed her hair while pulling her closer to him. Soon his hand began to slide over her shirt and caress her breast. Sitting up over the multiple blankets Atlas straddled Kyle as his lips kissed the side of Atlas' neck. Making its way back to her lips he whispered, "Attie are you sure? I don't want you to do anything you are not ready to do."

"Kyle 'Maybe' Noyes I've been ready to be yours forever and as long as you want me. I am yours and only yours," Atlas replied while going in for another one of his passionate long kisses.

Kyle's hands slowly began to unbutton her shirt, just allowing it to cover her shoulders and expose her breasts. He bent over and began kissing one while massaging the other one. Atlas' head was spinning with excitement and she braced herself on his shoulders. Soon she found herself lying on her back while he continued to bring out every ounce of pleasure he could with every touch. Using his tongue and lips Kyle traced her body from the torso to the top of her panties. Going up and down with kisses Atlas' felt Kyle's strong and muscular chest rubbing over her exposed breast.

Closing her eyes and allowing Kyle to work his magic was both ecstasy and torture for her. She wanted him, she needed him, but she knew she needed to be patient because the best was yet to come. Arching her back Atlas felt her head spinning as her body ached for his touch. Teasing her once more Atlas felt Kyle's fingers barely circling her over the material of her panties. Atlas opened her eyes and caught him staring deep into her. She knew he wanted her and she did all she could to contain herself.

Kyle's lips connected to hers once more as his fingers wandered into her soft and smooth center. As her lips separated Atlas could not help but let out a moan signaling she was ready for him. He however had other ideas finding other key spots to kiss as his fingers continued to transport her into wild, luscious, excitement. Atlas could feel her body betraying her and wetness invading her. He was driving her crazy with anticipation as his fingers explored each secret part of her body.

Atlas could no longer think her animal instincts began to take over. Using her feet she started to slide his pants off. She then placed her hands on his hips and pulled Kyle's torso over her body. Craving him to be inside of her, she said, "Take me I am yours." Kyle entered her and he placed his hands on the small curve of her back. With that gesture, they became one as Atlas's lips connected to his. They began rocking back and forth kissing, moaning, as their bodies found their flow and their rhythm was sync. As each wave of pleasure overtook them, Atlas could feel Kyle's manhood ready to erupt. Atlas was happy at this moment and wanted to ensure Kyle was satisfied with her as well. She smiled at him as he let out a loud moan and she felt his explosion inside of her body.

He kissed her gently as he helped her move to his side. Spooning their naked bodies together Atlas could feel Kyle's warm body holding onto hers. They needed to rest, but Atlas wanted to ensure Kyle knew he had finally conquered her and she was not going anywhere without him. Atlas decided to place her over his so he could feel her holding on to him while they slept. An hour later, Atlas rolled over to find that Kyle had slipped out of her grasp. Panic set in for several seconds and she looked around the dark room and could not find him.

Hearing a loud bag she stood up wrapped herself in a blanket and followed the sound into a dark room lined with supplies. There she found Kyle grabbing a shirt and putting it on. She reached around his waist, "Are we going to the rally point for our rescue?"

"No, I just came to get a shirt since you seem to like the other one so much," he said, holding onto her hands. He then spun her around and now they were facing one another, "You feel like maybe taking a shower and then getting some food in   us?

She nodded in agreement as he grabbed her and picked her up, "Where are you going, the showers are the other way."

"Not the private one. Wait till you see this one it will blow your mind," he said, giving her a killer smile and almost letting out a laugh.

As they made their way down one small corridor, Atlas could see a large bed and next to it a bathroom. Looking around in wonder she could not help but ask, "Whose room is this?"

"I think it was part of the contingency plan. It was probably set up for Dante and Tennessee," he said looking around, "or it could have been simply set up for Tennessee once she blew up the compound. I am not sure," he replied.

"Why would she do that? The compound seemed to be so safe and peaceful," she replied, trying to look around as much as possible but the light was extremely dim.

Sitting her on the bed Kyle walked into the bathroom and Atlas could hear the water running. She waited for a minute or two and then walked into the shower. Atlas stepped into the shower noticing that Kyle was standing there naked. She watched as the water tapped his tan skin. With his back turned to her Atlas admired silently his broad shoulders, muscular back, and arms. She almost blushed as she looked at his perfect butt, strong legs, and as she took a breath he immediately caught her peeking at him.

"Come on in the water is great," he said as his eyes sparked and he extended his hand.

Stepping under the water, Atlas' lips immediately locked into Kyle's and they began giving into one another passionately they began to tangle and become one. Atlas could not believe herself but in that moment all her heart wanted was to please him. She began kissing his powerful chest as his hands ran up and down her waist. Suddenly his magical fingers were once again teasing her most private and sensitive area. Opening her mouth just slightly Atlas let out a moan.

"Attie, tell me how you want me to make love to you. I will never stop satisfying you my love," Kyle said as he pushed her body into the glass door and lifted her with ease. His hand was inside of her driving her crazy as his lips began to hit her right breast and then her left. She could feel the heat of the excitement driving her out of control.

"Kyle I need you," she managed to say in between moans.

"You tell me when you are ready. I want you to enjoy every second we are together," he said as his strong gaze and huge smile watched her losing control.

Running her hand through her wet hair, and then bracing herself on Kyle's shoulders, Atlas found herself almost out of breath from the intense way he was making love to her, "Kyle you are driving me mad."

"You want me to stop?" he said, slowing down a bit while his fingers started to exit her center.

"No, just slow down a bit so I can catch my breath," she said, relaxing for a moment while staring at his deep hazel eyes.

"Attie I will do whatever you want me to do," pushing his finger slowly into her center making her feel silky and warm. A wave of passion came over her and Kyle guided her body onto his slowly fitting like a key to a lock. She could feel him inside of her, strong, and powerful. Waiting for his direction, Atlas let out another moan while Kyle braced his body. Her back was arched and she could no longer feel the glass on her back. It was as if she was floating in mid-air. Wrapping her legs around his waist and securing herself to Kyle Atlas enjoyed that intimate connection.

Opening her eyes, she watched him, seeking her breast, then shoulders, neck, and lips. As they kissed, he pushed himself into her once, twice, and they began an unwavering dance with one purpose: to reach the climax. She could feel her body giving into him as he devoured her over and over. The steam had covered their bodies like a cloud, and all that was left was their passion. Atlas yelled out, "Kyle!" he pushed into her harder while holding her tightly,

She closed her eyes realizing her body had surrendered to his every move. Opening herself was not easy but she loved every moment. Her mind began to travel when he felt herself climaxing once more and she heard him moaning, "Attie I love you." Her mouth found his as their tongues tango inside one another. They had given themselves to each other. Atlas could not believe Kyle was both gentle and a beast while making love to her. She could not imagine her life without him and found herself consumed by his touch.

Kyle gently lowered her down and began washing her body. Lathering her with soap and washing her body off. He ran his hands through her hair while Atlas lathered his body and cleansed him. Finishing their ritual, Kyle shut off the water and wrapped a towel around his waist and then ensured Atlas had one. He secured the towel around her body underneath her arm and tucked the material between her breasts.

"You alright," he asked, caressing her cheek with his hand.

"I have to admit I have never experienced something like that. I am not sure how to feel," Atlas said.

Kyle then lifted once more and carried her to bed, "Why don't you rest for a bit and we can talk about it later."

"Kyle do you love?" she asked as he placed her on the bed.

"With all my heart," he replied.

"Good because I don't ever want anyone else to make love to me but you," she replied with a devilish smile.

"Does it have to be over?" Kyle asked, lying next to her.

"Never," she replied, "because you are the love of my life."

Chapter 31

Steady My Heart

Making it out of the tunnels Atlas and Kyle hiked to the top of the mountain. Once there Atlas looked at Kyle asking, "Ready?" He nodded in agreement and she grabbed the rabbit's foot, but rather than activating it she looked at him raising her eyebrows.

"You right," he responded leaning down and giving her a warm, passionate, endless kiss. Atlas placed her hand over his chest and she could feel his heart beat and while they embraced she summoned the troops.

"It shouldn't be long now," she said looking into his eyes.

"Attie God only knows where we'll end up, but I want to make sure you know we will be together," Kyle said holding her hand. They could feel a strong gust of wind and as the helicopter approached, "Looks like our ride is here."

The helicopter hovered over the area, forcing each one of them to jump in. Kyle helped Atlas and then she reached out her hand to assist him. Once inside, the pilot instructed them to secure their seatbelts and put on their headphones,

"Welcome Officer Noyes and Deputy Martin. I have strict instructions to take you to the rally point west of

Cheyenne. I recommend you sit back and enjoy the view. We will be there in just a short time," he said.

"Are we the only team being rescued?" Kyle asked.

"Yes I believe the other agent from Homeland Security is on the hunt, and the FBI agent did not make it. I flew over his last known location but, that side of the mountain experienced a mudslide and the terrain is covered over. The assumption is with the combination of the height and those elements no one could have survived it," he said.

"Dante was an FBI agent?" Attie enquired.

"Yes it seems to be that way," he responded.

"I suspected something was up with him when you told me what he said, but I was not sure. I hope Ms. Anderson can clear this up," Kyle replied squeezing her hand.

In a matter of minutes, they landed in an open but secluded field that appeared to be a landing strip but Atlas was not sure. A black SUV was parked a short distance away, making their way to it Atlas held onto Kyle's hand. Reaching the car, Atlas took a deep breath as Kyle opened the car's door, she looked inside and saw Barb sitting in the back holding her cell phone.

"Welcome back you two. I am so glad you made it out alive," Barb yelled out as they sat inside the vehicle.

"Ms. Anderson, Attie, I mean Atlas has the drone sensors and Peter asked for you to have them analyzed," Kyle said without hesitation.

"Peter? Wow, he likes Biblical names," she said laughing out loud.

Atlas looked confused as she handed Barb her backpack, "what are you guys talking about? Peter right that is his name?"

"No Doll he is Lacota Lincoln but he does work for the Department of Justice. I believe you two served together right Kyle?" Barb clarified as the vehicle began to move.

"Yes Ma'am we did as a matter of fact, he saved my tail more than I care to say," Kyle replied and then continued, "Was he able to contact you after he left the compound and give you an update."

"He was. Don't you worry I will make sure Linc is safe. For right now he is on the heels of Tennessee. Lord, I hope he can catch her before she tries another domestic attack," Barb said looking at her cell phone.

"Do you need us to follow him?" Atlas said sitting up on the edge of the seat.

"No you two have done more than enough for me, your state, and your country. Right now I just need for you two to recover and get back on track. This next series will be an adventure that's for sure."

"Where are we heading?" Atlas asked looking out the window.

"Doll, we are heading home to the ranch. Kyle, where do we drop you?" Barb asked with a half-smile.

"Well, I am staying at the ranch with Rob and Ellie. Would you like to stay there with me?" Atlas said placing her hand over his.

"I would love to, but Atlas I want to do things the right way. I need to ask them first if they have space for me," Kyle started to say but was interrupted by Atlas.

"Of course, you lead and I will follow," she said.

"Well, good now that is settled. Let's talk about your future Kyle. I am sure you had enough of this gypsy life. Are you thinking about heading back to your agency in Cheyenne?" Barb asked as they started to recognize the fence line to the ranch.

"My contract with them has ended and to be honest I don't want to work far away from Attie. I never had the opportunity to hit the streets, but I hesitated about working in the same department. There might be a conflict and I don't want to mess with her career," Kyle stopped, "I mean your career. I have had mine with the military and you are just starting."

"Kyle, you shouldn't be held back because of me," Atlas added.

"Great!" Barb shouted, "There is an opening at the academy. Seems like Director Spinelli didn't work out. How could he when he was too busy schmoozing."

"Schmoozing?" Atlas repeated.

"You know kvetching Doll," Barb said placing her hand over Atlas' knee," he got caught putting his junk inside the wrong recycling bin."

"Oh wow," Kyle said he let out a huge laugh looking at Barb and then Atlas who all began to chuckle so hard until tears came out of their eyes.

The vehicle stopped, and Barb asked, "So you up for the job?"

"Yes, Ma'am, I would love to train the new recruits," Kyle said, reaching for the door handle.

"I will make those arrangements for you. That is fantastic!" Barb said stepping out of the vehicle, "Now why don't you two go and say hi to your friends while I go looking for my guy."

Atlas and Kyle walked up the stairs and knocked on the door. A few seconds later, Ellie appeared, "Oh my God, you both are back. Thank God we have been so worried," throwing herself into their arms.

"Well, had I known you would miss me so much, I would have been back earlier," Kyle said, hugging Ellie as Rob walked behind her.

"Please excuse my wife she has become a bit more emotional these last few days," Rob said pulling Ellie next to him and extending his hand to Kyle, "Welcome back soldier."

"Atlas I am so very happy you are here," Ellie said almost in tears.

"What is happening? Why are you so upset?" Atlas said, walking closer to Ellie.

"The pregnancy is kicking my butt. One moment I am happy the other I am crying I am not sure what is going to come out of my mouth next," Ellie said.

"Why don't we go sit in the kitchen and catch you all up," Rob suggested walking next to Ellie.

The group sat at the kitchen table as Rob began to explain, "The doctor called a few hours ago and he told us that Ellie's condition was a bit delicate."

Atlas began to panic, her face became flushed, and she started to tap the table with her fingers. Kyle immediately noticed, and took her hand to comfort and support her saying, "Go on Rob we are here to help in any way we can."

"It is not that big a deal," Ellie interjected, "except that I have to remain on bed rest."

"Since Ellie already had a miscarriage and because of her past injuries, the doctor feels it will be safer for them to stay at home," Rob explained.

"That is where you come in Atlas. I was hoping you didn't mind sticking around for a bit. I would ask Ava, but she and Levy are still traveling. I don't want to cut her adventure short. You know they want to experience everything together before he loses his sight," Ellie said.

Atlas looked at Kyle, and they both smiled before she said, "I would love to stay here as long as you want me here."

"As a matter of fact brother, I was going to ask if you could use a hand with the mustangs, and if you didn't mind me hanging out as well," Kyle added while half smiling at Atlas.

"Please tell me that means you two are finally together?" Ellie said, almost jumping out of her seat.

"Yes we are and we really want to make it work," Atlas said.

"Sounds like it is all settled then. Why don't you two head out to the east pasture? There is a very nice two-bedroom cabin that no one uses. It has plenty of space and privacy. You can rest for a while and come down in a couple of hours for dinner," Rob suggested, "in the meantime, my wife needs to put her feet up and maybe take a nap."

"Wait, I failed to mention that Barb is here. I guess she is out looking for Ben. In fact, I know she is looking for him because she called him her man," Atlas said.

"Crap! Do you think Ben knows that?" Ellie said, laughing.

"Maybe someone should warn him?" Rob said, laughing, handing Kyle the keys to the truck.

"You guys wanna catch up tonight? I am thinking maybe a bonfire would be nice. I haven't heard you sing in a while, Rob," Ellie said, standing up, "Or you, Kyle. A welcome home celebration."

Kyle reached and grabbed Ellie's hand, bending down and kissing her on the cheek, saying, "Congratulations, your baby is so blessed to have great people like you two as parents."

Rob gave him a frown, "you hitting on my girl?"

"Maybe, you know I would kiss you as well, but you are not my type," Kyle said, pulling on Atlas' chair as she stood up, "she is all I ever need."

"Alright, boys, let's leave this for another time and place," Ellie suggested, "nap, shower, food."

"We'll see you in a few hours," Atlas said, making her way out the door. Walking on the porch she noticed in the distance, "Look, I think that is Barb and Ben over there. You think we should tell them about the bonfire?"

"No, we should do what Rob said. Let's go settle in the cabin and move some stuff around. Maybe take a shower, food, nap, and let Ben and Barb figure it out," Kyle said.

"Are you always going to tell me what to do?" Atlas said, pulling away from him.

"You serious you want to pick a fight right now?" Kyle said feeling his blood pressure rising as they walked to the truck. He opened the door for her and helped her in while saying nothing as his mind was racing towards rage.

"Just a small one," she said when he got into the truck.

"A small what?" he said, putting the key into the ignition.

"A small fight," she responded with a smile, "just enough to get you all hot and bothered before we take a shower together, eat something, take a nap, and then repeat."

"You are so bad and yet so perfect for me," Kyle said, pulling her next to him as they made their way to their new home.

After settling into the new home and taking care of one another, Kyle and Atlas emerged at the meeting spot along with Ellie and Rob. The nice, crisp fire was a welcomed sight for everyone. Ellie smiled as she watched Rob pampering her with care. He brought over a comfortable rocking chair, pillows, and even a blanket. Ensuring she and their baby felt safe was his only mission.

"Hey guys, come join us. I got the fire started and dinner is on its way out," Rob said, watching the new couple slowly walking towards them.

"You need a hand, brother," Kyle asked.

"Not at the moment. I got plenty of chopped wood, but maybe in a few days, we might need to tackle some more. The weather is turning, and we don't want to get behind," Rob suggested.

"Relax, Rob, I am alright. You don't need to be worried," Ellie interjected, placing her hand over Rob's who was rubbing on her shoulders. Looking at him, she said, "It's just a baby. We got this."

"I know I am freaking out, but I can't stop worrying about you," Rob responded.

"I understand the feeling, brother, but you are not alone. Besides, Attie and I are here willing and able to work," Kyle said, holding Alta's hand.

"Yes, sure we are. You want me to go check on dinner?" Atlas stated, walking towards the back stairs to the main house.

"Why are you all making so much noise?" Ben asked as he made his way out of the house carrying a tray with food.

"Ben! I am so happy to see you. Here, let me take that from you." Atlas said, running up to him.

"Welcome back, my child," he said, nodding his head at her, "why don't you see if Barb needs help inside."

"Sure thing!" she responded, running inside the kitchen.

"I can see nothing has changed with that girl still lots of fire in her belly," Ben said, walking down the stairs and handing out neatly wrapped burgers. A few seconds later, Atlas emerged with another tray loaded with food, followed by Barb.

"Oh, let's get this party started. Dinner is served in Barb style. You take as much as you like. There is plenty!" Barb said, joining the group.

"You made enough to feed an Army woman," Ben added, looking at Barb.

"I made the essentials so no one would leave unsatisfied including you my Dear," she replied with a deviant smile.

Ben let out an unusual moan as he approached the fire. He looked around and noticed a hawk flying across the dark blue sky, "I sense a presence entering our circle." Reaching into his pocket, Ben took out sage, tossing it into the fire. "I am not sure if it's friendly or not. Just in case, I asked the

Great Spirit to guide it here if it's our ally and away if it's to be our enemy."

The wind picked up the smoke, bathing the guests and then taking it across the nearest path as if guiding someone into their group. Ben was focused on the fire, and everyone became quiet for several minutes. Barb stood up, walking next to him. She placed her arm around his waist.

Suddenly, they heard someone whistling as they made their approach. Atlas looked at Kyle, who had a great big killer smile as he gazed in the direction the smoke was signaling. He then took Atlas' hand and held it tight as if he was telling her not to move.

The whistle became more clear and louder as the person approached, "Good evening. I hope I am not interrupting, but I was told this was the safest meeting place in the region. And since I smelled the sage, I knew you were warning the enemy but welcoming a Dakota, a friend."

"Peter!" Atlas yelled out, " I mean Lincoln, wait, Linc, right," she jumped out of her seat and gave him a huge hug.

"Hey Lucky, I am so glad you were able to bring my brother home," Linc responded.

"Atlas, my name is Atlas," she said, reaching for his hand and leading him closer to the fire, "everyone, this is Linc. He was with us on our assignment. Let me introduce you?"

Kyle stood up to shake Linc's hand, leading to an embrace and several pats on the back, "why you here, Linc? Weren't you tracking Tennessee?" he asked.

"Yes, that got a bit complicated, and I got the message to return here for further instructions," Linc replied, looking at Barb.

"Well, Doll, I am glad you follow orders. She went underground, and it will take all we have to find her, but I am not concerned. Tennessee always comes up for air, and once she does, you will go after her. In the meantime, I thought you could use some homemade food, good company, and a few friends to refuel. I hope I didn't overstep by asking Linc to join us?' Barb responded.

"No, Barb, you did well. I can see Linc needs the vision to clear his path," Ben responded, dropping more sage into the fire. "We can start at first light, why don't you join us? The family is celebrating my grandchild and you are welcome to be here. The Dakota people are always welcome to share with us."

"Mitakuye Oyas'in, all my friends, thank you for welcoming me to your tribe," Linc said as he walked close to Ben. "The Great Spirit led me here. I need a clear vision so I can get back on my mission. Tennessee, she is very dangerous, and she needs to be stopped."

"Yes, my son, I will help you," Ben said.

"Well, Doll, I am sure Ben will get your warrior ready for a new adventure hunting Tennessee."

Authors Note

Dear Readers,

Thank you so much for all your kindness, support, and love. It has been a pleasure sharing these three book series "Love is…" with you. For the moment, the series has concluded; however, a new three-part series has emerged, starting with "Hunting Tennessee." The new romantic action adventure will feature Lacota Lincoln, aka Linc, who is hot on the trail of Tennessee, a highly intelligent ex-military female officer who is obsessed with the idea of destroying the American way of life. Her current plan includes dismantling all communications and the energy grid. Tennessee has managed to recruit a number of mercenaries who are just as disenchanted with the United States government and are fueled by the idea of extorting all the money they can before releasing their furry on their own country. Linc has vowed to track and shut their operation down for good. Follow this new action adventure throughout the Appalachian Mountains, crossing multiple states from Georgia to Maine and the Rocky Mountains, which include Colorado, Idaho, Montana, Wyoming, New Mexico, and Utah.

Warm Regards,

Jessica Jude Ziegler